CODE WORD: PERSEPOLIS

AN INTERNATIONAL THRILLER

DOUG NORTON

MAGOTHY
RIVER
PRESS

ISBN-13: 978-0-9994976-6-1

Printed in the United States of America

"Humans are caught—in their lives, in their thoughts, in their hungers and ambitions, in their avarice and cruelty, and in their kindness and generosity too—in a net of good and evil . . . A man, after he has brushed off the dust and chips of life, will have left only the hard, clean questions: Was it good or was it evil? Have I done well—or ill?"

—John Steinbeck, *East of Eden*

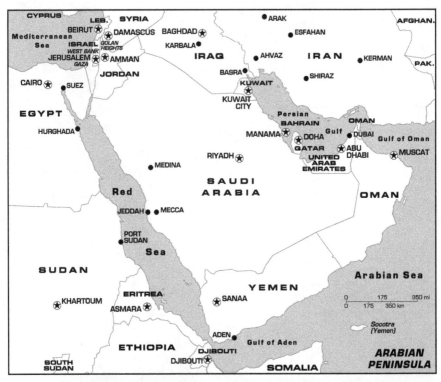

Strait of Hormuz

GLOSSARY OF ABBREVIATIONS
AND TERMS

ANGELS. Military air control term meaning altitude in thousands of feet.

AWACS. A military aircraft equipped for surveillance of a large area and for control of aircraft.

BANDIT. Military air control term meaning an aircraft identified as unfriendly. May be attacked if designated "hostile."

BOGEY. Military air control term meaning an unidentified aircraft.

CIWS. Close-in weapons system. A gun with an extremely high rate of fire used for defense against small boats, surface torpedoes, anti-ship missiles, and helicopters.

CSIS. Center for Strategic and International Studies. A highly respected Washington think tank.

COMINT. Communications Intelligence. Messages or voice information derived from the interception of foreign communications.

CYBERCOM. Abbreviation for the US Cyber Command, the military organization responsible for offensive and defensive cyber warfare.

DCS. Deputy Chief of Staff.

EA. Executive Assistant.

FOC'SLE. The forward portion of a ship.

GENERAL QUARTERS. The condition of maximum battle readiness aboard a warship. Upon hearing it announced, all sailors go to their assigned battle stations and prepare for combat.

HOSTILE. Military air control term meaning an identified unfriendly aircraft meeting the Rules of Engagement criteria to be attacked.

IAF. Israeli Air Force.

IRGC. Iranian Revolutionary Guard Corps. The IRGC is the descendant of the many militias that sprang up during Iran's revolution that began in 1979. Over time, as Ayatollah Khomeini consolidated power, these militias were amalgamated into a single armed force, controlled by the regime.

ISIS. "Islamic State in Iraq and Syria." Also known as DAESH, a transliteration of the Arabic acronym formed of the same words that make up ISIS in English.

MAD. Magnetic Anomaly Detector, a device used by airplanes and helicopters to detect submarines by means of their magnetic signature.

OPREP. Operational Report. The OPREP system prescribes the formatting of important, urgent operational communications such as reporting an emergency situation.

Ops. Slang term for the officer responsible to the captain for the planning and oversight of a ship's operations.

POSSUB. Abbreviation for "possible submarine."

NINETY-NINE. Military air control term meaning that the information that follows is addressed to all aircraft.

ROE. Rules of Engagement. In a situation short of war, the conditions under which an attack is permitted.

RTB. Abbreviation for "return to base."

SAM. Surface-to-air missile, an antiaircraft missile.

SIVITZ. Slang for Secure Video Teleconferences, known as SVTCs, pronounced "sivitz"

SKUNK. US Navy term for an unidentified surface radar contact.

SPECOPS. Special Operations, term for small, elite units such as navy SEALS and army Rangers.

SUPREME LEADER. The title of the most powerful authority in the Islamic Republic. He is the head of state and the commander-in-chief; he controls the executive, legislative, and judicial branches of Iran's government.

TALLY. Military air control term meaning an aircraft is in sight.

VAJA. Ministry of Intelligence of the Islamic Republic of Iran. The descendant of the deposed Shah of Iran's hated secret police, SAVAK.

WEPS. Slang term for the officer responsible to the captain for combat systems (weapons) aboard a ship.

XO. Executive Officer, the second in command of a military unit.

ZEBRA. Warships are deliberately divided into many watertight, fume-tight compartments so that fire or flooding in one part of the ship can be confined to the smallest possible area. Normally, the doors between the compartments are open or allowed to be freely opened and closed. When "Condition ZEBRA" is ordered, all doors are closed and may not be opened without permission from a central control station.

PREFACE

WELCOME TO THE THIRD OF the *Code Word* novels.

In the first book, *Code Word: Paternity,* bin Laden's avengers, directed by Al Qaeda's master bomber, Fahim, destroy Las Vegas with a North Korean nuke. The detonation hurls President Rick Martin into a universe that defies his humanism and demands self-sacrifice. Rick habitually buries emotions, sheltering behind rationality. He's confident that will still work, but he's dead wrong, and no one knows that better than his wife, Graciella (Ella) Dominguez Martin—except perhaps her old lover, former Marine general now congressman Ray Morales. After nuclear forensics point to North Korea's role in the destruction of Las Vegas, the United States retaliates with a nuclear strike that destroys a North Korean city.

In the second novel, *Code Word: Pandora,* Fahim launches a campaign of terror in America. But the wave of suicide attacks is not the deadliest of Fahim's schemes. He sets in motion an attack on a nuclear power plant that will rival 9/11 in shock.

Secretary of Homeland Security Ray Morales vows to get Fahim, but so too does Adel Ghorbani, leader of Iran's Quds Force, who fears Iran will be a convenient scapegoat and suffer the same fate as North Korea. In his determination to find Fahim, Morales violates the law and his own moral code, ordering that a captured terrorist be tortured to locate the hideout. Impulsively leading a raid on the hideout himself, Morales runs headlong into Adel Ghorbani and Quds Force.

Amidst the pressure of his reelection campaign, President Martin compromises to save lives and win votes by a means he abhors, thus infuriating the First Lady. She turns to Ray and for one explosive night they turn back the clock in their relationship.

An assassination in South Korea draws China and America toward war, thrusting Martin into a high-stakes encounter with China's president. Diplomatic, military, and covert action enmesh America, China, Korea, Japan, and Iran, forcing Morales and Martin into a struggle to defeat evil without becoming evil.

PROLOGUE

THE PERSIAN GULF—JUNE 1

LIEUTENANT LEE, THE OFFICER IN charge of the predawn bridge watch aboard the destroyer, concentrated on one ship's red navigation light among many in view across the glassy sea to starboard. It was a moonless night, but the waters surrounding his ship were illuminated by the dancing flames of an oil well platform flaring off natural gas. When Lee had taken over the watch from his yawning predecessor, who had been up since midnight, that officer had casually pointed to the red light. A check on the ops console had revealed the usual two lines of large ships, inbound and outbound, in one of the world's busiest waterways. The dots representing them on the console moved east and west with the ponderous precision of marching elephants. But the radar plot of this particular contact moved slowly and erratically, as a sailing dhow would move.

Dhows were a near-constant presence in the Persian Gulf, occasionally getting in the way of the tankers and warships as they sailed into and out of this body of water separating Arabs and Persians, Sunnis and Shi'as, who didn't much like each other. Generally, the dhows were adept at getting out of the bigger ships' way. Idly, squinting through the eyepiece of a pelorus, Lee took a visual bearing on the red light. He went to the ops console and rolled the trackball, cool and hard beneath his fingers, with a practiced movement. Yes, there was a phosphorescent blip on the bearing, and the display showed its range to be just under five miles. That could be a problem later.

Deciding to take a closer look at the dhow, or whatever it was, Lee moved through the darkened bridge with sure steps, threading shadowy equipment and men. Reaching the heavy, watertight door that opened to the starboard bridge wing, he pulled the long lever that opened it with a clank and stepped into ninety-degree heat, airborne desert grit, and smells of salt water and of oil. Raising condensation-fogged binoculars to his eyes, he saw only blurred white and darkness. Waiting for the condensation to clear as his binoculars warmed, he leaned against the bridge railing and commiserated with the sailor assigned as lookout about the heat and the talcum-powder-fine sand that lodged in the sweaty creases of the body and irritated the eyes.

A few minutes later Lee raised his binoculars and was rewarded with a clear view. Where there had been a red light, he now saw a green one. According to international maritime rules, that would be the sailing dhow's starboard running light. He deduced from this change from red to green that the sailing vessel had changed its course. It would now pass clear to starboard rather than cut across the destroyer's path. Lee smiled. Now he wouldn't need to alert the captain, who tended to be cranky when awakened, even though his standing orders required it.

Lee returned gratefully to the air-conditioned pilothouse, while the starboard lookout, sweating despite the last of a dying breeze, continued to observe the navigation lights. The breeze carried a rumble of engines starting, and he observed more intently. Lunging from hiding along the dhow's far side, a Boghammar patrol boat emerged; the three-hundred-horsepower outboards crowded on its transom were snarling. The lookout didn't need binoculars to spot it because it was throwing a rooster tail of white water. Urgently, he reported this to a sailor in the pilothouse.

The sailor called out the alert: "Starboard lookout reports a boat at zero five zero coming at us fast!"

Lee jumped up, spilling his tea, then rushed to the starboard bridge wing. He saw the rooster tail and heard the snarling outboards. The boat arrowed toward him, its compass bearing holding steady. He knew that meant a collision unless he maneuvered the destroyer quickly.

"All engines ahead flank! Captain to the bridge!" he barked through the open door. Jerking upright from his slump, the sailor at the control console rammed the throttle levers into their forward stops.

As the destroyer surged ahead, slowly gaining speed, the rooster tail kept to its course. It hadn't begun to slip behind them as Lee hoped it would. The speedboat, or whatever it was, arrowed toward him as he stood on the bridge wing, eyes wide and heart pounding. His tongue stuck to the roof of his suddenly dry mouth as his brain stuttered between the orders he might shout and his frantic attempt to understand what was occurring. The intruder was speeding toward them. Why? To launch a torpedo? A missile? To ram them in a suicide attack?

In response to Lee's order, the gas turbines used for speed howled as they took over from the plodding diesels. The sound of the bow wave increased to an angry hiss as white water creamed into an arc along the warship's cutwater. But the Boghammar could not be outrun. It smashed into the destroyer's starboard side at forty-five knots, turning its fiercely grinning occupant into jelly milliseconds before a contact-delay fuse detonated the fifteen hundred pounds of explosive it had thrust against the destroyer's hull.

* * *

NORTHWEST SYRIA

Nine hundred sixty miles away in the miserable, rubble-strewn remains of a town, a scarred, bearded ISIS soldier stirred restlessly in his sleep. His appearance belied the fact that he had once been, before he found his true calling, a clinical psychologist. In the heady days when the caliphate rolled across Syria and Iraq, its fighters capturing hundreds of *takfiri* soldiers, he had created and led a prisoner exploitation unit. He did not know it, in fact would never know because he would be killed tomorrow in an ambush, but one of the Iranian prisoners he had so skillfully sculpted into human bombs had just exploded.

BOOK ONE.

MARCH 1—APRIL 11

CHAPTER 1

ARLINGTON, VIRGINIA

Secretary of Homeland Security Ray Morales tried to stop his careening memories, but he couldn't. Guilt tugged at his shoulder as though he were carrying a sack of rocks.

As the Suburban rolled through Washington toward his home in Arlington, his mind pinwheeled: The crash landing in the Idaho forest, Phil's death, and Jerry's career-ending injury. Those were his fault. Then his own injuries, his capture, his rescue by Adel Ghorbani, and Ghorbani's contemptuous manipulation. Ray's face twisted with anger. Then Ghorbani had slipped away, compounding his failure and that of the administration and president he proudly served. He was forced to live the lie Ghorbani had set up. Outwardly he was a hero. But in fact he was a ticking bomb. If Ghorbani exposed him, Senator Arlene Gustafson would call for hearings that would reveal him as a fraud. And even now Gustafson was sniffing around.

Ray Morales was not a man who allowed himself to feel helpless, but he was perilously close to it now.

And that wasn't his only vulnerability. Last year America's security services had been desperate to capture the mastermind of a wave of bombings and shootings paralyzing the country. A would-be martyr, Ali Hadrab—captured just before he killed a food court full of people—was the key. And then the interrogation in the sterile, brightly lit room. Immoral as it was, it *had* to be done. But Hadrab's screams!

Senator Arlene Gustafson suspected what he had done, and his wife,

Julie, knew she was determined to take him down. Yet he couldn't tell Julie what Gustafson suspected. His refusal had accelerated the erosion of intimacy and trust in their marriage, which was already under strain. Julie was distant, planning to resume her old career at Booz Allen and steeling herself—for divorce, he feared. As the car neared his condominium, he could feel the storm coming.

* * *

They ate in alert silence, each guarding unshared fears and hurts, each searching for something to say that wouldn't lead to them, but not finding it. Ray, sitting stiffly in his chair, chewed the last bite of his dinner, takeout from a favorite Arlington restaurant. Julie, still working on her entrée and picking at her salad, looked at him with a carefully crafted expression that revealed nothing.

Her husband had thick hair, now more gray than black, and a ruggedly carved face bisected by a broad nose. His eyes were black and set off by squint-lines scoring his brownish, weather-beaten skin. His chest and shoulders loomed across the table, giving testimony to the record-setting shot-putter he had once been.

The familiarity of his appearance reminded Julie that beneath it lay unfamiliar territory, hinted at but not revealed by a woman who hated Ray's guts and knew things about her husband that he refused to share with her. She frowned.

"A penny," said Ray, breaking the long silence.

"Just a lot going on at Booz," she said, referring to the global consulting firm Booz Allen Hamilton for which she had once been a star consultant. That seemed a safe enough topic.

"Since Conklin announced his retirement last week, the whole top-level anthill has been stirring. Depending on who succeeds him as CEO, the company could see big changes. Nobody will feel secure until the new guy is in, and they know the winners and losers."

"Bobby Mandeville would take you back in a flash. You know that."

"Yeah, but if Pete Nakasone becomes CEO, Bobby's goose is cooked. Not a good time for me to go back to Bobby's division."

"But you two have been making plans for what you'd do when you came back aboard. Isn't Bobby going to resent it if you back off now? He was ready to go to bat to bring you back at the same level; now you back away, and he knows you've got no loyalty to him."

"Ray, this isn't the Marines! This is business. Bobby understands I have to look out for myself."

Ray shook his head. "I guess I'm still just a jarhead. Semper Fi and all that."

"Don't get snarky, Ray! You know I've always respected the culture of your Marine Corps, of your career. You need to respect the culture of mine."

Ray took a deep breath. "You're right, Julie. I apologize. May I change the subject?"

Julie smiled briefly and said, "OK."

Ray looked for a moment at his big hands, which were gripping the table edge.

"The new subject is Ali Hadrab."

Julie's posture, which had relaxed, stiffened, and her eyes widened. She put down her fork, locking her gaze on her husband's face. "Go on," she said.

"I said I couldn't tell you about what happened to him; maybe someday, but not now. I know you were hurt and offended by that. Please believe me when I say that I kept silent to protect you."

Julie felt her stomach drop and looked at him even more intently.

He met her gaze. "But after thinking about it, and seeing how it's a wall between us that neither of us can climb, I'm going to tell you if you want to take the risk of knowing."

"What do you mean, 'risk of knowing'?"

"After I tell you, you'll have knowledge of a felony. You could find yourself pulled into a conspiracy investigation, maybe charged with obstruction. Of course those charges wouldn't stick, but my enemies will try to smear you anyway. You might become too hot for Booz to touch."

After a pause she said, "I need to think about that, Ray."

He nodded and reached for her hand. She pulled it back. "Look, Ray. I already know you've done something that I never thought you would do. You slept with another woman. And you hid it as long as you could. I still don't know whether you would have told me if Gustafson hadn't forced your hand. Painful as it was, I could and did accept what you did. In a way it softened you, made you more fully human—you who had lived

Semper Fidelis all your life. For the first time I saw you fail and need my forgiveness. But *now*? Now you come out with another secret you've been keeping?"

"Julie, I thought we had worked that through. What happened between Ella and me at Camp David was a terrible mistake. It will never be repeated, not with her, not with anyone. And only the three of us will ever know."

"How can you think that way, Ray? Worked through means I haven't left you or thrown you out, not that I've forgotten. It will hurt me for the rest of my life. And it's not just the three of us—Gustafson suspects and will always be looking for a way to smear you!"

"Julie, we shut her down. She has no evidence, only a harmless photo she tried to spin into something else. A photo that we would discredit and use to make a fool of her."

Julie's eyes were wary. "I hope you're right. But it's still a possibility. And now another skeleton in your closet. And this one a felony? My God, Ray! How many more secrets do you have?" Julie studied her husband's face, then said, "No, Ray. I don't want you to blurt out another secret right now. Especially one that could ruin me with Booz."

"And," she continued, "you have other secrets besides this one. I understand you pretty well after fifteen years of marriage, and that's what I'm reading in your face and your silence. Other secrets. I don't know if I want to stay married to a man with as many secrets as you."

"I don't blame you for thinking that, Julie. I want us to stay married. How do we resolve this? Counseling?"

"Maybe, but I doubt it. What I need right now is time to consider all this. Time apart from you."

"If you had to decide now on our future, what would it be?"

"I'm not going there, Ray. I need time. We'll see."

Chapter 2

NEAR ABERDEEN PROVING GROUND, MARYLAND

THE CROUCHING FIGURE HUSTLED A paddleboard into the greenish shallows of the Chesapeake and hunched atop it. He rose high enough to take several short paddle strokes and saw his guards off to the left and right. He would be followed, but he didn't care. With the board gliding on glassy waters through which passed the small humps of dying swells, he had good stability standing on his legs. He made several deeper strokes, increasing his speed. Now confident of his lead, he began to take deep, regular strokes, settling into a rhythm. Not thinking about his pursuers, he concentrated entirely on building speed and reading the swells so that he could maintain his balance as the board shimmied with their passage.

President Rick Martin glanced behind him to his Secret Service detail, all of whom were new to the sport of paddle-boarding. He was rewarded by the sight of one of them losing his balance and pitching into the bay with a splash. He grinned. It felt good to be able to do something better than one of his nearly superhuman protectors.

He had made good his escape, however brief, from the weight of his office. As he stroked, enjoying the chuckling sounds of the board passing over series of wavelets, he felt as if the office he held—and had recently fought hard to keep through reelection—couldn't wrap its octopus arms around him, each sucker draining his energy and concentration with a different demand. It couldn't pull him into the tension and struggle and crisis management of the presidency. What wore him out were the number and variety of situations shouting for his attention. Often he felt like he was in a room filled with basketballs and had to keep them all bouncing. If he took the time to get one or two going well, another couple would subside to a roll.

Look at me! This is probably the best moment of my day, and I'm spoiling it with thoughts of my job.

He switched his train of thought to one of the many sidetracks in his mind and consciously embraced his surroundings. He was gliding near-silently through reflections of the shoreline on the water. A light breeze hit his face, and he was glad to be paddling into the wind, knowing it would aid him on his homeward leg. He felt a pleasing strength in his muscles as he stroked, three hard pulls on one side and then switching so that his course was more or less straight. As he slid by a weathered pier, a pair of cormorants watching his approach launched heavily from atop pilings. They dove down until their webbed feet were pressing against water, and a combination of windmilling legs and flapping wings brought them to flight speed.

His mind turned to First Lady Graciella Dominguez Martin—Ella, as she was known. Marriages lasting twenty-five years are held together by kids and mutual respect and romance and practicality. Theirs now seemed to be sustained mostly by practicality: their two kids were launched; romance didn't have the power it once did—although the Secret Service may have been surprised once or twice by the sounds coming from the presidential bedroom—and, greatest loss of all, respect was no longer mutual. He no longer had Ella's respect.

It was his fault. She had been a full partner and confidante as he built his career representing Maryland in the Senate and won his first term as president. And during that term they had long conversations about the issues of the day and, especially, about the deadly crisis of nuclear terrorism in America enabled by North Korea's leader, Kim.

The bare bones of that crisis with North Korea five years ago were straightforward, once stripped of the moral ambiguity that had made resolving the crisis terribly dangerous for America and agonizing for Martin. Al Qaida had purchased two North Korean nuclear bombs. Fahim al-Wasari smuggled one into Las Vegas and detonated it. The other was discovered before it could be detonated. After nuclear forensics had pointed to North

Korea as the source of the bombs, President Martin destroyed a North Korean city with nuclear-armed cruise missiles. China tacitly accepted this because it allowed the Chinese to replace the Kims, who had so bedeviled them for over fifty years.

In those days Ella had been one of the two people Martin had relied on most for encouragement and counsel. But then, when reelection loomed, he had shut her out after he made compromises without consulting her that she felt were betrayals of their shared principles. She had been right, but those compromises were necessary and temporary. And now she remained distant and polite but no longer deeply engaged after he had tried to resume their political partnership. He'd been awarded the Nobel Peace Prize for finally bringing peace and democracy to the entire Korean peninsula, but she refused to share his excitement. She'd been no more than arm candy at the ceremony in Oslo.

How do I get my partner back?

He feared she wouldn't want to come back if the secrets he was sitting on came out. *Ray Morales is a brave man, a patriot, and a friend, but the tactics he used to find Fahim al-Wasari will cause a scandal if they get out. And if Arlene Gustafson finds out ...* He winced.

This was a time when he envied his occasional ally, China's leader Ming Liu. As long as he kept the hierarchy of the Chinese Communist Party satisfied, Ming could suppress just about any bad news. China had the most effective internet censorship and suppression system on the planet. Martin criticized him for it but now would like to have one himself.

Experience had taught him that Ming was a smooth operator, a politician with strategic as well as tactical skill. Take his infrastructure and economic development initiatives. They were both a strategy to improve China's access to energy supplies and a tactic to gain leverage over certain other governments.

The Chinese were working hard in Africa. Martin doubted they'd see much success because they would come up against the same forces of corruption and tribalism that limited American influence there. But in the Middle East, economic assistance and a large dose of military cooperation were getting China closer to the Shi'as, most importantly the Iranians. Of course no other nation could count on the Islamic Republic of Iran because its policies were as varied as the differing interpretations of the

Koran brandished by regional rivals. But, for the moment at least, Ming's plan to enhance the quantity and security of China's oil supply by trading sweetheart arms deals for sweetheart energy deals was working.

A disturbance in the water about twenty yards to Martin's left caught his attention.

Once again I've let my mind spin away into the presidency! What's that over there?

The surface parted, and he saw a small brown triangle emerge and disappear quickly.

He recognized it as a ray. Hoping to get close enough to see it, Martin stroked gently, guiding his board to the left. He saw the ray's diamond shape and the flapping of its "wings" as it glided just below the surface. With each upstroke, the ray's wing tips broke the surface, displaying the small triangles that had attracted his attention. Happily absorbed, he paddled gently behind the ray until it dove out of sight.

Glancing at his watch, Martin saw that he had used half of the thirty minutes he allowed himself each day for relaxation and exercise. With a mischievous grin, he shuffled two steps to the rear of the board, which raised the nose clear of the water. Next he plunged his paddle deep to his right and pulled hard. The board pivoted in its own length, making a tight left turn. His Secret Service companions turned awkwardly in big, slow arcs as he scooted ahead of them toward the presidential "cabin" beside the Gunpowder River at Aberdeen Army Proving Ground. Martin loved showing his guardians that they weren't his superiors in all things physical.

Chapter 3

JERUSALEM, ISRAEL

J OSHUA ASKENAZI, PRIME MINISTER OF Israel, pressed the stem of his wristwatch. By its dim glow, he saw it was 3:20 a.m. A glance to his left told him that his wife, Shara, was sleeping. He rearranged his pillows, rolled over, and tried to quiet his mind and fall asleep. It didn't work. He sighed, then levered his bulk from bed, donned his robe, and padded to his study. There he sat, in a battered leather armchair, in the dark.

Iran.

His mind trod a well-worn path marked by so many danger signs. Mossad and military intelligence agreed that missiles capable of reaching Israel with nuclear bombs were being manufactured. Iran's missile tests were successful and demonstrated increasing accuracy. Iranian engineers had secretly assembled a prototype nuclear missile warhead, probably with Chinese assistance. Adel Ghorbani was recently put in charge of the program to develop a nuclear missile force, which meant the country would shake off its doldrums and move swiftly and purposefully toward the day when Iran's Supreme Leader would have a dozen or more nuclear-tipped missiles at his command. And the Supreme Leader hated Israel; he regarded its existence as an affront to Allah, to the Islamic Republic of Iran, and to him personally.

Israel was cursed with unfavorable circumstances: a small country surrounded by enemies. When the armies of those enemies breached its borders, Israel had only one choice: stand and fight, whatever the odds, for there is no space in which to retreat, regroup, hold, and counterattack.

Israelis can't do what the Russians did when the Nazis came at them, or the Chinese when invaded by the Japanese, or the Americans after being surprised at Pearl Harbor. In three wars during Askenazi's lifetime—wars in which he had fought—Israel had held when surprised and preempted when she had to. But now, with ballistic missiles, no Iranian need set foot in Israel to destroy the nation and its people.

Twice, Israeli prime ministers had faced this existential choice: destroy a newborn threat or hope that the adult it becomes will not strike. Twice they decided to take the safer course for Israel: destroy the threat in infancy. And those had not been easy decisions. If successful, a strike would bring down condemnation on Israel from Europe and North America, ignite rioting in Gaza and the West Bank, and upset Israel's own left-wing parties. It would, in all likelihood, cost the lives of some of those sent to do the job. If unsuccessful, the prime minister's decision would bring all of those woes and, in addition, make Israel look weaker and would savage his political standing. Askenazi's predecessors made the hard choices and destroyed Iraq's plutonium-producing reactor in 1981 and Syria's in 2007. Either of those countries, each sworn to Israel's destruction, could have detonated nuclear bombs in Israel without anything more than a truck to bring them in.

Now it was Askenazi who faced that choice. Iran had the missiles now and would soon have nuclear warheads to arm them. He believed that none of Israel's allies truly understood Israel's predicament. Its people were survivors and descendants of the most successful genocide in modern history, and they were still threatened by it. Israeli children must grow up with that. They must ride buses, play outside, go to movies, and attend school under a constant threat of a murderous attack, whether by a knife-wielding Palestinian, a bomb-wearing Saudi, or a rocket fired from Gaza by Hamas. No other people on the planet face such a pervasive, continuous threat to their lives. And no other people understood what that threat required of Israel.

He had spoken to President Martin once about this. "Mr. President," he said, "you speak to me of timing. You tell me the world still has time to eliminate this threat by diplomatic means. The missiles and warheads are not yet proven to work together. There are many things that could go wrong and prevent Iran's nuclear missiles from functioning. Be patient. We'll work this out.

"Mr. President, you are an educated man. You know that when one of your predecessors said nearly the same thing—be patient, keep calm, it's not so bad—that deferral condemned a million and a half Jewish children, *children*, to choke to death on Zyklon-B. Iran intends to use its missiles and nuclear warheads to bring an end to the very existence of the Jewish people in Israel. And do you not realize that such an attack would be avenged? Within hours, Iran would become a second radioactive wasteland. All of its many more children and grandchildren would be gone. The human cost of waiting would not just be eight million Israelis but eighty million more Iranians.

"You will say that Iran's Supreme Leader knows that and will never bring extinction to his own people. He will not use those nuclear missiles. But, Mr. President, history is full of disasters caused by leaders who failed to anticipate all the consequences of their actions. Hitler died in a bunker in the ruins of Berlin because he chose to attack Russia and had declared war on America. Tojo was hanged because, at his urging, Imperial Japan had attacked Pearl Harbor. Saddam brought about his own eventual execution when he attacked Kuwait, misjudging the ultimate consequences of that action.

"What is the American expression? 'Skin in the game'? Compared to me, Mr. President, you have no skin in this game. So don't presume to lecture me about caution and weighing all the risks and considering the larger picture!"

Alone in his study, Askenazi felt the weight of responsibility. His reproach had been satisfying to deliver, but he knew it had not dented Martin's confidence that America could measure the risk and balance all factors better than Israel. So he was back up against it: only he could make that calculation on behalf of Israel, on behalf of his nation's children and grandchildren and the unborn generations of Jews.

And to protect them, he knew he would do, *must do*, anything—whatever it took.

Chapter 4

A LONE IN HER CAPITOL HILL condo, Senator Arlene Gustafson contemplated the last bite of her salmon soufflé with regret. The senior senator from Minnesota and newly named chair of the Senate Government Operations and Oversight Committee had indulged herself this evening with a dinner she enjoyed both preparing and eating, complemented by half a bottle of Chateau Bonnet Blanc. Gustafson had two passions: politics and food. She was master of both, a Cordon Bleu chef and a two-term senator. It was Thursday, the last day of the congressional workweek, and she was privately celebrating her chairmanship. The committee luncheon had been a bit rushed so that members could catch flights to their districts. It was also strained because Arlene Gustafson was much more feared than liked by her colleagues, each of whom had felt the bite of her sarcasm and vindictiveness.

She carried her plate to a kitchen that any foodie would envy and returned bearing a spinach salad, which would cleanse her palate for the delicately flavored lemon sorbet to follow. She forked salad into her mouth, then raised her glass of Bonnet in a silent toast to the photo sitting on a nearby table of a young man in Marine dress uniform.

Matt had been so proud to be a Marine. Part of that, she admitted, was that she had been a helicopter mom, determined to show herself and others, especially her spineless former husband, that she could raise a fine strong son—masculine but sensitive, tough but compassionate, rugged but appreciative of art and music. Matt's decision to enlist was the first time he had ever defied her when she had a full head of steam about something. Neither tears, nor bribes, nor threats could dissuade him. Despite her objections, she had been almost as proud as Matt was when he graduated from basic training at Camp Lejeune. And it hadn't hurt her political standing either to have a son serving his country—especially as a Marine.

Damn Ray Morales!

She knew in her soul it was his fault that Matt was dead. If he had been willing to do the right thing when he was a Marine general, Matt would be serving in the Pentagon right now, a decorated veteran of two combat tours, and she would have had his appointment to the Naval Academy teed up. Morales could have stopped the court-martial in its tracks, but he refused, insisting that it would be improper. Matt's death was ruled a suicide, and technically it was, but to Gustafson, Morales was as responsible as though he had pulled the trigger himself.

Gustafson sipped the Bonnet, but its savor had been soured by her memories. She took her glass and plate to the kitchen, used a vacuum sealer on the bottle, and put it in the refrigerator. After making herself a cappuccino, she sat at her desk and read the letter she kept locked within it. It preserved the thoughts Matt had wanted to share with her as the final minutes of his life ticked away.

I love you, Mom, and I don't want to hurt you, but I can't stand it anymore. All I ever did right in my life was to be a good Marine. And now that's gone. And Andy's love is gone, too.

The chime of the doorbell brought her suddenly back to the present. Rising abruptly, she strode to the door, glancing at her watch, realizing then who it must be. Through the peephole she saw a familiar face: young, handsome, and—she thought—completely without character.

"You're early, Ralphie. I need a few minutes, and while I take them, you can clean up the kitchen."

Ralph Jacobson, the junior member of her office staff, gave a smile that was the opposite of his feelings and replied, "Sure, Arlene." As he put the dishes into the washer, he heard the rumble of the Jacuzzi located on the floor above the kitchen of the Capitol Hill townhouse. So it's gonna be one of *those* routines, he thought. *Why the hell do I put up with this?*

But he knew the answer, and it was compelling. So when his phone bleeped with an incoming text, he headed upstairs, carrying a glass and the Bonnet as his boss had texted. Opening the door to the master bath, he took in Arlene, neck deep in the roiling water, her faux blonde hair in a twist to keep dry and her eyes fixed on him as a cat might observe a mouse. The nearby massage table held a collection of oils and lotions. Her robe occupied the only hook, so, as usual, his clothes went on the floor as he peeled them off. She didn't allow him to place them on the massage table because, she said, that disturbed the karma. He knew from experience they would be damp when he dressed again.

* * *

"OK, Ralphie, we're done. Take care to lock the door on your way out."

"Of course, Arlene." Ralphie toweled off and pulled on his boxers.

"And make time this weekend to prepare a thorough analysis for me on Bush Two's black detention sites and the enhanced interrogation procedures authorized by DOJ. How they were revealed, who ran them, what laws were violated. Lots of detail. I want to be *the* Senate expert on this."

"OK." He gathered his slacks, shirt, and loafers and moved toward the door; he would dress, as he usually did, in the next room so that he'd have a dry place to sit.

"Oh, Ralphie, one more thing. You need to do something to build your stamina. That was a little disappointing."

A few minutes later, Ralph Jacobson was downstairs and heading for the door. As he slunk through the dimness of the living room, a flashing blue light got his attention. He stopped momentarily, then realized it was Arlene's coffee brew station signaling it was low on water. Then he spied something on the desk in his line of sight: a handwritten letter. Now that was a rare sight in a town where the players sent email with almost every breath. He knew his boss rarely handwrote anything. But handwritten communication was the choice for extremely sensitive stuff because it couldn't be hacked or wiretapped. He paused.

The noise of the Jacuzzi probably means she's still in it, not much chance she'd see me now if I take a look.

He sidled over to the desk and read both pages of Matt Gustafson's suicide note. A paragraph near the end staggered him: *Mom, we should never have left after my accident. I know that going to the police after hitting that man would not bring him back, but I have been ashamed of myself ever since. I want you to tell the police what happened. Please, Mom, do the right thing.*

Quickly, he snapped on the desk lamp near the document and photographed the pages with his phone. Then he set the note as he had found it, snapped off the light, and flew out the door.

Upstairs, Arlene Gustafson was aglow from the Jacuzzi jets and from Ralphie—his performance had actually been more than adequate. Then, against her will, she surrendered to her obsession of wanting to punish Ray Morales.

That arrogant bastard! I'm going to bring him down, hard! I'll subpoena his ass and break him in front of my committee.

But to obtain the subpoena she had to have a reason. The real one obviously wouldn't do. Arlene's mind, like that of most veteran senators, was a storehouse of the vulnerabilities of others. It didn't fail her this time.

Wait a minute—how about the proof Marty claimed to have found that Morales tortured that guy? But Marty couldn't deliver, claimed that the guy was killed in a drone strike and that was the end of it. Still …

Chapter 5

NEAR BEIJING, PEOPLE'S REPUBLIC OF CHINA

PRESIDENT MING LIU WAS IN deep shit.

He was wearing boots and gloves, of course, which would be meticulously cleaned by his staff, rather than being unprotected as were the traditional Chinese farmers he liked to emulate. It wouldn't do to have China's leader come down with dysentery. He smiled at the pleasure of being at work again on his beloved "farm." It was only two rice paddies and a vegetable plot, but it was enough to relieve the strains of his office for a few hours a week.

His grandfather had belonged to a Communist Party cadre who made the Long March with Mao, but then he fell afoul of the party owing to jealousies and careerism and was banished to a collective farm during China's Great Proletarian Cultural Revolution. After being "reeducated" by several years' farming, he resumed his climb up the party ladder. As a child, Ming had been entertained by his grandfather's wryly humorous tales of life on the collective farm and its methods of cultivation. He used some of those methods on his own tiny farm, and that's how he came to be standing in a foot of water, mud, and feces.

He used different cultivation methods on his two rice paddies. One, in which he now stood, he fertilized with human and animal feces. In the other, he employed the technique of raising fish in the water that covered the paddy and nourished the rice plants. The fish ate insects and parasites that plagued the rice and contributed their excreta to the water, naturally fertilizing the plants.

Finishing his work in the paddy, Ming entered a small greenhouse and began to inspect his tomato plants. They wouldn't be moved outside until the danger of frost had passed.

Damn, damn, damn! Spider mites again.

His defense against spider mites was spraying his plants with neem oil to kill the tiny pests. He arose from the squat he had assumed to inspect his tomatoes and strode to the small wooden toolshed next to his plot, trying to ignore his limo and security detail hovering nearby. For the next hour, the gods willing, he was just a farmer, facing no bigger problems than insects and weeds.

Ming was quite a big man, especially for a Chinese. He had the classic Han round face, full lips, and black eyes, eyebrows, and hair. His hands, now refilling his sprayer, were outsize. On a visit to the United States, he had met Michael Jordan. When the basketball icon saw his hands, he had said, "Man, I'll bet you could palm a basketball. Here, I'll show you what I mean." Ming grasped the basketball with ease, all the while wondering why shoes with Jordan's name were so popular in China since basketball was such a silly game.

Back in his greenhouse, Ming began to spray the tomatoes thoroughly, being careful to wet the underside of each leaf, where mites often lurked. He had found that gardening was not only an escape from burdens but also a time of useful reflection. He was facing reelection as the head of the Chinese Communist Party. He was confident of keeping his office, although not overconfident. He had spent the six years of his first term putting his people in place. They had consolidated their individual roles, eliminated rivals, and had been enjoying power and prestige. He was confident of their support at the party congress next month.

True, he had had to accept the reunification of Korea as a so-called democratic state. But China bore none of its huge cost and reaped benefits such as better trade relations with the former South Korea; an end to insult and embarrassment by North Korea's crude, shortsighted leaders; and an agreement that no US or UN forces would be stationed north of the former north-south border or venture north of it without China's agreement.

His political appointees would make that case for him vigorously, just as they would promote his global trade initiatives. Following his strategy, China would use, acquire, and build a network of rail lines, roads, ports, and sea routes connecting the country with Europe and East Africa. When complete, these logistics projects, plus the increased presence of Chinese military power, would improve the supply lines that presently made China's trade, especially in energy, expensive and insecure. His employment of China's economic and military power was already showing results, shaping the policies of many nations to benefit China. Soon, when energy supplies were secure and with the leverage of economic development loans to strategically located nations that couldn't afford to service them, Ming knew he would lead China back to its rightful place as the most powerful, prosperous, and influential nation in the world.

Since China was the world's largest energy consumer, the vital ingredients of her national power were large, reliable imports of petroleum, coal, and natural gas. To ensure sufficient energy, Ming knew he must see to the expansion of naval and air power so that China could react quickly to events that might threaten its interests anywhere.

The greatest danger to China's energy supplies was the rivalry between Iran and Saudi Arabia, between Shi'a and Sunni. Iran was not only a critical source of petroleum but had the potential to either enhance or reduce the security of China-bound tankers as they lumbered through the Persian Gulf and the Strait of Hormuz to reach the open sea and thence China. Ming had sent his navy to patrol the Persian Gulf shipping lanes, and he had tilted economically and politically in favor of backing Tehran as a balance to American support of Riyadh. Preventing war in the region was paramount to keeping petroleum moving to China at reasonable cost and with certainty. Ming understood that Iran, Israel, and America were key to this and maneuvered among them, playing them off one another to China's advantage. Iran especially needed China's support now since North Korea's assistance with missile and nuclear bomb development had ended abruptly with the reunification of north and south.

As for the United States, Rick Martin had won a second term, but the election had been close, and his party only controlled half of America's Congress. In the person of Martin, Ming knew he faced a proud man at the end of his career who was concerned about history's verdict. Ming felt he could use that to his own advantage. And America was still reeling from Fahim's terror campaign, so Martin had many things to distract his attention.

Ming's musing ended abruptly with the buzzing of his phone. He saw that the caller was the party leader in Shanghai, someone whom he could not afford to ignore today, not with the party congress only weeks away. Frowning, Ming accepted the call, bracing himself for a brazen proposal—probably infrastructure, since that was the man's family business—that would further enrich the powerful regional politician.

Chapter 6

VOLARIS FLIGHT 438 FROM TIJUANA braked to a stop at its gate at the Federal de Bachigualato International Airport at Culiacán, State of Sinaloa, Mexico. Among the passengers shuffling off was a slim, mustached man in his thirties. He was dressed like the international banker he was, in a dark blue suit, custom-made white pinpoint cotton shirt, Hermès tie, and wing-tip Ferragamo slip-ons. He carried nothing. Entering the terminal, he made his way rapidly to the street by a route with which he was clearly familiar. Once outside, he stepped purposefully toward a silver-gray Mercedes G-Class off-road vehicle with tinted windows. As he approached, a husky man emerged from the front passenger seat and swung open the rear door for him. The Mercedes immediately pulled away from the no-parking zone it had occupied and began to make its way northeast along Federal Route 280, followed by a blue Ford F-250 Raptor occupied by four men.

Emerging from the last of the city's *colonias* on Boulevard Francisco Madero, the two vehicles increased speed for twenty minutes, then slowed as they turned onto a side road that soon became potholed and then onto a gravel road that, though not paved, had no potholes. An hour after leaving the airport, the vehicles reached a circular driveway, near which were several armed men who waved them through. The Ford halted, the Mercedes continued to the door of a sprawling, two-story hacienda with white walls and terracotta roof tiles. Large urns with beautiful flowering plants flanked the doorway, unnoticed by the blue-suited visitor who had been passing through that doorway since childhood.

The visitor smiled at the majordomo near the door and went down a brightly painted hall. He knocked on a door whose heavy, dark wood gave off a satisfying thump. Without waiting for a response, he entered.

"*Federico, mi sobrino, bienvenido!*" said a man in gray slacks and a white linen guyabera shirt, much shorter and older than the one he greeted. "Tio Carlos," replied his visitor. "Uncle Carlos" was Carlos Flores Solano, head of the drug cartel controlling the trade from Sinaloa and Durango to Arizona, California, Chicago, and New York. He was probably the most wanted man in Mexico, but this did not stop him from using his condominium in Mexico City or several other trophy homes like this one around the country. The combination of vigilance, bribery, and ruthless power gave him impunity with Mexican authorities, although not with others. He was in danger from his competitors and from the gringos who held his predecessor, now sitting in a supermax prison north of the border. He trusted no one, except family—sometimes.

After an *abrazo* and admiration of several pictures of a newborn son on his nephew's phone, the older man got down to business: "Federico, let me tell you a story."

Even though he was family, Federico couldn't suppress a chill at those words, and the expression on his uncle's face revealed that he knew it. Carlos Solano was known for his storytelling, which always began with those words, often when his lieutenants were gathered in this room. Usually the stories were narco-gossip or tales of political chicanery, but occasionally one of the lieutenants would realize the story was about *him*, and it was a story of betrayal. The man's fear would grow before the eyes of all, until, in a quiet voice, Solano would say, "*Mi hijo, mi hijo, por que me traicionas?*" The man thus accused of betrayal would then be pinioned by guards and hustled away for interrogation and execution. For this quirk, Solano's street name was "*El Narrador,*" the storyteller. It had a purpose, as did all of his actions: it kept his lieutenants too fearful of him and of each other to challenge him.

"Federico, as you know, the ability to move products and people across borders and within societies without permission or detection has many uses. Occasionally, we put our skills to unusual but profitable uses."

Federico nodded.

"So," continued his uncle, "when an Arab highly sought by the Americans came to me for my assistance in bringing people and explosives into *el Norte*, for which he would pay handsomely, I agreed. The Americans' problems are no concern of mine, and the money was good, so we did as he asked."

Federico started to speak, but his uncle's raised hand stifled his question.

"Hear me out, then questions. Shortly after we agreed, I was approached by another person from the Middle East. This one was a senior member of Iran's Quds Force commandos. You know of them?"

Federico nodded.

"He paid extremely well for a similar service, although he didn't need to move explosives, only people. Unlike the first man, who specified delivery only to various locations within the states of Washington, Oregon, and Idaho, this second man required deliveries to both the east and west coasts of the United States.

"The first man was the now deceased terrorist Fahim al-Wasari, who led the recent jihad campaign in America," continued Solano. "He was tracked to a hideout in Idaho and killed in a raid led personally by General Ray Morales, the head of Homeland Security. In fact it is said that Morales himself killed al-Wasari in a hand-to-hand struggle. This was made known in many news reports.

"But here's a puzzle, Federico: shortly before the government forces raided the hideout of Fahim al-Wasari, we were asked with great urgency to transport five Quds Force men from Virginia to Coeur d'Alene, Idaho. That's very close to the place where Fahim was killed. Is there a connection? If so, there's something very strange going on between America and Iran that is happening in the United States itself. Think about it: Why would Morales, a senior government official well past his prime physically, personally lead a tiny raiding party in storming a terrorist camp? There were only three of them. One was killed, one badly injured, and Morales himself barely survived his encounter with Fahim.

"There must be something more to this," he continued, "something the Martin administration wants hidden. I want to know what that is. Perhaps I can use it to force Martin to slow his campaign against our products, which is far too successful. It's costing us millions! Besides that, there could also be a great deal of money for us in what I've just told you.

"We don't need to solve the puzzle, Federico, to benefit from our knowledge. President Martin has many enemies who would be happy to devote their considerable resources to solving it for their own political advantage. Just think, Federico, of the outcry if Martin had asked for Iran's help in eliminating Fahim. Or, if he did not, the outcry would be about the fact that Iran dispatched commandos to the United States for some purpose and that America's security apparatus was unable to detect them.

"Federico, your job is to take what I've told you and figure out how to leverage this knowledge into making us money."

Chapter 7

ARTY SANDERS HURRIED THROUGH THE door of The Dubliner on F Street NW. He was irritated by the soaking he'd gotten from the wind-blown rain that mocked his umbrella. Sanders was an opposition researcher, or "oppo." He was one of the very best, someone who could find dirt on Mother Teresa or at least make it appear there was dirt to find. That meant politicians and lobbyists needed him, but it did not mean they admired or respected him. But Sanders planned to move higher on the political food chain, not that he disliked his present work. He enjoyed having power over people, figuring out their secrets, and seeing their arrogance shrivel when confronted with them. But he wanted to become a partner to the powerful, not remain merely one of their tools.

Marty, a short, bald guy whose superbly tailored glen plaid suit disguised a couch potato physique, wasn't a fan of Irish pubs—too much carved dark wood for his taste—but Ralph Jacobson apparently liked this one. Seeing him at a small table wedged into the far corner, Marty waved and headed toward him. It was well into happy hour, and most of the green leather-topped stools lining the bar were occupied.

"Hey, Ralph. I see you beat the rain; you're not soaked like I am."

"Thanks for meeting me here, Mr. Sanders."

"Marty, please."

"OK, Marty."

A harried blonde waitress in a black skirt and white blouse materialized. Sanders pointed to the younger man's drink. "Another?"

"Why not?"

"More of the same for my friend and Jameson for me, neat."

After she left, Sanders said, "You like this place? It's not exactly a Capitol Hill watering hole, and I don't see many folks here your age, mostly old fogies like me here."

Jacobson smiled briefly. "Actually, that's why I suggested it when you invited me for a drink. You're a heavy hitter; I'm a lowly Senate staff peon. If we were at the Old Ebbitt, someone in the crowd there might wonder what's going on between us. And you know how suspicious my boss is!"

After the waitress had hurriedly delivered their drinks, Sanders raised his glass and said, "Confusion to our enemies." They touched glasses, the clink inaudible in the hubbub. Jacobson looked quizzically at the older man.

"Ralph, how long have you been with the senator?"

"It'll be three years next month."

"Congratulations. She burns out most of her young meat in under two years."

Jacobson bristled. Grinning, Sanders held up a hand, his sleeve pulling back to flash his Rolex Oyster Perpetual. He didn't miss Jacobson's eyes darting to it. "Now don't act like I've hurt your feelings. I know you're tougher than that. I'm an opposition researcher; it's my job to know stuff that people would rather I didn't. There's a big market for that in this town, as I'm sure you know. And I could use some help."

Jacobson's expression became less wary. He nodded.

"You know, Ralph, I see a lot of junior congressional staffers as I go about my business. Some of them are so naïve I want to slap 'em upside the head. Others are like frightened rabbits, terrified of offending the staff director. And then there are the ones who've turned bitter because entry-level jobs on the Hill are more servitude than legislating. You know what I mean?"

"I do. You've got to be tough, practical, and quick to figure out the games people play." Jacobson preened noticeably.

"But a few—and you're one of them—learn quickly what it takes to succeed, to move up the ladder, and have the brains and balls to do what that takes. I've heard that you do good research, and I like your style, Ralph. There would be a place for you in my organization, if you wanted it. You'd enjoy it. Nothing feels as good as watching one of those posturing politicians fold when you've got the goods on 'em."

Jacobson was smiling now.

"So look. Here's my proposition: Your boss has been a pretty good client. But recently she's gotten too full of herself. She stiffed me on some really juicy information, something worth a fat bonus. Nobody gets to do that.

"I want something on her, and given the special relationship I know you have with her, I'm betting you can deliver it. She'd figure out where it came from, of course, but you can tell her to stuff it because you work for me. Would you like to do that?"

Jacobson's eager expression was his answer.

But seconds later, it became twisted, fearful. "But she'll pull my security clearance. She'll blacklist me. I'd never work on the Hill again!"

"Ralph, you'll work on the Hill again but not under the thumb of some senator. You'll work on the Hill for *me*. Trust me, Gustafson's anger will be no more than pissing in the wind. Politicians will write fat checks to us for what we do. You'll walk into the Old Ebbitt, and committee chairmen will be buying you drinks. Everyone will know you're *Marty's guy* and what you know will make some and break others. And they're dying to find out, to get some tidbit they can drop later. 'I was having a drink with Marty Sanders's guy, Ralph Jacobson, and he told me, in confidence …'"

Jacobson nodded.

"Consider it settled, Ralph, if you have something for me. What can you bring to the party?"

Jacobson smiled and pulled out his phone. "Something you'll like," he said.

Twenty minutes later, Marty stepped outside, not even noticing that the rain had gotten worse. Some six months ago he had given Gustafson that picture of Ray Morales and Ella Martin, and it sure as hell deserved a bonus. Her contemptuous refusal had rankled, but it was more than that.

I know her mind. Hell, I should because my mind works exactly the same way. If she thinks she can bully you, she will. I'm going to slap her down; not ruin her, just show her she can't mess with me!

He smiled as a taxi swerved to the curb. Sometimes he amazed even himself with his ability to find dirt on politicians.

Chapter 8

JERUSALEM, ISRAEL

J OSHUA ASKENAZI SCRIBBLED ON A notepad as he sat in his study at six a.m. recalling yesterday's cabinet meeting. It had been, as usual, a mixture of the ridiculous and sublime, of the inconsequential and the existential. Twenty-one duplicitous prima donnas, he thought. That's what Israeli cabinets *always* were. When a country had thirty-four political parties vying for one hundred twenty parliamentary seats, that's what you got: coalition government is inevitable, and the result is predictable. No Israeli government had lasted its full term since 1988.

Yesterday his government once again began to unravel from ministerial egos, facts on the ground, and the single-minded focus of tiny political parties on a single piece of the thousand-piece jigsaw puzzle their prime minister must solve.

The finance minister, head of a party with only three seats in the Knesset—but seats essential to his majority—led off by threatening to resign. The head of the National Insurance Institute, one of Israel's many powerful career bureaucrats, had announced that his agency, which paid old-age pensions, would cease the practice of handing over "surplus" funds to Israel's general budget. The finance minister made it clear that she would pull her party out of the government if this decision was allowed to stand.

There had been an ultimatum from the minister representing the Jewish Homeland Party and their three votes: Mateh Binyamin, a settlement region of the West Bank, must be permitted to expand by twenty percent in the coming year. This one was a bit of a puzzle, thought Askenazi, as he sipped his second cup of coffee. What had set the minister off? Jewish Homeland always wanted to enlarge existing settlements and build new ones. And their leader always made dire threats to support his proposals. *But why now? Something's going on that I don't understand. I'll get Barak on it.*

The last of yesterday's bombs had been thrown by, appropriately enough, the defense minister. Leader of a party that fancied itself "the sword of Israel," the minister demanded a reprisal operation because some of the rockets fired from Gaza had escaped the Iron Dome defense system. Never mind that there were only three killed, all kids. Never mind that reprisal raids were deadly games of whack-a-mole that got Israeli soldiers killed but made little difference in the number of rockets fired from Gaza. And since all adult Israelis were required to do military service, the dead soldiers had relatives who criticized Askenazi sharply for every casualty. Not to mention the Left parties, who criticized him for every Palestinian death that couldn't be proven to be that of a Hamas fighter.

The prime minister's own army service had been in the Thirty-Fifth Brigade, the paratroopers. As if it were yesterday he remembered the night he and other new soldiers had marched up the winding trail to the ancient Jewish fortress of Masada, which had held out against Roman legions for three years. Every Israeli Jew knew that the fall of Masada had begun two thousand years in which Jews had no country. Askenazi and his comrades had sworn together on that torch lit night in the fortress, "Masada shall not fall again." Never again would Jews be without a homeland, no matter what that required.

Although he had worked hard to earn selection for the paratroopers, and had worn the brigade's red beret and jump boots proudly, he felt disappointment as well as pride when he thought of his army years. His goal had been to join Sayeret Matkal, the secretive and daring special reconnaissance unit, an organization that hand-picked its soldiers rather than accept applications. No one outside the unit knew how the selection process worked; only that those tapped for it vanished from their former units, with a one-word explanation: "Sayeret."

The Masada ceremony had been discontinued since his youth. When he became prime minister he ordered it reinstated and made a point of attending whenever he could. Watching young soldiers fresh from basic training take their oaths of allegiance to Israel and affirm—as he had and still believed—that "Masada shall not fall again" always moved and inspired him.

Askenazi worried incessantly about Iran. He worried not only about increasing Iranian power relative to Israel but about the willingness of Israelis to believe that Iran's threats to exterminate them weren't just rhetoric, like the Saudi's words. They meant it and soon would have the means to do it in one swift, terrible slaughter. *Are Shara and I the only ones who realize this?*

It was David and Goliath again. Israel's sling was its air force; Goliath's sword, Iranian nuclear missiles. Just like David, who would have been chopped to bits if he waited to use his sling and stones until after Goliath had gotten close to him, Israel cannot wait.

Joshua heard Shara moving about upstairs in their bedroom. The old house's floor creaked slightly as she made her way to the bathroom. He heard the toilet flush, which told him that it was time for her tea, their morning ritual. He invariably awakened a little after five a.m., while she slumbered until six or seven. Although they had household staff, he always made her tea himself, in her favorite cup, and brought it to her.

Joshua stood by their bed and waited fondly as Shara arranged her pillows just so, then reached for her tea. After forty years he still marveled that she was his wife—and much more. Vivacious, bright, and outspoken, she had accepted him only after a long pursuit. There were many who claimed she supplied the brains that had propelled a fame-hungry young man along his path to the prime minister's office. In fact, he and Shara were more balanced than those observers realized; both were brazenly ambitious and were fierce competitors willing to take risks. Shara's fierceness was calculating and thorough; Joshua's tended to be emotional and impulsive. Their success within the intricate patterns of Israeli politics was owed to both temperaments.

They sat in companionable silence for some time, then Joshua said, "Shamir is positioning himself to resign unless I order a raid into Syria in reprisal for those kids the rockets killed."

"And you don't want to."

"Shara, reprisals don't have any lasting effect. They kill a few of us, we kill a few of them, and on we go. And the more we use reprisals, the larger they have to be in order to satisfy people like Shamir and his party." Joshua threw up his hands.

"Joshua, you know that Hezbollah wouldn't be a serious threat without the support and leadership of Quds Force. Instead of tit for tat with Hezbollah, you should hit hard at Quds."

"But that would make Martin very angry. He worries about escalation. And Quds has helped America in Syria; in fact they still are helping. We have another fifty F-35s to be delivered in a few months. He or his allies in Congress might stop the delivery."

"Well, there is that risk, but Senator Gustafson would fight him hard if he tried that, and we could make it hot for him with our political action committee."

"That would be unnecessarily risky, Shara. I don't want to publicly challenge the man who will lead our most important ally for the next three years when we still have other options."

Shara nodded, then said, "You need to keep thinking about that. Iron Dome and bee-sting reprisals against Hezbollah aren't a sustainable way of protecting Israel from Iran's determination to destroy us.

"And remember God's promise to Joshua of Nun: 'Be strong and courageous; for you shall put this people in possession of the land that I swore to their ancestors to give them.'"

"Shara," he said, with the realization that he would never understand her spirituality: "I'm not Joshua of Nun!"

"Everything happens for a reason, Joshua. Perhaps that is the very reason that a man named Joshua is once again leading Israel."

Chapter 9

NEAR POTOMAC, MARYLAND

A N ISRAELI INTELLIGENCE OFFICER—WHO WOULD answer to the name of Hank Raeder at today's meeting—puttered along River Road north of Potomac, Maryland. He drove a battered silver Toyota Corolla. In his line of work he met a lot of people in out-of-the-way places, so he was always careful not to attract attention; hence he drove a heap. Of course, he was being tailed, probably by the FBI. As a member of Mossad's Washington station, he expected to be under observation. Since there was nothing illegal about what he was doing today, and he felt no obligation to protect the man he was meeting, he made only a cursory effort to shake the tail. He wasn't going to show them his best stuff when it didn't matter; letting them believe his tradecraft was mediocre would help him break surveillance another day, when it was crucial.

Usually he had an idea how the meeting would go, but today was different. He was meeting a guy who called himself William, who had secured the meeting by dropping a tidbit of his story: Ray Morales's heroic takedown of Fahim was not as it appeared; there was a drug cartel involved. The guy sounded American but had a faint Latin accent.

William's claim might be bullshit. But since truth was never essential, especially in relations among nations, even a bullshit story might someday be useful to Israel. And this story did have a certain logic to it. After all, it had always seemed dubious to Raeder that a guy Morales's age could go mano a mano with the world's most wanted terrorist and win. Or that he would even try it.

Spotting the left turn for Swain's Lock Road, he took it, and within a few minutes he reached Swain's Lock on the C&O Canal. It was a weekday afternoon, and few other cars were in the parking lot.

Clad in a Georgia Tech hoodie and Levis, he got out and sauntered past the whitewashed, two-story lockhouse, home of the tender in days gone by, and started across the short wooden footbridge to the far side of the narrow canal. As he reached the other side, he heard footsteps on the planks behind him. He stopped and leaned on the rail, gazing downward into the glassy canal, seeing his own reflection. As the footsteps approached, Raeder turned his head to glance casually at the approaching visitor, who had a pair of binoculars over his left shoulder.

"Mr. Raeder, I'm William," said the man, whose binoculars were the agreed recognition signal, as was the Israeli's Georgia Tech hoodie. Raeder noted William's anxious, darting glances at their surroundings. Everything about William screamed "amateur" to him.

"Pleased to meet you, William. Call me Hank."

"Let's walk, Hank."

They ambled along the towpath, the canal on their left, trees branching above them. "Hank, I know you're a busy man. So am I, so let's be brief."

Stooping to pick up a stone that he side-armed into the canal, William continued: "You know of the Sinaloa cartel, don't you?"

"Of course."

"I'm not part of that organization, but I represent a client who has access to their leader, Carlos Flores Solano. My client doesn't conduct business in narcotics, but he exchanges information with Señor Solano from time to time. My client asked me to tell you the following, which came from Señor Solano:

"Last summer the Solanos were hired by Iran's clandestine operations group, the Quds Force. I trust you know of it as well?"

Impatiently, the other grunted, "Sure."

William continued: "Using their drug-smuggling channels, the Solanos brought a group of Iranians, presumably Quds Force commandos, into the United States. About a month before the attack on Fahim's hideout in Idaho, they delivered them without incident to various locations on the east and west coasts. A few days before that attack, the Solanos received an urgent request to transport four Iranians from Crisfield, Maryland, to Coeur d'Alene, Idaho. Unlike the earlier 'deliveries,' these men were armed."

"So help me out here, William. What's the bottom line?"

"Hank, Coeur d'Alene is quite near the wilderness area where Fahim was operating his terrorist base. Does it not strike you as questionable that Ray Morales, alone after the plane crash had taken out his two companions, was able to successfully assault this base? He's a Marine, yes, but one man in his sixties against several terrorists?"

"So, you want me to believe the Iranians were part of Morales's plan; they were working together? That's pretty hard to swallow, William. Got any proof?"

"Not a smoking gun—not yet, anyway—but someone with the right interest and investigative resources could well find one, don't you think? And in any case, it would be interesting to investigate how Quds Force commandos operated in America for a month without detection by General Morales's organization, DHS. Or by the FBI."

"OK, it might be. But what's the deal you came to drive, William? You've given me this information for free. In my business that's the sign of a bullshit peddler. What are you holding back that you want to sell me, now that you've delivered your teaser? Or am I right: you're just peddling bullshit to see whether you can get me to destroy my credibility by passing it along?"

"Hank, I'm neither a poser nor running a false flag operation. I asked you to meet because my client is very, very concerned about the direction of American policy toward Iran. The idea that it is possible to do a deal with the Iranians and stop their nuclear program is naïve and dangerous to my client. Yet certain important figures in the American government, especially the president, believe the Iranians can be trusted. Whether or not there was collusion in Fahim's demise, the Quds operation I've revealed shows how wrong that is and how little they fear American power. They're playing America for a fool in the Middle East and now in America itself. You are Mossad. You know this is true.

"Israel's close relation and influence with the United States has earned you this gift from my client. You will be able to verify it. When Israel uses this information to strengthen American opposition to Iran, you will be advancing my client's interest as well as your own."

With that, William turned on his heel and strode back toward the parking lot, leaving Raeder to determine whether this was a gift or a trap. It took Raeder only moments to realize that if there was a trap, he could avoid it. And he had a theory about William's "client": it was most likely the Saudis. The director was going to be very interested in this. He strolled back toward his car, smiling.

Chapter 10

WASHINGTON, DC

"THIS THING COULD BE A disaster for us!" said Vice President Bruce Griffith to President Martin and Bart Guarini, the White House chief of staff. They filled the president's small private office nearly to overflowing. As usual when the three met, there was underlying tension. Griffith was an extraordinarily assertive vice president who had clashed with his boss many times, twice causing Martin to consider curtailing his duties. Guarini, with Martin since his first Senate campaign sixteen years ago, was his closest political associate apart from the First Lady. Guarini thought of himself above all as the president's political and personal protector, a loyalty that often brought him into collision with Griffith.

"Of course it could," snapped Guarini, a wiry six-footer with classic male pattern baldness. "But that's what we're here for," he continued. "Look, all she has is her word that Morales tortured a terrorist. We can discredit that, slow-roll our inquiry, fuzz it up, bury it with other news."

"Or we could admit that it happened," said Griffith, whose acne-scarred face saved his otherwise classic politician appearance from being too smooth, "but without our knowledge. Then we build on rather than oppose the hearings Gustafson is threatening. You know, 'follow the evidence wherever it leads.' She thinks she has us over a barrel, but she doesn't."

Guarini, observing the president's disgust at Griffith's proposal, said, "Mr. President, "there's no way hearings end well. No—we've got to convince Gustafson to lay off, or we buy her off, or scare her off."

"And we do that by … ?" said Martin

"Well, let's take them in order," said Guarini. "You could invite her for a face-to-face in the Oval."

Martin scowled, rocking back in his desk chair to look up at Guarini, who was leaning against the wall to the right of Griffith. In that posture, Guarini looked a little like a praying mantis. Griffith sat in the only visitor chair. Martin said, "So what would I say to her besides, 'please drop this. Ray Morales is a good man, and what he did saved a lot of lives'"

"Nonstarter," said Griffith, waving a hand dismissively. "Arlene Gustafson has been in this town too long to be awed by a meeting in the Oval, or even by the president of the United States. And we all know she blames Ray for her son's suicide and wants to destroy him."

"So what else might we try?" said Martin.

"She's ambitious, Mr. President," Griffith observed. "I think she even has hopes of running for your job someday. Maybe an important ambassadorship—Paris, London, Bonn, Tokyo. That would allow her to match her strong domestic experience with some foreign policy cred." Griffith regarded this option with special favor because it would make it harder for her to run against him in three years.

"I like that better than begging her to drop it," said Martin. "It's worth trying. What else?"

"Well, she sure would like to stop that oil pipeline extending from the Canadian tar sands from running through her state," said Guarini. The president nodded, hoping this meeting would eventually produce something he hadn't already thought of, then gave a "what else?" gesture with his left hand.

"What she wants most is Morales's scalp." Griffith's words hung in the air as if they were visible. He was willing to play Judas, ready to give up the man who had done more than any other to bring Fahim down, ending his terror campaign and salvaging Martin's reelection. Martin and Guarini glared at him. Guarini started to speak, but Griffith held up a hand, preempting him. "I know that's drastic. It's unfair. It might even seem dishonorable. But it's not. It's the sort of thing a former Marine general would understand, maybe even something Ray has done himself. Sometimes it's necessary to sacrifice a rear guard so that the main body has time to reach a defensible position."

"Mr. President," Griffith continued, "Your legacy is threatened if Gustafson holds open hearings to investigate the rumor that Morales found Fahim by torturing a detainee. And, *and*, we each know what else involving Ray Morales would inevitably come out under the grilling he would get. Morales won't lie under oath."

Griffith's unwelcome words were met with a long silence. Eventually, Guarini said, "OK, the third line of defense. What do we have to scare her off?"

Martin looked expectantly at his vice president, who had been the attack dog through both his presidential campaigns.

Though he actually had only a hope, not an idea, Griffith was happy to step up: "Well, Mr. President, it's no secret that she likes her boy-toys."

"Other than the novelty of a woman being a sexual predator, that's hardly a big deal," said Guarini.

"Right," snapped Griffith. "But I was alluding to the fact that she's run through a lot of younger men in her three terms. Maybe some of them were a *lot* younger than her current playmate. Maybe some of them had traffic tickets or misdemeanor arrests that she fixed with the DC cops. Maybe some of them had such questionable backgrounds that they got security clearance only because she leaned on the FBI. If we can delay her, stall her for a few weeks, I can probably come up with something." He looked at the president, his expression asking, "How about it?" President Martin, a disgusted look on his face, nodded: "OK. But we've got no more than a week to act. Bruce and Bart, keep me in the loop; let me hear your findings and ideas as they arise."

As he walked alone back to his own office, the vice president congratulated himself for having taken control of the meeting. He felt even more confident that he was going to be the next president. He'd positioned himself to be the savior of the Martin presidency and staked out the leading role in shaping how Martin would handle Morales's messes, the screw-ups that could keep him out of the White House and maybe even deny him the nomination.

Time for that dinner with Marty Sanders.

Chapter 11

TEL AVIV, ISRAEL

I T WAS A LONG AND vaporous cabinet meeting. In other words, typical. Put twenty-one politicians in a room, and that's what you get. That's why Prime Minister Askenazi, now presiding over them without much thought, never brought the important things to the cabinet until he had decided what to do and was ready to do it. His mind wandered as the finance minister spun a vision of the tax potential of Israel's new medical marijuana export industry. Germany, Austria, Australia, and Mexico were, he crowed, lining up to buy all that Israel companies could produce. And soon there would be other large customers. The tax benefit to the government could be three hundred million shekels a year.

Askenazi, meanwhile, worried about the entrenchment of Hezbollah in Syria and how that had changed the strategic equation for Israel. Until the Syrian civil war, Syria's border had been Israel's quietest. Back then it wasn't a source of rocket attacks or terrorist raids. Now it was ablaze.

The ministry of construction and housing, not to be outdone by his colleague, gave a glowing report of Chinese investment in Israeli infrastructure projects. He happily described his own role in obtaining Chinese funds for the new harbor at Ashdod and light rail projects in Tel Aviv, as well as millions invested in Israel's high-tech sector.

Prime Minister Askenazi managed to smile, nod, and make comments while his mind contemplated the seeming inevitability of another war between Israel and Hezbollah. Which was to say, between Israel and

Iran. Hezbollah's mid-level and senior leaders, cash, weapons, explosives, ammunition—they all came from Iran.

Would the spark come from Syria or Lebanon? And what about the army? Since 2004 the Israel Defense Forces had become so absorbed with what were really police operations that its readiness for full-scale war was questionable. The gap between the experience that its lieutenants, captains, and majors were amassing in policing and the experience they would need to employ their men in large-scale combat greatly troubled their colonels and generals. The senior officers had seen this cycle before, and the results had not been pretty.

Askenazi emerged from his gloomy prognosticating sufficiently to realize that the foreign minister, never one to be left out, was holding forth about her success in improving relations with Japan. She hailed increasing security cooperation, for example, annual national security dialogues in Tokyo and Jerusalem covering strategy, counterterrorism, and military technology. And the number of officers exchanged between the two nations' armed forces and security services had doubled on her watch. That of course led to comments from the defense minister.

The prime minister had a finely tuned sense of how long to let his ministers hold forth in reporting evidence to their party that they had advanced the party's agenda. When the defense minister paused for a sip of water, Askenazi thanked the ministers for their selfless work on behalf of the nation and adjourned the meeting. He decided the time had come to deal with the one item of urgent business on *his* agenda.

"Ya'el," Askenazi said, as the cabinet ministers left the room, some chatting cheerfully, the defense minister and his allies scowling. Director General of the Prime Minister's Office Ya'el Barak, whose role and relationship to Askenazi were similar to those of Bart Guarini to Rick Martin, came to his side. "Ya'el," Askenazi continued, softly, "What of Persepolis? Spare me your objections that I know so well—just give me an update."

"Yes, Prime Minister. We have obtained a unit, and our people are reverse-engineering it. As expected, they have, so far, found nothing we cannot copy or improve upon."

"Keep pressing them, Ya'el. And don't look so long in the face. This is only a precaution. I haven't decided."

Chapter 12

"MMM," SAID MARTY SANDERS. "NOTHING like that first puff on a fine cigar after a great dinner!" Vice President Bruce Griffith nodded and responded with a contented look as he completed the ritual of lighting his own Cohiba. They were on the veranda of the vice president's quarters, once the home of the officer in charge of the Naval Observatory, on whose grounds it sat. A light wind was blowing, chilling the air.

Griffith gave what he intended to be a sheepish smile. "I know it's a little cool out here, but Marilyn hates cigar smoke; gotta smoke outside."

"I'm fine, Mr. Vice President; no worries. Our dinnertime discussion was encouraging. You're the right man for the presidency, and I'm glad you aren't bashful about your candidacy. None of that BS about hanging back until the last moment because you need to defer to the president."

"Thank you, Marty. And here's the thing: I'm going to start building my team *now*, the best people, a team that will fight with me through the campaign and then serve in key posts in my administration, in jobs for the proven, the trustworthy. I hope you're ready to join that team when I call. I can't *actually* hire my guys now—the national party would balk at this early stage—but I can make pledges now to the folks I want beside me. Marty, you're one of them."

Griffith held out his hand.

Marty Sanders was far too cynical to believe he had just heard a commitment, but his heart gave a little jump anyway. *I'm going to have a job in this campaign and then in the White House; that will prove to those assholes who've been calling me a hack, a political garbage man, just how wrong they are. Ideally, a job that will let me screw over one or two of them.*

Shaking the offered hand, Sanders said with a big smile, "Mr. Vice President, it will be the greatest honor of my life to serve with you. What do you have in mind?"

"Marty, I want you close to me. I'll need your advice frequently. I don't know what title yet, but I want you on the campaign plane with me and then in the West Wing."

It was no surprise to Sanders that the vice president left himself so much wiggle room.

"Well, when you're ready to make it official, sir, you can count on me."

"I hope I can count on you before then, Marty. In fact, I *am* counting on you. Because there's a big potential problem right now, one that could keep me from being elected, maybe even keep me from being nominated."

Marty had figured something like this was coming and was probably the purpose for Griffith's trolling a shiny lure in front of him this evening.

"Sounds serious, sir. How can I help?"

"Marty, since you are close to Arlene Gustafson, I'm sure you've heard the rumors that there is more to Fahim's demise than what we've said publicly. That Ray Morales used, shall we say, irregular means to locate the jihadi safe house in Idaho." Griffith winked.

"Of course, sir." Sanders knew what was coming and had the urge to cut to the chase, but his desire to see Griffith uncomfortable won out.

"That might blow up into a huge national scandal. And it doesn't even have to be true, as you know, for that to happen. All it needs is endorsement by a heavy hitter, and the Martin administration, very much including me, will be smeared. I've been alerted that Gustafson's staff have been asking a lot of questions at the agencies, like FBI and DOD, that might be involved in such a thing."

Griffith's eyes bored into Sanders's. "I need your help to head this off, Marty."

"Well, sir, I *do* have some influence with Senator Gustafson, but you know how she is when she smells the blood of Democrats. Plus, she *hates* Morales; besides her son's suicide, she's never forgiven him for slapping her down during a public hearing. Yours is a big ask."

"If you're as tough and clever as I think you are, you'll get it done, Marty."

"Actually, I believe I can. I may need a little show of interest from you, sir. Can I count on that?"

"You can."

"Then I'll be on my way." The vice president walked Sanders to the front door. There the vice president gave him what Sanders thought of as "the sincere but threatening handshake," right hand gripping firmly, left hand on Marty's shoulder, piercing gaze into his eyes. He almost laughed.

Driving along Massachusetts Avenue, Marty could hardly believe his good fortune: now he knew exactly how he would employ the explosive suicide note he had so recently obtained from Ralph Jacobson and what advantage it would bring him.

Chapter 13

I T WAS SURPRISING HOW QUICKLY it all unraveled. Senator Gustafson held Ray Morales responsible for her Marine son's suicide; she was wrong about that, but it didn't matter. What mattered was that she chaired the Government Operations and Oversight Committee and had the power to bring Ray Morales before that committee. Ignoring White House requests to desist on national security grounds, she plowed ahead with her plan to haul Morales before her and humiliate him.

"This hearing of the Government Operations and Oversight Committee will come to order." Senator Gustafson had emphasized her words and her authority with a sharp gavel smack that resounded in the small room used for classified hearings.

As the hearing began, the senators settled into their seats. Seated at a table facing her, and feeling less confident than he appeared, Ray had silently repeated his mantra: *don't volunteer, set everything in context, and don't show anger.* In her opening statement, the chair noted that the hearing was classified top secret and that it was to look into all the circumstances surrounding the killing in Idaho last year of terrorist Fahim al-Wasari, leader of a virulent jihad in America that killed hundreds.

"Secretary Morales, do you have a statement you wish to read?"

"No, Madame Chairman," said Morales, with what he hoped was an earnest look on his face.

"Might that be because you believe you have something to hide?"

Morales's jaw clenched momentarily before he said, "Not at all, Madame

63

Chairman. It is to expedite this matter. We are here today because you have not been satisfied by prepared statements. I don't want to waste the committee's time, or mine, with another one."

"Very well, we will proceed. Each member will have five minutes for a statement or questions during this first round. I call on the senator from South Carolina, Mr. Thompson."

Though he was a Republican probing a leading figure in a Democratic administration, Thompson's questioning was cautious. Morales was a national hero for leading the attack that put an end to the worst period of domestic terrorism in living memory, one that had taken victims in seventeen states. That Morales had been wounded in the struggle made him even more a heroic figure. Other senators exercised the same care, and the first hour of the hearing passed without damage to the position that Morales intended to hold.

The floor returned to Senator Gustafson. "Secretary Morales, how were you able to locate Fahim, when he had eluded every resource of this government for so long?"

Morales's pulse accelerated. This was the beginning of the line of questioning that would test his ability to deceive without lying under oath. His attorney had urged him to take the Fifth Amendment, but he had refused.

"Madame Chairman, an alert police officer captured a would-be martyr seconds before he blew himself up in a crowded food court. The terrorist, who identified himself as Ali Hadrab, didn't know the location of Fahim's base, but he knew enough to enable an aerial search team to find it eventually in the backwoods of Idaho."

"You mean he gave up that information voluntarily?"

"I don't think he realized the significance of what he said. He described how he had been smuggled in via Mexico by a drug cartel and how he was handed off to Fahim. But the rendezvous was far from Fahim's base, and the terrorist was blindfolded while being driven there. He was an untraveled young Arab with limited English, stunned by his failure at the food court. It's no surprise that he didn't know how important his few data points were to become."

With the hint of a smile, Chairman Gustafson said, "You didn't answer my question, Mr. Secretary. Did he give the information voluntarily under questioning within the limits of Army Field Manual 2-22.3, which defines the lawful scope of interrogation methods?"

Morales felt wetness in his armpits. Tension filled the room like an explosive vapor needing only a spark to detonate. The row of senators gazed at Morales, some with eagerness, some with apprehension. Staffers scribbled furiously. Morales's attorney looked down at the green felt tablecloth.

Morales looked Gustafson in the eyes and said, "No, he did not."

"And who ordered this unlawful interrogation?"

"I did."

"Who supervised it?"

"I did."

"Madame Chairman! Will you yield the floor for one question?"

Gustafson shot a look promising retribution at the junior senator from Texas and said, "I will not! The gentleman will have his turn in order."

Turning again to Morales, she said, "So you are admitting under oath that you ordered and supervised an illegal interrogation!"

"Admitting is not the right word. There is no guilt in what I did. It had to be done to protect America and Americans. I did my duty."

"Duty is no protection against the consequences of breaking the law. You broke the law."

"Madame Chairman, I will accept the consequences of breaking the law. I trust this committee will weigh what I did against the law and also against the consequences of my not having done it. I am prepared to answer to the Congress and the American people."

His eyes scouring the row of senators, Morales continued, with more heat than he intended: "Madame Chairman, have you ever personally seen a human being with his intestines hanging out? Ever seen a medic trying frantically to keep a kid whose leg has been blown off from bleeding to death?

"No, you have not. And until we got Fahim, scenes of carnage were being repeated daily across America, in schools, malls, and restaurants. It was my duty to do everything in my power to stop the carnage. I did what was necessary to save lives."

After a brief, stunned silence, every senator demanded the floor. Gustafson gaveled them into silence.

"We now have an extraordinary and grave matter before us, one the committee did not anticipate and can hardly believe: A cabinet officer ordered and then supervised the torture of a detainee. And he sees nothing wrong with his brutal, illegal act!"

Jabbing her finger at Morales, Gustafson said, "Do you think you are above the law, Secretary Morales? Did you think you could come before this committee, brazenly reveal your crime, and we would excuse it or ignore it?"

Morales leaned forward and said, "Madame Chairman, if telling the truth under oath is brazen, then I am brazen. I take full responsibility for the interrogation." Morales paused, his gaze measuring the committee, and continued: "and for its results."

He rolled on: "At a time when we were clearly being bested by Fahim, when we had no leads, when you and others were rightly pointing out that the administration was failing in the most basic responsibility of any government–protecting its citizens—we captured one of the killers. A few moments—"

"Secretary Morales," interrupted Gustafson, "we already know about your failures. You are wasting the committee's time."

"Let me finish, Madame Chairman! It is not a waste of time to remind the committee of what was at stake at the moment of Hadrab's capture. The safety we enjoy today must not blind us to the peril we faced then.

"A few moments ago you called me brazen. That word would certainly describe the fanatic we confronted on that night. He was defiant, projecting the hate that had propelled him into that food court with an explosive vest and the intent to murder as many Americans as possible. And I knew that there were others like him, somewhere, awaiting Fahim's command to kill Americans anywhere they could."

"Secretary Morales," said Gustafson, "the fact that you were clueless in the face of Fahim's attacks doesn't mean they couldn't have been stopped by lawful methods. The nation obviously needed a more energetic and competent person in your job. I'm aware that the president was considering firing you. You tortured Hadrab out of desperation to save your job."

"You're wrong again, Madame Chairman. I had Fahim tortured to save American lives. Madame Chairman, you are correct that eventually the vast resources of this nation's law enforcement would have located Fahim's base and captured or killed everyone there. But you seem to overlook the reality that the time passed before then would have been counted in deaths as well as days. How many husbands, mothers, and children would you have sacrificed? Are the hundreds of dead Americans invisible to you?

"Because they weren't invisible to me that night as I confronted a defiant fanatic whose only goal was murdering as many innocents as possible. They, the citizens it was my sworn duty to protect, were the reason I refused to let Hadrab hide Fahim and his band of killers. I hope, Madame Chairman and committee members, that any of you would have done the same."

Morales sat back, folded his hands on the table, and scanned the nine senators before him. He felt the satisfaction of someone who has said what he needed to say. And while some senators gazed at him like hungry raptors, others nodded and returned his gaze with respect.

"We'll see, Secretary Morales." Turning to her right, Gustafson said, "We will proceed in regular order. Senator Carothers, you have the floor."

"Secretary Morales," said Carothers, "from your words moments ago, you would have us believe that the end justifies the means. That is the essence of the case you make for torture." After a short silence, Carothers said, "What is your response, Secretary Morales?"

"What is your question, Senator?"

"We will not accept game-playing, Mr. Secretary. *Do* you believe that the end justifies the means?"

"I believe that's a judgment each of us must make whenever we face the question. Does the end of public safety justify the incarceration of tens of thousands of Americans? Does the end of keeping you and your constituents free and safe from conquest by a foreign power justify the killing that such protection sometimes requires? Judging by your voting record, Senator, I'd say that you agree with me that sometimes the end *does* justify the means."

"Do not presume, Secretary Morales, to equate my voting record with your brutality!" Carothers looked at Chairman Gustafson, who said, "The witness will show proper respect for this body and its members, or be cited for contempt!"

"Senator Carothers, I meant no disrespect," said Morales. "I apologize for giving offense. I do think, however, that in this setting we owe it to each other and to our country to be candid. I will do all I can to keep my candor from causing further offense."

As Senator Carothers was glancing at papers before him, the senior senator from Massachusetts said, "Madame Chairman, I request the floor at this time in order to follow up on this important line of questioning."

Gustafson looked at Carothers, who nodded.

"The senator from Massachusetts, Mr. Philimont."

"Thank you, Madame Chairman.

"Secretary Morales, in your response you said something along the lines of 'every situation must be judged in light of its circumstances.' I think that's reasonable, if not always noble, and certainly we in politics are familiar with that approach. It would be helpful to understand that framework as you saw it at the time. Please walk us through your decision process that night."

"Certainly, Senator. American citizens were under constant attack; anywhere people gathered was under threat. We—the government and DHS and other agencies charged with security—were, by and large, failing to prevent attacks. We were, with few exceptions, unable to intercept the killers before they had detonated their suicide vests or started cutting down the people around them with automatic weapons. More and more Americans were opting to remain at home and take their children out of school."

Morales paused, shuffling the papers in front of him. Then he continued, "It was no exaggeration to say, as Senator Gustafson did in a speech last October, that the social fabric of the country was tearing apart, our economy was sputtering, and our defenses were ineffective.

"And then, Providence smiled on us. Enabled by alert citizens, a courageous police officer had time to wrestle Hadrab to the ground and prevent him from detonating his vest. Suddenly, we had an opportunity, one there was no reason to hope would be repeated anytime soon: to interrogate someone who had been dispatched on a suicide mission. Someone who surely knew where the terrorist base was. Ali Hadrab was potentially the key to ending our bloody national nightmare. Within hours he was being interrogated. And he was defiantly uncooperative."

Morales's attorney covered the microphone with one hand and whispered in Morales's ear.

"Madame Chairman, may we recess for ten minutes to allow me to consult my attorney?"

With a gleeful look, Gustafson said, "Yes, Secretary Morales, by all means consult your attorney. I'm not surprised he wants to counsel you. The committee will recess for ten minutes. We will resume promptly at eleven fifteen."

Chapter 14

Washington, DC

IN THE CORRIDOR, MORALES LISTENED to his attorney's forceful whisper: "Ray, you're about to set yourself up for prosecution and jail time. Think it through again. You owe it to yourself and to Julie to take the Fifth!"

"Frank, I'm between a rock and a hard place. There's only one way to reduce damage, and it's *not* claiming self-incrimination. I appreciate that you're trying to look after my best interests, but nobody knows those better than I do. I'm going through with this!"

Back in session, Morales resumed: "I knew that every day the nest of terrorists remained safe was a day in which attacks were being planned, martyrs prepared, killers let loose among us. We were losing this fight at the time. I was confident that we would eventually locate and kill or capture the jihadi terrorists, but if I let this particular killer control the situation by remaining silent, many more Americans would die before we prevailed. I decided I would authorize whatever measures it took to wring information from Hadrab."

Morales's attorney looked like he was watching his client raise the guillotine blade above his own neck.

"And you were successful, weren't you?" said Senator Philimont. "You made a tough call, and it was the right one."

"Madame Chairman," said Senator Carothers, "I request the floor for a follow-up question. I ask my colleague from Massachusetts to grant me the courtesy I gave him."

At a nod from Philimont, Carothers said, "And 'whatever it took' was what, Mr. Secretary? What did you do to this helpless young man?"

The palms of Morales's hands, interlocked on the table before him, grew sweaty. He placed them flat on the table. To his right, his attorney was observing his own steepled fingers planted on the table, with his lips compressed in a flat line.

"Senator, the skin of one thigh was peeled back using a surgical instrument. The procedure was extremely painful but not life-threatening. Almost immediately, Hadrab broke and began answering questions."

Silence. The senators looked at one another, then at Morales.

"And who did this 'procedure' as you call it?" said Carothers.

"An interrogator, at my personal direction and in my presence," said Morales flatly. "A physician treated the wound and gave Hadrab a pain reliever after he began answering."

The nine senators stared with disbelief. They had just heard a cabinet officer convict himself of a felony by his own testimony.

Chairman Gustafson made a show of looking at her watch, then said, "Clearly this has been an extraordinary session, one in which a cabinet officer admitted defiantly, even proudly, to a crime. We have a lot of work ahead of us. The committee stands in recess until two o'clock."

Morales remained seated, a contemplative expression on his face. Covering the microphone before him with a meaty hand, he said to his attorney, "Well, Frank, not a bad morning. We kept the biggest cat in the bag."

* * *

Arlene Gustafson sat at her desk, surrounded by staff offering encouragement, advice, and refreshment, a prizefighter between rounds, scenting a knockout victory.

"Senator, you've got him now," said her chief of staff. "Morales stands convicted by his own sworn testimony."

Gustafson bit into her club sandwich, tasting sweet victory as well as the food. "He's not going to wriggle out this time. I'm going back after this recess and dissect him like a frog in biology lab."

"Senator, the White House is calling—the vice president," said Gustafson's administrative assistant. A hush fell. Gustafson smiled and said,

"Give me the room, please." The men and women filed out, her chief of staff lingering in hopes of being asked to stay, but he was not. When he had closed the door, she picked up the receiver and spoke in a clipped, confident tone.

"Arlene Gustafson."

The vice president's voice filled her ear, its tone reminding her of a long, warm, and insincere handshake: "Hello, Arlene. A little bird told me you're doing quite a number on Morales. Where are you going with this?"

Gustafson smirked. "That remains to be seen, Mr. Vice President. I'll go wherever the testimony leads me. I hope you didn't call to ask me to go easy on him. He sat there and admitted breaking the law as if he were bulletproof. Well, I'm going to show him he's not!"

"Why is the White House calling? Martin must be getting pretty nervous, having you reach out like this. Or are you the one who's worried? Thinking about the nomination?"

"Arlene, really! You know better than that. I'm going to be the candidate. I'm going to be the next president. There is nothing that ties me or the White House to a former Marine gone rogue. If we decided to, we could help you hang him and make this whole thing a speed bump three years from now, when it matters. You've been in this town long enough to know that.

"Actually, this call is to give you an opportunity to head off a scandal of your own, one that would keep you from ever being voted Senate majority leader. That would be a shame, Arlene, because you've been working toward that for years, and it's finally within reach. And, actually, you'd make a damn good majority leader because the others are scared of you.

"Arlene, where were you on February seventeenth, two thousand and twelve?"

"Hell, I don't know. I ran my first Senate race that year, so I was probably out campaigning. What's it matter?"

"Arlene, your son's suicide was a tragedy. It wasn't Morales's doing. You really should let that go."

"How dare you bring Matt into this! And don't try to tell me Morales had nothing to do with it. He could have stopped that court-martial. If he had, Matt would still be alive!"

"Well, Arlene, I'm bringing Matt into this because he *is* in it. He carried the guilt of what the two of you did on that February night for the rest of his life. And he wrote that in the suicide note he left you.

"The president has a copy of that note. He's so furious at what you're trying to do to his friend Ray Morales, that he's ready to do something I never thought he'd do: use the information in Matt's note to bring you down. I'm calling to help you avoid that, Arlene."

Gustafson jumped, then sat rigid, her face working. After a pause she hissed, "You couldn't possibly have a copy of Matt's note! This is a bullshit attempt to scare me."

"It's not bullshit, Arlene. Let me quote you some: 'Mom, we should never have left after my accident. I know that going to the police after hitting that man would not bring him back, but I have been ashamed of myself ever since. I want you to tell the police what happened. Please, Mom, do the right thing.'"

Arlene Gustafson's heart raced, and her pupils widened. *No! I've never shown that note to anyone. It's in my desk. This is impossible!*

Griffith waited in the pregnant silence.

"Even if that were genuine, which it isn't, you can't prove it's authentic."

"Arlene, Arlene, you and I know that it is authentic. It's in his own handwriting, and there's no lack of samples for comparison in his military record. And we also know that public records the press will dig out will establish that a hit-and-run death occurred that night and that you had spoken at a fund-raiser near the scene. And Matt was with you at that fund-raiser. This circumstantial evidence, plus the authentication of Matt's handwriting, will be enough to stop your colleagues from electing you majority leader. You know a lot of them hate your guts and would find the courage to vote against you if they had justification for taking you down."

"I'm not afraid of that fight! I'll win, Bruce, and if, *if* you become president, I'll block every one of your judicial nominations. And I'll shred your cabinet picks. Screw you! Screw the president, too!"

"Arlene, I'm not surprised to hear that. I've always respected your courage and willingness to fight. That's why I've convinced the president to offer you this deal: He'll force Morales to resign. We'll call it for health reasons; after all, he was banged up in the crash and wounded by Fahim. You can kick his butt all over the hearing room this afternoon, but that's all. No recommendation for prosecution. After today, you let this go. He resigns. That's it. We move on."

Gustafson took a deep breath, removed her reading glasses, and rubbed her eyes. She stared at her son's picture in his full dress Marine blues. She thought of the other things he'd said in that note. *Matt's memory is sacred. Even though this is a fake, even though I could beat it, I don't want the press exhuming his memory and picking through his life.*

"Bruce, I'll make this deal: Morales resigns; Matt's note stays between us. If it ever comes out, everything Morales has done comes out. And I believe there's more to what happened in Idaho than we found this morning."

"Arlene, you drop this entire investigation or no deal. No more digging. No prosecution. No press conference. No leaks. This just goes away."

"I agree."

"Goodbye, Arlene. I wish I could be there when you hammer Morales this afternoon. He's such a self-righteous Boy Scout!"

BOOK TWO.

APRIL 12—MAY 13

Chapter 15

WEST PALM BEACH, FLORIDA

THWAK! THE INSTANT RAY MORALES heard that sound he knew the bunt was too hard. He saw the ball skid toward the third baseman, who gobbled it up and made a throwing motion toward first, then lobbed it toward the other baseballs scattered around the pitcher's mound.

"*Suave manos!*" said the coach standing next to the batting cage. "*Suave como las tetas de su novia.*"

Like the other Spanish speakers around the batting cage, Morales chuckled at the coach's reference to the anatomy of the youngster's girlfriend. The unsuccessful bunter, a strapping kid from the Dominican Republic, tried and failed to suppress his own amusement before the next ball shot out of the pitching machine. Sure enough, his distraction caused him to whiff completely. This brought a chorus of ribald Spanish from the other Minor League hopefuls practicing the art of the bunt at the Washington Nationals' spring training in West Palm Beach.

Morales, wearing faded jeans, a red Nationals t-shirt, and a white ball cap sporting the team's curly "W," felt glorious under the warm Florida sun. He was bathed in the sounds and smells of baseball—the *smack* of a fastball into a catcher's mitt, the chatter of players and coaches in English and Spanish, and the odor of new-mown grass. Baseball was emerging from hibernation, and he was trying to consider no universe larger than spring training.

Morales hadn't been able to truly relax for years. But now he was out of government, and there could be no buzz of a crypto-protected smartphone summoning him to face either an actual crisis or a bit of government stupidity spotlighted by some alert journalist. The National Counterterrorism Center neither knew nor cared where he was, and Ray loved that.

But he couldn't suppress all thoughts of the recent past. He was depressed by Julie's absence and pained by the reasons for it: his admitted infidelity and her shock and disgust after he told her the true reason for his resignation. He felt disgusted and weak over breaking his marriage vows. His feelings about torture were more complicated. Torture was illegal and immoral and often didn't deliver actionable intelligence. But in this case, it had, ending a devastating campaign of domestic terrorism. He had done his duty but didn't give himself a moral pass. Raised a Catholic by his Mexican immigrant parents, he believed he would face divine reckoning for this and other acts of violence he had committed or ordered.

It was early afternoon, and Morales had been at the park, which the Nationals shared with the Houston Astros, since it opened at ten. Dropping his small rucksack from his shoulders, he eased his two hundred fifteen pounds onto one of the metal bleacher seats near a batting cage where pitchers were taking their swings. These were National League pitchers, who had to take their turns at bat like other players. They took hitting seriously but not without humor; they constantly teased each other about the hot shots, bloopers, and whiffs in batting practice.

Morales watched and listened, sipping water from a plastic bottle. After a while he became aware that the Nationals' ace pitcher was eyeing him. He realized he had been recognized and soon noticed the ace pointing him out to teammates. When the coach tending the pitching machine called a halt, the man ambled over to Morales, followed by several other pitchers.

Speaking across the waist-high chain-link fence separating the field from the bleachers, the pitching star said, "General Morales, right?"

"That's right."

"Surprised to see you here."

"Well, in a way I'm surprised to be here," said Ray.

"Didn't know you were a fan."

"I am. A big one. It's just been a while since I had time to go to a ballpark."

"Yeah, I can imagine. Listen, sir, what you did in Idaho, getting that raghead? That took guts. I know some people are saying you screwed up, went rogue, and got fired. That's bullshit. Americans are damn lucky you had the balls to take him out.

"Thank you, sir. I'd be honored to pitch a game with you in the stands. If you get a chance to come to Nats Park, let me know, and I'll get you seats right behind the plate."

With that, he and the others sauntered off, leaving Morales both moved and shamed by his words. He wondered whether the lie forced on him by Adel Ghorbani would come out, whether Julie would forgive him, and what he was going to do with the rest of his life. That must include dealing with Adel Ghorbani, who had saved his life with the casual mercy of a Roman emperor and manipulated him into living the lie that—as he had just been reminded—was increasingly intolerable.

Chapter 16

THE GULF OF ADEN

COMMANDER WEN CHAO, OF THE People's Liberation Army Navy, squinted into the glare of a cloudless afternoon on the cerulean sea in Pirate Alley. Wen, a wiry five feet four inches tall, did his last set of pushups, hands and feet protected from the hot metal deck atop the destroyer's pilothouse by a woven rice-straw mat. Toweling the sweat from his face and neck, he scampered down the metal stairs to the pilothouse and entered the cool shade therein. Although nothing was said, the body language of all the men on duty in the pilothouse showed that Wen Chao was captain of this Chinese warship, a Type 52D destroyer named *Nanking* on patrol in the waters of the Gulf of Aden near Socotra.

Wen didn't linger. "Officer of the Deck, I'll be in my cabin." The watch officer, who knew this without being told because it was part of his skipper's daily routine, replied, "Yes, Captain."

Once in the cabin, Wen showered quickly, using as little water as possible because one of the ship's freshwater distillers wasn't working now. If they couldn't get it fixed, he faced a difficult decision: whether to request permission to leave patrol for repairs in the Port of Djibouti. Halfway through a six-month deployment from the ship's home port, Qingdao, they were doing pretty well at keeping *Nanking* in fighting trim. He had been on another destroyer, not in command, where mechanical failures had turned the ship into a hell for the crew, short on water and frequently without air conditioning in the hundred-degree heat. Problems with sensors and weapons had made that ship virtually useless as a warship, but the patrol continued because to ask for permission to enter port for repairs was to lose face. He would not be so stupid as to repeat that fiasco, but he was reluctant to leave station for repairs to the distiller.

Attired in crisp khakis, Wen returned to the pilothouse and seated himself in the chair reserved for him alone. Another day without pirates. He knew the crew was getting bored and stale. *He* was getting bored and stale. Years of naval patrols had quelled piracy along this shipping route for the time being. But still, *Nanking* and her sister ships were there to show the Americans and others that China can protect its cargoes on the Silk Road, to remind the Indian Navy that the Indian Ocean wasn't India's, and to fly the flag on port visits to the Philippines like the one made two months ago to Manila.

With a sigh Wen opened his file of radio dispatches and other paperwork and turned most of his attention to them. But not all, for no captain ever fails to have a part of his mind sensing the ship's motion, the sounds of hull and machinery, and, when in the pilothouse, the actions of the watch standers. The ship hobby-horsed easily, heading into dying four-foot swells from a distant storm. The bow knifed through them without throwing spray or shuddering from their impact as it would have if they'd been wind-driven and possessed momentum.

Wen had been lost in his papers for about half an hour when the bridge-to-bridge radio came to life with a burst of heavily accented English. "Pan-pan, pan-pan, pan-pan. This is the Panamanian flag bulk carrier Gulf Banker requesting naval assistance in position thirteen fifty-three north, fifty-two decimal three east. I am being shadowed by a pirate boat, over."

Wen's head snapped up from its gaze at the papers on his lap. He was pleased to see that the quartermaster of the watch was already plotting the Gulf Banker's position. "She's bearing one three two, about twenty miles from us." The watch officer's eyes met Wen's. He nodded, and the officer said, "Helm, come right to one three two. Make your speed twelve knots. Commence transition to turbines."

The captain and the watch officer each did some quick math in their heads. "Captain, figuring we'll be at twenty-five knots in about ten minutes, I make it about fifty minutes to her position."

"Sounds about right. Tell them. And launch the helo!"

Grasping the microphone of the bridge-to-bridge radio, the watch officer transmitted, in his own heavily accented English, "Gulf Banker, Gulf Banker, this is the Chinese warship *Nanking*. We are twenty miles from your position and will reach you in fifty minutes, over."

They waited for the Gulf Banker's acknowledgement but heard instead, "Gulf Banker, Gulf Banker, this is the United States Navy destroyer *Agerholm*. I am proceeding to your position at thirty knots and will arrive in twenty-five minutes, over."

Wen's eyes flashed, and he slammed his palm against the folder of messages. "Watch officer, resume patrol at ten knots! Stand down the helo."

Wen appeared to return to reading his papers, but in fact he hardly saw them. He believed that, someday, Chinese officers wouldn't need to learn English in order to speak to other ships; the others would have to learn Chinese. And he would live to see that day.

Wen looked to the future with confidence because he believed the American navy was fading and his navy was rising. He had done these damned patrols nearly his entire career, as the Chinese navy learned how to operate far from China, how to refuel and replenish stores and ammunition from supply ships at sea, how to repair its equipment, sometimes without parts.

We've mastered all that, thought Wen. Now, it's time for some action, like showing the Americans that the South China Sea is *ours*. And maybe we'll soon have an opportunity to show what we can do. Next week we end this stupid patrol and set course for the Persian Gulf, to watch over our tankers.

Chapter 17

WASHINGTON, DC—ONE WEEK LATER

W HEN RAY MORALES REACHED THE Daiquiri Lounge of the Army and Navy Club, not far from the White House, Marine Lieutenant Colonel Jerry Thomas awaited him at a table in the corner, near the floor-to-ceiling windows looking out on McPherson Square. His former military assistant at the Department of Homeland Security rose as he approached and, ever the Marine, waited at attention until General Morales offered his hand before extending his own.

"Hi, Jerry. Good to see you looking chipper and without a bandage in sight," said Morales.

"Thank you, sir. You're moving pretty well yourself; I didn't see much of a limp as you came across the room." Thomas's face was split by a grin revealing that he truly liked his former boss. In contrast, his eyes held a hint of guilt.

After they were seated, Morales said, "So tell me, Jerry: how's the fight to get flight-certified again?"

"I've still got a ways to go, sir. It's my eyes; the head and neck trauma messed with my color vision. The docs tell me that's a rare but not unheard of result of injuries like mine. You know the rule: colorblindness is medically disqualifying for a military pilot. But the docs also say that, in some cases, color vision returns. I'm hoping I'll be one of those cases."

Morales frowned, then looked quizzical. "So what have the personnel wienies got you doing now?"

"Well, they're under the illusion that I understand how Washington works, so they've made me EA to the DCS Ops and Plans."

"Well, that's a pretty good billet for an oh-five, Jerry. Lotta E-Ring face time, and, as I can vouch, you'll make your boss's life a lot easier. I still have enough influence to suggest that you be rewarded for it."

"Yes, sir, thank you, but in comparison to getting a squadron command, it sucks."

Morales grinned briefly. "Still telling me like it is, huh, Colonel? Be a little patient. The Corps usually takes care of the good ones, like you, in the end."

A server appeared and took their drink orders, a daiquiri for Thomas (after all, they sat in the room where the drink was first introduced to America) and a Miller for Morales.

"General, if I'm out of bounds here, I know you'll tell me. So I'm going to ask: What happened in Gustafson's committee?"

"For you, Jerry, not out of bounds. I can't tell you everything, but the bottom line is they hung me out to dry. Once their voters were safe again, the senators felt able to criticize what I had to do to make them safe, what *we* had to do. Your name did not come up, and I didn't mention it. By the lunch recess it seemed pretty damn clear they were going to recommend that I be indicted for the federal crime of torturing a prisoner. But somehow—I don't know how—the White House found a way to make Gustafson back down. The vice president called and told me and my counsel that he had set up a deal: in return for Gustafson not recommending indictment, my resignation—supposedly because of my injuries. I thought about telling him and the committee to go screw themselves and make my case in open court, but that would have dragged you and the doc and others into it. And besides, I was pretty fed up with being in government. So I took the deal."

"Thanks for covering my six, sir. What we did to that terrorist had to be done. It's hard for me to imagine what the White House has on Gustafson that would make her back down, make her walk away without your scalp. And it's beyond amazing that none of her committee members or staff have speculated about the help we got."

"Well, the reason I copped to torture was to keep them from going there. I'm surprised, too. But everyone knows Gustafson's vindictive as a Sicilian capo and will probably be the next Senate majority leader. I figure that once the vice president forced Gustafson to fold and she gave her committee its marching orders, they'd be inclined to obey. The Democrats wouldn't want it to come out, and the Republicans are scared of Gustafson. They each made their calculations and decided that either supporting or attacking me isn't worth the price she'd exact."

Thomas's face became solemn; he took a deep breath, held Morales's eyes, and said, "Sir, a lot of what went wrong for us is my fault. It was my idea to go after Fahim on our own. And I should have seen that gully in the meadow when I made the low pass just before landing there. I nearly got us all killed. And I *did* get Phil killed."

"Jerry, it was my decision to go for him, not yours. And yours weren't the only eyes that should have seen that gully. You're *not* solely responsible for Phil's death in the crash—that's on me, too. Really, more on me than you because I was in charge."

"You've never filled me in on what happened after the crash, General."

"Well, Jerry, you've certainly earned the right to know. Let's take a walk." Ray Morales scribbled his membership number and signed the check; then the two strolled through the club's lobby, filled with busts and photographs of prominent military men, down the front steps, across Fourteenth Street, and into McPherson Square. Morales set course along I Street, heading west. The rush-hour throng had disappeared, into bars for happy hour or into the nearby Metro entrance for the outbound commute.

"Jerry, I was thrown out of the plane, seat and all, unconscious. I had knee and foot injuries and probably a concussion. I came out of it when someone kicked my foot; I opened my eyes, and there was this Arab-looking guy in Levis and a plaid shirt, pointing a gun at me. Turns out it was Fahim. He pushed me toward his hideout at gunpoint but got careless, and I jumped him. Shook his gun loose, but he was able to grab it first.

"That really pissed him off. He said he was gonna get his special knife and cut off my head … slowly. He shoots me in my good foot to be sure I can't get far, then leaves to get that special knife of his. After a few minutes I hear a shot; then after a few more minutes, I see another Arab guy standing over me. And guess who? General Adel Ghorbani, commander of Iran's Quds Force."

Thomas's lips silently mouthed "no shit?" and his eyes popped.

"Yeah, Jerry, no shit! Long story short: Ghorbani and a handful of his guys had come looking for Fahim at the same time we did. They shot him—that was what I heard while lying there—dumped his body near me, gave me the pistol used to kill him, and boogied. I'm not the hero who killed Fahim; I'm the schmuck he captured, who'd be dead now except for Ghorbani."

Abruptly, Thomas stopped walking. "So the Quds Force mounted an operation to get Fahim, and they fooled us all completely. We never got a sniff of them."

"That's right, Jerry. So you can see why the Martin administration preferred the fairy tale that we were successful in the end, that I killed Fahim."

"So what about this Ghorbani, sir? And why did he come after Fahim?"

"Jerry, this is way beyond your security clearance, but you deserve to know: He's no longer head of Quds Force. Now he's in charge of leading Iran's nuclear missile program. Clandestine, of course. He must be one of the most powerful men in Iran.

"As for why he came after Fahim, and came personally? I'd love to know. Someday, somehow, I'm going to catch up with him, and this time I'm not going to be lying at his feet!"

Thomas emitted a low whistle. "So what do you think of him, sir? Any impression of him? Is he another nut case?"

"Well, my impression was formed when I was lying on my back in a world of hurt, so who knows? But he didn't seem like a nut case to me. And as he was leaving, he said something like this to me, in pretty clear English: 'You Americans are fools to think you can stop us from getting our own bombs. We're going to have them, and we're going to destroy the Jews and dominate the Arabs as we did in the days of Darius. Get used to it.'"

BOOK THREE.
MAY 14—AUGUST 28

Chapter 18

TEL AVIV, ISRAEL

"PRIME MINISTER!"

Ya'el Barak spoke as he darted through the door that connected his cubbyhole to Askenazi's office. Askenazi looked up from a stack of papers.

"The reprisal strike that went into Syria this morning—apparently we killed Zana Jahandar!"

"Apparently? Apparently? What do you mean apparently? I need to know!"

"Apparently because we haven't seen his body and Hezbollah has made no announcement."

"Why wasn't I told? The air force did this on its own? Get Rivkin in here!"

"He's already on his way, sir. But this was a surprise. We had no intelligence that Jahandar was going to be there. This strike was to eliminate a senior Hezbollah commander. Jahandar was with him."

"Who else knows this?"

"The Iranians, of course, and our intelligence analysts and their superiors."

Askenazi bolted from his chair and began to pace. He stopped, stared at the floor, then resumed. He stopped again, looked at Barak, and said, "Get out an announcement that we targeted and killed him. Do that immediately! And be sure the analysts keep their mouths shut."

"But, Prime Minister—"

"Go! Go!" said Askenazi, pointing to the door.

As Barak bolted for his office, Lieutenant General Dan Rivkin, chief of the general staff and Israel's most senior military officer, arrived.

"What the hell, Dan? Are you running your own foreign policy now? How could you go after Jahandar without my permission?"

"We didn't know, Prime Minister. The mission for the two aircraft was to put a five-hundred-pound guided bomb into the home of Hezbollah's deputy commander in Syria. That was cleared with your office."

The prime minister waved that aside and said, "Dan, we're going to announce that Jahandar was the target! Can those pilots keep their mouths shut?"

"Of course, Prime Minister! They're Israeli Air Force officers. But, in any case, they don't know who they were after. Our pilots are never told who, just where and when to strike."

"Khamenei is going to go nuts! And Martin as well."

Rivkin nodded. "Prime Minister, I'm going to put us on Condition Jericho. That's one notch short of general mobilization."

"I know the readiness conditions, Dan! Now go do it.

"Ya'el," shouted Askenazi. "Clear my schedule. National security team meeting as soon as humanly possible. And make the arrangements for me to go on television this afternoon."

As soon as General Rivkin left, Askenazi closed his door and called Shara: "We've just killed the head of Quds, Zana Jahandar!"

"How? Why didn't we talk first?"

"It was an accident, Shara. An air strike targeting a top Hezbollah leader in Syria hit Jahandar, who was with him. It got them both. I've decided to announce that Jahandar was the target. We're going to get blamed anyway, so we should make what we can from the situation. I'm going on TV this afternoon."

Shara didn't answer right away. Then she said, "Joshua this is the hand of God. Jahandar was delivered to us, as the Hittites were delivered to Joshua of Nun.

"Yes, seize this opportunity to project Israel's strength and determination! We are not willing to sit passively and take the rockets and raids as if they weren't planned by Quds, funded by Quds, and launched on orders from Quds. This will be a great moment for you, Joshua!"

* * *

WASHINGTON, DC

"Yeaaaah?" said the president of the United States as he took the predawn phone call from the watch officer in the Situation Room. He felt the mattress move and knew that Ella had also been awakened.

"Sir, NSA is pretty sure from a burst of Iranian communications that someone just took out Zana Jahandar."

"Who? Where?"

"They don't have much, sir. The where is Syria; the who isn't determined. The Iranians don't seem to know for sure, but the COMINT says they of course suspect Israel."

"Is that all you've got?"

"Yessir."

Rick Martin put the phone down and answered the question in Ella's eyes. "Somebody just killed the new head of Quds Force."

"Israel?"

"Maybe, but I'd think they would give us a heads-up. The Kurds, the Saudis, and Iraqi Sunnis certainly all have motive. And so, of course, do we, for anyone who's compiling a list of suspects."

"So what happens now, Rick?"

"We have a very busy day."

Chapter 19

QOM, ISLAMIC REPUBLIC OF IRAN

MAJOR GENERAL ADEL GHORBANI, ATTIRED for the occasion in the Revolutionary Guard Corps uniform that announced both his rank and his courage, entered the room and saw a mass of milling, posturing men, each wearing a white or a black turban: the Council of Guardians. After the Supreme Leader, Ayatollah Ali Khamenei, they were perhaps the highest authority in Iran's murky governance. The Leader wasn't present.

Ghorbani noticed two other uniformed men, the heads of the army and Quds Force counterintelligence. Their faces revealed that they were in trouble. Undeniably there had been a major security failure. How else could the Israeli Air Force have targeted the leader of Quds Force at the meeting in Syria? The fact they had been summoned meant that the long knives were out.

Three military men present and two of those under a cloud. That told Ghorbani he was an especially valued advisor to the Supreme Leader, even after having stepped away from command of Quds Force. In fact, the absence of any military other than he and those about to be interrogated meant that he was the Leader's most trusted military advisor, invited to evaluate their responses.

Confidently, Ghorbani worked his way through the bleating herd of guardians, who would be the only ones seated at the table with the Supreme Leader. He took a lesser but strategically located seat, on the Leader's right and in his line of sight. He sat, relaxed, hands in his lap, wearing confidence like a thousand-dollar suit. His face was peaceful yet sinister—the perfect don't-screw-with-me expression.

The Supreme Leader entered and was immediately surrounded by gesticulating, gabbling guardians. He waved them off as if they were annoying insects and took his seat at the head of the table.

"Brothers, let us come to order," said Khamenei. For the next hour the members of the council ranted against the Jews and their enabler the United States, and they loudly debated the appropriate retaliation, trying to outdo one another in the horror and scale of Iran's vengeance.

Many of these men seemed otherworldly to Ghorbani. Just as their predecessors did during the war of Iraqi aggression, they demanded actions that would produce many martyrs but leave Iran worse off. They believed their own chants that the Jews and the Americans were cowards, easily outwitted nonbelievers who could be frightened off by the willingness of Iranians to become martyrs for Islam and Iran. But Ghorbani had fought them both for years, and he knew the guardians were wrong. Just as they themselves had no taste for martyrdom, neither did many other Iranians, who were not infatuated like the Saudis with this route to Paradise. And they seemed to have forgotten that President Martin ordered a nuclear strike on North Korea several years ago in retaliation for a spectacular attack on Las Vegas.

If we go too far, he will do it again—to us. Until we have our own bombs.

"General Ghorbani," said the Leader. "Though you are no longer its leader, you know Quds Force better than any in this room. You have fought the Jews—and the Americans—and handed them stinging defeats. And General Jahandar was your battlefield comrade and loyal deputy. What are your thoughts?"

Ghorbani felt a spike of excitement. "Leader, I have heard the outrage of us all at this crime done by the cursed Jews, which is just another in a long string of attacks on the Iranian people since our nation was born in glorious revolution. Many good ideas have sprung from the lips of the guardians. I would not presume to select among them; that is a matter for you and you alone. But I haven't heard discussion about the most fearsome power of Israel, its nuclear weapons. They can destroy the city where we sit, and many other cities, with the press of a button. We cannot now do the same to them. This situation produces a clear limit on what we can do and, indeed, eliminates some of the best ideas I have heard today. Where we find ourselves now shows how much we need to have the only suitable counter to this threat: nuclear-armed missiles that can incinerate Israeli cities."

"And what would you, who lead the nuclear weapons program, have us do now, to bring us to the moment we can do as you suggest?"

"Leader, we are at the point now that the development of the weapons and of the missiles to deliver them must come together. If you grant me authority, I can accelerate missile development as I have accelerated weapon development."

"And when could you have nuclear missiles ready, General?"

"Since I am not now in charge of the missile program, I don't have sufficient information to give a certain answer. But, surely, I can do it within a year if given full authority and priority for resources."

"We cannot wait a year, General."

"Several of the ideas I have heard today would make an excellent first response. For instance, destroying an Israeli embassy, which Quds could do easily. Then, when our missiles are ready—and the Jews and Americans have relaxed, thinking they have survived our retaliation—we launch our army at them, and their ultimate response will be checkmated by our missiles. Once we have a nuclear missile force, we have many more opportunities to destroy the bastard state Israel."

"I'll consider your request, General Ghorbani. But today I have another project for you: resume your post at Quds and begin wreaking Iran's vengeance on Israel."

"It will be my highest honor, Leader." And, thought Ghorbani, with this mission I am now the most powerful general in Iran.

* * *

Javad Ahmadi, president of Iran, took another sip of coffee as he sat at his desk reading the popular newspaper *Kayhan*. He wrinkled his nose at the simplicity and cant—he was Oxford-educated before the revolution—but continued reading in order to know what the masses were being fed. Their diet, of course, was the brutal and arrogant murder of General Jahandar by the Jews. The Supreme Leader and the Council of Guardians had made plans to punish Israel and its supporters for this act of war. Javad sucked his teeth and shook his head. He had not been included in any of those discussions—he, the president of the Islamic Republic, its highest nationally elected official! That meant he was losing power again to the clerics and the military. Ahmadi was determined not to allow himself to remain sidelined.

He continued his glum march through the paper, quickly scanning the pages before him on his computer, occasionally pausing to read an entire article. About three-quarters of the way through his dutiful journey, his dark brown eyes glittered, and he sat up straighter at a memory triggered by what he'd read.

He ran a Google search. It took five variations of search terms before his vague memory took precise form on the screen. He smiled as his thought began to turn into a plan.

Chapter 20

NEW YORK AND BRUSSELS, FIVE DAYS LATER

THE EVENING NEWS PRODUCER THOUGHT that anchor Carleton Fiske looked nervous, almost flustered, during the final countdown to air time, but when the set went live, Carleton was in his usual calm, all-knowing persona.

"Good evening after a day in which Middle East violence spread to Europe. At midmorning in Brussels, the Israeli Embassy was devastated by what appears to have been a mortar attack, launched from a rooftop about half a mile away, according to Belgian authorities. Iran's Quds Force claimed responsibility. At least thirty-eight people, including Israel's ambassador, were killed in the explosions and fire that followed. Let's go to our Brussels correspondent, Philip Holmes."

Holmes appeared before a pulsing background of flashing red lights, black-clad security forces, and the smoking shell of a three-story building. "A terrible sight, Philip. What's the latest on this situation?"

"Carleton," he said, speaking over the wailing of sirens, "the death toll has now reached forty-three. One of the survivors told us that she thinks there were about one hundred people in the building, which was hit after the business of the day was well under way."

"Well, there's no question about who did this and why, is there? Do Belgian authorities have any leads yet as to how the Quds Force was able to get in position to do this in broad daylight?"

"Not at this early moment. Police are canvassing the neighborhood as we speak, seeking anyone who may have seen something suspicious. As we saw after the Charlie Hebdo killings in France, when the perpetrators were traced to Belgium, this country—and Brussels in particular—has a very big challenge with internal security. As the location of European Union headquarters and of NATO headquarters, Brussels is literally the crossroads of Europe. More foreigners live in Brussels than do Belgian citizens. And Belgium does not have the internal security resources of, say, France or of Germany. By the way, somewhat ironically, the Belgian government has just thrown a heavy security cordon around Iran's embassy here."

"Thanks, Philip. Be safe out there."

Carleton Fiske's wise countenance filled the screen again. "For the Israeli government's reaction, we go now to Tel Aviv."

Joshua Askenazi appeared, flanked by General Dan Rivkin and by the leader of Askenazi's major opposition party: "I will be brief because our actions will speak louder than any words of mine. Today all Israel stands united in anger and grief at this vicious attack on our embassy in Brussels. The murder of these diplomats—and of dozens of Belgian employees—is completely disproportionate to our elimination of a single terrorist leader. Iranians will come to bitterly regret their government's rash and brutal decision to escalate."

He turned away, ignoring shouted questions.

* * *

WASHINGTON AND TEL AVIV

Rick Martin, at his Oval Office desk attended by Bart Guarini, Secretary of State Anne Battista, and Secretary of Defense Eric Easterly, heard the Situation Room operator say, "The prime minister is on the line now, Mr. President." With a shrug and raised eyebrows, he glanced at his advisors and picked up the handset.

"Joshua, my condolences. This is a terrible day, not only for Israel but for the world."

"Thank you, Rick. I appreciate your sympathy, but what I need is your support."

The president scowled and said, "America is Israel's ally and friend, Joshua."

"That's good to hear reaffirmed now, Rick. You know we are going to have to strike back at Iran, swift and hard. I will try to keep you informed in advance but may have to act first, if circumstances demand."

Martin threw up his hands and silently mouthed "shit!" Then he said, "Joshua, I'm not writing a blank check. You know our separation of powers. Don't put us in a situation where we can't help as much as we'd like to. We need to talk before you act, prepare the way on the Hill—you know."

"Rick, I'm surprised to hear you hesitate about an opportunity to hurt Iran and particularly Quds Force. After they dared to run that operation in your country, you know that Iran can't be trusted and that Quds must be crippled."

Martin was on guard for this conversation but completely unprepared to hear those words. He felt a chill; anger shot through him. He squeezed the handset and glanced, narrow-eyed, at the group around his desk. Thankfully, it didn't contain anyone not already privy to that explosive information.

"Joshua," he said, drawing out the name in a tone that said a line had been crossed, "the United States will deal with that. It's our problem—it's *my* problem. It is *not* part of Israel's issue with Iran."

"Of course, Rick. I understand how embarrassing that is for you, and I leave it in your capable hands. And now I must go to a cabinet meeting. Thank you for your call and your support." He was gone.

Face flushed, Martin slapped his hand on the desk. "That SOB just threatened us. How the *hell* could he know about Ghorbani's operation? And how *much* does he know?

"Well, I'm not gonna be blackmailed!" The president's mouth set in a hard, flat line, and a vein pulsed in his temple.

Chapter 21

TEHRAN, ISLAMIC REPUBLIC OF IRAN

IMAM PARIZAD HASHEMI GAZED AT the hundreds of men, including President Javad Ahmadi, kneeling before him on prayer rugs that covered the floor of the mosque. He lifted his gaze to encompass the many women in the rear of the mosque. Hashemi always felt the great honor of his position as a provisional Friday prayer imam, appointed by the Supreme Leader, but today he felt especially proud because of Ahmadi's presence. He also felt deep, burning anger.

"Faithful, we celebrate the martyrdom of Zana Jahandar, murdered by the Jews."

Hashemi pointed to the images of Jahandar that gazed upon the worshipers from the walls. "Iran will respond tenfold. Hundreds of Jews will die as we avenge his death. The destruction of their Brussels embassy is only the beginning. It is the duty of all the faithful to kill Jews whenever and wherever they can. We will destroy the Zionist abomination! Our brothers in Lebanon and Syria are even now raining missiles upon them!

"But we know that the Jews did not do this alone. The martyr Jahandar's killers flew American aircraft. The pilots received their training at American bases. The bomb that killed the martyr Jahandar was made in America.

"Faithful, you know how the Great Satan has tried for more than seventy years to crush our religion and our nation. Like all American presidents, Martin wants to humiliate the great nation of Iran, while it is the Iranian nation that has humiliated the US in the world and will continue to do so. Thank God we are strong and getting stronger! Over the past many years, the US has attacked us, imposed the nineteen eighties war on us, and waged any propaganda and economic war against us that it could, but in this encounter, the real victor has been the Iranian people and the Islamic Revolution. Our revolution has shaken the foundation of global arrogance led by the United States and international Zionism, and their failures continue at the hands of the Resistance Front, which is inspired by the Islamic Revolution."

The Imam was pleased to see that his anger was readily absorbed by his audience.

"Iran's defensive power will not allow the United States to reach its goal, which is spreading war in the Islamic World. The worldwide-hated Saudi regime, which only enjoys the support of the United States, will not be able to continue its warmongering policies in the region due to the authority of Muslim states including Iran, Iraq, Lebanon, Syria, Yemen, and Palestine. The enemies' conspiracies are continuing, and for this the armed forces are constantly thinking of building new advanced defense capabilities and increasing their means to defend the country's borders. If our enemies had been able to do something militarily against us so far, they would have done that by now. We must say that they are never capable of inflicting heavy casualties on us. Our enemies cannot fulfill their dreams!"

A growing number of men were on their feet, shouting "death to the Jews, death to America," and punching the air with their fists. Some were waving Iranian flags. Imam Hashemi gestured to reduce the tumult, and the shouts became fewer. Many resumed their kneeling positions.

"But we have not only survived; we have become an even greater, more powerful country. Now we will slap the face of the world's bully! It is time to use our great power not only to kill Jews but to devastate America and its apostate Saudi vassal by blocking the flow of oil. I declare righteous and binding the fatwah of Mufti Barati. It is our duty to close the Strait of Hormuz through which this oil flows day and night. Yes, this will require us to sacrifice, but the Iranian people are resilient. And any who, in these great and historic days, fail in their duty to observe this fatwah are traitors to the revolution!

A young man in a business suit arose and shouted, "Death to all traitors to the revolution!" Others took up the cry and soon the faithful were chanting "Death to all traitors" in a rhythm that seemed to shake the building.

Hashemi waited, holding the worshipers in the palm of his hand and feeling the rush of power. Gradually, the crowd grew quiet. He let suspense build. He could see rapt attention on hundreds of faces, each staring at him as though he held the keys to the gates of Paradise. It was the most sublime moment of Hashemi's life.

He spoke forcefully into the silent mosque: "The one who will lead us in dealing this great, crushing blow is our president, Javad Ahmadi." Then he bellowed, "Death to traitors. Death to Jews. Death to the Great Satan!"

The crowd's answering roar grew to the scream of hurricane winds, destroyer of all they encountered. Then it changed quality, grew deeper, slower, more powerful yet. It became a beast whose heartbeat was the enraged chant: "Death to traitors. Death to Jews. Death to the Great Satan!"

The faithful surged through the mosque's doors into the streets. Placards with Ahmadi's picture and others with a cartoonish image of a hook-nosed Jew arm in arm with a clownish Uncle Sam were handed to them as they emerged.

Chapter 22

TEHRAN, ISLAMIC REPUBLIC OF IRAN—THIRTEEN DAYS LATER

J onas Garvey was nervous and hoped it wouldn't show in the news segment he was recording, standing about twenty yards from angry demonstrators in Tehran. It was a really large demonstration—"mob" would be more accurate—not a small one the cameraman had to frame carefully for maximum impact.

"As you can see," said Garvey, "emotions are running high in Tehran over the presumed role that the United States played in Israel's targeted killing of Quds Force leader, Zana Jahandar. Despite President Martin's flat denials of US involvement or foreknowledge, Iranian streets have been in an uproar against the United States as well as Israel since Imam Hashemi made that accusation. He also endorsed another cleric's fatwah calling for Iran to block the Strait of Hormuz.

"It's worth noting that Iran's president, Javad Ahmadi, has engineered a remarkable surge in popularity among many Iranians, such as those behind me. Ahmadi, who is the highest secular leader in this theocratic state, had recently borne the brunt of popular anger over difficult economic conditions. Ahmadi has gotten himself out of the doghouse by becoming the champion of a proposal made two weeks ago by an obscure mufti at the Houzeh Elmiyeh Seminary in Qom. Mufti Hosan Barati, citing passages in the Koran, issued a fatwah calling on the faithful to close the Strait of Hormuz to infidel shipping. Barati's interpretation of Koranic passages triggered a theological debate in this nation of eighty-one million, ninety percent of whom are Shi'a Muslim. So far none of the most senior clerics, the grand ayatollahs, have backed Barati's fatwah. But Imam Hashemi, a high-ranking prayer leader, reportedly at Ahmadi's urging, endorsed the fatwah last week at Friday prayers in Tehran. Ahmadi has gone all in on it, speaking in favor at rallies and in the media. While some still blame him for the weak economy, others believe he's just the man Iran needs now as its president."

Six thousand one hundred twenty-six miles away in New York, anchor Carleton Fiske said, "Jonas, what does this fatwah mean for America, for that matter for the world?"

"Well, Carleton, the best answer to that, unsatisfying as it is, is 'it depends.' It depends on how the theologians line up on the scriptural issues. If one of the grand ayatollahs were to support Mufti Barati's position, prospects for closing the strait would be considerably increased. If the Supreme Leader, who is the ultimate theological and political authority in this country, were to approve the fatwah, I believe Iran's forces would take action to close the strait."

"Well, could they do that, Jonas? Do they have the military punch to shut the door, so to speak, to the Persian Gulf, with all the impact that would have on the world's energy supply?"

"Once again, Carleton, it depends. One scenario could be that they declare the Strait of Hormuz closed, send their navy of small boats out to patrol it, and none of the tanker companies challenge it. After all, tankers are huge, unarmed, and full of flammable cargo. Each loaded tanker is worth millions of dollars. Most of them fly flags of convenience, which makes it technically not the business of the US Navy and other large navies to protect them in this scenario. So the ships might simply stay where they are and wait for diplomatic action to clear the way for them."

"Hasn't something like this happened before, back in the nineteen eighties?"

"Yes, Carleton, it did. At one point in the eight-year war between Iran and Iraq, tankers came under attack by both sides. In order to keep the oil flowing, the United States encouraged the ship owners to reregister—they call it 'reflagging'—their tankers in the United States. Once those ships started flying the Stars and Stripes, the US Navy began convoying them through the Persian Gulf, which was then a war zone between Iran and Iraq. The Navy even sent a battleship to escort convoys. In the spring of

1988, the Navy mounted a one-day operation called Praying Mantis and sank or severely damaged half the warships in the Iranian navy."

"Thanks, Jonas. That's fine reporting. Be safe!"

* * *

THE PERSIAN GULF

The destroyer reeled from the force of the explosion, slowing and twisting to starboard. Men who had been sleeping were now drowning, their berthing compartments suddenly open to the sea. Everyone in the pilothouse was flung to its ceiling, then dashed to the deck. That brief flight was fatal for several. A man with his face laid open from nose to scalp staggered to the aft bulkhead of the pilothouse and triggered the general alarm. It wasn't needed—no one had slept through the explosion and shock wave.

Lieutenant Lee staggered to his feet and gazed with surprise at the bright white of the bone projecting through the skin of his left forearm. He glanced toward the entrance to the pilothouse, hoping to see the captain scrambling through the door, but he was disappointed. Grabbing his junior watch officer by the shoulder, he told the man to get on the bridge-to-bridge radio and broadcast a Mayday. Next he called the ship's communication center with an order to report to fleet headquarters that they had been attacked and were badly damaged.

"Lee! What happened?" The watch officer jerked his torso around and saw the destroyer's executive officer, or XO, second in command, lurch through the door, tripping over a sailor writhing on the deck.

"We were rammed by a speedboat full of explosives. Have you seen the captain?"

"No, and I doubt we will. His sea cabin looks smashed to hell, and there was no answer when I yelled. Any more hostiles around?"

"If there are, we're screwed. I've got no steering control, and the mains are offline. The emergency diesels have kicked in, so we've got electricity to run fire pumps and power the radios, but we're sitting ducks."

"OK. Work on getting the main engines going, then head for the nearest land. Maybe we can save her, maybe not. But if we can beach, at least we won't go down. I'm going to supervise the firefighting. If we don't get fires under control, nothing else will matter!"

But as it turned out, something else *did* matter: the tons of water rushing into the ship's hull through the hole blasted by the suicide boat. The ship's gas turbines, at full throttle when the Boghammar struck, continued briefly to drive her ahead, and that forward motion rammed seawater into her hull. The inrushing water spread rapidly through watertight doors that were open since no attack had been expected. The destroyer listed to starboard, the angle increasing rapidly. With a speed that amazed Lee, the ship rolled onto its starboard side, then turned turtle. He was among those who were able to fight through twisted steel and swim clear of their ship before it sank. Not many did.

Lee began to shout, attempting to gather other swimmers and develop a plan for survival. Soon cries of pain, fear, encouragement, and command could be heard across the water.

The shouts and cries were in Chinese.

Chapter 23

THE PERSIAN GULF

A FLASH FLICKED ALONG THE ENTIRE horizon to the northeast of the Arleigh Burke class destroyer *Agerholm*, the second US Navy vessel to bear that name. Everyone on the bridge of the warship saw it and after a noticeable lag heard a sharp, powerful sound like the strike of a boxer's punch. The retina tends to hold bright images that surge across it, so after registering the flash and boom, most of the observers then saw in memory a column of fire erupt briefly above the horizon. Everyone with binoculars lifted them and looked at the intensifying glow on the horizon, an orange-red pustule on the face of the darkness. "Somebody's in a world of hurt!" said a voice out of the dimness of the pilothouse.

"Signal Bridge, OOD," barked the officer of the deck as he keyed the intercom. "How did that look from up there?"

"Like a big-ass explosion, sir. We've got the Big Eyes on it now. Something's burning like hell a little over the horizon."

The officer of the deck depressed the intercom button for the Combat Information Center, or CIC: "Combat, OOD. We just saw and heard a big explosion on the horizon, about thirty degrees on the port bow. What've you guys got out there?"

"Sir, we've got that Chinese destroyer and Skunk Delta—the radar contact that tracks like a dhow.

"Wait one!"

The OOD endured the pause with irritation, then heard, "Radar also picked up a high-speed surface contact between Delta and the Chinese ship

106

for just a couple of sweeps, then it disappeared. Mighta been just one of those radar ghost contacts we get out here, but it looked pretty solid while it lasted."

"Roger that," replied the OOD. Turning toward the chart table, he said, "Quartermaster, be sure you log all this!"

"Aye, sir!"

"Mr. Porter, point us over that way while I call the skipper," said the OOD.

"Aye, aye, sir." The officer named Porter quickly took a compass bearing, then said, "Helm, come left to course zero three one" As *Agerholm*'s bow swung obediently, the OOD called the captain.

* * *

The pipe shrilled, then the bo'sun's voice boomed throughout *Agerholm*: "Now all department heads to the bridge. That is, all department heads to the bridge." Those words over the ship's announcing system drew quizzical looks from sailors awakened by the ship's maneuvers and by the sixth sense that seaman develop for danger at sea.

Waiting on their arrival, Captain Mort Greenhouse huddled with his number two, XO Harry Blackburn. "Harry, I want you to lead the Rescue and Assistance Team. We'll be over there in about thirty minutes."

"Aye, aye, sir."

"Bridge, Combat," announced the intercom. "We're hearing a distress call from a Chinese destroyer, the *Nanking*. Signal strength strong, so it must be pretty close. Those transmissions from *Nanking* are on the compass bearing of that Chinese guy we've been tracking, so we think it's them."

Greenhouse's eyebrows shot up. "This is going to get interesting, XO!" Clapping him on the shoulder, the captain said, "OK, Harry. I know you want to get at it—off with you!"

As the XO hustled away, Greenhouse turned to the five officers responsible for the ship's major functional areas. "OK, guys, looks like we're going to help a Chinese destroyer that's burning, maybe sinking, too. Rescue and Assistance Team. Probably using fire hoses from our deck, if I decide to get that close. Chief Engineer, we're going to set modified Zebra. Have Repair Two and Three ready to go topside if I need 'em. Air, get the helo into the hangar—I don't want it damaged if we go close aboard to fight fires. But be ready to move her out and launch.

"Questions?"

"What about an OPREP, sir?" said the operations officer, referring to an emergency operational report.

"Send it. Our position and intentions. Tentative identification of the distress ship as *Nanking*. And get Lieutenant Oswald up here. I'll feed her info for more OPREPs as we go."

Greenhouse scanned the faces of the four men and woman he would be depending on to handle this dangerous, complex situation. Pleased with what he saw, he said, "Go to it, gang. Let's do this right."

Climbing into the high pedestal chair that was lettered "Captain" across its back, Greenhouse said, "Officer of the Deck, call away the Rescue and Assistance Team. Wait five minutes, then set General Quarters, modified Zebra."

Settled in his chair, Greenhouse reviewed the orders he had given and, satisfied that he had done all he could for now, considered what lay ahead. He would approach the burning ship from upwind, being careful to judge the ships' relative drift rates. He knew from experience that his ship sailed downwind like a kite and would probably drift faster than the other vessel. If he let *Agerholm* get too close, she could catch fire. He knew that there was another, bigger risk than that. If fire reached the other ship's ammunition magazines, both ships could be sunk in a giant explosion. But that was a risk that had to be taken if they were to be more than mere witnesses to the ship's struggle.

Reaching to key the intercom, Greenhouse said, "Combat, Captain. Send me up a tablet with everything you have on the *Nanking* class."

He keyed the intercom again. "Air, this is the Captain. Is Lieutenant Commander Putnam there?"

"Here I am, Captain."

"Putt, I may need your birds for medevac. Have you got a configuration for that?"

"Yes, sir. I'll get with Doc right now."

Greenhouse looked to the port side of the bridge, saw the figure he sought there, the ship's navigator. "Hey, 'gator. I need bearing and range to the closest port with decent medical facilities."

"Thought you might, sir. It's Jebel Ali in Dubai, one six zero about sixty miles."

"OK. Tell Ops I need her to start working on emergency dip clearance to enter port with mass casualties."

"She's already doing that, sir."

"I love it when you guys are ahead of me!"

An operations specialist materialized beside his chair. "Here's the scoop on *Nanking*, sir." Thanking him and wishing he could remember the man's name, the captain leaned back in his chair and began to scan the tablet. He had just begun scrolling through it when Lieutenant (junior grade) Oswald, the assistant supply officer, arrived at his side. "Sir, you wanted to see me?"

"Yeah, Sara. I've got a different job for you. Here's the deal: If this is what it looks like it is, we're gonna be on a direct feed into the White House. Washington will scream for information like we've got nothing better to do than answer questions. So, your job is keeping them off my back. Write up what's going on. Don't get colorful, just facts. Actually, there will be damn few facts. Call 'em estimates. About every fifteen minutes, show me what you propose sending out. Got that?"

"Yes, sir."

As Greenhouse scanned the horizon, he felt the forceful vibration of *Agerholm's* four gas turbines of one hundred thousand horsepower driving her up past thirty knots. The glow was now spiked with flames. The navigation lights of a large ship were near those flames. Probably a tanker, he thought. Trying to help, but with a huge, unwieldy ship, flammable cargo, no small boats, and a tiny crew, that skipper couldn't do much but hope swimmers could reach his ship's side and have strength enough left to climb a very long ladder.

And what the hell happened over there? Accident? Attack? Better be sure the crew keeps a sharp eye out; don't get fixated on the rescue, there may be somebody around who'd go for us, too.

Greenhouse decided to spend his last few minutes of relative calm centering himself and saying a few prayers. Then he thought of one more thing he ought to do and slid from his chair. "Bo'sun, pipe all hands for me."

Following the shrill of the bo'sun's pipe, Greenhouse's voice over the general announcing system reached every part of his ship: "This is the captain speaking. Here's what's going on: A Chinese destroyer is on fire, not far from us. We don't know what happened to her, whether accident or attack. As you can feel, the engineers are driving us at Flank Three to get over there and rescue survivors. We're going to have a lot going on: the Rescue and Assistance Team, helo ops, and maybe, just maybe, we'll have to defend ourselves against something that attacked them. You've trained for this; now it's show time. I need all hands focused on their jobs. Let's all be especially careful to remain situationally aware. If we all get focused on rescue ops, we might get sucker-punched. Now let's do it!"

Chapter 24

A s *AGERHOLM* SLICED THROUGH THE waters of the Persian Gulf at thirty-three knots, the sky signaled the approach of dawn. Lookouts strained to spot signs of the stricken ship or its crew, but they saw nothing. The flames had disappeared. On the oh-one level, one deck above the ship's main deck, the boat crew and members of the Rescue and Assistance Team readied the RIB, the ship's rigid inflatable boat, for launching. Up and down the main deck, other crew members rigged cargo nets ready to drop down for swimmers to climb aboard. The ship's three rescue swimmers prepared their gear and discussed their initial plan. The mess deck, the cafeteria-style dining area, was filled with tables that would be used to treat survivors. "Doc" MacMichael, a senior chief hospital corpsman with special training in trauma management, was busy there with his two assistants planning to triage and then stabilize a large number of burned and bleeding survivors. The ship literally hummed with vibration from the two huge props driving it forward and the universal, purposeful activity of the crew.

Captain Greenhouse was in the Combat Information Center for a review of the overall situation above, below, and around his ship. He would soon be busy on the bridge and wanted to fix the overall tactical picture in his mind before that occurred.

"Here's our last position on *Nanking*, Captain," said the TAO, the tactical action officer, gesturing to the operations summary console. "Datum Alfa is the spot we estimate she went down. It's about seven miles from Iran's territorial waters. Over here's the port of Bandar Abbas. We've tracked several small, high-speed contacts leaving Bandar and heading this way. They're unidentified but could be Iranian missile boats."

Greenhouse's raised hand cut her off. "That could be trouble. Get us some air cover."

"Working on that, sir." She rolled her trackball to a glowing dot on the operations summary display. "This track is Skunk Delta; we believe he's a sailing dhow. And this big mother of a contact is the tanker Global Resource that's stopped near Datum Alpha, trying to render assistance."

"Have we got comms with her?"

"Yes, sir, on bridge-to-bridge."

"How about the air picture?"

"Not many tracks, Captain, and all are squawking commercial."

"And sonar?"

"It's less than two hundred feet deep here, water conditions are very poor for sonar, and there's lots of noise from all that shipping traffic. Right now sonar holds no contacts, but, realistically, we're just about blind."

"Well, keep 'em jacked up anyway. It may have been a sub that got *Nanking.*

"OK. Everyone listen up!" The captain's voice was crisp and carried throughout CIC: "I'm going to be focused on the rescue. We're all depending on you in here to watch our six. We don't know what happened to *Nanking*, but she might have been attacked. We're at GQ, but a lot of sailors are off station helping on deck. We need as much warning as possible to get them back to their stations if something starts to look suspicious.

"TAO, you've got my permission to engage any threatening contacts. If you've got time, use the 1 MC to warn the guys on deck to clear away from the guns, especially Mount 51. My present intention is to search thoroughly for survivors and only then head for Jebel Ali. I may decide to send the helo with the worst injured while we're still searching for others."

"Understood?"

A chorus replied, "Aye, aye, sir."

Captain Greenhouse took several steps toward the short ladder leading to the bridge, then stopped. "TAO, what are we hearing from Naval Forces Bahrain or Fifth Fleet?"

"Not much, sir. Fifth Fleet watch officer says he's attempting to get us some air cover from *Stennis*."

"That'd be nice," said Greenhouse over his shoulder as he climbed the ladder with firm steps.

Greenhouse emerged onto the bridge to the familiar refrain from the first sailor who saw him: "Captain's on the bridge." A few steps took him to the bridge-to-bridge radio, a unique unit located in the control station of every oceangoing vessel, whatever its flag. Squeezing the transmit button, Greenhouse hailed the master of the Global Resource.

"Captain, please tell me the situation there."

"The ship sank not long ago. We have not found many survivors. I have five aboard now, two of them badly burned. Do you have a doctor?"

"We have an infirmary and a highly trained medic. If you wish, I'll take them aboard."

"Yes, yes, that would be best. I don't think we could get them safely from our deck to your boat. Do you have a helo?"

"Yes. I'll send the helo as soon as possible."

"Have the survivors said what happened to their ship?"

"They seem to be Chinese, Captain, and we have no one who speaks it."

Hanging up the microphone, Greenhouse punched the intercom and said, "TAO, Captain. Did you copy what we just said on channel sixteen?"

"Aye, sir."

"Then make it happen. And once the burned are aboard, the helo is to search for other survivors."

"Aye, aye, sir," said the TAO. Moments later the ship's announcing system blared, "Now set the helo detail."

"Mr. Samuels, how far to the Global Resource?"

"Twenty-one hundred yards, Captain."

"Very well. Slow to five knots. Let's ease in carefully."

Greenhouse's eyes sought and found the officer of the deck, who was on the far side of the pilothouse: "OOD, I need to know if the pilot can launch safely with us lying to. I don't want to go charging away from here in order to give him launch wind, unless I have to."

The captain looked again toward the scene of the sunken ship. The dawn breeze carried the stink of *Nanking*'s fuel. The Global Resource had many of her deck working lights turned on and loomed off to starboard, her illuminated bulk as long as ten blocks in Greenhouse's hometown, New York City. He glanced at the operations console to orient himself, then gazed in the direction of Datum Alfa, the point where *Nanking* had slipped under. Nothing.

"XO reports the boat ready for launch, Captain, and requests permission to lower away."

"Have we got good comms with them?"

"Yes, sir, on the PRC-66," said the officer of the deck, pointing to a sailor wedged into a corner of the bridge with an olive drab backpack radio.

"Permission granted to launch the boat, but tell the XO to remain aboard. No point in him being out there when it's too late to save that ship"

With nothing to do for the moment, Greenhouse stepped out onto the starboard bridge wing and observed the boat lowering smoothly to the water, where it rode alongside the slowly moving destroyer for a moment, then cast off and pulled away to search for survivors. He heard the pilothouse door open and then the voice of the junior officer of the deck: "Captain, the TAO reports we have control of Slingshot three one four, a flight of two Hornets. On station time two hours, and they'll be relieved on station as necessary to maintain coverage."

"Thanks, Mr. Porter. Nice to know we've got some firepower overhead if we need it."

He stepped back into the pilothouse, where he was greeted with "Captain, COMFIFTHFLEET is on the horn for you. He's on channel eight."

Greenhouse stepped to the operations console and took the radio headset proffered by the sailor seated there. The sailor got up, and Greenhouse slid into the chair.

COMFIFTHFLEET, this is *Agerholm*, over."

"This is COMFIFTHFLEET actual. How're you doing, Captain? Bring me up to speed."

Greenhouse gave a succinct description of the situation, concluding with his pending request for diplomatic clearance to enter Jebel Ali and debark the survivors.

"I'll see that you get the clearance. What's the tactical situation? Any idea how *Nanking* went down?"

"Admiral, we saw and heard a big explosion, then flames over the horizon. But we don't know what caused the explosion. The tanker skipper didn't see anything—just the explosion and fire. The tactical picture is quiet at the moment, but we're tracking several high-speed contacts headed this way, so that could change quickly. We have control of a pair of *Stennis's* Hornets."

"Well, stay alert Captain. With all the talk in Iran about closing the strait, this could be the beginning of something bigger. Exercise care not to provoke the Iranians, but protect your ship."

"Is there anything you need from Fifth Fleet now?"

"Not at this point, Admiral. But the air cover I've got is my ace in the hole. If you can be sure it remains continuous, I'd appreciate that."

"You got it. Good luck, Captain. COMFIFTHFLEET, out."

A sailor wearing headphones said, "OOD, the foc'sle has survivors close aboard. Request all stop." The junior OOD looked at him, and Greenhouse nodded, saying, "Do that, Mr. Porter. And let the tower know."

Agerholm drifted slowly ahead as her momentum bled off. Rescue swimmers scrambled down the netting to help survivors aboard. When he glanced again at the foc'sle, Greenhouse saw three men wrapped in blankets getting the once-over from one of Doc's assistants.

"Captain."

Greenhouse turned to see Hospital Corpsman Second Class Walker with a wet, blanket-wrapped figure next to him.

"Captain, this man speaks some English. He says he is an officer of the *Nanking* and has something important to tell you."

The Chinese officer saluted, and Greenhouse returned it.

"Captain Sir. *Nanking* … fast boat with big bomb. Sink very fast. Thank you for help us."

"Thank you for that warning. We'll be alert. Do you know where your captain is?"

"I think he killed."

Greenhouse couldn't think of anything to say except "I'm sorry," so he said that. Walker shepherded the Chinese officer toward the mess deck.

Stabbing the intercom button with his index finger, Greenhouse said, "TAO, Captain. A Chinese officer told me their ship was attacked by a fast boat with a big bomb. Sounds like a suicide attack to me. Be sure that gets out in the next OPREP."

Greenhouse climbed into his chair, leaned back, and flopped both feet onto the footrest. No sooner had he come to rest than a thought popped into his whirring brain. He sat up, leaned forward to reach the intercom, and said, "TAO, Captain. As soon as the foc'sle is ready to get under way, commence an expanding square search around datum, track spacing one quarter mile." That done, he resumed his relaxed posture, mind still working in high gear.

Six thousand miles away, at about 9:30 p.m. in Washington, calls were summoning the National Security Council to the White House.

Chapter 25

"MR. SECRETARY, THERE'S A NAVAL incident in the Persian Gulf. The NSC will meet ASAP. Your car is outside now."

Eric Easterly, in Levis and his favorite green cardigan sweater, muttered something, shoved his phone in a pocket, bookmarked the novel he was reading, and looked apologetically at his wife, seated near him in a cozy earth-toned wingback chair.

"Flap in the Middle East; the NSC is cranking up."

She blew him a kiss and returned to her book; sudden interruptions and hurried departures were just part of their life together. Not so different from many years ago while he was a Navy SEAL, although not dangerous. She had told him then he could be a SEAL or her husband, but not both. He had chosen her, and now, many years removed, he was the secretary of defense. As he seated himself for the short drive to the White House, he punched speed dial for the chairman of the Joint Chiefs of Staff, General "Mac" McAdoo of the US Air Force.

Secretary of State Anne Battista, very put-together in a gray Ann Taylor suit and near-perfect blonde hair, didn't get the message until the Delta Shuttle landed at LaGuardia Airport. In a gesture that amused her security officers, she made a practice of turning off her email on short commercial flights; she said everyone needs at least one place for solitude, and these flights were hers. She was traveling to the UN for meetings the next morning. Her security detail, which observed no hiatus in communication in-flight or elsewhere, had already arranged a red-light-and-siren trip to the

US Mission to the UN, where a secure video- teleconference system would permit her to join the NSC meeting.

John Dorn, national security advisor, was already in the West Wing because it was his routine to come in after dinner on Sunday to get a head start on the week ahead. Dorn was a persnickety fifty-three-year-old bachelor whose career was his life. None of the staff had ever seen him in the White House without a tie, and Sunday night was no exception, although he was attired in a sport coat and tan Dockers rather than his usual navy blue suit.

The Situation Room watch officer had notified him first, and Dorn had made the decision to summon the others. He also had called the family quarters, giving President Martin a quick assessment and telling him the NSC would be available soon. As usual, the president had responded cheerfully; Dorn knew that Martin, despite the gravity of situations requiring an unscheduled NSC, secretly welcomed them because he had so much more freedom of action in foreign affairs than domestic matters.

As Dorn swung through the White House Mess to scoop up a couple of chocolate chip cookies, the Situation Room staff prepared the smallish Presidential Briefing Room for the meeting. Knowing that neither the secretary of state nor the chairman of the Joint Chiefs of Staff were in Washington, they prepared only for the president, Secretary of Defense Easterly, Dorn, and Chief of Staff Bart Guarini. Awaiting each was a briefing binder, a legal pad, a tablet PC, a sterile phone (all phones were collected at the entrance), a water tumbler, and a ceramic cup with the attendee's name and title. Coffee was set a-brewing on a sideboard, on which were various snacks, including the chocolate chip cookies that were thickening Dorn's waistline despite his efforts to cut back.

General MacAdoo, attired in an olive drab Nomex flight suit and a battered leather jacket with his name and command pilot wings on a patch on the left breast, was asleep in the VC-10 bringing him back from a meeting in Brussels followed by a day of hunting and dinner with his German counterpart. A staff sergeant awakened him and delivered a cup of black coffee. As McAdoo was picking up Secretary of Defense Easterly's call, his military assistant came from the aircraft's communications module with a one-pager from the National Military Command Center that he handed wordlessly to his boss. The military assistant had, by the thinnest of margins, escaped the sin of allowing his boss to be caught flat-footed by *his* boss.

Bart Guarini, scowling, left what was shaping up to be a *very* pleasant evening with his latest girlfriend. Candles, wine, soft music, the aphrodisiac of power—and now *this*! As he slid into the back seat of his White House Pool car, he shot the driver a look that said, "Don't you even *think* about smirking."

In the White House Family Quarters on the third floor, Rick and Ella Martin were discussing the conversation they had just completed with their twenty-three-year-old son, Mark. "Rick, he's really not happy in accounting. We both know that. And he hates the cold weather in Boston. You need to let him know that it won't be the end of the world if he leaves PWC and takes some time to reevaluate."

"Ella, he's just coming to terms with the world of work. After all, he's been out of college barely a year. He needs at least to get his CPA, even if he's going to chuck it with PWC. That CPA is an important credential, and in another year he'll have it."

The president's phone bleeped. It had a unique ring for John Dorn, so they both realized immediately their conversation about Mark was going to be pushed aside. Rick was secretly relieved; Ella knew that and was exasperated.

"Yes, John?"

"Sorry, Mr. President, but we've got a situation developing in the Persian Gulf. A Chinese warship, a destroyer we think, has sunk near the Strait of Hormuz. We don't know whether it had an accident or was attacked. One of our destroyers was not far away and is in the process of rescuing survivors. Given all the talk in Iran about closing the strait, our ship could be at considerable risk. I've just called the NSC and will have the team together soon. I'll let you know when we're ready for you, sir."

"OK, John. Are the Chinese or the Iranians saying anything yet?"

"No, sir. We think the sinking occurred only about an hour ago. The Chinese, as you know, are rarely quick to make public statements when surprised by something. As for Tehran, if the Iranians didn't do it, they may not even know what's happened yet."

"OK, John. I'll see you in a bit."

"So, saved by the bell, are you, Mr. President? You get out of having this discussion that you don't want to have about our son?" Ella's grin soaked up some of the sarcasm of her words.

"We can certainly talk it over until I have to go, Ella."

Which can't be soon enough. Mark just needs to suck it up.

Chapter 26

USS AGERHOLM, THE PERSIAN GULF

T HE LIGHTER SKY IN THE east announced the arrival of nautical twilight, the period before sunrise in which mariners can see the horizon clearly enough to use a sextant to determine their positions. Normally at this time the chief quartermaster and some of his assistants would be using sextants to take sightings on morning stars. They did that even though satellite navigation was able to determine *Agerholm*'s location with greater precision. It was a skill that, if not practiced, would be lost. But not this morning. They were instead scanning the surface of the Persian Gulf for survivors, for debris that might be worth salvaging for investigation, and for bodies.

The bodies, as they found them, were laid out in the ship's gym, the exercise equipment having been shoved out of the way alongside the outboard bulkhead. *Nanking*'s only surviving officer viewed the bodies and was able to identify eight of the eleven before they were encased in body bags.

As the sun's fingers splayed upward from the eastern horizon, Captain Greenhouse was back in his chair on the bridge, eating a baloney sandwich and sipping carefully at a steaming cup of coffee. By leaning out of his chair and craning his neck, he could see the operations summary console to his left, over the shoulder of the sailor operating it. The ship's track glowed in white on its green screen and formed a series of interlocking squares, each leg ending with a jog farther from the estimated point where *Nanking* had gone under.

Five miles out is enough, decided Greenhouse. He knew the tide and current weren't especially strong now, and there was no wind, so nothing would have drifted far from where *Nanking* sank. Next, repeat the track, but working in toward the place the ship went down. That would be enough. Greenhouse ambled into CIC and approached the TAO.

"How's it going, Judy?"

"We're grinding it out, sir. We'll be five miles out when we finish this leg. Do you still intend for us to work back in from there?"

"Yep. And once we've done that we'll head for Jebel Ali. Let me know fifteen minutes before we're done with the search pattern.

"How're your troops doing? Are you rotating them off for some breakfast?"

"We're going to relieve the watch in about twenty minutes, Captain."

"That means you, too, Ops. I'm going to need you clearheaded when we put together our after-action report in a few hours."

"I'll be good to go, Captain. Weps is relieving me."

Greenhouse gave her a thumbs-up and left CIC to begin the second of his tours of the ship, sizing up the crew's mood, observing their work, stopping to ask questions here and there. As he reached the foc'sle, he felt the ship's engines backing and looked up at the bridge. The junior OOD was on the port wing, attempting to halt *Agerholm*'s progress alongside another body. He watched as Bo'sun Purdon pointed at one of the rescue swimmers, who dropped feet first into the water twenty feet below. Sailors swung a davit outboard and lowered a Stokes litter, a unique stretcher design that permitted carrying casualties up or down steep stairs and even vertical ladders. The junior OOD had done a good job of positioning the ship, and the litter nearly landed on the body. As Greenhouse and the deckhands watched, the swimmer positioned the litter beneath the Chinese sailor's body, clipped on the hoisting wire, and signaled for the deckhands to haul away. As the dripping, lifeless form on the litter was swayed inboard, Greenhouse felt a moment of sadness for a family somewhere in China.

The phone talker standing at Purdon's elbow got the faraway look that meant he was concentrating on hearing something over the headset he wore. His message was short: "Captain, TAO says high-speed surface contacts from Bandar Abbas are still coming our way. He recommends you take a look yourself."

"Tell him I'm on my way to CIC."

Arriving in CIC, Greenhouse joined the TAO, now the ship's weapons officer, at the ops summary console.

"There they are, Captain. Look a little like hornets busting out from a nest."

"Anything else going on?"

"No, sir. The AWACS controller confirms that other surface and air traffic is routine, everyday stuff."

"Can somebody get a visual on these guys?"

"I just sent the Slingshots to take a look; we should know soon."

"OK."

Greenhouse returned to the bridge.

As if reading Greenhouse's mind, the intercom announced, "Bridge, TAO. Slingshot three oh one has a visual on the high-speed contacts. They're Iranian missile boats, estimated to be Thondar class. We presently hold them at thirty-two miles, speed thirty knots." Absorbing that, Greenhouse realized the contacts would be on top of them in a little more than an hour.

"What's their armament, TAO?

"Four C-eight oh ones, range about twenty-five miles."

Greenhouse recalled that the C-801 was a sea-skimming missile with a warhead of about 350 pounds. If the five fired simultaneously, the odds were that at least one missile would get through the barrage from *Agerholm's* defenses. One hit probably wouldn't sink his ship, but it would do a lot of damage and kill some—maybe many—of his crew. And three or four missile hits could put them out of action or sink them like *Nanking*.

Greenhouse considered the possibilities. Tell the fighters to take them out now? Or wait to see if they shear away, keep their distance? But what if they did shear away? They could still launch missiles at *Agerholm* from twenty-five miles. That might have been what happened to the Chinese destroyer. But if he took them out soon, at that range, would he "provoke" the Iranians?

"TAO, Captain. Report to COMFIFTHFLEET that we hold five Thondars at about twenty-five miles and closing. Unless otherwise directed, I will take offensive action to protect my ship if they make missile launch preparations. Got that?"

"Yes, Captain."

"Also," continued Greenhouse, "begin calling the Iranian boats in the blind on bridge-to-bridge. Broadcast that they will be considered hostile if they approach us within ten miles. And let me know when they get to fifteen miles."

"Aye, aye, sir."

"Captain," said the OOD from the other side of the pilothouse, "the tower says our helo is on final approach and requests we maintain course and speed." A quick glance around told Greenhouse they could do that safely, so he said, "Will do. Green deck."

A long ten minutes passed, during which Greenhouse stared tensely out the pilothouse window, face expressionless. He was operating under the Rules of Engagement, or ROE, that permitted him—indeed required him—to shoot first if he believed *Agerholm* was under imminent threat of attack.

But this was not war. So what was, right now, an imminent threat of attack? During this deployment, *Agerholm* had been buzzed several times by Iranian missile boats coming very close aboard, with no harm done.

What's different now? The Israeli assassination of one of Iran's most important military officers, Jahandar, followed by Iranian threats to close the strait and then the sinking of *Nanking*. Maybe that signaled that any ship in these waters would be attacked.

He leaned to his right and keyed the intercom: "TAO, Captain. If these boats get to twenty miles, I want the Slingshots to discourage them. Try some flares, but no hostile action."

Soon, *Agerholm*'s air intercept controller radioed the flight leader of the Hornets from USS John C. Stennis: "Slingshot three one four, Checkmate, over."

"Three one four," replied the flight leader.

"Three one four, we want you to discourage those missile boats you identified a few minutes ago. Do not attack them, but see if you can scare them off with a high-speed, low-altitude show of force pass, expending flares."

"Checkmate, are we cleared to use ordnance?"

"Not at this time, except as permitted by self-defense rules."

"This is three one four, wilco."

The flight leader, Lieutenant "Moonshine" Moonie, took a deep breath and looked at the five boats, their wakes like arrows in flight toward *Agerholm*. He knew the Thondars had antiaircraft machine guns and could well have shoulder-fired SAMs, too. Dipping below ten thousand feet was risky. But the first pass would probably be a total surprise to the boat crews.

"Rebel," he radioed his wingman, Lieutenant (junior grade) Carl Yellich, "you make the first flare pass. Come at 'em out of the sun. I'll hold a perch at angels ten. When you're done and returned to a perch, I'll do the same. We'll keep it up until they get the message. If they fire on us, we get above ten and take 'em out—all of them—with Mavericks. Got that?"

"I got it, Moonshine."

Moonie watched from ten thousand feet as Yellich maneuvered his Hornet into position. Yellich dropped out of the sun, which was on the starboard quarter of the boats, and screamed over them at a hundred feet, flares winking and sparking behind his aircraft. As Yellich climbed rapidly to ten thousand, Moonie saw the boats slowing. But as he watched, they continued toward *Agerholm*. He positioned himself astern of the boat group, then rolled in for a low pass. Once again the sky above the boats winked and flashed with flares, and Moonie's aircraft made a thunderous roar as it passed over them. He pulled up sharply and resumed his perch at ten thousand feet.

"Checkmate, Slingshot three one four, over."

"Go, three one four."

"We've made two low-altitude, high-speed passes. The boats have slowed but continue on about the same course."

"Roger, three one four. Hold at safe altitude and await instructions."

"Three one four, wilco."

The quiet bustle of the bridge was broken by the intercom: "Captain, TAO. The lead Thondar is at twenty miles and continuing to close."

Captain Greenhouse had expected this. In past encounters, Iranian boats had rarely been deterred by flares. The US Navy had used this tactic often enough that most Iranian skippers understood that it did not mean imminent attack. He felt all eyes on him.

"TAO, tell the Slingshots to make a strafing pass with the aim point offset a thousand yards."

"TAO, aye."

Greenhouse knew he had crossed a line that would be hard to justify to higher authority if this went south. He was taking a huge risk, not for the strategic aim of avoiding conflict that could spin out of control, but for his crew and his ship. It came down to this: He could be passive, or he could be active. He'd be damned if he was going just to sit in his chair with fingers crossed and wait for whatever fate—or the Revolutionary Guard—delivered.

His decision could go badly wrong in at least two ways. One or more of the Iranian skippers might decide he was under attack when those bullets hit the water ahead of his boat and decide to launch a missile. Or he might fire at the American fighters overhead and perhaps bring one down. Or it could go right: the boats might stop or turn away without attacking. The next few minutes would determine whether his order would prevent destruction and death or cause it.

* * *

Deftly selecting guns on his stick while he maneuvered his aircraft, Moonie set up for an attack with a twenty-millimeter cannon, with a thousand-yard offset from the target. Then he rolled in, his Hornet screaming down. He kicked some rudder, twitched the stick, and saw the pipper in his head-up display settle across the lead boat. Touching the trigger button, he heard the loud staccato of the Vulcan six-barrel cannon in the Hornet's nose and felt the shudder as it spewed five hundred rounds at a point half a mile ahead of the Iranian boat. He saw a flash of white as the slugs hit the water, then all was behind him as he pulled out.

"Moonshine, I think that did it," radioed Yellich. "The lead boat is doing a one-eighty."

"You sure he didn't take a shot at me?"

"Yes, I'm sure!"

"Too bad, I was hopin' …" Switching back to Checkmate's frequency, Moonie said, "Checkmate, they've done a one-eighty. We'll keep a visual on 'em, and if they turn back toward you, we'll remind 'em that's not allowed."

The intercom on *Agerholm*'s bridge crackled to life: "Bridge, TAO. Is the captain there?"

"Listening, TAO."

"Sir, looks like the Slingshots chased them off. They're making a big turn to the south, like they're heading back to Bandar Abbas."

Relief flooded over Greenhouse. "Roger, TAO—real glad to hear that! But stay alert—the longer we're here, the more chance the Iranians are going to send folks to see why."

Standing at the ops console in the pilothouse, Greenhouse thought again about the admiral's words of caution. Don't provoke. He'd already pushed beyond his limits defined by ROE. They'll be back, he thought. Not much sense in hanging around longer. We arrived on the scene quickly, and we've done a thorough search of the area. We've got seventeen survivors, two badly burned, and eleven bodies.

Greenhouse turned toward the OOD. "Time to head for Jebel Ali. There's nobody left alive out here, and we've probably got all the bodies there will be until the floaters start to come up in a couple of days. Take the 'gator's course for Jebel Ali but at only twenty knots. No use acting like we're running away."

Greenhouse saw his XO enter by the door from CIC. "Captain, I've just come from Doc. He's pretty worried about the two burn cases and would like to helo them to the hospital in Jebel Ali. I gave Putt a heads-up, and they're doing the preflight now. It's about sixty miles to feet dry."

"Let's do that, XO. Helo detail whenever Doc's ready."

Chapter 27

THE WHITE HOUSE

R ICK MARTIN WALKED BRISKLY ALONG the south portico of the White House on his way to the Situation Room, which was actually a group of rooms manned around the clock by a team of military and civilian specialists. "No, Aaron," he said into his phone, "for now I want you to stay at GW with Helen. It's early days on this; we both know that. I'll send for you if anything of significance develops." He listened for a moment, then hung up. The president had been told that what the wife of the director of national intelligence had suffered did not appear to be a stroke. But right now he wanted the director to be with his wife in the emergency room of George Washington University Medical Center, not in the Situation Room.

By his second term, Rick Martin had walked many times into a hastily assembled meeting of the National Security Council, or NSC, and he intuited that this time, thankfully, he was not likely to have to make a save-the-world decision. As the Marine in dress blues opened the door for him, Martin said, "Thanks, Corporal." Once inside he slid into his chair at the head of the table and noted that only Bart Guarini, Eric Easterly, and John Dorn were physically present. Framed in wall-mounted screens were Secretary of State Anne Battista, General "Mac" MacAdoo, and CIA Director Shelby Wohl. Mac's features were grainy and faded in and out, probably, Martin thought, because he was airborne.

"OK, what's going on, John?"

"Mr. President, about three hours ago a Chinese destroyer, *Nanking*, blew up and sank in the Persian Gulf, not far from the Strait of Hormuz. We know this because one of our Fifth Fleet destroyers, *Agerholm*, happened to be near enough to see and hear the explosion and render assistance, although *Nanking* had sunk before our ship arrived. We don't know why *Nanking* blew up. We have had no communications from the Chinese government or any of the regional governments. But we know, of course, that senior officials in Iran have been advocating that Iran close the strait to the shipping of all infidels. This might be their way of announcing that."

"Or it might be a gigantic screw-up by the Iranian navy, or it might be that something aboard *Nanking* just blew up," said the president.

"Exactly, sir. Rather than speculate, let me tell you what we know by way of reports from *Agerholm*. The only living Chinese officer, one of seventeen survivors aboard *Agerholm*, reported in his limited English that a boat with a bomb was responsible. No identification of the boat. It apparently caught them by surprise. *Agerholm* is en route to Jebel Ali in the United Arab Emirates to deliver the survivors for medical exams and repatriation to China. We have a Chinese linguist en route to Jebel Ali and hope to pump the officer a bit more before a representative of the Chinese government arrives.

"Two of the survivors are badly burned, and they were flown to a hospital in Jebel Ali by *Agerholm*'s helo. The ship will arrive in Jebel Ali in about three hours. We're keeping this quiet, but you should know, Mr. President, that *Agerholm* recovered a considerable amount of debris in addition to eleven bodies, and this may provide us with some useful intelligence."

Rick Martin's active listening and intellectual curiosity were familiar to the NSC members, so no one was especially surprised when Martin asked, "Where's the Chinese linguist coming from? I wouldn't have thought we had any in the Middle East."

"Actually, Mr. President," said Shelby Wohl's talking head, "she's coming from Africa. As you know, the Chinese are working hard to increase their influence there, so we have some assets in place to keep an eye on them."

"OK, thanks, Shelby.

"So," continued Martin, "what if this is the first move in Iran's plan to block the Strait of Hormuz? What's our response?"

"If I may, Mr. President," replied Anne Battista: "while freedom of navigation is one of the cornerstones of our foreign policy, in this case we may want to soft-pedal a bit to see what Beijing will do. Iran is a major player in Ming's strategy to increase China's energy security, and Chinese expertise is a major factor in Iran's missile and, probably, nuclear programs. If Iranian forces sank *Nanking*, it's a huge setback for cooperation between China and Iran and a big hit to mutual undertakings important to each of them. And this Sino-Persian incident, if that's what it proves to be, would be a boon for two of our important allies, Israel and the Saudis."

She continued: "On the other hand, it's less severe for us. We can afford to let the Chinese swing in the wind rather than follow our usual practice of taking the diplomatic and military lead to solve this problem."

"I rather like that approach, Anne. I'm really tired of having Ming gripe about our insistence on freedom of navigation in the South China Sea. Let him find Chinese shipping interfered with, and we'll see what he does!"

"I hear you, Mr. President," said Secretary of Defense Easterly, "but it might be to our advantage to swat the Iranian navy hard now, so we don't have to do it later, when it would be a different ball game if they have nukes by then. We could send *Iowa* in, covered by a carrier air wing and shore-based assets from our base in Qatar, and she could blow the hell out of Iran's naval bases, in response to their closing a vital international waterway."

"Still trying to find a use for the world's only battleship, Eric?" said Martin with a grin. During the second term of Martin's predecessor, reactivation of the battleship *Iowa* had been forced on a reluctant administration and navy through the determination of several members of the House Armed Services Committee. *Iowa*'s recommissioning was the quid pro quo for the committee's support for construction of another nuclear aircraft carrier.

Easterly bridled a bit, then said, "Sir, she's perfect for a show of force in the Persian Gulf. Very heavy firepower, none of it putting pilots at risk, and able to take a hard punch if the Iranians can land one."

"Eric, you could say the same thing about a destroyer like *Agerholm*, couldn't you? Don't the destroyers have lots of cruise missiles that would do the same thing? Or, for that matter, a submarine could launch a swarm of cruise missiles." The president was partly yanking Easterly's chain and partly asking a serious question.

"Mr. President, *Iowa* and *Agerholm* may pack the same punch, but they don't have the same swagger. I wouldn't want to risk *Agerholm* in the strait in a freedom of navigation scenario. Too much chance the first Iranian shot might be lucky and cripple her. And if she stands off and shoots from a hundred miles as she is designed to do, it could appear sneaky rather than bold.

"But *Iowa* was designed not only to deliver a massive punch but to take one as well. If we send her in there for all the world to see, you've got a Clint Eastwood moment. 'Go ahead, make my day.'"

Easterly continued: "You're still getting questions about what Ray Morales did in Idaho, Mr. President. If *Iowa* goes steaming through the strait—and, even better, if they take a potshot at her, and she blows away Iran's naval bases with her sixteen-inchers—that story line will fade."

The room was silent for a moment; then the president said, "Anybody else want to weigh in?" When there was no reply, he said, "Anne and Eric, those are two contrasting and interesting ideas. And, actually, we might be able to combine them: do a joint operation with the Chinese to reopen the strait. Right now, we don't know what Ming will do, and that's a big problem. So I'd better ask him. Let's adjourn for now, and we can reconvene after I've spoken with Ming."

Martin looked at the wall clock set to Beijing time. It was nearly noon. "Right now Ming probably doesn't have any more information than we do—in fact he probably knows less than I do right now. I don't want to embarrass him, so I'll give him some time and call tomorrow morning, say, about nine our time." He looked at his chief of staff, who nodded, but then said, "Mr. President we need to reach a decision about public disclosure before we adjourn. Are we going to announce this now? Wait for the Chinese or someone else to announce it?"

"Bart, we don't yet know what this means," replied the president. "All we know is that a Chinese warship blew up and sank and that one of our warships rescued survivors. If we announce only what we know, we leave it to others to put it in a larger context. Which may be sensationalized and spin public opinion off in some crazy direction."

"But, Mr. President, if we don't reveal what happened immediately, we risk being criticized again for covering up," replied Guarini.

"And there's another aspect to that decision, Mr. President," said Anne Battista. "Unless we want to set an adversarial tone with China, I should call their UN ambassador here in New York tonight—or maybe ask for a meeting—and tell him we've rescued some of their sailors and taken them to Jebel Ali. Our ambassador in Beijing should make the same report to the Chinese government, now. I really think we should do both of those things at once, regardless of the decision on timing a public announcement."

"OK, I agree with that, Anne," said the president. "And as for the public announcement, let's have the Pentagon make it tomorrow morning."

Bart Guarini's expression said he was uncomfortable with that delay, but he knew his boss and realized he wanted to end the meeting. He said nothing.

General MacAdoo's voice interjected from the wall speaker: "Since we're reaching out to China about the crew, I should give my counterpart, General Ma, a call with the same information, Mr. President."

"In that case, I should call Minister Chen," said Easterly, slightly irritated as he always was when reminded that his subordinate had his own channel into the Chinese military."

"OK, but I think that's enough in the backchannel," said the president. "Be sure you all sing from the same music."

He glanced around the table and at the secure teleconference screens, then said, "Thanks, John. Good night, all."

Chapter 28

THE WHITE HOUSE

THE NEXT MORNING PRESIDENT MARTIN settled himself in his chair behind the Resolute desk in the Oval Office. With him were National Security Advisor John Dorn and Chief of Staff Bart Guarini. Somewhere in cyberspace, the president's lead Chinese language translator-interpreter listened for the leaders' first words, his stomach fluttering as it always did before one of these conversations got underway. The protocol was that Martin's linguist translated his words into Chinese and Ming's translated *his* leader's words into English. Each linguist also listened intently to the other's leader and to the translation and, if he thought it faulty or deceptive, could speak privately to his own leader.

When the sivitz—secure video teleconference—connection was established, Rick Martin and Ming Liu eyed each other, game faces on and pulse rates elevated. Martin spoke first: "Good evening, Ming. I want to add my personal condolences and cooperation to the sentiments expressed to your government several hours ago by mine. The loss of a fine new ship and most of her crew is shocking and upsetting."

"Good morning, Rick. Thank you for your sentiments and for the swift action by your ship to come to the aid of ours. Although we have not yet been in direct communication with our officer, it appears from the single message we received from *Nanking* before she went down that her loss was due to a surprise attack. As you said, the ship was new. Her crew was well trained; it's most unlikely that she sank from some error or internal catastrophe."

"Ming, since the sinking, I've had an intensive examination made of all intelligence that might bear on it. We have found no smoking gun, as we say, but, of course, with the turmoil in Iran caused by those wishing to close the strait, I have to wonder if Tehran was involved in some way." Martin knew he was baiting Ming a bit with that comment, since relations between China and Iran were better than the United States wished.

With anger escaping his usual poker face, Ming said, "Whoever did this made a great mistake. We will not rest until we find them and hold them accountable." Martin couldn't help thinking that what Ming said was very much like what Prime Minister Askenazi had said and what he himself had said after a terrorist attack. He couldn't resist the opportunity to chide his Chinese counterpart about the practice of free navigation that China flouted in another part of the world.

"Ming, I offer America's full cooperation to ensure freedom of navigation in the Persian Gulf and, indeed, all over the world. To that end, let both our countries call for an emergency session of the UN Security Council to look into this outrage and to warn those in Iran who want to close the strait that America, China, and other nations will oppose them strongly."

"I agree, Rick. Let us do that."

"I'll instruct my UN ambassador immediately," said Martin, pleased with the thought that Ming hadn't missed his jibes and was fuming about the shoe being on the other foot.

* * *

BEIJING, PEOPLE'S REPUBLIC OF CHINA

Ming Liu's irritation was evident after his conversation with Martin. He paced the aisle of the Boeing 737-700 aboard which the People's Liberation Army Air Force was returning him to Beijing after meetings and a speech in Shanghai. It had been there, in the headquarters of the Shanghai region's People's Liberation Army commander, that he had taken the American's call. He had been expecting it ever since he had first learned—via the American ambassador—of *Nanking*'s sinking. The memory sharpened his frustration. He hadn't heard of the sinking until he asked General Ma. Ma insisted that he wasn't told either until he'd called Admiral Yi. Yi had kept quiet because he lost face when the ship sank and because he had only the single report from the ship to go on. Ming was realistic about these failures, acknowledging that he and his countrymen were not good at coming forward with bad news, and any of his other admirals would probably have behaved as Admiral Yi had. So he didn't act on his first impulse, which was to fire Yi.

But I will make him miserable for a while!

Martin's motivation was transparent. He wanted to use this incident to drive a wedge between China and Iran. He had no subtlety about him, just like all Americans and especially their politicians. He wanted to rush to the UN and get the Security Council involved. Americans confuse knowledge with wisdom. They are very good at knowing things; their spies and sensors around the world are excellent. But in their rush to turn knowledge into action, they often act unwisely. For now, China will support America in the Security Council. But Ming resolved that when he had all the facts and had considered them carefully, he would choose China's best course, including perhaps stepping aside as the Americans rushed in.

Ming could hardly believe the Iranians could be serious about closing the Strait of Hormuz. President Ahmadi had just made a statement to that effect, but surely they didn't mean to act on it! Could they be as foolish as to think that China, their largest trading partner and, with North Korea gone, their only reliable supplier of essential military technology, would tolerate that? China needed Iran's oil, and Iran needed China's money and access to the world banking and finance network, from which it had been effectively banned by American sanctions. Deprive the two nations of this relationship, and both would soon be suffering. Even the Supreme Leader, despite his crazy Islamic ideas, should be able to see that. But, Ming conceded, perhaps he cannot. Or more likely, the power struggle between him and Ahmadi has reached the boiling point, and now a faction of the Iranian military—the Revolutionary Guard, say—was taking its orders from Ahmadi.

But Ming was not yet ready to accept that *Nanking*'s attacker was Iran. It certainly could be, either some crazy person acting on his own, transported by religious zeal and ambition. Or it could have been on orders from the Supreme Leader. But Iran was such an obvious suspect. What about another player, someone who wanted to hurt China or Iran or both? The Israelis? They certainly want to see Iran deprived of China's support, and of course their American patron would owe them for weakening China by cutting off its oil supply. Or the Arabs. Any of them would like to see Iran weakened, but the Saudis were probably the most likely to act on that desire. And then there was ISIS and other Sunni transnational groups. Or even the Americans?

Ming ended his speculation. *I will let Martin believe I am with him but will consider all the possibilities and the facts before deciding on China's response. And right now I will call President Ahmadi and remind him of China's interest in free navigation of the strait and of his country's need for things that only China is willing to provide.*

Chapter 29

MACDILL AIR FORCE BASE, FLORIDA

GENERAL "RIFLE" REMINGTON LEANED BACK in his chair and fixed a hard stare at the visage of Vice Admiral Tyler Watson, who appeared on sivitz from his headquarters in Bahrain. Remington, the commander of US Central Command, didn't like doing important business over sivitz. He much preferred face to face, where he could feel emotions as well as hear words and see carefully controlled faces. But sivitz was better than the secure telephone. "So, Ty," said Remington to his subordinate commanding the Fifth Fleet, "now that the ayatollahs have announced the strait is closed, what's the worst that does to Fifth Fleet?"

"Well, General, that depends on our mission. If it's just force protection, no problem, as long as this fracas stays subcritical. We're about three hundred fifty miles from Bandar Abbas, and with *Stennis*'s air wing plus air force fighters at Al Udeid, we own the air—assuming cooperation from the Saudis, of course. The Iranians aren't going to even get within range of us. 'Course, if they start lobbing missiles at Bahrain, that's a bigger problem.

"On the other hand," Tyler continued, "if our mission is to fight our way through Hormuz, it could get dicey. Once in the strait we'd be within range of Iranian cruise missiles and air, as well as subject to attack by fast torpedo and missile boats. And there'd be a threat from subs, too. Their Kilo-class subs wouldn't operate in the strait—shallows and water quality are terrible for sub ops—but they'd wait just outside, in the Indian Ocean. Those nine-man midget subs they've built on their own could be a torpedo threat—or maybe a suicide attack threat—in the strait itself. But the biggest problem is mines. The Iranians used 'em often in the tanker war back in eighty-two, and they have thousands in stockpile. If we let them lay a field across the strait like a gate they've shut, we're into months to get the strait fully open for business again. That's what I'd do if I were the Iranian commander."

"What would you do about it if they lay a minefield like that?" said Remington.

"I'd have to run a mine clearance operation like the one in 2003 after Operation Iraqi Freedom. That could take weeks or even months—and that's after we had taken out Iran's anti-ship cruise missile launchers and established full air and sea control in the strait. With the exception of a few unmanned underwater vehicles, none of our minesweeping platforms could survive if the Iranians were free to attack 'em. They're designed only for clearing mines."

Lieutenant General Troy Krongaard, the US Air Force commander in the region, sat next to his boss General Remington. He said, "No worries about the Iranian air force. Their pilots have so little flight time that we would take 'em out quick. But finding and eliminating their cruise missile batteries, that's very hard. We know it from the Kosovo operation in '98 and '99 and from chasing the Iraqi Scud batteries in 2003. They shoot and scoot. And until they shoot, they're almost impossible to find from the air or by satellite. Iran has hundreds of them with enough range to hit the Strait of Hormuz. We're probably looking at a month, at least, to get 'em."

Frowning, Remington said, "Too long. Ty, how would the Iranians lay the minefield? Would we be able to catch 'em at it, and how long would they need to really shut the strait? Do you think they've started already?"

"Well, if it were me, I sure as hell would have started before declaring the strait closed. But we keep a pretty close eye on that area and haven't detected unusual numbers of IRGC boats there. They could be using their subs to lay mines, but that's a pretty slow process with the ex-Russian Kilo class. And our Global Hawk and satellite passes over Bandar Abbas show no more than one of the Kilo subs away from its berth at a time. So my guess is that they haven't laid many mines yet."

"And how long if they go at it full bore?"

"I'll have to get my guys to work that out. But they don't need to lay many to cause a big problem. A Kilo can lay around eighteen mines each trip. Let's say they manage to sneak in three trips. In that narrow, crowded shipping lane, even with it far from fully covered with mines, pretty soon some tanker is gonna hit one. And once that happens, shippers are going to stop sending tankers through the strait, at least until they can evaluate the true risk."

"So," said Remington slowly, "in political and commercial terms, the Iranians could put a kink in the world's crude oil supply hose quickly, even if it was a pretty thin minefield. And it would take us weeks or more likely months to get rid of it. Is that how you would sum things up, Admiral?" growled Remington.

"General, Fifth Fleet could certainly reopen the strait, but it would take weeks to months if the Iranians mine the area thoroughly. If we want to reduce the time to reopen the strait, then Washington needs to let us go after the boats and subs that are laying mines, whether we catch 'em in the act or take 'em out while they're in port loading up."

"So what would your destroyers do while mine clearance took place? Sit in Bahrain?" said Remington.

"That's about it, sir; wouldn't want to send 'em into the strait until the mine threat is negated and the sub threat is manageable."

"That's not going to play well in the press," said Remington, "so it won't play well in the White House, either. The Iranians will crow that we're afraid to challenge them, and if you just sit there ..."

Watson, knowing Remington's personality well, decided not to say anything; after all, that was a statement, not a question from his boss. Then he had a new thought: "General, if we want to be seen as doing something forceful, how about if you get me *Iowa*? It will take a couple of weeks for her to get here, and Washington can pitch that as giving diplomacy time to work, while winding up to throw our Sunday punch if it doesn't. Of course, she's really not our Sunday punch, not anymore, but she's huge and tough and can fire one-ton explosive projectiles over twenty miles. And while the minefield could sink her, if we have it mapped by the time she gets here, she can probe the strait without trying to breach the barrier. If the Iranians smack her with a missile or a suicide boat, they won't cripple her or sink her the way they would one of my destroyers. And if they attack her, it will give Central Command an excuse to blow the hell out of Iranian military sites along the coast."

Remington smiled. "I like that, Admiral." He turned to Marine General Bob Hurley, the deputy director for operations, and said, "Bob, get to work on that."

Chapter 30

NEW YORK CITY, NEW YORK

JULIE MORALES, WEARING A TEAL pantsuit and white blouse with throat ruff that successfully walked the line between business and femininity, hustled to the escalator leading to the tracks beneath New York's Penn Station, hoping to catch the five p.m. Acela home to Washington. Minutes later she was in her seat in Club, pumps off, briefcase in the overhead rack, gazing contentedly at a glass of chardonnay and what Amtrak called a "cheese board." It was actually a plastic tray of soggy crackers and wilted cheddar, but she attacked it with gusto. The train pulled out on time, cars yawing from side to side as they slowly traversed the old, uneven roadbed and rails beneath the city.

Julie felt great about the presentation she had completed two hours ago. She had really grabbed the attention of a huge potential client with her pitch on the benefits of artificial intelligence apps to make more accurate predictions, automate decisions and processes, and optimize employees' time. She was confident of landing some of the client's business soon, which would give her a major client within her first month back at Booz Allen.

You've still got your mojo, girl!

Julie wished things were going as well with her other new start: her four-star Marine being a house husband. Not that things were bad. Ray had adjusted well. He'd been a poster child for physical therapy and could walk without a limp, although the ankle damaged by Fahim's bullet still kept him from running at full tilt. And he almost seemed to enjoy being in a daily routine after three years of urgent calls in the dead of night, of the chaotic life during Fahim's American jihad, then that crazy attack on Fahim's camp, and finally the brutal investigation by Gustafson and her committee. Ray wasn't addicted to the adrenaline rush of crises and was nothing if not resilient. He had come home from Nats spring training seeming at peace with what fate—and Arlene Gustafson—had dealt him.

Their marriage, though, was not doing as well. She couldn't let go of Ray's night with Ella. Even though Julie believed his insistence that it was a terrible mistake that would never happen again, it would always hurt. She would never have left Ray while he was serving in office, recovering from that idiotic raid that nearly killed him, and being savaged by Gustafson. But what about now? What gnawed at her was that she had trusted Ray and he betrayed her. Julie was trying to believe he would never betray her again, about anything, but it was hard while she knew he was still keeping some secrets.

There's stuff that Gustafson knows about my husband, big stuff, which he won't tell me. I really don't know if I want to stay in this marriage!

What kind of a human being could order what he had done to that terrorist kid? And then walk into the room and question him as he lay there in blood, pain, and terror? And later try to justify it by saying it was his duty?

Julie was many years beyond the naive idealism that she and her friends had exhibited in college. She understood that war was evil, brutal, merciless—and sometimes the best of an array of bad choices. She knew that those who had dedicated themselves to fighting America's wars had been indelibly marked by what they had seen and done. And that Ray was one of them. But she had never before known the details of any of the bloody episodes he had gone through. Now she knew exactly what had been done—at Ray's bidding—to the helpless young man on that stretcher. And Ray had wanted to keep it a secret from her, like that night with Ella at Camp David.

And yet, she told herself, maybe she shouldn't be so put off. For twelve years before she met Ray, she had been a business process consultant. She worked with some clients and some colleagues who lied, cheated, and ruined lives in the pursuit of money and power. She didn't play that game, but she hadn't turned away in moral outrage, either. If what Ray did was an abuse of power, it wasn't the first time she had associated with someone she knew was abusing power.

Do I find it revolting because the abuse of power was physical, because actual blood was spilled? And if so, is that valid? Or is it merely self-indulgence?

Perhaps she was expecting more of Ray than was reasonable. His action, after all, did not gain him anything, only put him at risk. And he knew that at the time. Maybe she just needed to accept his love and love him back and move on from their inside-the-Beltway past.

Ray had gone, literally overnight, from full speed ahead, as one of the most consequential officials in government, to full retirement. His active, inquiring mind and energy now found little outlet other than household chores and physical fitness. He had taken those on with his usual determination; their houseplants had never had it so good, their kitchen was a model of efficient arrangement, and grocery shopping was managed as precisely as the supply line of a Marine regiment.

And still, even though he must be feeling useless, unappreciated, and cast aside, he was supporting her wholeheartedly in the re-launch of her career.

She asked herself what she would have done in Ray's place. If she had felt compelled by duty to do something she knew was illegal and immoral, would she tell her husband? He had to choose to maintain safely within law and morality while the deadly attacks continued, or to risk both prosecution and his soul to get information that might stop them. And circumstances had demanded an immediate decision. What would she have done? Which choice would really have been the moral one? And either way, would she have shared it with Ray?

Maybe I just need to accept his love and love him back and move on from all the inside-the-beltway, cable news, talk-radio crap.

Chapter 31

NEW YORK CITY, NEW YORK

THE PERFECTLY COMBED, CRISPLY SUITED news anchor said, "So how are Iranians reacting to their government's decision to close the Strait of Hormuz and international anger about what many are calling a brazen defiance of international law? Here's our chief foreign affairs correspondent, Charles Delany, to weigh in.

"Charles, you're just back from Tehran. What did you learn?"

"Carleton, this certainly is topic number one on the street in Tehran. It has grabbed the attention of Iran's people as nothing else has since the nuclear deal was signed in 2016. But unlike the mood then, which was largely optimistic, this time it's one of caution, alertness, and concern about what may come out of this.

"It's fair to say that this caught most people by surprise. The fatwah of Mufti Hosan Barati had largely fallen on deaf ears. He's a pretty obscure character, and in this country of many legal scholars, fatwahs come and go, many never noticed, much less acted upon. But President Ahmadi grabbed the issue and swiftly brought it to national prominence as a vehicle for increasing his stature. This issue went from a gleam in Ahmadi's eye to the attack on the Chinese destroyer *Nanking* almost overnight."

"So, do people support this decision?" said the anchor.

"Initially, many were angry with the government, but as the response of the US, China, and most western nations became perceived as belligerent and disrespectful of Iran, opinion changed radically. Whatever their initial feelings, now most Iranians whom I spoke with—from journalists

144

to clerics to street vendors—stand with their government. It's become a matter of patriotism. And since all Iranians under the age of about seventy-five have been taught repeatedly in school and mosque that America, the Great Satan, is always looking for excuses to damage Iran's interests and overthrow its government, public opinion levels blame at American aggression. Within the house of mirrors that is Iranian politics, what began with Israel's assassination of Quds Force leader Jahandar has now become a confrontation with America. In short, the government now enjoys strong public support for closing the strait and defying American demands to open it."

"But, Charles," interjected the anchor, "anger at America is, as you say, pretty much instinctive. But what about *China*? Why in the world pick a Chinese navy ship to attack, rather than an American one? And isn't China's response likely to be, in the long run, worse for Iran than America's?"

"Good point, Carleton. But, while governments and geopolitical wonks know how essential China is to Iran as a trading partner and as a supplier of military technology and hardware, the average Iranian—and I daresay the average American or European—isn't aware of that.

"As for targeting a *Chinese* warship, that's truly a mystery. There are many crosscurrents in Iran's mix of religion and politics, but none of the experts I spoke with could explain this in terms of factional conflict. Several suggested that it was just a mistake, a product of the fog of war. It's worth noting that Iran actually has *two* military structures. One is a conventional military organization of air, land, and naval forces. This organization predates the Iranian Revolution of 1979. During the revolution many militias and paramilitaries sprang up. They were eventually consolidated and brought under government control. Today this military structure is known as the Iranian Revolutionary Guard Corps, or the IRGC. Both the regular military and the IRGC report directly to the Supreme Leader. It's as if Iran had two Pentagons, to offer an analogy in American terms. That seems, as least to me, to have the potential for confusion."

"Charles, before I let you go, what about China's reaction to the sinking of the destroyer *Nanking*, apparently by an Iranian suicide boat?"

"Carleton, that is perhaps one of the most interesting things about this situation. Although China has had military skirmishes over the years since its major role in the Korean War of 1950 to '53, those have all been at its borders. The Chinese have fought both the Indians and the Russians over the location of those borders. But this is the first time that a unit of the Chinese military, the People's Liberation Army Navy, has been attacked away from China's borders or home waters. It is, in a sense, a 'welcome to the club of global powers' moment for Beijing. America, Russia, France, and Britain, the other four permanent members of the UN Security Council, have each brought their dead home from far-flung military operations. But, for China, this is a first, at least in the twentieth century and to date in the twenty-first.

"No nation or organization has claimed the attack that sank the *Nanking*. And the Chinese government, while publicly vowing to hold the attackers responsible, hasn't made any accusations of culpability. We can only wonder what the Chinese may be saying behind the scenes to the government of Iran, which, since it declared the strait closed, has to be the prime suspect."

"Thanks, Charles. Now for a sense of how Americans are feeling about this tense situation, here's Lupita Miranda, our national political correspondent. Lupita?"

"Carleton, in contrast to the rapt attention of the Iranian public—and probably the Chinese public—Americans don't seem to be concerned. As you know, our most recent nationwide poll shows that only about twenty percent of Americans believe that the closure of the Strait of Hormuz is harmful to the United States. With our own shale oil and natural gas now so plentiful, the price of fuels in America hasn't moved up much. Most Americans believe we are energy self-sufficient. While that's not strictly correct, when it comes to the petroleum products that matter most to the average citizen, gasoline, diesel, and home heating oil, we are very close to that point. And I hardly need to point out that Americans are thoroughly disenchanted with military action in the Middle East. On the other hand, a majority of Americans are aware that one of our navy ships, the destroyer *Agerholm*, rescued the Chinese navy men who survived the sinking. Americans are proud of that rescue but have little interest in the rest of the story over there."

"And what about the reaction from the White House and Capitol Hill, Lupita?"

"Would you be surprised if I told you that it mirrors public opinion?"

she replied, smiling. "The Martin administration has joined with China in requesting an emergency meeting of the UN Security Council but has made no statement about what it might do to reopen the strait if the UN is unable to. And, like the public, the administration has praised the quick and courageous work of the crew of USS Agerholm. As for the Hill, all quiet except for praise of *Agerholm*."

Chapter 32

TEHRAN, ISLAMIC REPUBLIC OF IRAN

DESPITE HIS IMPECCABLE REVOLUTIONARY CREDENTIALS—IN 1979 he had left the American college at which he was enrolled to return to Iran and build an Islamic republic—Adel Ghorbani cheerfully acknowledged that the Great Satan had at least one virtue: the hamburger and its little brother, the slider. He loved sliders and had just savored several, along with fries, at Gumbi restaurant, near his apartment in the Qeytariyeh neighborhood of Tehran. It was, as far as he knew, the only place in Tehran—probably in Iran—that offered sliders.

Ghorbani took another sip of the thick, sugary coffee he loved. As he sifted through the events of the past week, he worried that they were beginning to spin out of control. It reminded him of the revolution. Then, events and opportunities had overwhelmed common sense in a rush of empowerment. Nobody told the students to seize and occupy the American embassy; they just did it, with no thought beyond the excitement of the moment, of the heady feeling of power. And Iran had lived with the events that flowed from that occupation ever since. One of the most significant decisions made by Iranians in the twentieth century was taken by a bunch of kids with no plan for what came next. He feared that the sinking of the Chinese destroyer and the closing of the Strait of Hormuz were equally heedless and would have even worse consequences.

After days of confusion and finger-pointing, the regime discovered that *Nanking* had been attacked and sunk by a rogue sailor of the IRGC navy. Whether he was a young zealot whose desire for martyrdom had been given purpose by rhetoric about the strait, or, as some asserted after an examination of his computer, he was an agent of ISIS, it didn't matter beyond Iran's ruling circle. An Iranian navy man, using an Iranian navy patrol boat, had sunk the destroyer. So, just as in the seizure of the American embassy, a rationale was manufactured after the act

Ghorbani sighed, disgusted, and lit another cigarette. He realized it was unwise to do that, to let his feelings show in this public place, this place where he was known and, probably, watched.

After the revolution, we didn't abolish the secret police; we replaced the Shah's with our own, VAJA.

After the sinking, he had gone immediately to the head of the Chinese engineers assisting the missile programs and apologized. He had nearly shamed himself self before the self-righteous, slant-eyed little prick. A lot of good it did! The engineers hadn't been withdrawn, but they had stopped work. The threat of leaving was clear. He had also gone to the leader of the nuclear physicist group, and that was even worse because Iran's prototype missile warhead was so close to being ready to test. And a successful test was crucial: he had to be confident that the nuclear warhead would function after the punishment of riding atop a rocket and plunging through the atmosphere encased in a reentry vehicle glowing from friction.

It wasn't that they couldn't test their warhead without the Chinese scientists. But assessing the explosion itself, sucking every bit of data from the nanoseconds before the weapon blew apart, and drawing the correct conclusions from the various isotopes remaining in the debris—these were things the Iranian scientists and engineers lacked the experience to do confidently. Not to mention figuring out what had gone wrong if the warhead failed to detonate. Ghorbani worried that if Iran tested without the Chinese, his nation would enter a period of maximal risk, when it had revealed that it had the bomb but didn't yet have an operational nuclear missile force or know all that was needed to produce reliable nuclear weapons.

But even that wasn't the worst of the problems caused by the sinking of *Nanking*. Ghorbani's greatest worry was that, having outraged and frightened the most powerful nations in the world, Iran's test of a nuclear weapon would not just increase the risk of an Israeli-American attack on nuclear facilities; it would *trigger* such an attack. Israel and America would shout that a nation that had done something as irrational as Iran just did in closing the Strait of Hormuz *could not* be allowed to develop a nuclear-armed missile force. And the Chinese, who before *Nanking* would have sided with Iran and called the Jews and the Great Satan warmongers, would either remain silent or even agree with them.

As he sat and smoked, Ghorbani cursed Javad Ahmadi for seizing on a ridiculous fatwah from an insignificant mufti. Ahmadi's motive was clear enough—to save his skin. But why did the Supreme Leader allow him to carry out that fatwah, ruinous to Iran? *He* was under no threat. He could have allowed Ahmadi a role in retaliation without giving the order to close the strait through which flowed the petroleum lifeblood of Iran's most important ally.

Ghorbani recalled the premature order to attack Khorramshahr in the War of the Eighties against Iraq. It was stupid, but as a troop commander he had to figure out how to make the best of it. He reminded himself that he did it then and that he had a plan for now.

But today his position was both more powerful and more vulnerable. Reporting directly to the Supreme Leader, Ghorbani commanded a force that would be very dangerous to the government if it were not completely loyal. That's why he was watched—and why what he had in mind could easily be construed as treason.

The first part of his plan was relatively safe. There was a way that the Leader and Ming Liu could work this out, each claiming victory, even though neither wanted to take the first step. But he was confident that he could convince the Leader to do that.

But the second part was very dangerous, depending on the discretion and cooperation of a proud man he had treated with contempt.

Will he even listen to my proposition? Does he still have access? Will he do as I ask, in secret? So many risks! Should I take them?

Chapter 33

ARLINGTON, VIRGINIA

IN THE KITCHEN RAY MORALES whistled off-tune but cheerfully as he poured hot coffee into Julie's travel mug. In the night just past, they had shared their most enthusiastic lovemaking in years. As she pecked Ray's cheek and headed for her commute, Julie chuckled to herself over how simple Ray sometimes was. Good food and good sex were often all it took to give him contentment.

But Ray's delight in the return of passion and in the recovery he perceived in their relationship faded as the day stretched emptily before him. He didn't want to go to his office at CSIS—he had spent so much time there with so little to do that he felt pitiful. Even the interns gave him looks that he interpreted as saying, "Don't you get it, General? Nobody cares what you think or know anymore." The Nationals were traveling today, so no ballgame. And it was too early to allow himself to attack the only remaining event in his day, a workout.

In the weeks following the hearings and his resignation, Morales had received many invitations to appear on talk shows and news broadcasts. He had turned them down, partly to avoid putting himself back in Arlene Gustafson's gun sights but also because he was ashamed of his misjudgments in the pursuit of Fahim. He didn't want to revisit his foolhardy decision to personally go after the world's most wanted terrorist, accompanied by only a lone Department of Homeland Security agent, Phil Hoskins, and his military assistant, Jerry Thomas. Phil was killed, Jerry might never fly a Marine fighter again, and he himself now had to live a lie. Live it until Gustafson or Ghorbani exposed him, which he feared either still might do.

He had also received several feelers from publishers: "Americans want to hear your story, General Morales. Not only your daring foray into Fahim's Idaho terrorist base but also all about the dedicated, selfless fight you and your DHS team waged to defeat his jihad in America."

When he and Julie had discussed the first such offer, they quickly concluded what the pitches really meant: "let's package up all the juicy tidbits and gory details and then sell a lot of books and split the money." No, he had decided, a sensational book would cheapen the sacrifice of Phil's life and the really tough decisions made by the president.

There was one proposal, though, that he hadn't rejected. That was to write his autobiography, with as much help as he wanted. The writer suggested by the publisher was a respected former journalist with impressive book credits.

"General," the publisher had said, "your life story is truly inspiring. Growing up in San Antonio, you might have become another Tex-Mex kid in the barrio. But your parents sacrificed for you and your sister, imbued you with their work ethic and integrity, and both of you became successful. You worked for your dad's painting business after school, except during football season. You studied hard, got top grades. Won a competitive appointment to the Naval Academy. Commanded a battalion in combat with distinction. Excelled in every assignment and became the chairman of the Joint Chiefs. And then you decided to resign from that post as a matter of conscience because you couldn't support President Rogers's plan for the pullout from Iraq. No chairman had ever done that—and events proved right your insistence that her plan was flawed. Appointed to a vacant congressional seat by the governor of Texas, you became a close confidant and advisor to President Martin during the crises with North Korea. Then DHS.

"That's a story people will want to hear. It's a story that could change the lives of disadvantaged kids. We want to tell it."

Julie had cautioned him that this might be just a softer pitch for the same sensationalism, so he would need a contract that gave him absolute control. But it might, indeed, become an inspiration to some kids and their parents. And, she had said, writing it might help him sort out his options for what comes next. He was still mulling it over.

Morales heard the phone ring again. Annoyed, he punched the button on his phone to find out who the hell had called twice in the last couple of hours without leaving a message. This was his personal cell, and the relative few who had the number were unlikely to behave that way.

"Morales!" he grated.

"General, this is a fellow general to whom you owe your life," said a voice with a strong accent Ray couldn't quite identify. But the words, of course, identified the caller exactly. His anger flared, was replaced by caution, and then by curiosity.

"OK, I understand who you are. Why are you calling me? And how did you get this number?"

"How I got this number is of no matter compared to the reason I have called. I assume that you, like me, having seen the face of war, do not want war between Israel and Iran. The danger of such a war is increasing rapidly."

"If that is so, it's been caused by Iran closing the Strait of Hormuz and sinking a Chinese warship," interjected Morales.

"And the Israeli assassination of Zavad Jahandar had nothing to do with the situation?" Ghorbani paused, then continued: "Let us not waste time playing games, General. It is what it is. The sinking was the work of a single navy man, his mind twisted by ISIS when they held him captive. And perhaps, just perhaps, the Israelis are telling the truth about killing Jahandar. Those events are history. The question now for the two of us is, Will we do what we can to prevent a war that will destroy at least two nations? By this call I am demonstrating that I am willing to risk my life to prevent a war."

Morales, wishing he had the means to trace the call, said nothing.

The caller continued, "You know who I am and who I work for. I can guarantee he won't start a war with Israel if you can get a promise of certain things from your president."

"I'm not in government anymore. I'm a private citizen. There's no way I could guarantee what our president might choose to do. And even if I could, why should I?"

"I saved your life that day. Have you no honor?"

That stung, Ray admitted to himself. *Adel Ghorbani saved me from a beheading by Fahim. He didn't have to do that. He could've waited until Fahim had killed me and then shot him.*

"OK, you *did* save my life. But only because your mission didn't require that you kill me. You told me so as I lay on the ground. Why were you after Fahim? What brought you to the United States?"

"That is for another time. I cannot stay on this call much longer, so listen carefully. Israel wishes to destroy my country. Unfortunately, we have just offered Askenazi a pretext for attacking us. And he is preparing to do that, very soon. If your CIA doesn't see Israel's preparations, it is blind! America is the only nation that can prevent Israel from doing this and beginning a slaughter in the Middle East." He paused. "Yes, you understood me: a slaughter. We may or may not have nuclear weapons today, but we have others even more terrible. You know what I mean. If Israel attacks us, we will use them.

"We are neither a nation of fools nor of martyrs, so I make America this offer on behalf of our Supreme Leader: prevent Israel from starting this war, and we will enter negotiations to limit our nuclear weapons and those of the Jews to a number that will not threaten either of us with a first strike. Yes, supposedly neither Israel nor Iran has nuclear weapons, but let us not live in a dream world. Tell your president this. I will contact you again in two days to hear your answer. Do not be so foolish as to believe America can stall until Israel attacks us. Two days!" He was gone.

"What the hell?" muttered Morales. *Was* that Adel Ghorbani? Since so few others knew the full truth about Idaho, and he trusted them to keep silent, it must have been Ghorbani. But was Ghorbani telling the truth? That was a harder question.

Ghorbani had just claimed that, if attacked, Iran would use weapons even more terrible than nukes. He probably meant chemical and bioweapons, thought Morales. And he acknowledged that Iran had nukes of its own, or could have on short notice. Neither claim was a total surprise, but if true, that meant the cost of attacking Iran must be recalculated. That was what Ghorbani hoped to gain if he were lying—or by revealing truth if he were not. Morales was glad it wouldn't be up to him to decide which. And besides the threat of holocaust, Ghorbani had offered an arms control negotiation that would be very attractive to President Martin. Like every president in his second term, Martin was eager to build his legacy. How could he resist an opportunity to bring Israel and Iran to the table?

But what if Ghorbani was playing a lone game? What if he wasn't really acting at the behest of the Supreme Leader? He might be a truth-teller but unable to deliver on his promise.

Well, all this is way above my pay grade, and I'm glad of that. I'll ask Bart to set up a meeting with the president. As he reached out to Chief of Staff Bart Guarini, Morales realized the meeting would be the first time he and Rick Martin had met since the hearings—and Camp David.

Chapter 34

"THREE MORE MISSILES YESTERDAY AND twenty-seven dead. Our Arrow interceptor missiles just can't stop them all," said Israel's prime minister to his wife as the early morning sun streamed through the window overlooking Balfour Street.

"When will the army be ready, Joshua?"

"They're ready now, but Martin threatens serious consequences if we send troops into Syria and Lebanon to get the missile launchers. He doesn't believe that we killed Jahandar accidentally. He thinks that if we take only defensive measures, he can negotiate a cease-fire. He's wrong, but I'm going to give the air force a few more days of strikes against the launchers. I'm not ready for that kind of break with America yet."

Shara's eyes flashed, and her voice hardened. "Martin is bluffing, Joshua! He cannot afford to cut off the F-35 deliveries and support when we are under attack like this. The blowback in American politics would be too much. He'd be hanging the shame of abandoning Israel around the neck of his party, where it would stink for a long time. That's not the legacy he wants to leave. And now he needs us even more, with Iran's closure of the strait."

"Shara, the Americans have been walking away from us for years, foot by foot. Their nuclear deal with Iran sold us out. We found out then that we have less influence with them than before. Israel's all-out opposition to the deal didn't stop it. Walking back the F-35 deal wouldn't be as bad—he could get away with it. Besides, the American public has become focused on the strait crisis, and many of them blame Israel for it because we killed Jahandar."

"Joshua, you know as well as I do that Iran has assembled its first missile warheads. How much time will it be before they have operational nuclear warheads sitting on dozens of missiles, missiles that we already know we can't stop?"

"Shara, they've blundered. Since they sank *Nanking*, the Chinese have stopped helping them. That will set them back. They've never tested a complete nuclear missile delivery system, end to end, so they can't be confident theirs will work."

Shara's eyes were alight. "And that buys time for us to strike before Iran has its nuclear missiles and Israel must live forever under that threat. Under its cover, Iran will launch even bolder terror attacks. Joshua, you *cannot* let that happen! Once again we see the hand of God. Sinking a Chinese warship was surely not their intention; they were led to do it. Moses told Joshua that God goes before him. God will not fail you or forsake you, either."

Joshua arose and began to pace. "I will not be the last prime minister of Israel," he said quietly.

He halted beside their bed, and their eyes locked. "It's time for Operation Persepolis, Joshua."

"Yes!" said the prime minister of Israel, his fist striking his palm.

* * *

QOM, ISLAMIC REPUBLIC OF IRAN

Adel Ghorbani sat comfortably, or so he endeavored to appear, in a chair on the Supreme Leader's right, facing him as he sat behind his desk. The day before, when his assistant had told the Leader's secretary that he needed to speak with the man about the "special program" he ran, he had received an appointment for today.

"So, General, what is it about our nuclear missile force that is so urgent that you need to tell me immediately? I have given you every resource. Surely there is no great problem!"

"You have, indeed, Leader. And we are very nearly ready to test. But it's not the bomb itself that concerns me."

The Supreme Leader's eyebrows shot up. "Something with the missile, then?"

"No, there are issues with the missile, but we know how to solve them, along with our Chinese assistants."

"Good, good, because I have important news for you about the test. The Great Satan and others are gathering forces to push their way through our Strait of Hormuz. We need to show them how foolish such an attempt would be. And what better, more fitting way to do that than to test our bomb now? They would know then that we have the means to incinerate Israel and any foreign forces that do not respect our control of the strait. Hormuz is *ours*, leading into *our* waters."

Ghorbani felt as much alarm as he was capable of feeling after more than fifty years of surprises, ambushes, and intrigue. Shifting mentally from his plan for reconciling with China, he marshaled his thoughts to deal with a man who was even more impulsive and ignorant of military realities than he had feared.

Careful that neither his expression nor his tone would reveal his thoughts, Ghorbani said, "Leader, that would indeed put the infidels and the cursed Saudis on notice that we have become the most powerful Islamic nation in the world. It would indeed frighten them."

"As I thought!" interjected the Supreme Leader. "And to make them even more fearful, you will test our bomb above our strait."

Ghorbani fought back his rage at this man, who would blunder into the total destruction of Iran just as it was on the brink of becoming the most powerful, feared, and respected nation in the Middle East. It was all he could do to hold back the shout that thrust against his lips: *You fool!* But he managed outward calm. This was too important for emotion.

"Leader, I admire your boldness. Perhaps you should have been a soldier. We will need to plan carefully for this test and its outcome.

"Prior to the test we must evacuate Bandar Abbas and our military bases there and at Chabahar. Radiation and fallout from the blast will otherwise kill everyone. We must also go on our highest defensive military alert to be ready to defeat the massive Israeli, American, and even Saudi air attacks that will follow very soon because they will be terrified of an Iran with the bomb."

The Supreme Leader said nothing, but Ghorbani saw that the manic gleam was gone from his eyes. Now to give him a way to back down.

"While we are making these preparations, Leader, I suggest we take another very powerful action, one that will please the Chinese and catch the Americans off-guard. It's a bold action that only you could take."

Seeing the Leader preen slightly and nod, Ghorbani continued: "You can speak directly to President Ming Liu and resolve the issue that stands between us. Neither of our countries benefits from the current situation, in fact, quite the opposite. The Chinese have ceased their important assistance with our military programs. And we have cut China off from a critically important source of energy."

"If you are about to suggest that I disrespect us by apologizing, know that I will never do that. China's demand for an apology and for compensation I will never grant!"

"I would never be so foolish as to think that, Leader! But the very boldness you showed by taking control of our strait allows you now to resolve the issues between our two countries with honor. And cunning. Ming Liu will respect you even more."

The Supreme Leader leaned forward on his desk: "I will listen and consider your idea."

* * *

CAIRO, EGYPT

"The special flight has landed, Mr. Ambassador," said his secretary.

Ambassador Saul Goldstein disapproved of meetings such as this one. Israel's ambassador to Egypt, like every ambassador of every nation throughout human history, didn't like it when his government conducted important business on his turf without including him. But sometimes it happened. And sometimes, he admitted to himself, it turned out to be good not to have known about the proceedings. But today it rankled that the Egyptian government knew more about whatever this was than he did.

At Cairo West military airbase, Israel's top military officer, Lieutenant General Dan Rivkin, chief of the Israeli General Staff, paused for a moment before descending the stairs jutting from the cabin of the unmarked Gulfstream G-150 that had carried him to Egypt in what he hoped was total secrecy. He took a deep breath. What lay ahead might be the most important conversation of his professional life.

As his black sedan bumped through Cairo streets, its smoked glass windows impenetrable from outside, Rivkin wondered how long it would be before the Egyptians told the Americans about this meeting. He couldn't blame them. Israel, too, collected choice tidbits that it tossed to the American government to demonstrate the value of their relationship. And, who knows, the Saudis themselves might tell the Americans. Many of us in the Middle East seek their favor. It's damn demeaning!

His car, with Egyptian military license plates, was waved into the compound of the embassy of the Kingdom of Saudi Arabia and then into its garage. Rivkin was pretty sure that his Saudi counterpart, Prince Abdullah bin Abdulaziz, would have surmised at least the topic of their meeting. He doubted that Abdullah had come with an open mind. He himself would not have. He would be looking for the trick, the deception. In this case there would be none—but in a way that made his proposition harder to sell. And since Israel had asked for the meeting and agreed to hold it on Saudi turf, Abdullah would feel he had the upper hand.

"Danny, how are you?" said Abdullah in English, arising from the couch as Rivkin entered the room.

"I'm fine, Double-A, and hope you're the same," replied Rivkin, following Abdullah's lead by using the nickname he had received when they were students together in America's National War College. Rivkin took this as a signal that Abdullah would at least hear him out.

"So, Danny, I trust you had an uneventful journey? May I offer some refreshment?"

"I'd appreciate that, Double-A. How many years since National?"

"I've stopped counting the years—it's a little depressing to me that there are now so many of them. Who could have predicted when we were classmates in Washington that we would meet like this! Or that our classmate Ray Morales would become chairman of the Joint Chiefs of Staff."

A young man brought them cool yogurt drinks and withdrew.

"So, Double-A, to the business of our meeting. First, I appreciate your willingness to see me. This meeting is a risk for both our countries, but the situation in our region warrants accepting risks. I know that you have watched the failure of American diplomacy to end Iran's nuclear weapons ambitions. You know, as do I, that they are developing and testing missiles of sufficient power and reliability to carry nuclear warheads. Would you agree with me that Iran will soon have such ballistic missiles?"

Abdullah nodded.

Rivkin continued: "And they are not far from having those missiles ready to carry nuclear warheads. They have, in fact, built a prototype missile warhead, using a proven Chinese design. Iran is nearly ready to deploy a nuclear missile force that will threaten both of our countries.

"By closing the strait, Iran has now demonstrated beyond any doubt that it is a dangerously unstable nation, one certain to lurch in unpredictable directions. What could be a better illustration of this than sinking a Chinese warship and cutting off the oil China needs? How could this possibly come out well for Iran? It shows the irrationality of the country's leaders, leaders who will soon have a force of nuclear-armed ballistic missiles."

Abdullah nodded, expressionless.

"We—Israel, Saudi Arabia, and other Sunni nations—cannot allow this to happen. We know very well what Iran plans to do after it becomes a nuclear power: wipe Israel from the earth and dominate every nation in the region, especially Sunni nations. For Israel and, if I may say so, for the House of Saud, it has become a question of when, not whether, to take military action to prevent this disaster.

"Israel believes we must act now, within weeks if not sooner. We are prepared to strike and destroy Iran's nuclear facilities."

"If you do this," said Abdullah, "you must succeed. You must destroy *all* their facilities. Some are buried deep. And far from Israel. There must be some you haven't discovered. How can you be sure you will not miss one and provoke the nuclear attack you intend to prevent?"

"We cannot be absolutely sure. As you know, there are no certainties in warfare. But the risk of doing nothing is much higher than the risk of doing our best to destroy Iran's nuclear program. We have excellent intelligence, highly trained and motivated pilots, and aircraft with certain capabilities that their American manufacturers did not give them. At the least, the Iranians will need years to reconstitute their nuclear facilities. We are going to strike. The decision is made.

"But you are right," continued Rivkin, "that when we strike, we must be successful. So I am here to suggest that, in your own self-interest, you permit our strike aircraft to pass over your country and our tankers to station in your airspace for a few hours. As you know, this will greatly enhance our odds of complete success. And your odds of preventing Iranian domination of your country."

"Danny, you present this plan of yours with the usual Israeli arrogance. You tell me 'we are going to do this, and you'd better help us if you want to save yourselves.' You put us at risk in the service of Israel's interests and then ask for our help."

"Double-A, this is not arrogance. It's the opposite. We need your help to succeed with this strike! And we're willing to trust you with the details of it: time, numbers of aircraft, routes, refueling positions. We are not demanding, we are asking; asking for your assistance when we do something that is very much in your interest. Our countries are not friends or allies and never will be. But a nuclear-armed Iran is an existential threat to both our nations. We are prepared to risk virtually our entire air force. And we are asking only that you close your eyes for a few hours!"

"No, you are asking much, much more! If we do as you ask and still you fail to cripple Iran's nuclear program, we face an even bigger risk of retaliation than Israel. Israel has nuclear weapons that would deter the Iranians from using their own. We do not. Iran could use a nuclear bomb on us without fear of retaliation in kind."

"Double-A, with your assistance we *will* succeed!

"And look at the situation now," continued Rivkin. "Khamenei and others curse the House of Saud every day. Every Friday, imams inflame hundreds of thousands across Iran against you. Iran has attacked your oil fields using the Houthis. They have put a noose around the neck of your economy by closing the strait. If we do nothing, sooner rather than later you will face a nuclear-armed Iran determined to subjugate you and emboldened by its control of the strait.

"Really, Double-A, your best chance to avoid that is to help us now!" Rivkin looked intently at Abdullah, tension wrinkles showing at the corner of his jaw.

Abdullah cocked his head and looked away. Then he said, "I will present your proposal to the Crown Prince."

"Will you recommend it?"

"I will consider it."

Prince Abdullah rose and extended his hand. "Safe travels, Danny."

Chapter 35

THE WHITE HOUSE

WHEN HE WAS USHERED INTO the president's small private office, Ray Morales was surprised to find him alone. He wondered about Guarini's absence and what it might mean for the meeting. After a handshake, Ray sat in the only side chair this cubbyhole permitted.

"Ray, I want to tell you that I'm sorry I had to let you go. When you had Hadrab tortured, you sacrificed yourself to save the lives of others as surely as if you had thrown yourself on a grenade. Measured on the scale of loyalty and fidelity to duty as you saw it, you deserved better from me. But that's not the only scale a president must use."

Ray felt patronized but stifled his anger, wondering where Martin was going with this.

"I had also to consider the record I was leaving for my party's candidate to run on and the standard my response to torture would set."

"Mr. President, I understand that. I served at your pleasure and never expected a pass. And as you said, I did it to save lives. I didn't do it for you or your administration, and I knew it would be a huge problem for you if it came out." Ray stopped himself from veering into defensiveness. "How did you get Gustafson to back off?"

Martin squirmed and shifted his gaze to a point over Ray's left shoulder. "Bruce did it. He told me I shouldn't know how, so I let it go."

"You know she hates me. She'll probably come after me again."

"Bruce assured me that he had a way to silence her permanently on this topic."

Ray looked disbelieving but said nothing.

Martin fiddled with a letter opener on his desk, looking as if he were on the cusp of saying something important about Gustafson, but then said, "I want to hear about your conversation with Ghorbani, and so does Bart." He flicked a switch and asked the chief of staff to join them.

As Guarini entered, his sour expression revealed his feelings about his boss meeting privately with Morales. It was political dynamite for him to be in the White House at all.

"OK, Ray," said Guarini, "you asked for this meeting. What have you got for us?"

"Now hang on a minute, Bart," said Martin. "I was just going to offer Ray something to drink."

"I'm fine with water," said Morales, gesturing at the carafe on the side table. Ray glanced at a grim-faced Guarini, standing at the president's right, then turned to Martin and said, "Mr. President, thanks for agreeing to take this meeting yourself. I realize there's political risk involved in that alone."

"Ray, just about everything I do or don't do has political risk. I appreciate Bart here trying to talk me out of meeting you, but I owe you too much for your help over the years to stand off. Besides, I did more ducking for cover than I should have when Gustafson came after you. I feel pretty bad about that—although I still believe what you did to Ali Hadrab was wrong. That is, I hope, water under the bridge. I'm anxious to hear what you've got for us today."

"Mr. President, yesterday I got a phone call from General Adel Ghorbani. I believe it was truly him; he knew some things about the shootout in Idaho that only he—plus you and a very few others—could know. He gave me a message to pass to you and set a forty-eight-hour deadline for receiving your answer through me.

"The message is this: The Iranian regime believes that Israel is going to attack Iran very soon, using as justification Iran's actions in the strait. If that happens, Iran will unleash 'terrible weapons, almost as terrible as nuclear weapons'—those were his words—on Israel. I think he was threatening to use chemical or bioweapons.

"Ghorbani has devoted his life to making Iran the top dog in the Middle

East. He wants to prevent the Israeli attack, avoiding mutual suicide. He said that if you assure Iran that America will prevent the Israeli attack, Iran is prepared to enter talks to limit its nukes and Israel's to a number that doesn't threaten either country with a first strike. He told me he speaks for the Supreme Leader on this. And he was emphatic that this offer was only good for forty-eight hours."

"That's a bullshit offer, a sucker deal!" said Guarini. "We save them from a clear and present danger, and in return they agree to sit down and talk for months if not years! And that's if we can get the Israelis to negotiate, which I don't think we can." His expression mirrored his words.

But Rick Martin looked interested. Foreign policy was by far his favorite aspect of the presidency, and while he no longer believed he could bring all opponents together, he still had great confidence in his ability to find a way forward. After all, he had won the Nobel Peace Prize in his first term for the reunification of Korea as a democratic nation.

"Well, there's a lot to unpack yet, but it may be worth pursuing," Martin said. "Not on the terms Ghorbani offered but on others.

"Today's intelligence briefing had an item on possible Israeli attack preparations," he continued. "There are apparently signs that some analysts take to mean the Israelis are gearing up for a large number of air strikes at a very long range—or maybe these signs are no more than practice runs, training."

"I don't see how we could *really* know about an Israeli attack in time to stop it," said Guarini. "I hate to say it, Mr. President, but I think that, during the campaign, Rutherford and his people convinced Askenazi that we weren't to be trusted. You and the Israeli PM aren't exactly buddies, sir."

"You're right," said Martin. "He doesn't trust me, nor I him. If I need to shut down an Israeli preemptive attack and have no personal relationship of trust to draw on, what else have I got to work with?"

"Nothing but the really big sticks, sir," said Guarini. "You can tell Askenazi that he's on his own if he attacks, that the United States won't lift a finger to help Israel deal with the response. You can throw in the end of all aid to Israel's military programs. And, of course, pay a big political price for doing that."

"And I haven't got a clue," said Ray, "whether Ghorbani truly speaks for the Supreme Leader. He might be freelancing, genuinely trying to prevent war, but in the end won't be able to deliver on Iran's piece of the bargain. Or he might be running a deception to drive a wedge between the United States and Israel. Or maybe he's just trying to get his name off our kill list."

"Which takes us back to where I was when I walked into this room," said Guarini. "This really comes down to nothing. There are so many unknowns and risks that his offer, even if genuine, amounts to nothing we should act on.

"My recommendation, sir, is *no deal.*"

"Ray, what's your evaluation?" said the president.

"I'm with Bart, sir. Although I owe Ghorbani my life, I have no relationship with the guy, nothing to vouch for his credibility. Since he's survived as long as he has, he must be clever and ruthless. He's surely betrayed lots of people along the way. We shouldn't trust him."

"OK, then we don't trust him," said the president. "But we don't tell him no, either. Tell him this: We are committed to Israel's survival but not to Iran's destruction. We are interested in his proposed negotiation but need more to go on. Best would be if Iran immediately stopped claiming authority over the strait and opened it to all shipping. Under those circumstances I'm prepared to guarantee Israel will not attack Iran, and we will sponsor negotiations between Iran and Israel to reduce the danger of war. Or, if Ghorbani can establish to our satisfaction that he speaks for the Supreme Leader, we can then discuss what the US is prepared to do to prevent a preemptive attack on Iran by Israel.

"Bart will write that up for you, Ray. And Bart, take Ghorbani off the kill list, at least until we sort this out."

Martin stood up. "Time for my next meeting. Ray, it's good to see you looking healthy! We'll be hearing from you soon, I'm sure."

The president shook Morales's hand and left them. Guarini turned to leave, but Ray put a hand on his shoulder, and Guarini halted.

"Bart, what did Griffith have on Gustafson to make her back down? They were getting ready to hang me high, and she was loving it."

"I'm sorry, but I can't tell you that. All I can say is that she won't come gunning for you again." He paused, and his tone shifted: "Tell me, Ray. How are you doing? You and Julie taking some time off to smell the roses?"

"Bart, time off is all I've got. I'm damaged goods. I've got a title and an office at CSIS but only because the CEO there is a former Marine. As for Julie, she's doing a great job of rebuilding her career at Booz Allen."

Guarini said, "That's a damn shame, Ray," and seemed to run out of words, a look of sadness on his face. After a moment he shrugged and gestured for Ray to precede him through the door.

Chapter 36

SHILO SETTLEMENT, WEST BANK, ISRAEL

S IRENS WAILED, AND THE CHILDREN, grades one through six, filed into the shelter, chattering as they walked. Teachers hustled them along, trying to move them quickly without frightening them. They were attending Lieb Primary School in the West Bank settlement of Shilo, about thirty miles north of Jerusalem. Just before the sirens sounded, the hard-looking men with Shara Askenazi had pressed fingers to their earbuds, then began to hustle her to an armored limousine protected front and rear by army Humvees. She looked surprised, then grim. After a few steps the security leader made a largely intuitive decision: too late for speeding away. He halted and reversed the group herding Shara to the street and led them instead to the shelter.

Five miles away, the Iron Dome sector control station was a scene of intense concentration and rapid decisions. The long-range, Russian-designed rockets Hezbollah had launched from Lebanon to the north were clearly visible on their displays, a swarm of red dots. Within minutes the dots were within range of the variety of weapons that constituted Iron Dome. Tamir ground-to-air missiles went for them, creating fiery collisions that trailed flaming debris to the ground. Rapid-fire antiaircraft weapons atop armored vehicles opened up on the nearest rockets, spraying glowing tracers like fireworks across the sky.

Suddenly the sector commander, who was beginning to feel good about the battle so far, stiffened in his chair and snapped, "Say again, Citron Tree Control."

He heard, "We hold a ballistic missile at two three three degrees inbound your sector. Engaging in ten seconds, but it's a crossing shot at extreme range. Be prepared to pick it up if we miss."

"Oh, shit!" The officer commanding the Iron Dome sector slammed his palm on the table. Iron Dome wasn't designed to destroy ballistic missiles. Nonetheless, he barked orders for all Iron Dome weapons under his control to open fire, sweeping a sector from two two zero to two five zero degrees. He was throwing up a curtain of metal and explosives as if spraying water with a hose, hoping the descending missile warhead would plunge through the curtain and be blown apart. The officer knew the warhead was descending steeply to its target and, even if struck by Iron Dome, would probably crash into the selected spot, but he did everything he could with what he had.

The Iranian warhead stabbed downward and found its target, Lieb Primary School. Passing easily through the roof, second story, and floor, it struck the shelter of reinforced concrete and structural steel and skidded sideways without penetrating fully, then exploded in the earth alongside the shelter. The high explosive completed the job the warhead's kinetic energy had begun. When first responders arrived seventeen minutes later, they found the shelter thrusting from the ground, blown upward through the school's ground floor by the blast. The shelter, of the latest design, had survived the shock, overpressure, and fire remarkably well. Its occupants had not.

Ninety-three minutes later, Joshua Askenazi's convoy pulled up at the edge of an area secured by yellow tape. The prime minister flung open the armored Humvee's door and jogged, zig-zagging among chunks of concrete, splintered furniture, and tattered books. His foot caught an upthrust length of rebar, and he staggered, then caught his balance. An army major intercepted him, trying to slow his rush toward the dangerous edges of the crater. Askenazi pushed him aside and rumbled on. Reaching the lip, he shouted to a medic below, "Where is she? Where is my wife?"

The medic gave a small shrug and gestured to the remains of the shelter. Askenazi began to clamber downward, slipping as loose earth gave way. The delay allowed the army officer, now accompanied by Ya'el Barak, to place his hands atop Askenazi's shoulders and thrust him into a sitting position.

"Get your damn hands off me, Major!"

"Joshua, my friend," said Barak, gesturing the major to release the man

Barak had served for seventeen years. "Stop, Joshua. She's gone. She's no more. She would not want you to see her as she is. She would hate that!"

Eyes filled with tears, Joshua Askenazi glared at Barak, then bowed his head and slumped. "Yes, of course. You're right." His voice cracked. "She was so beautiful. So wise. She was everything to me. How am I going to live without her?" His shoulders shook, and tears came. He pounded the earth, now softened from firefighting water. Barak stood beside him, one hand on his heaving shoulder, and gazed at the blackened concrete that hid the remains of Shara Askenazi, twenty-eight schoolchildren, two teachers, one classroom aide, three journalists, and four security officers.

Joshua Askenazi lurched to his feet, threw back his head, and bellowed into the blue, cloudless sky: "You'd better be with me, you old bastard, because I'm calling you on your promise! You're going to deliver them into my hands, and I'm going to destroy them! And after I've done that, you can do with me as you wish."

He wiped his eyes and started toward his Humvee with long, urgent strides. "Come on, Ya'el. We've got things to do."

Ya'el Barak hustled alongside his boss, wondering who else had seen and heard Joshua Askenazi's personal declaration of war on Iran.

* * *

Her state funeral in the Knesset chamber was attended by every Israeli political and military figure of consequence. And by the First Lady of the United States, Ella Martin, beside Vice President Bruce Griffith; by senior officials from the major countries of Europe; also by the wife of the general who ruled Egypt; and—to the surprise of many—China's premier.

Sitting silently, wishing his own heart would stop beating, Joshua Askenazi took in the flags, rich tapestries, and solid gold menorah. He knew she was pleased at the setting, top-class as she always had insisted. Afterward her coffin, encased in the sky blue and snow white flag of Israel, was escorted by a military honor guard to Mount Hertzl cemetery. Someday, perhaps someday soon, he would join her there, in the nation's national cemetery among the great and the brave of Israel.

He owed her so much. From the beginning of their political career, Shara had made the critical decisions. The fierce will, the strategic vision, the shrewd compromises needed to form a governing majority in the

Knesset—these were mostly Shara's. He would be happier if he had the massive coronary his doctor had threatened when warning him about his weight and blood pressure.

Unlike most Israelis, Shara had believed adamantly in the existence of a spirit world that overlapped the physical one. Joshua had assumed that this was yet another way in which she was an original, someone who reveled in her own power and in being unconventional. Now, feeling the central support of his life torn from under him, he ached for her to be proven right, if only for a single hour to say goodbye. Sharing her belief became his connection to Shara.

Chapter 37

ARLINGTON, VIRGINIA

R AY MORALES CLEARED HIS THROAT nervously as he waited for Ghorbani to call as he had said he would. He felt out of his depth: still a Marine, not a diplomat. He worried that he would be drawn into something harmful to the country. If this negotiation went south, and it very well might, would he be thrown under the bus again?

When the hell is he gonna call? We're down to twelve hours or so from his deadline. Is he playing with me, waiting until the last moment?

With Julie in New York, Morales had been pacing their apartment alone, not wanting to leave lest this call come in when he was in a public place. He was tired of reading. The Nats were at home, but he dared not go to the ballpark. And anyway, the game wouldn't start until just after seven p.m., and it wasn't yet noon. He was about a quarter of the way into a thriller, but it hadn't grabbed him. He slid open the door to their small balcony and stepped outside, aware of but not seeing the Potomac and Memorial Bridge before him.

The phone rang.

"Morales."

"Well?"

Anger shot through Morales. His brows drew down in a lowering scowl. Someday, he swore to himself, he would puncture that arrogance. But not now. He said, "I've spoken to the president and have his response to Iran's offer to negotiate the reopening of the strait."

172

"Negotiate! Negotiate? We are not negotiating. You can accept our offer or accept the continuation of the present situation."

"The United States has no particular problem with the present situation," said Morales. "We have no particular problem with China exacting a high price for your destruction of *Nanking*. And there are many in the United States, some of them in high positions, who would have no particular problem if the Israelis decided to eliminate the threat of an Iranian nuclear weapon. And Iran made that more likely by killing Shara Askenazi."

"Which happened only because Israel assassinated Zana Jahandar!"

They fell silent, each waiting for the other to put their conversation back on the path both knew it needed to take if war between Iran and Israel was to be avoided.

"We are two soldiers trying to prevent more of the unnecessary death we have each seen in the past," said Ghorbani. "Let us try our hardest to do that."

"Here is President Martin's reply," said Morales, evenly. "The United States is committed to Israel's survival but not to Iran's destruction. Iran's illegal closure of the strait makes it much harder for the United States to support Iran in anything. If Iran were to reopen the strait to free passage of all ships, that would facilitate US efforts to prevent war between any nations in the region."

"Tell your president this," barked Ghorbani. "If he is truly committed to Israel's survival, he will prevent Israel from attacking us. Israel's attack preparations are forcing us to consider using our nuclear weapons before they are destroyed. I understand, and so do you, that even as it dies, Israel will retaliate with nuclear weapons. But Israel will *not* survive, no matter how effective its attack is. We have the means to assure that. And so the ultimate result of an Israeli attack will be the death of two nations. President Martin has the opportunity to prevent the greatest disaster ever to strike the Middle East. I hope he will act now, before it is too late.

"Unless we see evidence very soon that Martin is taking steps to prevent Israel's attack, Iran will have no choice but to consider all measures."

"As you said, General, I will transmit your response to my president."

"Be quick. Things are very complicated here."

"Goodbye."

Morales stood unmoving, gazing out the window. Ghorbani had just claimed that Iran in fact had nuclear missiles and would launch them if Israel attacked. Was he telling the truth? Morales was glad he had recorded the call.

The analysts are going to have quite a time with this conversation!

Chapter 38

ABERDEEN ARMY PROVING GROUND, ABERDEEN, MARYLAND

E LLA WASN'T AFRAID OF RICK'S first reaction. It would not be overt anger or indeed any uncontrolled emotion. President Rick Martin was a man totally in his head, someone who buried his emotions as deeply as possible.

Still, this was really hard: finding the right moment and the right words to begin the revelation that she had slept with Ray Morales. She knew that Rick had felt her emotional absence since the election. She believed he wanted to return to the intellectual and emotional partnership they had before the campaign. But he hadn't reached out to her about these things. Was he, too, struggling to find the right moment and the right words?

Was now the time to do it, in the sitting room of the guesthouse at Aberdeen Proving Grounds, alongside the Chesapeake, Rick's favorite spot to unwind and enjoy the water sports he loved? Though the temperature didn't call for one, a fire was crackling beneath the driftwood mantelpiece. They had dined on the porch, watching the backlight of sunset behind them paint the clouds over the bay, refusing to let the strain they felt keep them from this much-loved ritual. She looked at Rick sitting to the left of the fireplace, reading a thriller by one of his favorite authors, David Ignatius.

"Rick," she said.

He looked up, his expression revealing that he was at an especially engrossing point in the book. She almost veered away from her moment of truth but decided to go ahead.

"Rick, there's something important I need to tell you. I've been looking for the right moment; this may not be it, but I've kept this secret too long already."

Her husband's face grew serious. "Secret? OK, Ella. What is it?"

"Rick, we grew so far apart during the campaign. I hated that. Instead of sharing each day's events, discussing how to play the big-money donors—remember how ridiculous some were?—or talking about our plans for the second term, we hardly spoke at all, and that was mostly by phone. I felt like you rejected me, no longer respected my thinking, shut me out. I was so unhappy! And then I got really angry when you flipped on 'good guys with guns.'"

As she paused to gather her courage, Rick said, "I know Ella. I was wrong to put our partnership in a box and put it on the shelf. I'm glad you've brought this up, and I want to talk about it. I want to get back to how we were before the campaign."

Ella took a deep breath. "I do, too." Her voice broke, then thickened as she fought the lump in her throat and the burning in her eyes that preceded tears. "But before we can do that, you have to know something I did in my depression and anger: I slept with Ray Morales. One night, and it will never happen again, but I did it."

As she expected, Rick absorbed the blow with outward calm, the way she had seen him absorb so many surprises as president. He put the book down, put his hands in his lap, and stared at her with a neutral expression. The he crossed his arms across his chest and looked away, into the fire. Ella resisted her urge to say more.

Turning back to her, Rick said, "When? How did it happen?"

Ella knew he was defaulting to attorney-thought, seeking facts without acknowledging the accompanying emotions. But that's who he was. An only child, he had grown up in a household where his parents screamed at each other. One of his deepest determinations was never to lose control. She resolved to meet him on the ground he had chosen, within the protective cloud of facts.

"Last October I was just about out of my mind from the feeling that you and Bart were managing me, like one of the donors we used to laugh about. And your approach to both the campaign and homeland security seemed wrongheaded to me. You were unwilling even to hear my opinions, or at least that's how it seemed to me.

"While you were out of town—you were always out of town—I asked Ray and Julie to join me for dinner at Camp David. I knew that Ray respected my thinking and would hear me out about the campaign and about safeguarding Americans from Fahim's murderers. I hoped to get my concerns to you through Ray. The morning we were to meet for dinner, Julie told Ray she was sick, didn't feel up to the travel, and didn't want to give us her bug. Ray told me that Julie asked him to go ahead with the dinner.

"When Ray walked in the door of Aspen Cabin," Ella continued, "I was so glad to see him. At that moment, I guess he represented all I was missing in life. A few alarm bells went off, but I ignored them. Remember, I was really angry at you. As we ate dinner in front of the fire, I found myself thinking what a handsome, smart man he was, how the world was upside down, and this was time out of time. I guess I was an emotional wreck. And I could feel that he was still attracted to me. By the time dinner was over, I had decided that, for one night, nothing mattered except being with Ray."

Her husband shifted in his chair, nodded, and said, "I get that. So how did it happen? Did he come on to you?"

"Honestly, no, he didn't. But he didn't back away, either. We went for a walk, and when we got back, he was helping me take off my windbreaker, and suddenly we were kissing … He spent the night.

"Next morning I knew what a mistake we had made, and so did Ray. We agreed that it would never happen again, that we were each committed to our spouses and marriages. This had just been another of the tragedies caused by the terrorist campaign that had turned life in America upside down. I have to say that I think Ray was more upset than I was. I felt it was a terrible mistake; he felt it was a failure to do his duty, to keep his marriage vows. He was really crushed. I said that, as long as nobody ever found out, the damage would be limited to the two of us. He agreed that was best."

"So there must be some reason you're telling me now. What is it?"

Ella felt nauseated. Now came the part she dreaded most. "Arlene Gustafson got wind of this and has threatened to go public. You know how she hates Ray. He, Julie, and I met with her—while Ray was in the hospital—and convinced her that with the three of us united in denying it, she would end up looking like a vindictive fool. That shut her down. But I'm afraid she'll return to it. You know she's like a dog with a bone when she's out to get somebody."

"So, until a few minutes ago, Julie knew, but I didn't?"

Ella ducked her head. "Yes," she whispered.

Rick pursed his lips. "So, why did you keep me in the dark after Ray told Julie?"

"I wanted to see whether we could repair the campaign damage first, to return to something like our old partnership."

"So do you now believe that Gustafson is about to start her smear campaign?"

"Not specifically. But there's something else from that meeting in Ray's hospital room. When we didn't fold before her accusations about Camp David, Gustafson tried something else: she asked Ray about someone named Ali Hadrab. Ray got furious and told her she was about to cross a classification line; if she did, he would see her destroyed. I don't know who this Hadrab is, but clearly Gustafson thought she could use him to ensure Ray's support for her campaign to get her son buried at Arlington despite his court-martial and less-than-honorable discharge. She wasn't fazed by Ray's threat; she just let him know that unless her petition to get Matt into Arlington was granted, he'd have to explain Ali Hadrab."

Ella saw her husband's jaw muscles flex. Then he spoke: "That's very bad news, Ella. I can't tell you about Hadrab, but if she goes public with rumors about him, it would be even worse for our administration than your night at Camp David."

Ella, noticing that he had said "our" administration, wondered if that was a signal. Maybe. But Rick seemed to be taking her news about Hadrab harder than her revelation of infidelity. She fumbled for words to bridge the gap.

"She's an awful person, isn't she? What can I do to help get us out of this mess I caused?"

His rationality and innate fairness kicking in, Rick said, "The fault goes way beyond you, Ella. You've stumbled into something truly awful that we are trying to manage as best we can."

Ella recognized that his remark was an escape hatch either of them could use to avoid discussing her infidelity. But she didn't take it.

"What about us, about you and me, Rick? After what I've done ..."

As a litigator Rick Martin had never wanted to wing it when cross-examining. No litigator does. It had become a life habit; he always sought to delay conversations until he had the opportunity to develop a plan. But Ella was not to be put off.

"Talk to me, Rick. What are you feeling? How do we go forward after Ray and I betrayed you and Julie?"

She held his eyes, her need keeping him from looking away.

"I'm surprised, hurt, embarrassed."

"Angry, too?"

"No, you two didn't set out to betray me. It wasn't planned. Neither of you is a person who could do that. I'm sad but not angry.

"How do we go forward? I guess one day at a time. I'm still absorbing this."

Ella knew that her husband was suppressing emotion, going into his head now, and would be there for a long time. He could leave their future open-ended; that was his personality. But Ella needed some form of closure.

"Rick, please give me something to go on. Do we have a future together?"

"Of course we do, Ella. But it's too soon for me to know beyond that."

Ella knew she shouldn't push for more from her emotionally armored husband.

"All right, Rick. I'm going for a walk now. You can come if you want." Her tone made it a plea rather than statement.

He looked at her and shook his head solemnly.

Ella stood, hovering awkwardly for a moment, and then went to her husband and kissed him on the cheek. He didn't react or look at her.

She was barely out the door when her tears came. The Secret Service agent posted in the hall looked away.

* * *

TEHRAN, ISLAMIC REPUBLIC OF IRAN

Qasem was in the sixth hour of his eight-hour shift monitoring Tehran's cell towers. He had been doing this job for three years, and the titillation of eavesdropping on private conversations was long gone. Still, occasionally he would come across something interesting, like a high-ranking cleric proposing a sexual encounter with another man. Or a government minister being upbraided by his wife. But even with the possibility of occasionally delicious voyeurism, it was all he could do to get through the stultifying boredom of most shifts. That's why he almost missed this particular call.

The software that continually sampled cellular transmissions was programmed to sound an alert for certain words in Farsi or Arabic. It was also programmed to alert for certain languages, among them English and Hebrew. Because the clerics controlled much of the machinery of oversight, many of the alert-words had to do with apostasy, a crime the clerics especially detested. Qasem found listening to such conversations even worse than just waiting for an alert to sound, so it was with reluctance that he clicked the button that channeled the conversation into his earphones. When he realized the conversation was in English, he felt a little spark in the pit of his stomach. He immediately initiated recording.

Qasem understood some English because he enjoyed watching old American westerns featuring cowboys, ranchers, Indians, and the cavalry. He understood "two soldiers," "general," and "death." As his concentration increased, Qasem realized one of the English speakers had a strong accent. He alerted his supervisor, who initiated a procedure to locate the cell tower. The tower was in the northern section of Tehran, an area that was home to senior officials, near Qeytariyeh Park.

Eight hours later an analyst within the Herat, the signals intelligence branch of the army, was translating the conversation into Farsi and wondering if he was playing a part in capturing that most dangerous and despicable of enemies, a traitor to the Islamic Republic.

* * *

JERUSALEM, ISRAEL

Sleepless again in his grief and worry, Joshua Askenazi was pleased by the stumbling of Iran, the nation he was determined to destroy. *They've really stepped in it now, unless they are even crazier than I think they are.*

Closing the strait on which one of the world's great powers depends for importing its petroleum couldn't possibly turn out well. The UN Security Council had met in emergency session and condemned Iran's action. Even the Russians voted for that resolution. On a second resolution, one declaring that Iran's action was a threat to peace and security—the UN's equivalent of fighting words—only a Russian veto had prevented the majority approval from taking effect. Save for the Russians, Iran was isolated.

And the Chinese were demanding an apology and reparations for the ship they claimed that Iran attacked without provocation. It had taken a full four days before Tehran announced that Iran had sunk *Nanking* "for violating the territorial waters of the Islamic Republic." The satellite tracking records of at least three nations disproved that claim. Clearly the sinking had taken the government by surprise; that was obvious from the delay in acknowledging it and from the weak justification finally offered.

His latest intelligence brief had informed Askenazi that there was a furious debate swirling around the Supreme Leader, between those who wanted to call the attack on *Nanking* a mistake and throw Ahmadi under the bus and others who felt the event had united the Persian people behind their government in a way not seen in years. The latter group had won—at least for now.

This confusion and disagreement was another sign that the time for Persepolis was near. And when that had been accomplished, Shara would be at peace. He felt her fierce, confident spirit, more now in some ways than he had before they killed her. During her life, he had never really shared her spiritual convictions, her confidence in God's promise to Israel. Now, surrounded by skeptics and the silent reminders of her life—the large portrait recently hung in his office, her favorite cup waiting in the pantry for another morning together that would never happen—he reconsidered her faith. He felt closer to her whenever he did so. God's eternal covenant with Israel might or might not be real, but, as an act of faith in Shara, on the day of her death, Joshua Askenazi had laid claim to it. It fed his rage at Iran as a bellows feeds glowing coals.

Chapter 39

R AY MORALES ENTERED THE SMALL, private study adjacent to the Oval Office and, at the president's gesture, closed the door.

"You slept with my wife, Ray. We need to talk about that!" Martin's eyes flashed, and his hands curled into fists at his side as he stood near his desk.

She told him!

The president's blunt words, uttered without preamble, surprised Morales. Rick Martin was never one to reveal emotions, and only rarely did he show anger. On the other hand, this wasn't quite anger. It felt to Morales more like a dutiful protest than the fury of a husband confronting his wife's lover. He kept his face neutral and met the president's gaze.

Morales said, "OK." Each man stood waiting for the other to speak.

Finally, arms outspread, the president said, "How could you, Ray? I thought you were one of the very few trustworthy people in my life."

Though Martin's demeanor seemed stilted, Morales nonetheless felt the weight of his betrayals. He took a deep breath. His shoulders drooped for an instant, then he straightened and met Martin's insistent gaze. "There are no words that will undo what happened. It wasn't planned. It just *was.* It was my doing, not in that I forced myself on Ella but that I ignored the warning bells ringing in my brain from the moment Julie dropped out. You were away somewhere campaigning. And it wasn't only you I betrayed. I betrayed Julie even more."

"And what about Ella? Did she come on to you?"

Ray shook his head. "You shouldn't blame Ella. You should try to understand how she was feeling and why."

The president looked down and rubbed the toe of his shoe across an imaginary spot in the carpet, then spoke softly: "I know how she felt and why. She felt ignored and betrayed. And she was right. I shut her out of the campaign and then betrayed her by working with the NRA during the worst period of Fahim's attacks."

He looked at Ray. "I know that it looked like I had sold my soul for the election, but it saved lives."

"If we account for the people that were shot by mistake, I'm not sure that it did, sir."

The president shrugged. "Maybe you're right. But at the time it was the right decision."

"Well, sir, we both know a lot about hindsight."

Martin paused a beat, deciding how to take that remark, then replied, "You mean Ali Hadrab."

"Yep."

"You were wrong to torture information from Hadrab, Ray."

"Yes, but at the time … Plus, you were glad when we used that information to kill Fahim and stop the shootings and bombings."

Arms folded across his chest, Rick Martin glared at Morales, who met his gaze. Martin broke eye contact, dropped his arms to his side, and said, "Yes, I was. I guess there are some things we will never know for certain in this life. You make the call and move on. No do-overs."

Morales nodded.

The president said, "I think we're done with these topics, Ray. Unless you …"

"Yes, sir. We're done."

There it was again: that odd detachment. Morales shrugged mentally and waited.

The president held out his hand, and Morales took it. Leaning over his desk, Martin flicked a switch. "Bart, can you come to the study?"

As Guarini entered, Morales caught a flash of curiosity in his eyes. *He's curious about my ten minutes alone with the president. And he'd be surprised to know that in those ten minutes we said what needed to be said about that night at Camp David and about Hadrab.*

"Take a chair, Bart. Ray has news from Ghorbani."

Guarini seated himself with a disapproving look at Morales.

"Let's listen to their conversation," said the president. Guarini pulled out his ever-present notepad. The three listened intently to the recording captured by Morales's cell phone. When Ghorbani threatened to use nuclear weapons the president's eyebrows shot up.

"Do you think they've got them? And why am I learning this from Ghorbani, not our intelligence?"

"Ghorbani's trying to rush you into coming down on Israel, Mr. President," said Guarini. "He's trying to spook us with his vision of a nuclear apocalypse in the Middle East but not offering any evidence. The reason you haven't been briefed is our guys don't have the evidence to make that call."

Expression neutral, Martin said, "What's your take, Ray?"

"Bart may be absolutely right. Ghorbani gave us a dire warning but made no attempt to build a supporting case. For what it's worth, he seemed to me to be genuinely worried, but I don't know him at all. He could have been feeding me a line.

"But these days I'm completely out of the intel loop," continued Morales. "For all I know there may be trace evidence of an Iranian bomb and an Israeli deep strike that haven't bubbled up to your level. We all know the spooks will hold back until they've tried to reach consensus; maybe it's time to shake the tree and see what falls out.

"Askenazi has been threatening a strike on Iran's nuke program for years. Now he has a personal motive for hurting Iran, too. And just going by the news, he's been quoting his namesake a lot in his speeches. That 'Promised Land' stuff may be just to keep the ultra-religious parties in his coalition. But, still, I'm not ready to dismiss Ghorbani's warning and his threat as a disinformation play by Iran."

"Neither am I," said the president. "For now, this goes no farther than the three of us. If it leaks that we are talking to Ghorbani—and what he told us—we'll have a disaster! Bart, put a squeeze on our spooks and be very, very careful how you do it."

"Yes, Mr. President," said Guarini. He stood, and Morales followed suit.

Martin reached for a folder on his desk, then said, "Ray, what about

Ghorbani? Do you think he'll reveal the operation he ran here? That's a big shoe that hasn't dropped, not yet anyway."

"I don't know. He might try to use it to coerce you. But it would be dangerous for him to spill it. That operation enabled us to get Fahim and stop his terror campaign. That was a campaign many Iranians welcomed. He could be accused of helping the Great Satan." Morales shrugged. "I know that sounds weird, but so are Iranian politics."

The president nodded. "Why do you think he ran the operation, Ray?"

"That's one of a lot of things I want to ask him someday, when we meet again."

"Meet again? What do you mean?"

"Mr. President, someone has to meet Ghorbani face to face, see whatever evidence he has of Israeli intentions to launch a deep strike. I'm the one to do that."

The president looked skeptical. "Maybe, Ray. But that seems to me to be a long way down the road."

Chapter 40

JERUSALEM, ISRAEL

Y A'EL BARAK PUT DOWN HIS cigarette and let his mind drift for a moment as effortlessly and purposelessly as the smoke rising from the ashtray. He knew he should cut down, but tackling his tobacco addiction seemed one stress too many and, unlike the others, one he could ignore without consequence to anyone but himself. He looked at his watch. Nearly eight p.m. and his boss was still in the office. Barak had sent the staff home an hour earlier.

Since Shara's death, Joshua Askenazi spent much more time in his office. Yet Barak saw little in the way of increased output from this time. It was still a chore to get the prime minister to sign routine documents. Askenazi's in-basket remained a pile. He made no demands for the staff to devise new programs to address festering social issues. He had cut back visits to government agencies and military units, settlements, and schools—activities he formerly pursued with gusto.

So what was he doing in there for all the extra hours? Well, one thing was some project with Dan Rivkin. They had spoken many times on the prime minister's direct private number. Barak had never been included, which was unusual. Even more unusual was that on occasions when Rivkin had called while he was with the prime minister, he was asked to step out. And there had been a number of deliveries by armed military courier that Askenazi had never discussed with Barak.

There were other troubling occurrences. On several occasions after Askenazi failed to respond to his knock, Barak had opened the prime minister's door and entered to address some issue. The prime minister was doing ... nothing, or so it seemed. Barak was a little worried: on one occasion he had listened with his ear to the door—feeling overdramatic and silly—and heard what sounded like a muffled conversation. Yet when he entered, the prime minister was alone. On another occasion, the prime minister was seated in one of his side chairs, positioned directly in front of a life-sized portrait of Shara, gazing intently at the painting and scribbling on a notepad. He seemed to be in a state of reverie, because he did not react to Barak's entrance. Barak sensed that for a few moments his boss didn't realize he was in the room. When he noticed Barak, he said, "You know, Ya'el, she was more than the light of my life. She was my wisest counselor and the bravest person I ever knew."

After one more drag, Barak stubbed out his cigarette and took the few steps to the door of the prime minister's private office. His knock drew an invitation to enter, spoken with Askenazi's usual force.

"So, Ya'el, how many times do I have to tell you? You don't have to be here every moment that I am. Believe me when I tell you that every minute you have with your wife and family is precious. But since you are here, we shall discuss something important."

Barak was relieved that his boss seemed entirely normal. "As you wish, Prime Minister. But what about your dinner? Shall I have something sent up?"

Askenazi patted his considerable belly and smiled. "I'm not exactly starving, Ya'el. And this will only take a few minutes."

Turning away from Barak, Askenazi gazed at the portrait of his wife, and Barak thought he heard a few soft words.

"Sit, Ya'el, sit! Don't be so formal."

Askenazi arose, looked at Shara, and began to pace. "Ya'el, the security— no, the survival—of Israel rests on our shoulders, yours and mine. Truly, of course, the responsibility is mine alone. But I depend on you. You are my right hand, my Gideon. Because I alone bear this ultimate responsibility, it is my right and my duty to act alone if necessary to meet it. The cabinet, as you know, are a collection of quarreling, self-serving weaklings. I would never take them into my confidence on a matter crucial to Israel's survival. So this conversation remains between you and me."

He halted in front of Barak and gazed fiercely into his eyes.

"Yes, Prime Minister. I understand."

The prime minister looked toward Shara, nodded, and resumed pacing.

"Ya'el, I believe we are nearing the time when Iran will act upon its vow to destroy us. Iran will do so with nuclear weapons and ballistic missiles, which it will soon have in sufficient quantity, thanks to Chinese assistance. I cannot let that happen."

"But, prime minister," Barak rushed his words as if speed lent them weight. "Your intelligence briefings do not predict that it will be soon. There is no confirmation that Iran has any operational warheads. They've never tested a nuke. They've never tested a complete nuclear ballistic missile system."

His skin grown ruddy, Askenazi gave a dismissive wave. "They have no need to test the Chinese warheads because the Chinese have tested them. Ya'el, there are many in this government, including our military, who are determined to ignore reality. Like their predecessors before the Yom Kippur War, they deny because they don't want to face what is required of them!"

"Ya'el," he intoned, "we must make ready Operation Persepolis."

Barak was worried, but he had seen the prime minister operate this way many times in the years he had served him. He would often state as settled something that was still an open question in his mind. It was one of his ways of gauging reactions, of testing the waters.

"Prime Minister, Persepolis has always been intended as a last-ditch measure. We do not have the military capability to create a permanent barrier against all forms of Iranian aggression."

"Ya'el, I am disappointed in your thinking. True, we cannot create an impregnable defense against every weapon from every enemy. But we can create a barrier in the minds of our enemies. We can show the Iranians—*and* others—that we will *never* be cowed by their weapons or their numbers." Askenazi cut his eyes to Shara, then back to Ya'el Barak. "Just as the tribes of Israel overcame their enemies when they trusted God's promise that they would never be defeated, we can strike Iran in a way that will make the Iranians fear to attack us. David did the impossible with his sling and a stone, and the Philistines marched away. We can do the same—"

"Prime Minister." Askenazi's upraised palm halted Barak's speech.

"Ya'el, it is the end of a long day. One like it will follow tomorrow.

Enough for now. Go home and hug your wife and children and show them that you love them."

As Ya'el Barak drove home, he tried to find a comforting explanation for all he had observed since Shara's death and, especially, tonight. But he couldn't.

Chapter 41

THE WHITE HOUSE

"**M**ING," said President Martin after preliminaries were completed, "the longer the world's two leading maritime nations accept Iran's illegal action, the more damage is done to the very idea of freedom of the seas. Both our countries are harmed by that.

"Do you think," he continued, "that you can get Volkov to stop blocking our Security Council resolution?"

Martin, at his desk in the Oval Office with John Dorn and Bart Guarini nearby, waited for the translation of his words and Ming Liu's response.

"No, Rick. Iran is Russia's most important partner in the region, since Syria is useless. Besides, Russia might as well have a border with Iran, since they share the Caspian Sea and are separated on land by only a few miles of territory belonging to insignificant countries. And Volkov is not going to slap the Supreme Leader in the face over an action that helps Russia by driving up the price of oil."

Martin paused to let that topic die, then said, "Forgive me, Ming, for not asking sooner, but how are the men from *Nanking* doing?"

Ming realized that he was being baited. By asking, Martin was reminding him that Iran attacked and sank a Chinese warship. And implying, perhaps, that an American warship would not have been similarly caught off-guard? Ming pushed his anger into the background before speaking.

"All are recovering, thank you. They received excellent treatment aboard your ship."

"The sea has its laws that all seamen observe and have for hundreds of years," said Martin. "A mariner always helps other mariners in trouble. And another of those laws is that the high seas are open to passage by all. Iran violated that law and lied about your ship's position in a weak attempt to justify what cannot be justified."

I know where this is going, thought Ming. The Americans are going to use their navy to force open the strait. And Martin wants China to join forces with America to do that.

"Ming, China has been very patient with Iran. You've given the Supreme Leader time to investigate the matter, and he surely knows the truth. Yet he continues to deny it and refuses to acknowledge China's justified demand for apology and compensation."

In other circumstances Ming would have been happy to wait for the impatient Americans to deal with this situation. But China had been triply insulted: first by the attack, second by the obviously false Iranian claim, and third by Iran ignoring China's demand for an apology and compensation for the loss of the ship and men, men whose families must now manage without them. And some on the Central Committee and on the Military Committee are waiting for the chance to criticize inaction.

Ming replied, "China's patience is not endless, but it is not yet exhausted."

"I have a proposal for your consideration, Ming: Let us jointly demand that the strait be opened to the ships of all nations by a certain date, perhaps several weeks from now. And let us back that demand by a joint military operation, if necessary, to remove Iranian mines and then escort ships of all nations in and out of the Persian Gulf. This would be similar to the anti-piracy operations that our navies have done so effectively for the past ten years or more."

"Rick, I hope you understand that China has no interest in changing the government of Iran and will not be a party to any attempt to do so. And we will not become pawns of Israel. If China is to participate, Israel must not be involved in the operation, in any way. Nor the Saudis. Were either to be part of this operation you propose, the Iranians, seeing that their worst enemies were involved, would view it as an attack."

"I understand, Ming."

"Understanding is not the same as agreeing, Rick. Do you accept those conditions?"

Martin, in the Oval Office, saw both his national security advisor and chief of staff wince. Dorn scribbled a note, "Much harder without Saudi bases."

Nodding his thanks, Martin said, "Ming, our aircraft will need to use Saudi bases to provide air cover for our ships—and yours. We would be using the bases under an agreement signed many years ago. Tehran could not credibly claim this was a new measure allying America, China, and Saudi Arabia against Iran. With that caveat, I agree that neither the Saudis nor the Israelis will be involved."

"That's troublesome, Rick. If an American aircraft that takes off from Saudi Arabia attacks an Iranian boat that is interfering with our operation, the Iranians will not be calmed by the legal nicety that you mentioned.

"I will have to think about this, Rick, and consult my colleagues on the Military Committee. But let us take a first step. Let us direct our military leaders to make a plan for our consideration, then speak again."

Another note from Dorn: "Suggest a date soon for talk again."

"Well, let's do that. And let's tell our military men to work swiftly! I think they should be able to develop a plan in five days or less. Let's plan to examine their ideas then, or sooner if possible."

* * *

After the call, Ming Liu lit a cigarette from the battered metal case that his father had carried when he fought in Korea in 1951, which had come back to him after his father's death in an American air strike. That was good, he thought. I have bought at least five days to consider the proposal sent by this General Ghorbani, who claims to speak for the Supreme Leader. Ghorbani's proposal, if genuine, would get our oil flowing again. But would it cause oil prices and shipping costs to return to normal? It might not, if the Americans are skirmishing with Iran in the Strait of Hormuz.

Chapter 42

BEIJING, PEOPLE'S REPUBLIC OF CHINA

Gᴇɴᴇʀᴀʟ "Mᴀᴄ" MᴀᴄAᴅᴏᴏ ᴏꜰ ᴛʜᴇ US Air Force, chairman of the Joint Chiefs of Staff, was tired, grumpy, and over-caffeinated. He had flown fourteen hours and then hustled through Beijing smog to the office of his Chinese counterpart, General Ma. That office was almost as respiration-challenging as the streets because Ma chain-smoked. The tall, athletic, silver-haired Mac and the short, pot-bellied, balding Ma made an odd couple, at least visually. But they had worked together during two Korean crises and developed a sliver of understanding and rapport. Once again they found themselves charged by their heads of state with an urgent, difficult task: to create the first-ever plan for an American-Chinese military operation. In the Korean crises they had worked out plans that had permitted their military forces to operate coordinately but separately. Operating together would be more difficult.

The top generals, lesser navy and air force officers, and interpreters sat facing each other across a polished dark-wooden table. A large chart of the Persian Gulf, covered with symbols for military units and firepower, was projected before them. An American navy captain had just finished briefing on the positions and relative strengths of military forces in the Persian Gulf.

MacAdoo said, "So that's how we see the situation today, General. I think you will agree that opening the strait will require breaking *in* with the forces our countries are assembling in the Indian Ocean, rather than breaking *out* with the forces now in the gulf."

General Ma said, "Minefields are very effective in confined areas, whether on land or sea. They can do a great deal of damage to an attacker while not risking a single defender."

MacAdoo was familiar with Ma's tendency to make statements that begged questions, rather than ask the questions themselves. Sometimes he simply acknowledged Ma's statements and waited, or moved to another topic. But today he needed to get Ma engaged, and quickly, so he said, "Captain Hogue, give General Ma a rundown on the mine clearance plan."

With a mouse click, Hogue projected a chart of the Strait of Hormuz, on which the minefield was shown as a series of red dots. "General, we've been using unmanned underwater vehicles to hunt and map the mines," said Hogue. "Although we estimate that Iran has a stockpile of three to six thousand mines, they have few platforms capable of laying them secretly, so the rate at which they are building the minefield is on the order of perhaps fifteen to twenty mines in a twenty-four-hour period. We are able to locate and map the mines about as fast as they are emplaced."

Hogue continued: "The Strait of Hormuz is about one hundred seventy-five miles long and narrows to only twenty-one miles wide. The narrowest part is quite shallow, no more than about one hundred twenty feet. This is the most attractive area to lay a barrier of mines, because it's closer to Iran, and in those water depths, all types of mines are fully effective. So—no surprise—that is where most of the mine-laying is occurring. As you see from this slide, the mine barrier runs roughly north-south across the shipping channels from Iran's Larak Island to Oman's Quoin Island. Larak Island has a Revolutionary Guard garrison and a battery of Silkworm missiles. Although Iran has several hundred sophisticated mines, such as the EM-52 and the MDM-3, the majority of their inventory are bottom-moored contact mines. That type of mine is a very old technology but quite effective in locations like the Strait of Hormuz."

"Yes, the EM-52 is an excellent mine," interjected Ma. MacAdoo thought he detected a twinkle in Ma's eye as he praised the Chinese-manufactured mine. Holding Ma's gaze, MacAdoo raised his eyebrows. Without changing his serious expression, Ma said, "Yes, it is ironic that we are facing our own weapons. Those missiles you call Silkworms are so old that I assume you have learned effective countermeasures. If not, we will be glad to provide them."

"Thank you General. Our staffs will compare notes on that, I'm sure. What about the EM-52?"

"If you encounter them, we will send men to deal with them," replied Ma. "And of course you face your own weapons as well: Iran has F-14 fighters plus Phoenix and Hawk missiles. Presumably you will share with us your intimate knowledge of those weapons."

Touché, thought MacAdoo. *And since neither is now in use by us, I'm happy to do that.* "We will, of course, General.

"But let us concentrate on the central matter that our presidents directed us to address: what forces we each will assign to the mission of clearing the Strait of Hormuz and how they will work together."

"Yes," replied Ma. "I emphasize that China will not be part of any attempt to change the regime in Iran. China believes this situation can be resolved through negotiations and that our military forces are only a demonstration of resolve. Therefore, China will provide a destroyer and a logistics-support ship."

"But, General, those ships can't sweep mines. Removing the mines is our goal."

"China believes there are few mines and good-faith negotiations with Iran will lead to their removal by the same forces that planted them."

I flew fourteen hours to meet this guy, and now he stiffs me? MacAdoo controlled his well-known temper, but just barely. "General Ma, I must say that I disagree strongly. Two tankers have struck mines, one of them loaded with oil for China. No oil is being exported via the strait, including Iranian oil. The delivered price of a barrel of oil to China has risen sharply. Iran shows no sign of willingness to negotiate. Are you saying China is willing to tolerate this situation? Can *afford* to tolerate this situation?"

Ma's eyes were black pools of defiance in his round face, his lips a horizontal line. "Once again, the United States rushes to use military force. China sees no wisdom in that course. Do what you feel you must do. At the appropriate time, China will provide the naval forces I mentioned."

I've just been told to go screw myself, thought MacAdoo. *I oughtta just walk out. But I can't. I need to nail him down as much as possible on the ships.* "And what is the appropriate time, General?"

"When my president decides, General."

That's it! thought MacAdoo. He rose, saluted General Ma, and said, "I will convey this information to my president." He stalked from the room, his staff officers trailing, looking shocked. Their Chinese escort scrambled to get ahead of MacAdoo to usher him to his car. As he strode quickly along the corridor, MacAdoo hissed to his nearest staff officer, "Tell me I haven't just wasted about thirty-six hours!"

Suddenly, a Chinese officer darted from a room just ahead of the group and spoke rapidly to their escort, who stopped so abruptly that General MacAdoo nearly collided with him.

"General," the escort officer said in English, "General Ma asks that you please go into that room, alone." MacAdoo looked surprised, then irritated, but he entered the small room to his left. He was alone until Ma appeared a few minutes later.

"General MacAdoo," said General Ma through his interpreter, "You must learn patience. I, like you, have my orders. But I want you to know that the People's Liberation Army Navy will not let the death of its comrades go unavenged. This is not only a manner of honor; it is a matter of practicality. If we tolerate this attack, there will be others. We will not tolerate it!"

MacAdoo, his mouth set grimly against his still-boiling anger, nodded.

"General MacAdoo, when the time is right, China's navy will join with America's to teach Iran a severe lesson. But the time is not yet, and I can't exceed my instructions. So let us make plans but do it subtly. China's naval attaché in Washington is a skillful and experienced officer whom you may trust to work with your naval planners. He will report directly to me on this matter. Through him, let us make a plan for the day we will return to Iran the fire and death they gave to the crew of *Nanking*."

Ma offered his hand and MacAdoo grasped it firmly, holding Ma's gaze and encouraged by what he read in it.

Chapter 43

ARLINGTON, VIRGINIA

J ULIE MORALES STOOD IN THE tile-floored entryway to the Arlington condo, her coat dripping from rain she hadn't expected. Her miniature umbrella, snatched from its nest in her briefcase, had protected her hair but not much else. As she hung up her coat, her mind returned to the idea that hit her in the elevator: *it's like he's back in the game.*

A few minutes later she was nestled in her chair of the two positioned in front of the fireplace, shoes off. Within it colorful flames danced; yes, with the artificiality of gas, but so convenient! She cupped her mug of coffee, microwave-bitter but welcome, and picked up the thread of her elevator thought.

When Ray had gotten home from spring training, he seemed to have accepted his situation: a hero fallen from grace unjustly but fallen just the same. He got his days organized, hung out his shingle at CSIS, threw himself into physical fitness, and moved on. These days, the old zest was missing, but so, too, was the depression of his first weeks out of government. He was coping, and there was hope for a future in which his abrupt resignation was no longer the subject of demeaning rumors.

But now there was something else: a sparkle in his eyes, a higher energy level … a different affect. I've seen this before, she thought, when Ray is fully engaged in something of great importance. *What's going on? Surely, he's not keeping secrets again? When he was in government, I could accept that there were things he couldn't tell me. Now, though, if something so significant is going on that it has changed his demeanor, he should tell me. And I shouldn't have to ask.*

She heard their door open and turned, seeing Ray as he greeted her. Her posture stiffened, and she no longer lay back in her chair.

"Where'd that rain come from? It wasn't forecast."

"It got me, too. Come sit by the fire."

Ray trundled to the kitchen, grabbed a Miller Genuine Draft from the refrigerator, and dropped into his chair. In moments he had his coat, tie, and shoes off. He took a deep drink and lounged for a moment. Julie thought he seemed relaxed but somehow also alert. He looked at her, then held his index finger to his lips. He scooped up the TV remote from the coffee table and launched a local news program, turning up the volume higher than necessary. Then he perched on the arm of her chair, leaned toward her, and said, in a voice she could barely hear above the TV, "Julie, I've got a secret to tell you and this time it doesn't involve a crime." She saw a twinkle in his eyes, and relief swept through her.

Ray settled in his chair again and continued softly: "I'm in contact with Adel Ghorbani. We've become the channel as Khamenei and Rick try to work out a solution to the Strait of Hormuz crisis. Ghorbani called me and passed along a message from Khamenei. It wasn't very encouraging, but it was a beginning. I met with Rick and Bart and then delivered our reply, which was far short of what Ghorbani wanted to hear but interesting enough to keep the ball rolling. Now I'm waiting for the next call."

"Ray, I'm glad you're able to help. God knows we don't need a new war in the Middle East! But be careful. Rick's already let you take the fall once; don't give him the opportunity to do it again."

"Yeah, that bothers me, too. In the big picture of his presidency, keeping me at arm's length was the smart thing to do. But it hurt me. A lot. And when we met, he said something that was sort of an apology—the way politicians do—but it wasn't, not really.

"But this isn't about me. Or you. I think we're headed for a fight to reopen the strait. That fight could spread pretty quickly. The Israelis and the Saudis would love to get us drawn into war with Iran. They would happily pile on, and, in a war, we'd need them. The next thing you know, the Russians and the Syrians are in it, too, backing Iran. And in the general confusion, a lot of sidebar conflicts would ignite, like the Turks going after the Kurds in northwest Syria and Hezbollah taking total control of Lebanon. And who knows what the Chinese would do—they could be tempted to support Iran because they need the oil and have investments there.

"So it's worth a lot," Ray continued, "to keep those first shots from being fired in the Strait of Hormuz."

"What about this Ghorbani character?" Julie leaned forward, and her worries tumbled out: "Can you trust him? What do you know about him? He could be setting you up now, you know. And I hope you don't feel like you owe him for saving your life in Idaho!"

"No, I don't feel I owe him anything for what he did in Idaho. His mission was to get Fahim, not me. I was a surprise, and he turned that surprise to his advantage by realizing that my presence offered him a story to hide his team's tracks. I don't think saving my life was anything more than a snap judgement, a tactical decision. And it could have gone either way—he said as much.

"Adel Ghorbani is clearly one of the most powerful men in Iran," Ray continued. "In theory, as the head of Quds Force, he answers to General Jafari, head of the Iranian Revolutionary Guard. But he is equal in rank to Jafari and in fact often speaks directly to the Supreme Leader. These days he runs both their overt missile development programs and their covert nuclear weapons organization. In that position he surely has direct access to the Supreme Leader. And the Supreme Leader is the ultimate authority over everything and everyone in Iran."

"OK, he's a major player. How about trust?"

"Trust doesn't figure into it for me. I don't trust him, and I'm sure he doesn't trust me. He's no fanatic; that seems clear from what we know about him. Like quite a few young Iranians before the revolution, he attended college in the US. He was a student in Illinois when the revolution exploded, and he rushed back to Iran without graduating. He's religiously observant but not committed—he's never had anything to do with the clerical side of the Iranian power structure. In fact, as a young military commander during the Iraq war, he took some risks to limit Iranian casualties from several of the clerics' stupid military demands. I doubt that Ghorbani thinks closing the strait was a good idea. And speaking of trust, he's got real skin in the game: given what almost happened to President Ahmadi, if it gets out that Ghorbani is in touch with me, it could get him disgraced, even killed.

"He's not married, has no family we could find. He's devoted his life to increasing Iran's power and influence in the Middle East. You remember his parting words to me in Idaho, right? He said, 'You were fools to believe you could stop us from having nuclear bombs. Iran will destroy the Jews and dominate the Arabs as we did in the days of Darius. Get used to it.'

"I think he can be trusted to pursue that goal," Ray continued. "And that means we may be able, from time to time, to trust him about certain, limited matters. I mean things that advance his goal with little harm to us or our allies."

Julie stood. "OK, Ray. I get that. But what are you getting into? Do you want to put on your combat boots again? I sure hope not—you've done enough! Service to our country got you forced out of DHS, and it nearly got you killed in Idaho!"

Ray rose, moved close, and grasped both her hands in his big ones. "Julie, this is too important and too fluid to draw lines in the sand. I can't say where this is headed, and I can't rule out an active part. But I know I'm over the hill for fieldwork. Fahim taught me that in Idaho. By rushing in I got a good man killed and another one so injured he may never get back to flying Marine fighters."

Recognizing the slippery slope in her husband's words, Julie worried that this wasn't going to end well for their marriage. But she agreed with him about the danger of a big war in the Middle East. And his relationship with Ghorbani might be the only means to prevent it.

Julie threw her arms around Ray's neck. She hugged him, then stepped back and looked into his eyes. "Don't keep me in the dark, Ray. I'm going to worry if I know what you're doing. It'll be even worse if I don't. And that would be more than our marriage can stand."

Chapter 44

"AT LAST WE'VE SHOWN OUR power to the world!" said Grand Ayatollah Ravjani. "We've shown the world the Americans are toothless cowards. Their ships are trapped in Bahrain—may all Arabs be cursed—they are afraid to face our navy."

"God is good!" declaimed two lesser clerics, whom Adel Ghorbani considered Ravjani's toadies. He held himself carefully in check as he listened to members of the Council of Guardians maneuvering under the gaze of Iran's Supreme Leader. They had been at it for nearly an hour.

"Now is the time to hold firm to Allah's promise that the Strait of Hormuz is Persian, ours by right," concluded Ravjani.

"All Iranians know this, and we will fight to the death for our right to the strait," said President Ahmadi, relishing his new status as darling of the clerics. With a sly expression he turned to Ghorbani: "You are quiet today, General. Surely you have something to contribute to this discussion."

Ghorbani's face remained impassive, though his eyes were chilling as he returned Ahmadi's glance. "Like all our soldiers I am eager to fight the Americans. Soon there will be hundreds of their airplanes in our skies: tempting targets for our air force. They will fear to enter the strait until they have fought our pilots and missile batteries. Eventually they will enter the strait with many ships. They will pass through waters turned red by the blood of our martyrs. Then they will be in our trap, fat targets for our submarines. After our brave submariners are martyrs, we have hundreds of small, fast boats to attack the remaining Americans. Still unable to defeat us, the Americans will then be shamed into bombing our cities. But we will wait in the rubble and then, when their invading armies approach, rise from the dust and attack like djinns. We can never be defeated because we do not shrink from death as the Americans do. Allah will welcome thousands of our martyrs to Paradise, as he did in the war of Iraqi aggression, but we will prevail, just as we did then. And I will be leading fearless soldiers to ultimate victory, just as I did then."

Make *that* into a charge against me, you cretins, thought Ghorbani. He felt a fierce satisfaction at the confusion he saw in the eyes of several clerics and at the hint of amusement he observed in the Leader's glance around the table after his words had been absorbed.

"But what of our oil exports? Of the oil the Chinese buy in huge quantities?" said a guardian who had been a supporter of Ahmadi's predecessor.

"The Iranian people will eat dirt if they need to in order to protect our sovereignty and carry out Allah's will!" said Ravjani

"And what of the Chinese ship *Nanking*?"

"It violated our sovereign waters. The Chinese, too, must accept that Iran is to be respected," replied Ahmadi.

"Yes," interjected Ghorbani, "They will be surprised when I do not beg them to return their engineers. Our missile program will succeed without them because Allah wills it!"

"General Ghorbani," said the Leader, who had hardly spoken during the council's discussion. "How much will the missiles be delayed without the Chinese engineers?"

Ghorbani quickly considered alternative responses and the outcome of each, then said, "Leader, it will take about another year to compensate for China's foolish withdrawal of the engineers. I will drive the team hard. We will overcome this obstacle much faster than the cursed Jews of Israel expect, and then we will destroy them at your signal."

All eyes were on the Leader, who said nothing, merely raised his eyebrows. Discussion faltered as the individual guardians considered the significance of the exchange. Which way was the wind blowing? They were saved from needing to choose by the muezzin's call to prayer.

* * *

TEHRAN, ISLAMIC REPUBLIC OF IRAN

It was evening when Ghorbani's driver returned him to Tehran. As they neared his neighborhood, Ghorbani decided he wanted a snack and told his driver to drop him at the San Marco ice cream shop on Qeytariyeh Boulevard. Best ice cream in Tehran. It was crowded, as usual—no wonder, thought Ghorbani as he waited in line, conspicuous in his uniform but not caring. Soon the shop's manager pulled him aside and offered nervously to get his order. A few minutes later, cheerfully clutching a cup of creamy vanilla sprinkled with pistachios, Ghorbani set off through Qeytariyeh Park for his apartment.

His thoughts returned to the meeting that had consumed, counting the drive to and from Qom, half his day. Worth it, though, because of his brief exchange with the Leader. And his nominal superior, General Jafari, wasn't present. That must have been the Leader's doing and was a good sign.

As he strolled through the nearly deserted park, savoring his ice cream, thoughts too dangerous to express raced through his mind. The Council of Guardians are idiots. They care mostly for their individual reputations and power; that's understandable, but what seems nearly beyond belief is that they don't understand what closing the strait means for Iran in terms other than the Koran. Iran is bleeding because no oil passes through the strait. It's as if we have slit our own wrists as well as those of the cursed Saudis and are waiting to see who dies first.

The Leader understands—but what game is he playing? At least he knows that a delay in the missile program dictates a delay in the bomb test. I made my point: this strait nonsense is holding up the bomb test. And he wants the bomb test!

"General Ghorbani."

The voice came from behind him, and Ghorbani knew from its confidence and accent that he wasn't being accosted by a thief or a beggar. Was it the Basenji? No, they wouldn't dare. Was it Mossad? No, Mossad would just shoot him without a word if harm was their intent. Nonetheless, his hand went to the holster of the pistol on his uniform belt. Deliberately, he turned around.

He saw a man partially in shadow about ten feet away. Ghorbani detected uncertainty and fear in the man's posture; it was not that of an attacker or a security officer but of someone poised for flight. But something about the figure signaled sincerity as well as anxiety, so Ghorbani made none of the offensive moves he could have and instead said, "Yes."

"General, you don't know me, but I owe you my life. Basra, 1987, Operation Karbala-5. You canceled an assault that had been compromised, despite pressure from the generals. My unit was to lead that assault. We would have been slaughtered."

Speaking more softly, the man continued: "I am a loyal Iranian. Not a traitor. But in 1987 you taught me that sometimes the leaders can be wrong, and when that happens, true patriots act to protect the nation's best interest. So, I am here in Qeytariyeh Park tonight to tell you this: Not long ago, VAJA monitored a conversation in English that raised many eyebrows. The identity of the speakers could not be established, but one of them was connecting through the cell tower near us. All conversations relayed on this cell tower are now receiving special attention. I have seen a list of the numbers being monitored, and yours is one of them. By telling you this, I have repaid my debt to you. This is the only warning I will give."

The man turned and walked rapidly away. Ghorbani removed his hand from his holster and put it to work spooning ice cream as he continued his walk home, thinking about the man's words. So he was on the watch list of VAJA, the secret police. By the time he got home, he had reached a decision.

Chapter 45

USS AGERHOLM, THE PERSIAN GULF

"SONAR CONTACT, BEARING TWO SIX three, range two thousand four hundred yards. Classification possible sub."

Lieutenant Jan Palmer, tactical action officer for the port watch section, looked at the display to the right of her chair in *Agerholm*'s Combat Information Center and registered the new symbol, glowing malevolently off the starboard quarter of her ship. Moments after the contact announcement, she heard another voice, this one from the pilothouse: "No surface contacts on that bearing." Speaking into her headset mike, she said, "How's it look, Sonar?"

The petty officer in charge of the sonar watch section replied, "Pretty mushy right now, but we had several solid pings in the past few minutes. Also a possible aspect change. This shallow water makes everything harder to figure out. Lots of echoes from bottom objects."

"Let's get a little help from Seasnake one zero," said Palmer, nodding to the antisubmarine air controller to her right.

"Seasnake, this is Checkmate. I hold POSSUB bearing two seven zero, two thousand from me. Left to three two five for MAD."

Palmer settled into her chair, eyes fixed on the computer display, observing the dots that represented *Agerholm*'s progress through the water and others that depicted the possible submarine and the ship's helo, Seasnake. The possible submarine's phosphorescent trail of red dots wavered in a sinuous pattern, but the trend was clear: parallel to *Agerholm*'s track. If this was a sub, it was stalking them.

205

"Checkmate, Seasnake one zero. Madman, Madman, Madman."

Palmer tensed. *Agerholm*'s helo had just reported the presence of a large magnetic object at the location of the suspected sub. Submarines are magnetic objects. She keyed her microphone and said, "Bridge, TAO, based on MAD, reclassifying as probable submarine."

Seconds later, Palmer said, "Sonar, TAO. Let's throw a little shit in the game. How about we turn toward the contact and run over top of it? If it's a sub, he may maneuver to get away, and you'll hear machinery noises."

"Sonar concurs."

"Bridge, TAO, come right to course two two seven to close the probable sub."

"Torpedo room, TAO. Prepare to fire number three tube. Snake search, floor one hundred feet."

"Torpedoes, aye."

"Sonar reports high-speed screw noises on the bearing of the contact!"

Palmer knew those screw noises meant that fifteen hundred pounds of torpedo was coming at her ship at forty-five knots and reacted immediately. "Tube three, fire! Bridge, TAO. Recommend left hard rudder, all ahead flank three to comb the wake!"

"Stop the problem. Stop the problem," said a new voice over the announcing system.

Palmer pounded her fist in frustration on the arm of her chair. She had failed in the simulation.

Captain Greenhouse, who had been sitting silently nearby, moved to Palmer's side. "Jan," he said, "that was a good, aggressive move. In a scenario where we were protecting a carrier against a sub that popped up close aboard, it would be the best thing to do. But that's not the problem situation. Today we're hunting subs, just us and Seasnake. Your turn in set us and the sub up for an exchange of down-the-throat shots. If you had stayed away and used Seasnake to attack, you could have gotten a kill with much less risk to *Agerholm*."

"Yes, sir. I blew it."

"You didn't blow it, Jan. If you had done nothing after the Madman call, *that* would be blowing it. You reacted quickly with one of the possible moves in this situation. It just wasn't the *best* move.

"Now do another run. And remember, when we get under way from Bahrain, it won't be a simulation."

Clapping her on the back, Greenhouse turned away and left CIC. That was one stop on the walk he was taking through his ship, as he did nearly every day. It was one of his defenses against the "bubble," the isolation of command. He wanted to see and feel and hear and smell his ship. To have off-the-cuff conversations with sailors that he surprised by turning up unexpectedly, sometimes in the darndest places. In his first week in command, he had told the chiefs and officers that he did *not* want them showing up whenever they got word the captain was in their territory. Since he made it a rule never to come down on one of them directly for something he heard or saw, unless it was imminently dangerous or a gross violation of regulations, they stopped fearing his wanderings. He used his firsthand knowledge discreetly but effectively, as a supplement to the reports he received through the chain of command.

Strolling aft along the main deck passageway, he came upon a sailor working one of the heavy powered buffers to put a shine on the newly waxed deck. Every section of *Agerholm* was the responsibility of a specific sailor. Some accepted the daily chore of keeping it shipshape grudgingly; others embraced it. This sailor was somewhere in the middle; he obviously wanted to be done with this, but he felt satisfaction at the results of his labor. Greenhouse reinforced that with a few complimentary words, then said, "Seaman Roberts, what did you think of that business with *Nanking*? Were you out on deck?"

"Yes, sir. Helped one of the Chinese guys down to the mess deck so doc could check him over."

"What sort of shape was he in?"

"Didn't seem hurt bad, but his eyes were looking way off somewhere else. And he was gabbling in Chinese at me. Wish I could've understood him.

"You know, Captain, we made most of the news broadcasts right after that. Got email from my parents and my girl about it. They were impressed."

"Well, we were right there, and this crew knew what needed to be done and how to do it. Your drills paid off. I hope you'll remember that.

"Thanks for keeping this passageway sharp. I think everybody appreciates living aboard a clean ship."

As Greenhouse continued his walkabout, he was thankful for the opportunity that had come *Agerholm*'s way. Actually doing something, instead of only practicing, put a spring in the step of most of the crew. And hearing about it from home was a boost. They'd been deployed four months now and done little that had meaning for the families and friends awaiting their return in two more months.

And there was something else, which watching the antisubmarine drill had brought home: they were in a dangerous neighborhood, one where things could go from boring to life-threatening without warning. *Agerholm* was a large, sturdy ship, but it could be turned into a burning, sinking death trap for its crew, as *Nanking* had been. Seeing what had happened to *Nanking*—the bodies they recovered, the injuries of the crew they rescued— was, he hoped, a wake-up call for any who were growing complacent.

* * *

An hour later, in his cabin, a combination studio apartment and office cube, Greenhouse jotted a few notes about what he had seen and intuited, then toggled his computer awake. He skimmed through a swamp of emails, only a few of which were of immediate importance. Making sure his crew had access to the information and absentee ballots needed to vote in two months did matter, but it wasn't what occupied his mind. And besides, he thought gratefully, he had a terrific executive officer who stayed on top of that stuff so he could concentrate on the big picture.

The smirk that came with that thought revealed that Greenhouse had no big picture to think about. Nobody has one at this point, he thought.

His mind churned. Are we going to negotiate the reopening? Will we force the strait open with ships like *Agerholm*? What are the Iranians doing in the strait while we sit in Bahrain? You can bet they are laying mines. Will we just watch while they make it ever harder to force the strait open?

He knew that the *Vinson* carrier battle group was on the way, so they'd have two full carrier air wings for cover, plus air force. *Iowa* was also on the way, in fact less than a week out. The air force had beefed up the expeditionary air wing in Qatar. What would happen when all the pieces were in place? And what will the Chinese do? Are they just gonna take this, shrug off the *Nanking*? *Agerholm* now had five Chinese linguists aboard, hustled over from the states. Was someone thinking about a joint operation to clear the strait?

The admiral had invited all the skippers into port to attend his morning brief, but so far it had yielded information, not plans. Greenhouse knew there were about two dozen tankers sealed inside the Persian Gulf, plus a bunch of containerships and others. He wondered, How long before they will try to get out? The oil-producing Arab countries are furious—except Iraq, which is politically paralyzed between anger at the loss of its oil revenue and pride because the Iranians are Shia brothers.

What a mess! No, not a mess, a boiler with an ever-larger fire beneath it. Pretty soon it's gotta release steam, or blow up. Either way, Agerholm is going to be in the middle of it. I have to be sure we're ready.

Chapter 46

BEIJING, PEOPLE'S REPUBLIC OF CHINA

MING LIU, IN A DARK suit, snowy shirt, and ruby-red tie, sat behind his rosewood desk in an office as large but not as often seen as that of the man in Washington with whom he was speaking. On the wall behind him was a painting of the Great Wall of China, its lines of stones seeming to flow over the hilly terrain like the scales on a dragon's sinuous body. Positioned to his right rear was China's flag with its blood-red field and yellow stars. The walls behind him were book-lined. On a credenza below the painting of the Great Wall, some photographs: a black-and-white photo of a young army officer—his father who was killed in the Korean War—and four color shots of Ming with his wife and children. The big desktop was uncluttered despite hosting a white phone, two large red phones, a small stack of briefing folders, and a desk calendar.

His interpreter sat at a small table against the wall but positioned within Ming's field of view because Ming found it helpful to observe the man's body language. Although Ming and Rick Martin saw each other over the secure teleconference link between Beijing and Washington, neither could extract information from the other's tone of voice and inflection, as they were adept at doing at meetings in their respective native tongues. This was because tone in English conveys emotion, but tone in Chinese primarily differentiates one word from another. So Ming relied on watching his personal interpreter off-camera and listening for private comments from him. Once the teleconference began, President Martin didn't waste any time before pursuing a direct line of questioning.

"Yes, Rick," said Ming, "General MacAdoo is correct: one of our destroyers and a support ship will participate in the operation to reopen the strait, if military action is necessary. We will also send a minesweeping ship if it comes to that. Although I do not believe such action is necessary yet, as you know, our vessels are approaching the position of your aircraft carrier, to be ready if force is needed. I believe all the necessary military-technical arrangements have been agreed to between Ma and MacAdoo."

I know he'd like us to provide more ships, thought Ming, but he won't ask.

"Excellent, Ming. I wish you and I were as clear on *when* we are going to send our forces in to open the strait as we are on *how* we will do it. How long are you prepared to wait on our diplomatic efforts? Are you seeing any signs of flexibility from Tehran?"

No, thought Ming, but I'm not going to tell you that. "We see signs that many powerful figures in the government are urging the Supreme Leader to reopen the strait. I think, Rick, that China is better informed than America on discussions within the Iranian government because we have full diplomatic relations and many contacts within Iran's government."

"Ming, we, too, have conversations with senior Iranians. One has suggested that, if we keep the Israelis under control until the Supreme Leader feels able to lift the blockade, he will soon after be able to announce his willingness to negotiate limits on Iran's nuclear weapons and Israel's. What's your reaction to an arrangement like that?"

Excellent, thought Ming. Iran isn't the only threat to our oil supply. The Israelis—that excitable Askenazi—could start a war that would hurt China worse than this blockade. *Any* war involving the Persian Gulf, regardless of its source, would be a big problem for us.

"China would support that, Rick. But, as I'm sure you know, many Iranian officials claim to be in the Leader's inner circle, and most of them are not, of course. How can you be confident this senior official has influence with the Leader? And where do matters stand? Does your contact offer a timetable for the resumption of shipping?"

After a pause longer than that required for translation, Martin replied tartly, "I have full confidence that General Adel Ghorbani has influence with the Leader. But we are in a period of quiet now because he has not responded to our latest proposal. It's a bit frustrating."

"Rick, it's good that you are willing to wait on developments in the discussions that your emissaries and mine are having with Iranian officials. I'm glad you recognize that we have the greater stake in shipping through the Strait of Hormuz and will not use force just yet. Hopefully, either your channel through Ghorbani or ours through our ambassador will prove fruitful soon."

"Ming, I hope so, too. But neither of us can allow this to continue much longer. Not only is there the interruption of China's oil supply; American presidents have said on many occasions that the United States will not tolerate closure of the Strait of Hormuz. I'm not going to walk away from that. And, in addition, I'm sure your military as well as mine is saying that the more time we give Iran to emplace mines, the longer and more dangerous will be our operation to remove them."

* * *

After the call ended, Ming Liu retrieved his father's dented cigarette case from his pocket and lit up. How interesting, he thought. So General Ghorbani is in conversations with the Americans, too. He is indeed a formidable presence in this struggle, apparently as influential as the senior clerics. But can he deliver what he offered China: free passage for China-bound oil in return for our remaining aloof from whatever military action the Americans take and for condemning it at the UN?

Ming considered his options. Leave the Americans isolated if they attack? See if Ghorbani will sweeten his offer by selling oil to China at a discount? And what does it mean that Ghorbani has now gone silent?

Even though the Iranians attacked *Nanking* without any provocation and then lied by saying the ship was in their waters, Ming didn't want to join the Americans in attacking Iran. In the long run, good relations with Iran were crucial to ensuring China's oil supply. But above all, China's tankers must pass through the strait again soon. China *must* regain its normal oil supply!

Chapter 47

CONGRESSIONAL COUNTRY CLUB, BETHESDA, MARYLAND

"Nice, Mr. Vice President," said Marty Sanders as he and Bruce Griffith observed the arc of Griffith's drive.

"Marty, out here, it's Bruce," said Griffith with a smile.

Sanders, clad in lime green trousers and a yellow shirt, settled himself into his stance at the third tee of the Congressional Country Club's Blue Course. After a backswing more fluid than usual, he got off a pleasing drive. The ball lanced down the fairway, lower than he wanted but true. Smiling, he picked up his tee and handed his club to the caddy, who hustled off to mark their balls. It was a gorgeous day, in the high seventies with low humidity, and both men were in a jovial mood as they climbed aboard the golf cart they were sharing so they could speak privately as they played. Sanders was elated about more than his golf shot. He was enjoying the perks of being on the Griffith team, such as golf rounds like this, a White House pass, and being greeted by name by the vice president's Secret Service detail. Around town he was now a bet to be covered, someone who would be an insider if there was a Griffith administration, and it showed in deference from headwaiters and ingratiation by lobbyists.

As they rolled toward Marty's ball, Griffith said, "So how's your favorite senator these days?"

"Hah! She'd like to strangle me but doesn't dare. We've got her, and she knows it. Especially now that she has her eye on Senate majority leader."

"Do you think we've got enough to keep her quiet until after the election?"

Marty assumed his most confident tone and said, "It's a lock. Like you, she needs to be clean as a whistle to win. She wants to be majority leader more than she wants to screw Morales."

"I question that. She truly hates him."

"Bruce, I've known her for years. Not even revenge is a higher priority than running the Senate. You can take that to the bank. And after you're president, you'll have plenty of ways to keep her quiet about Hadrab *and* about the Iranians."

Griffith's expression said he wasn't sure, but he moved the conversation on. "Let's talk about the primaries. What do you have on Nelson?"

"I've heard that during his first term he had a fondness for a certain intern in the Congressional Research Office. She wasn't the first. When his wife got wind of this chick, it was the final straw. When she told him it was either a quiet divorce on her terms or an ugly one naming his hottie, she got her way and a pile of money. We can leverage that, and to give it a bit more pop, I'm pretty sure I can get his playmate to decide that it wasn't consensual."

Griffith smiled. "Nice, Marty! I definitely picked the right guy."

"Thanks, Bruce. I've been in this business a long time. I've got something on just about everybody—or I can get it."

Sanders noticed the change in Griffith's expression and was pleased that his message had been received: *Hey, Brucie, don't think you're the only one with power in this relationship.* Deciding to sheath the stiletto he had just flashed, Sanders said, "But, on the other hand, I'm not much up on the politics of what's going on now in the Middle East."

Griffith's expression showed his irritation at the nerve of the Iranians for creating a crisis that interfered with his plans to win the nomination and the presidency. "There's a lot to it. But first, let's hit."

Sanders, about two hundred yards from the green on a par four hole, pulled his five wood into the trap in front of it to the left. Griffith, whose drive had carried about twenty yards farther, used a two iron to put his ball just short of the green.

Back in the cart, Griffith picked up the thread: "Foreign affairs is tricky because you hardly ever have much control over the other players. This situation in the gulf is trickier than most because you've got the Chinese, Saudis, Israelis, and Iranians all up to their necks in it. And the Turks and the Syrians are hovering like vultures, waiting for a juicy scrap to fall within their reach. Like we used to say in the air force, it's a real fur ball."

Sanders knew that Griffith had been a protocol officer during his two years of air force duty but liked to use fighter pilot slang.

"So this closure of the Strait of Hormuz is a real problem for me," continued Griffith. "Whatever Martin does, including nothing, he pisses someone off real bad. And that rubs off."

"But don't most Americans think this is somebody else's problem? I mean, with shale oil and fracking and all?"

"They do, but they're wrong. The pie's pretty big right now. But about sixty percent of the proven oil reserves in the world are in the Middle East. You take away sixty percent of the big pie, and in the long term there's not enough to go around. And in the short term, closing the straits takes about 20% of the world's daily oil consumption right off the table. That amount can be made up from other sources, but then the price goes up. Americans who drive cars, or heat with oil, or buy anything manufactured with petroleum get hit right in their wallets. If the strait stays closed, voters will soon feel the hit and be mad as hell at the president and the party in the White House."

Griffith stopped the cart and watched Sanders take two strokes to get out of the trap. Griffith strode to his ball and chipped it within about five feet downhill from the pin. "That's how it's done, Marty!"

When their caddy had walked away to tend the pin, Griffith concluded his lesson on the unfortunate linkage between foreign policy and elections: "So the main thing is, we gotta get the oil tankers moving again, and we gotta do it without a war. A nice little dustup like the First Gulf War would be OK—but that's not in the cards. If the shooting starts, that wild man Askenazi—he thinks he's leading Israel to the Promised Land—will want to pound Iran and remove that threat to Israel once and for all. That would start the fur ball to end all fur balls."

Chapter 48

THE WHITE HOUSE

A S SHE OBSERVED THE CONTROLLED bustle that precedes a speech from the Oval Office, Press Secretary Samantha (Sam) Yu thought it had almost a feeling of routine—weighty but practiced. Since this was the seventh Oval Office broadcast for Rick Martin and his staff, each of the eleven people in the room knew exactly what to do and how to do it efficiently. Still, she thought, this room is so special, its walls have heard so much history. An Oval Office speech could never seem ordinary.

The president spoke a few words to permit technicians to check sound levels in the three systems in use to ensure that audio would always be available, then settled into his opening demeanor, a serious but calm expression on his face. The director moved to his familiar position off-camera but directly in the president's view and counted down from ten to air time, fingers ticking off the final five seconds.

"Good evening, my fellow Americans. Tonight I want to describe for you the situation in the Persian Gulf, specifically the narrow body of water that connects it to the oceans of the world. I'm speaking of the Strait of Hormuz."

Prior to going on air, staff had questioned his use of the term "Persian Gulf," even though it was the accepted term for the body of water separating the Arabian Peninsula from Iran. Some felt the name conveyed acceptance of Iranian control over those waters and thus was inappropriate in a speech intended to convey exactly the opposite. President Martin told them that, in this case, geographic convention trumped nuance.

After describing the impact of cutting off sixty percent of the world's proven oil reserves and explaining the maritime law that mandated free passage through the strait, the president came to the meat of his message.

"Although we do not have diplomatic relations with the Islamic Republic of Iran, we have numerous channels of communication with that government. We have employed all of them in an attempt to understand Iran's rationale for closing the strait with minefields and to resolve any legitimate concerns or grievances the Iranians express.

"Let me be clear that the unprovoked Iranian attack on the Chinese navy destroyer *Nanking* is nothing other than an outrage and a deadly flouting of international law. We stand firmly with the government of China in condemning this offense and with all the nations of the world that respect and rely on the right of passage through international waters—which the Strait of Hormuz and the Persian Gulf most assuredly are."

Now, thought Yu, we get to the parts that will keep me busy as soon as he finishes. She leaned in slightly from her perch on the arm of a couch positioned off-camera before the president's desk.

"Virtually every maritime nation in the world has condemned Iran's actions. The UN Security Council has demanded that Iran reverse its actions by clearing the mines it has laid—and continues to lay—and permit trade to resume its peaceful and necessary journey through the strait. Iran has so far refused.

"I believe it is time to take action to reopen the Strait of Hormuz. Russia used its veto to block the joint American-Chinese UN resolution that called for using all necessary means to reopen this vital waterway, while all other members of the Security Council voted in favor of it. So the United States and China have agreed to act jointly. One week from today, unless the mines are being cleared and Iran has declared its intent to permit passage, America and China will use all means necessary to remove the mines and open the strait to the peaceful voyage of all seafaring nations."

* * *

BEIJING, PEOPLE'S REPUBLIC OF CHINA

At six fifteen in the morning, Ming Liu, habitually an early riser, listened with much less attention to the remainder of Martin's speech, the part where he assured everyone that this would not lead to war and invited the government of Iran to climb down from its perilous position. Ming's mind was assembling and reassembling the puzzle it had begun working on when Adel Ghorbani proposed the deal.

Switching off the TV, Ming swiveled his desk chair to face the window in his small home office. Beijing was facing another day of foul-smelling smog, and he was trying to peer into a murky future. Ghorbani's offer of unobstructed passage of China-bound ships, assuming it was valid, was appealing. And, of only slightly less importance, it gave a better opportunity to restore fruitful commercial relations between China and Iran, a flow of trade and investment that was good for both. Why shouldn't he make a deal with Iran if it enabled oil to flow and China's economic and military power to grow? And when they did, it would make him the most consequential ruler of China since Mao.

Martin's speech had just made the cost of accepting Ghorbani's deal higher. Unless he directed his foreign ministry to deny any agreement between America and China on the use of force, he gave the appearance of agreement. So if he later pulled out of the military operation, China would be seen as going back on its word. An unreliable partner, untrustworthy.

In some ways that impression mattered little. America and China would never be close allies anyway. But it would make it harder to obtain the trade and military agreements he sought to restore Chinese hegemony. It would also confirm Japanese and Korean distrust of China—but that was a historical given. Probably the biggest downside would be the difficulty that an untrustworthy reputation would inject into his efforts to forge stronger ties with India.

All that being said, Ghorbani's deal *was* appealing to Ming, but he wondered whether Ghorbani could really deliver. The Supreme Leader must approve, and Ming had no way of knowing whether he would.

On the other hand, whether by cold-blooded calculation or careless incompetence, Iran had killed two hundred thirteen Chinese navy men and sunk one of China's newest front-line warships. Not only was that outrageous; it was also embarrassing. Many armchair admirals were posting, "How could *Nanking's* crew have been as careless as to fall victim to a sneak attack by something not much larger than a waterski boat? And what does the rapid sinking of the ship from a single hit say about the battle-worthiness of China's navy?"

Ming scowled and began to pace the small office.

The members of the Military Committee of the party, which Ming chaired, were furious. While General Ma, the vice chairman, would keep his disapproval between the two of them, others on the committee would voice sly criticism. While the honor of the People's Liberation Army Navy didn't mean much to Ming, he conceded Ma's other point: that unless China held Iran accountable, this attack would embolden others to attack, if not China's warships, then its tankers and cargo vessels. And Ming was personally irked that Iran's Supreme Leader had ignored China's demands for an apology and reparations for loss of life and property.

If the Americans decided to force the strait open with or without China, as they seemed certain to, it meant fighting in the Persian Gulf. Even if China-bound ships were granted passage by the Iranians, safety wasn't theirs to give. The Persian Gulf and the strait would become a battleground between America and Iran. All tankers would have to wait for safer conditions, and he would have no influence over when those conditions would be achieved. If China joined the naval force, he would have influence. And with China and America cooperating—for the moment anyway—Iran would have less incentive to resist the mine clearance operation. The day that China-bound tankers could safely resume voyages would be hastened.

As he had nearly four years ago with North Korea, Martin had maneuvered Ming into grudging support of military action that Ming strongly preferred to avoid. Ming was angry at that but consoled himself in knowing that Martin would be gone in three years, while he, by cooperating with Martin this last time, would outlast him in power by many years. And he could easily outwit and manipulate either of Martin's likely successors, Griffith or Rutherford.

Ming Liu had become China's leader and had stayed in power partly because he knew when to accept the least bad outcome and move on.

Well, I have a week before I will have to commit or decline. A lot can happen in a week.

* * *

THE WHITE HOUSE

Six thousand miles away, another Han Chinese was also wrestling with the consequences of Martin's speech. Sam Yu stood at the podium of the White house press briefing room.

She called on a reporter. "Martha?"

"Aren't we at risk of sailing into an Iranian trap in the narrow, shallow waters of the Strait of Hormuz? My Pentagon sources tell me that the navy is worried that we will be sending ships intended for standoff combat into a tight space where swarms of Iranian cruise missiles and suicide speedboats will be at close quarters, where they can do real damage. One source said it's like a long-armed prizefighter allowing a short-armed opponent to get close enough to land punches."

"Wow, Martha, I didn't know you were a boxing fan!" Yu's grin drained the sarcasm from her words. "Look, the navy's not rushing in there willy-nilly. The battleship *Iowa*, the most heavily armored ship on earth, will be arriving in the region in a day or two. Can we agree to leave the military questions for the Pentagon to answer? Larry?"

"I hope you're not just going to refer me to the State Department!"

"Try me!" said Yu, popping up on the balls of her feet like Serena Williams waiting to receive a serve.

"Look," said Larry. "We've had a rocky relationship with China. Trade issues. Intellectual property. Its support of North Korea until the last hours of the nuclear crisis. But now we're cooperating militarily against China's most important oil supplier. Has something big shifted in China? Has the Martin administration adopted a new strategy? Are we now looking to partner with China?"

"Larry, the administration didn't orchestrate this crisis. It came out of Tehran. It's not our opening move in some new strategy. We are standing up for an aspect of international law that's vital to our economic well-being: the right of merchant ships of all flags to pass through international waters unmolested as they transport goods around the world. It happens that's also vital to China. In this crisis, our interests seem to be aligned, so we're working together. If this leads to increasing cooperation across a range of issues, wonderful. It's not a new strategy, it's simply an application of the strategy we've had from day one: build coalitions of nations willing to work together for the common good."

Yu's wide grin told them all that she was pleased with her ability to turn a debate over foreign affairs into an opportunity to declare the administration's support of motherhood and apple pie. But she couldn't help worrying a little bit: It was out of character for the Chinese to cooperate with America in a way that could damage them economically. When push came to shove, could China be counted on?

Chapter 49

TEHRAN, ISLAMIC REPUBLIC OF IRAN

YAZDAN LAJANI DIDN'T KNOW WHAT to do next. He pushed his plastic chair, uncomfortable despite the pillows he had bought for it, back from his tiny desk, hardly larger than the MacBook Pro resting atop it. He gazed vacantly out the small barred window of a room where eleven other intelligence analysts sat at equally small desks in equally uncomfortable chairs. Partly from the tingle in his bladder and partly to gather his thoughts, he went to the men's room. He urinated, washed, combed his hair, and stared at his reflection: brown-black eyes flanking an aquiline nose and short, curly black hair and beard. He splashed water on his face, dried it with a paper towel, and walked slowly back to his desk.

Let's take it from the beginning. Inshallah, this time I will solve this puzzle. What do I know?

He knew that Fordow was beyond the combat radius of an unrefueled Israeli Air Force F-15, F-16, or F-35 with a full bomb load. He knew that Iran's uranium enrichment plant there was buried too deeply to be destroyed by the conventional bombs those aircraft could carry. He knew that the Jews had three Boeing 707 tankers, and they could each provide enough gas to refuel five strike aircraft on a single mission deep into Iran. That would allow a deep strike by only fifteen aircraft, inadequate for a massive simultaneous attack on all of Iran's special facilities.

Besides those facts, he had collected a few tidbits meriting consideration. There were indications that the Israeli Defense Ministry had contracted with Israeli Aerospace Industries to modify C-130J transports to refuel

F-15Ds and F-16s. They were already equipped to refuel the 707s and helicopters. Was that because the Israelis were preparing for the day, not far off, when the 707s would be too old for service? Was it because they wanted to use the 707s for something else, some new mission, and the C-130s were to step in for deep-strike refueling? Or was it because they wanted to significantly increase their deep-strike refueling capability by adding the nine C-130s to their three 707s? That would more than double the strike size to about thirty-three aircraft. That number *might* be sufficient.

An Iranian intelligence agent on a cleaning crew at the main aircraft maintenance facility of the Israeli Air Force had reported seeing early-model F-15s—the A's and B's—being modified by the addition of conformal fuel tanks that would nearly double their flight range. That was an expensive, difficult modification that the Israelis had never before made to these early, less-capable F-15s. Why do it now?

An Israeli blogger who had proven reliable in the past in leaking intelligence asserted online that the Iron Dome's missile defense software was being modified to permit concentrating all its resources along a single threat axis, rather than all-around defense.

Was this unusual amount of activity a precursor to a Jewish attack on Iran? Or was it just a coincidence that a series of modifying activities were occurring now?

Am I missing something? What?

Yazdan Lajani had no time to pursue these questions. All his superiors were interested in was information about the Israeli reaction to Iran closing the strait. What more could he do?

* * *

THE INDIAN OCEAN, GULF OF OMAN

"What are you still standin' there for? You old farts don't move around enough to burn the calories you already got on that tray"

"Give me three more bacon strips, sonny. I was a battleship sailor long before you came into this world. The reason we're here is you kids couldn't hack it. So shut yer gob and gimme my bacon!"

Grins on the faces of both men—the young sailor serving the mess line and the gray-haired, slightly pot-bellied man demanding bacon—showed this was just trash talk between shipmates.

With extra bacon secured, the gray-haired sailor carried his tray to a metal table on the mess deck of USS Iowa, the only battleship in the world and the oldest seagoing ship in any navy. *Iowa* owed her third recommissioning, several years ago, to members of Congress who had decided for a variety of mostly self-serving reasons that the US Navy needed a working battleship.

At the time, the chief of naval operations hadn't wanted her but knew it wasn't worth angering members of the House Armed Services Committee. Among other problems that the chief had with the return of a battleship was that there was very little on hand of the unique ammunition for a battleship's huge guns. He intended to slow-roll her updating and recommissioning until the legislators became enamored with their next boondoggle, then quietly slip her into the oblivion of the National Defense Reserve Fleet.

As things had turned out, though, his successor was glad she was available because a series of crises in Korea and in the Middle East called for her unique political and military capabilities. Designed and built during World War Two to withstand onslaughts of Japanese suicide bombers—kamikazes—*Iowa* was so heavily armored and well protected by rugged, combat-proven damage control systems that she could shrug off the missiles, torpedoes, and suicide boats that third-tier navies and jihadis could throw at her in a surprise attack. When it came to taking a punch and then returning a bigger one, analog beat digital every time.

With the shrunken US Navy's reluctance to expose destroyers and cruisers, much less its few hugely expensive nuclear carriers, to the sort of suicide attack that had taken out USS Cole, America had pulled its warships back from volatile regions. Not its submarines, but in the political context they didn't count because they couldn't be seen. A navy that had once thumbed its nose at powerful counterparts like the Soviet Navy by cruising their home waters now stayed out of harm's way. The US Navy's visible presence was much diminished and contributed to an impression from friend and foe alike that the United States was a declining power.

And so *Iowa*, once considered a bad joke by the admirals, had become a valued asset. The production of ammunition for her sixteen-inch turret guns was resumed. Every combatant commander wanted her in his region, to poke her bow into dangerous places with relative impunity. She wasn't capable of making much difference in twenty-first-century war at sea with an opponent like China, or even Russia, and probably wouldn't last long in such a scrap, but she was just dandy for the Persian Gulf.

Because she was from another era of naval armament, twenty-first-century navy men and women lacked the skills and experience to operate her most important attributes: three triple-barreled gun turrets that could heave tons of high-explosive projectiles over twenty miles. Gunners with experience in the operation of her massive, complex sixteen-inch gun turrets were found only on the navy's retired list. A similar issue existed with her power plant. Her gigantic propellers were driven by turbines supplied with steam from boilers at six hundred pounds per square inch, an arrangement long since discarded in favor of gas turbine propulsion. She needed experienced boiler operators.

And so the call went out, and the navy was flooded with applications from gray-haired former battleship gunners and boiler men. The best of these, mostly retired chief petty officers and warrant officers, were selected, and they joined, or in some cases rejoined, *Iowa*'s crew. They called themselves the Old Goats. Every navy ship has an irreverent nickname by which it is known throughout the fleet. *Iowa*'s crew proudly christened her the "Goat Boat."

Now the huge vessel from the past slipped through the predawn wavelets of the Indian Ocean, parting them with surprising stealth. Her rugged outline could barely be seen in the light of a fingernail moon. Fearless—nothing else of her size and power existed in these waters—but alert, the apparition from a bygone century idled near the eastern entrance to the Strait of Hormuz. For now, she would not risk the minefield stretching south from Larak Island to Quoin Island. But she would trail her coat and await a reaction.

Eyes unawed by the behemoth's bulk observed her electronically from the Iranian shore, near Bandar Abbas. "I have lock-on. Request permission to fire." A squat man with jug-handle ears turned to his companion, who was as tall and regal as the first man was dumpy. The body language of each of the six men in the darkened room deferred to the tall one. None but the squat one met his eyes. "Do it," said the tall one. The squat one turned to the man who had asked permission and said, "You may fire."

The modified Aegis fire control system that had been grafted onto *Iowa* detected the launch of three Silkworm missiles. It simultaneously tracked the missiles, computed their launch points, readied the ship's close-in weapons system, or CIWS, and directed two of the ship's three massive gun turrets to lob a pair of one-ton shells at each of the launch sites.

Sounding like an electric drill magnified a hundred times, the CIWS spewed depleted uranium slugs at the incoming Silkworms. Two of the Silkworms exploded in flight. The third bored in, shedding pieces of its airframe as it covered the final quarter mile. At that moment the remaining Silkworm was like nothing so much as one of the kamikazes the ship had been designed in the past century to withstand. The missile struck *Iowa*'s starboard side at the base of one of its many gun mounts. The mount launched skyward atop a piston of flame and disappeared into the night.

A minute later, flames from the damage were dwarfed by tongues of fire lancing from two of the three sixteen-inch guns in turret one and two of those in turret three. Just under nineteen miles away, four tons of high explosive atomized itself with a series of blasts heard and felt for miles. Dirt, rock, metal, and bits of the squat one and his companions rained briefly from the altitudes to which they had been flung. Then silence. Aegis swept its gaze about hungrily, hoping for other targets. Finding none, it sulked into standby.

Iowa continued as before, while damage-control parties quenched the flames and dealt with pipes and power cables damaged in the explosion. Since *Iowa*'s presence there owed to her tough hide and sixteen-inch guns, smaller guns like the one blown skyward were considered superfluous and had been left unmanned.

With barely visible damage—about twenty feet of twisted, smoke-blackened metal at the main deck of her nine-hundred-foot hull—*Iowa* loomed in the night-blackened waters, as if to say, "Is that all you got?"

Chapter 50

QOM, ISLAMIC REPUBLIC OF IRAN

"I KNOW THE REAL REASON YOU'RE here. It's about China." The Supreme Leader's face was as blunt as his words to Adel Ghorbani. The two sat in the Leader's office, with its dark, heavy furniture. In the center of the room, partly covered by the Leader's desk, a nineteenth-century Meshed rug in burgundy with a bright floral design signaled the stature of its possessor. Two walls were filled by bookcases displaying the beautifully bound works of religious scholars; one wall displayed photographs of the Leader with heads of state, including Ming Liu. The remaining wall had three large windows overlooking the square four stories below.

The Leader's aggressiveness was no surprise to Ghorbani. The Supreme Leader was a powerful individual with feelings of inferiority that he worked to suppress by attacking others. He had reached his position by virtue of his obeisance to his predecessor, who had forced the Council of Guardians to select him over more senior clerics.

Adapting to the Leader's mood, Ghorbani said, "Not entirely, Leader, but let's discuss China first. Now is the time to seize the initiative, to cut the legs from under the Great Satan by boldly restoring our good relations with China. Only you can do that. Only you can defeat the self-serving maneuverings of Ahmadi and Rajavi. You've heard them in the Council of Guardians. You know they have no goal beyond advancing themselves and holding back rivals. They have no concrete proposals, only objections and concerns and big ideas that have no chance for success in the reality that Iran faces."

"I will never apologize to the Chinese. They are an ugly people. They attack the faithful in China. They are the worst sort of infidels!" The snarl in the Leader's voice and his jabbing index finger underlined his words.

"And you are expressing the will of the Iranian people when you take that stand, Leader. We will never apologize!" said Ghorbani, with a fist-pump.

"But," Ghorbani continued, "There is no need to apologize. Above all, Ming Liu needs to get tankers moving through the strait, to resume the flow of oil to China. The economy on which his rule depends is the world's largest consumer of energy. And the need is growing. Ming's agreement with the Americans is only an alliance of convenience. He knows that America is inevitably China's enemy, as it is ours. When you offer him free passage for China-bound tankers, he will be only too happy to withdraw from the military operation. And *Nanking*'s blunder into our waters and its consequences will be no more than a footnote to the historic alliance between Iran and China."

"But why," responded the Leader, "offer China a way out of the crisis it had created by sending its warship into our gulf? Let Ming sweat until he comes to me! The arrogance of the man—demanding an apology from Iran!"

"Because, Leader, after we have reached agreement with China, when the Americans attack us in the strait as they have threatened, it will be clear to all that they are aggressors whose aim is war on Islam. Their plan will be exposed for what it is: a flimsy excuse to attack the Islamic Republic and all true believers, a plan the Chinese would have no part of. It will be Martin who'll look unreasonable and bent on violence, not you, who negotiated a settlement with China. In that atmosphere, the cursed Jews will find no support for their plan to strike us. They will be stymied by your bold move.

"Our trade with China will recommence. And, *and* … China will resume its assistance with our missile and nuclear programs!"

As he watched the color of anger leave the Leader's face, Ghorbani believed he had won. His tension began to fade. "I will do it," said the Leader. "But I will *not* rely solely on international pressure to defeat the Jewish attack. We must end the threat of it entirely. You hear what Askenazi is saying about the Jews being destined to control everything from the

Euphrates to the Mediterranean. This time he will back down, as you say, but he will continue to plot our destruction.

"So I will deal with China, and you will do *this*: within thirty days, you are to have three missiles ready with warheads of the proven Chinese design. I refuse to depend solely on the forbearance of that pig Askenazi. And you are to have Quds warriors ready to kill Askenazi, his defense minister, and his military chief. The Jews will be so shocked that they won't be able to strike us."

Stunned, Ghorbani said, "Leader that may not be possible! Thirty days isn't enough time to plan such a Quds operation. And please understand that the marriage of a nuclear warhead to a missile is very delicate and complicated. It normally requires flight testing and modification. I will look at our production schedule and accelerate it wherever possible, but thirty days is not long enough. I can probably get it done in sixty days." A faint sheen of perspiration appeared on Ghorbani's face.

The Supreme Leader looked at Ghorbani with fiery eyes and said, "All right. Sixty days. But no more!"

* * *

Adel Ghorbani's stomach pained him as he began the familiar hour-and-a-half ride from Qom to Tehran. The pain was always in the same spot, a combination of burning and stabbing. He assumed it was an ulcer, and he had been living with it for years. If the West ever embargoes antacids, I'll be in real trouble, he thought, as he unwrapped a Tums tablet and popped it into his mouth. The familiar chalky taste foreshadowed relief.

But there was no pill he could take to relieve his fear for Iran. In sixty days he would have to hand the Leader control of three operational nuclear ballistic missiles. He knew where the Leader would send them: Haifa, Tel Aviv, and Dimona: Israel's main seaport, its economic hub, and the facility producing plutonium for nuclear weapons. The assassinations that the Leader had ordered would not prevent a nuclear response from Israeli that would devastate Iran. Such a suicidal plan was not Allah's will. It couldn't be!

I have to prevent this madness! But how?

Chapter 51

WASHINGTON, DC

AS HE WALKED THE FAMILIAR route from the Oval Office to the Situation Room, President Rick Martin could almost hear a clock ticking, counting down the days, hours, and minutes until Iran's week to comply with his ultimatum would end. We're getting nothing but mush, he thought.

The Canadians who were representing American interests in Tehran had nothing more to report than what was broadcast on TV: large rallies denouncing the Great Satan, with much shouting, flag-burning, effigy-hanging, and chest-beating. In New York, in private talks with Iran's UN diplomats, their responses swerved from pure propaganda to nuanced problem solving and back to propaganda. Surveillance of the strait had revealed no sign that the Iranians were removing mines or preparing to do so. Ming was keeping his own counsel and holding America's operation at arm's length, keeping his military out of contact. And Ghorbani had remained silent. Had he been betrayed and thrown in prison? Martin had a bad feeling about it all.

He made eye contact and nodded in response to a crisp salute from the Marine who had opened the door for him. Inside the Situation Room waited his entire national security team. Also present was Bart Guarini, and Martin was pretty sure that in an adjoining room were the heads of the CIA and the National Security Agency; General Remington, the military commander responsible for the Persian Gulf; and a clutch of staff experts. A full house and a single subject: opening the Strait of Hormuz.

He could tell from the tension he saw and felt that this was going to be another of those meetings where the others thought, "Thank God *I* don't have to make this decision." By this, his fifth year of making such calls, Martin had found a way of dealing with the pressures. He said a prayer, then made the best decision he could. Later, he prayed for forgiveness for the evil he had inevitably done or tolerated in order to accomplish good. Sometimes, he thought, the good proved to be illusory while the evil was real. *And each time, it takes a chunk out of my soul.*

"OK, John, let's get started," said Martin. "I didn't have time to read the agenda. This is about climate change, right?"

Smiles and chuckles around the table, but nervous ones.

"Mr. President, we'll begin with Lieutenant General Ferrara, Joint Chiefs operations director, who'll brief us on the present military situation in the region."

Ferrara entered and worked his way through a slide deck as he described the minefield and Iran's anti-ship cruise missiles, aviation squadrons, and naval forces. Once he had finished and exited the room, Martin turned to the chairman of the Joint Chiefs of Staff and said, "OK, Mac. Boil that down for us."

General MacAdoo propped both elbows on the polished table, steepled his fingers, cocked his head to the side, and spoke in a gravelly baritone: "Mr. President, Iran shows no signs of preparing to remove the mines. Reopening the strait against Iran's will is doable, but it will take about two months—maybe more. Before our minesweepers can enter the strait to do their work, we'll have to eliminate Iran's cruise missile batteries, chase off or destroy their tactical air, and force their navy into port or sink it. We're looking at a major air and naval campaign in which we will take losses and will, despite every effort, inflict significant civilian casualties."

"So," said Martin, "the questions are, should we take that on, extend the deadline, or find another way to open the strait?" His tone and expression gave no hint of his thinking.

"Mr. President, there's another factor at play here," said Dorn, who motioned to the director of national intelligence. "Aaron?"

Director Aaron Hendrix cleared his throat and said, "Mr. President, we are seeing signs that Israel may be preparing to carry out large-scale air strikes against Iran."

"How sure are you, Aaron? After all, Israel's air force is *always* prepared to launch strikes."

"We assess medium-to-high confidence, sir."

"Do you guys always have to hedge your bet to reach consensus? Which is it, Aaron, in *your* opinion?"

"High, sir."

"And what makes it high?"

"Recently, Israel's top military officer, General Rivkin, met secretly in Egypt with his Saudi counterpart. We think the Saudis have signaled that they'll look the other way when an Israeli strike on Iran passes over them. And if the Saudis have agreed to it, then Jordan will also have agreed. Those agreements would offer Israel's air force a better path to hit Iran.

"There are other things, but that's the big one. That shortcut *significantly* improves the odds that an Israeli deep strike would succeed."

Martin grimaced and threw up his hands. "Come on, Aaron! The Saudis don't even acknowledge Israel's right to exist."

"It's the Middle East, sir. The enemy of my enemy—"

"Anne, Eric, what do you think of this?"

Secretary of State Anne Battista, half-glasses perched low on her nose, nodded her graying blonde head and said, "Well, it wouldn't be the first time Cairo was used for a secret meeting between Israel and an Arab country that officially has no relations with it. Both Israel and Saudi Arabia have embassies there, so ..." She shrugged.

Martin shifted his gaze to Secretary of Defense Easterly. "Eric?"

"One of the big challenges for an Israeli air strike meant to destroy Iran's potential for nuclear missiles has been distance. If Aaron's information is correct, the Israelis might have solved the distance problem because they can safely station refueling aircraft in Saudi airspace. The other problem for the Israelis is uncertainty about the location of all sites in Iran's program. Obviously, they can't destroy sites they can't find. And, of course, some of the known sites are deep underground, beyond the reach of anything but a nuke or a MOAB."

"MOAB. That's a huge conventional bomb, right?"

"Yes, sir. The GBU-57 Massive Ordnance Penetrator. The troops call it 'mother of all bombs,' or 'MOAB'." Thirty thousand pounds apiece, each with a five thousand pound explosive charge in a super-hard warhead designed to burrow deep into ground, concrete, or just about anything."

"Do they have any MOABs?"

"Not any of ours, sir. But the Russians have a similar weapon and …" Easterly shrugged.

"What about that, Aaron?"

"We hear rumors of a 'special new weapon.' But there are always those rumors. Israeli R&D lives in a state of perpetual threat of war. The Israelis are constantly tweaking weapons or coming up with new ones.

"But to Eric's point, there are a couple of things going on that, *if* you posit that they have a MOAB, could be attack preparations. C-130s, the only military aircraft they have capable of carrying a MOAB, have been observed performing an unusual maneuver that might be practice for a MOAB drop. And El Al's new Boeing 737-900 extended range models have been withdrawn from service. The reason given was reconfiguration of the cabin seating. But if the cabins were stripped out and fuel bladders installed in place of seats, this aircraft would have the range of a deep-strike tanker.

"But I must emphasize, sir, that this is conjecture. The C-130s could be practicing that maneuver for other reasons. And we have no hard intelligence about conversion of those Boeing jets."

"So let me attempt to sum up," said Dorn. "The Israelis *may* have solved some of the challenges of a preemptive strike on Iran's nuke missile development program. But there is no convincing evidence that they actually *have* done any of those things. So I suggest we put that aside for now and focus on the strait."

"OK, then back to my question," said Martin. "Do we attack at the end of the deadline, extend the deadline, or do something else?"

"If I may, sir," said Bart Guarini, "I'd like to hear more about how this would unfold militarily. What's the sequence of events and timing?"

"Yes," said Martin. "Mac, tell us more about the plan."

"Yes, sir. There are two main pieces to this job: making the strait safe enough for our minesweepers to work in, then locating and removing or destroying the mines. The first part is the hardest and will probably take the longest.

"Iran's cruise missiles are on mobile launchers. We've had considerable experience trying to hit mobile launchers, and it's not encouraging. The launchers are very hard to find until they shoot, and then they go into hiding again so quickly that it's hard to catch them. Iran has hundreds of these, and General Remington estimates a month of air and missile strikes to manage that threat. Iran's relatively few tactical aircraft can be eliminated quickly. The same is true of their surface ships and patrol boats. The subs are tougher because of water conditions in the region. However, those conditions work against the subs as well as our sub-hunters, so by the time we've eliminated the cruise missiles, the subs should be sunk or driven off.

"When we're ready for the mine clearing, our mine countermeasure forces—ships, helos, and robotic underwater vehicles—will have a relatively straightforward task. Remington estimates that, if not interfered with by Iranian forces, they can have a path cleared through the minefield in about two weeks. Clearing every single mine will take much longer, but ships would be able to pass through the strait within the swept channel."

"So," said Guarini, "you're saying we have at least a month of combat against Iran, with the likelihood of significant civilian casualties plus losses of our own, before we can start to work on the purpose of the whole thing, opening a path for ships."

"That's our best military estimate, sir," said MacAdoo, bristling a bit.

"Mr. President, I don't think that's politically sustainable," said Guarini. "Combat on that scale is going to look like—and in fact could become—full-scale war with Iran. There's nothing surgical about this. I don't think Americans would support going to war to reopen the Strait of Hormuz. I think they could be persuaded to support combat on a lesser scale, including some casualties, but not the plan Mac just described.

"I'm not criticizing the plan, Mac. But if your troops don't have at least most of the public behind them, we risk having to draw back before they accomplish the mission."

The room was pin-drop silent. Guarini had just done his job. Everyone else felt the need to stay in their own lane while the chief of staff was free to roam.

Rick Martin was unsurprised. He had seen the same polls that Guarini had. But America had issued an ultimatum. He said, "Well, if that's not politically feasible, what is? Extending the deadline?"

"Perhaps," said Battista, "we could find a third party to mediate. The

UN or the Qataris—they've got pretty good relations with Iran despite Saudi pressure on them. I can get my folks to take some soundings."

"But that would be a pretty obvious back-down, Anne," said the vice president. "We can't afford to look weak."

"Well, there's another negotiated solution we could try. Let's assume that Tehran reads the military situation as we do—using force to resist the reopening of the strait could lead to full-scale war with the United States. I doubt the Iranians want that. After all, there've been no further attacks on the navy since *Iowa* demonstrated the response that attacks would bring.

"All they have to do to comply with our ultimatum is *announce* that they are reopening the strait and *begin* the process of clearing their mines. If they do that, we could give them a lot of time to do the job, during which we could perhaps negotiate an agreement managing the issue."

"Negotiate an agreement managing the issue," mocked the vice president. "What the *hell* does that mean, Anne?"

Battista flushed. "Right now I don't know, Bruce," she snapped. "What I'm trying to do is find a way to keep us out of a war that most Americans don't want and won't support. What suggestions do *you* have in that department?"

"I think we can borrow from both your points to find a way," said Guarini. As usual, he served as the president's dealmaker. "I think you're right that the Iranians can see the same danger of war that we do, and they don't want it. Look, we're assuming they'll attack our minesweepers. But maybe they won't. Maybe they know where that would lead and don't want to go there. And we've got the Chinese with us in this. Probably the Iranian government doesn't want to make things worse than they already are with China. Let's send the minesweepers and a Chinese ship into the strait under heavy air cover, maybe escorted by *Iowa*, and see how they react. If they don't attack, we sweep the mines, and this thing is over. If they do, we have strong justification for mounting the military campaign that Mac's given us."

"Sir," said General MacAdoo, "we're now talking about major changes in the military commander's plan. I think General Remington should be part of this discussion."

"Not yet," said Easterly, more sharply than he intended to. "We're discussing this at the concept level. Now is not the time to get into the weeds about tactics."

MacAdoo reddened but said nothing in reply.

"Mac," said the president, "what do *you* think about Bart's approach?"

"I understand the politics of it, sir," said MacAdoo. His body language said far more.

Dorn caught the president's eye, saw him nod slightly, then said, "All right. Mr. President, I recommend we have General Remington look at the approach Bart suggests and get back to us with a plan."

"Let's do that. Thank you, all."

Chapter 52

TEHRAN, ISLAMIC REPUBLIC OF IRAN

I T HAD BEGUN AS A tingling, just a feeling he got when his subconscious was beginning to see small objects bobbing, spinning, and drifting in the deep pool of his mind. Like when an archaeologist uncovers enough fragments to sense more there to see, a bowl or a cup. Indeed, Yazdan Lajani thought of himself as an archaeologist of the present, assembling opinions, conjecture, and occasionally demonstrable conclusions from fragments of information he had sifted from the internet, agent reports, public statements, interrogations, trade data, the ebb and flow of electronic communication, and anything else that caught his attention.

Yazdan came to believe in his theory the way Columbus had believed there were lands and riches beyond the sea. But his bosses in Iran's intelligence organization were unconvinced—or more aptly put, were unwilling to be convinced because his was not a message that snapped into place, Lego-like, with the received wisdom that Israel would never dare initiate a war with the Islamic Republic.

Like Italian Cristoforo Colombo when he had approached the king of Spain, Yazdan Lajani was both running out of options and had entered a foreign land when he stepped into the office of Adel Ghorbani. And also like Columbus, Lajani had to travel far, bureaucratically speaking, to obtain an appointment with the commander of Quds Force and head of the nuclear missile program. But he had persisted, and here he was.

"Thank you for seeing me, General."

Ghorbani, seated at a desk with neatly arranged stacks of papers to the left and right of a yellowish blotter, looked up, gazing at Lajani with inquisitive eyes.

"Be seated, Lajani, and tell me why you risked a visit to someone your boss regards with suspicion." Lajani's prominent Adam's apple bobbed as he swallowed hard and took the chair centered in front of Ghorbani's desk.

"I am not a brave man, General. But I have what some call a foolish devotion to truth."

"Then by all means speak your truth."

"General, the Israelis are preparing to attack all your nuclear and missile sites. So many signs point to this. Yet many, including my superiors, believe that because it would trigger a war the Israelis cannot win, they would never do that."

"Of course they're preparing, Lajani. They've been preparing that attack for at least ten years. Planning to rip the heart out of your country's worst enemy is what military organizations *do*. But what makes you think they *will?*"

"Many things. We have an agent within the IAF Munitions Division. She has learned that the Israeli company IMI, which manufactures many of the bombs, rockets, and artillery shells used by Israeli armed forces, obtained a Russian deep penetration bomb last year. It's similar to the ones the Americans call MOAB. After examining the Russian bomb, IMI has begun manufacturing them."

"Yes, I know of the MOAB," said Ghorbani. "And I know that it weighs far too much for any of the Jews' combat aircraft to carry."

"General, you know of Israel's Yellow Bird squadron of C-130J Hercules transports, do you not?"

"Of course. They're based in the Negev, poor bastards."

Lajani continued: "The C-130s have been observed by Egyptian intelligence—and we have contacts there, Shia brothers—at an Israeli bombing range. They approach at very low altitudes, fifty to one hundred feet, then climb steeply just before reaching the target. At about five thousand feet they release a large object from their cargo bay. It slides out their rear doors, as if it were a pallet of food or ammunition. But they're not rehearsing a cargo delivery method, because these objects have no parachutes, other than the small ones that pull them out of the cargo bay.

They free-fall. These transport aircraft have never before been observed at a bombing range. And never have they been seen to maneuver in that way.

"The American bomb weighs thirty thousand pounds. And the C-130J has the lift capacity to haul a thirty-seven-thousand-pound payload from Ramat David Air Base to any of our special facilities that I know of."

"And your conclusion is?" said Ghorbani, stroking his silver-black beard.

"The Yellow Bird squadron is preparing to drop MOAB-type weapons on your facilities, General. What else could it be?"

"I don't know ... maybe they're now able to deliver fuel bladders that way without bursting them. Maybe it's a huge napalm canister. And even if you are correct, this becomes a new capability but not necessarily one the Jews would dare to use. You said 'preparing' to attack. I say what you saw was *practice* to attack, which is not the same."

"General, during your military studies, surely you reviewed the 1973 Yom Kippur War. You know that the Jews were caught by surprise, not because attack preparations were undetected, but because the Israeli high command and government refused to see them for what they were. They didn't believe the Egyptians would dare attack; ergo, what was observed could not be attack preparations."

Ghorbani nodded.

Lajani let the information brew in silence, then said, "Israel paid dearly for its leaders' refusal to acknowledge truth."

Lajani paused again, then said, "Remember the Osirak reactor in Iraq, General? No one thought the Jews would dare strike it. But they did. And more recently they destroyed the Syrian reactor, the one being built with North Korean help."

"All right, I'll give you that. But striking Iraq and Syria is not striking Iran. Taking out all our buried facilities would be much harder than hitting those single targets, unprotected and close to Israel. Refueling would limit them to a few strike aircraft. In fact, unless their planes overflew Syria and Iraq or Jordan and Saudi Arabia, they wouldn't have enough fuel to return."

"True, General. But I have also seen evidence that the Israeli Air Force is converting several El Al Boeing 737s into tankers for strike aircraft. And right now Iran has many powerful enemies besides Israel. The Americans, of course, but perhaps the Chinese, too. And especially the cursed Saudis. Who can say they wouldn't just ignore a strike on us as it passed over them?"

Ghorbani's face had changed from skeptical to thoughtful. "I can see why your conclusion isn't popular," he said.

"Bring me all your raw intelligence on this matter. Tell no one you are doing so."

* * *

WASHINGTON, DC, AND BEIJING, PEOPLE'S REPUBLIC OF CHINA

"So how hard should I push Ming to assign more ships to the joint strait force?" President Martin's words were addressed to the three men and a woman seated on the couches and chairs in front of his desk in the Oval Office.

"I think the fact of China's *participation* is more important than how much they contribute," said Secretary of State Battista.

"I agree," said Secretary of Defense Easterly. "We don't have the technical means to actually integrate Chinese ships into our battle group. Besides the language issues, our computer networks don't exchange information."

"And shouldn't!" interrupted the vice president.

"As I was saying," resumed Easterly, glaring at Vice President Griffith, "however many ships the Chinese provide, they will operate on their own, in their own area. Mac is a little miffed that they're not making more effort, but he's satisfied with the one destroyer and a minesweeper. Actually, Mac said they may have a nuke sub in the area, too, based on a couple of brief, inconclusive sonar contacts."

"It's time, Mr. President," said his translator. Martin squared his shoulders, took a sip of water, and punched his speakerphone.

"Good evening, Ming."

"Good morning, Rick."

"Ming, we've observed no sign that the Supreme Leader is going to comply with our demand that he clear the mines and reopen the strait. Is it the same with you?"

"We see no active preparations, but the Iranians could be waiting until the last minute. I'm not yet ready to assume we must use force."

"Nor am I. But I believe we should be clear between us what we will do if the deadline passes without compliance. As our military leaders have agreed, we will send minesweepers, escorted by an American destroyer and a Chinese destroyer, to clear the minefield. I'm sure you agree that this is a minimal force, nothing that could be called an attempt to bring down the regime?"

"I do, but it is what the Iranians think that is most important. And with your aircraft flying from Saudi Arabia and Qatar, they will be alarmed and angry. They will see an Arab-American conspiracy to weaken Iran."

"Ming, those aircraft will do nothing but patrol outside Iranian airspace unless the ships are attacked." As his eyes scanned faces, Martin saw the vice president reddening and Easterly looking pleased as he scribbled on a notepad.

"Just the same, I believe the Iranians will see it as a provocation," rejoined Ming.

Martin read the note from Easterly: *The planes can sit strip alert and still be overhead in minutes. I could live with that.*

"Ming, we've been through this before. You agreed to this plan."

"Rick, I can offer a way around this issue. I have spoken with the Supreme Leader. He will allow free passage to ships of any country that respects Iran's sovereign rights."

Vice President Griffith appeared ready to explode. The secretary of state and Bart Guarini looked relieved, and Easterly was unreadable.

Martin said, "Respects Iran's sovereign rights. What does that mean, Ming?"

"That's to be determined. But the point is that Iran is offering to negotiate the reopening of the strait. And China will not participate in use of force while diplomacy still has promise."

And that, Martin realized, was Ming's bottom line. He couldn't ignore it unless he wanted to do this alone. And he didn't.

"Ming, that offer is like a thief negotiating how much stolen money to return! This may be a promising development, but I fear it may simply be a ploy to undermine the unity of the many seafaring nations that condemn Iran's actions."

Ming remained silent. Martin sighed, looked around the room, and seeing no reaction except Griffith mouthing no, said, "But we shouldn't ignore it. Let's direct our foreign ministers to issue a joint statement announcing this development and extending the deadline."

After ending the call, Martin looked around at those gathered in the Oval Office and said, "Well, one thing about this job: it's never boring. So what do you think?"

His face scarlet, Bruce Griffith blurted, "*Damn* those Chinese. We should never have trusted them!"

"This was never about trust, Bruce," said the president firmly. "It was about working to solve a common problem."

"Ming led us out on a limb, and he just sawed it off! Let Ming back down, but we shouldn't. We should stand by what we told the world: one week, or we come in."

"I don't see it that way," said Battista with a shake of her head. "While Iran's offer was made *to* China, it isn't *limited* to China. Yes, this could be no more than a shrewd move by the Iranians to split those allied against them. But it could also be a way out of this without either sending the minesweepers in nearly defenseless or mounting an air campaign that could land us in another Middle East war."

"Eric?" said the president.

"Exploring this offer doesn't change the military situation significantly. Yes, it gives them the opportunity to enlarge the minefield, but enlarging it doesn't really change our immediate challenge, clearing a channel. I don't see a military problem with putting the joint operation on hold."

"OK, go to work on this," said Martin. "As for me, it's time to congratulate the winner of the National Spelling Bee.

"Bruce, stay with me a minute."

Martin came from behind his desk and stood, arms folded across his chest, as Griffith approached, walking stiffly and scowling.

"Bruce, what would you have us do when China threatens to pull out? We need China to have skin in the game."

"You mean more than the destroyer and its dead crew?" snapped the vice president.

"That's only part of it, Bruce. Don't you realize that with a Chinese ship escorting the minesweepers, the Iranians will think twice before attacking them? Do you really want to be running for president with a war going on, a war that began on *our* watch?"

"I'd want even less to be running on the record of an administration that had caved to Iran!"

"Bruce!" Martin visibly held back a moment. "Thanks for your counsel, Bruce." Martin's tone was dismissive. Griffith jutted his chin and stalked out of the Oval Office.

Turning, Martin saw Guarini standing by the door that separated their offices.

"Bart, you need to let Bruce know that I'm not having any of his 'deep background' grumbling about this—nor any by his staff. If he wants my backing to sit in this office, he better stay on my team."

"My thought, exactly, sir. I'll take care of it. And something else: Why did the Supreme Leader make this offer to negotiate? Could it be for the reason you gave, to split us and the Chinese? But maybe it's because he genuinely believes Israel is about to attack. Maybe Ghorbani is telling the truth."

"And Ghorbani's still quiet," said Martin. "We've *got* to get that channel open! I've *got* to have more to go on before I risk a break with Israel. Ray's the only one who can do that. Tell him I need him to do whatever it takes to get back in touch with Ghorbani. And, Bart, make sure he has any authorities he needs."

Chapter 53

J*UST WRITE. AT THIS STAGE don't concern yourself with telling an orderly story in strong prose. Making it orderly and interesting is my job. Yours is to remember and to write it down.*

Ray Morales remembered the words of his coauthor as he sat at the keyboard. The man who had said that, Nicholas Tibbets, wasn't a ghostwriter. His name would appear on the jacket. Morales preferred it that way, and so did Tibbets, who had written several books "with" public figures from business and politics. Before accepting the book deal that would link him to Tibbets, Morales had read those books and felt they were solid and honest, without the sensationalism he was determined to avoid.

So he had signed, and now it was time to write. Tibbets had said it didn't matter where he began; one thing would lead to another. The more he wrote, the more he would be able to write.

So what were the major phases of his life and life's work? He grew up with a sister, the children of legally immigrated Mexican parents, in the Tex-Mex culture of San Antonio. Nothing extraordinary or interesting in that; there were thousands of kids like him in Texas.

But in his senior year of high school, he took his first steps down the path that would lead him to his life's work, service to America. He applied and was chosen by one of Texas's senators for appointment to the Naval Academy in Annapolis. Looking back, he supposed his appointment had been due to many things: excellent grades, four letters each in football and in track—he had been a tackle and a shot-putter—a ticked box for his heritage for both the senator and the academy, and, perhaps, his essay. He had written that he wanted to serve his country by being a Marine officer.

Morales grinned. Twenty-four years after graduation, he had returned to Annapolis as the director of English and history and a senior Marine. The Corps always assigned one of its high-flyer colonels to this billet, to spot and then lobby midshipmen who had the right stuff to choose a commission in the Marines and also to serve on the admissions board and keep an eye out for more of the same. From that experience he could imagine how he had once looked to the senior Marine: a big athletic kid who might help two Academy sports, had good grades, got good test scores, and wants to be a Marine. That colonel would have taken his application and run with it, selling him hard to other board members. The unknown colonel's advocacy was soon justified by three letters in track, selection as commander of a company of midshipmen, and commissioning as an officer of Marines. But really nothing exceptional in all that. Two hundred others in his class had become Marine officers. He could duly cover it in a short chapter.

But there was a delicate issue during those Annapolis years. He scratched his chin and frowned. He had met Graciella Dominguez, a Princeton student, after a track meet, and they had been hot and heavy for two years before drifting apart upon graduation as he devoted himself to the Corps and she to Columbia Law. That was where she had met Rick Martin. And now she was Ella Martin, First Lady of the United States. And last year there had been Camp David. That momentary mutual weakness was hidden from view, so the less said about their former relationship the better. But if he didn't mention her in his book, surely someone would dig up their college romance and question why he hadn't mentioned it. That would lead in a dangerous direction. Well, he had plenty of time to decide how to handle it.

After fifteen minutes at the computer, he had not written anything.

Tibbets had said he could begin writing anywhere, at any point in his life, and the two of them would fill in, upstream and downstream, from there. So what were the most significant events of his career in the Marines? He smiled, thinking of an early event that only another Marine infantry officer would truly appreciate: he had had a great gunnery sergeant during his first assignment.

About two weeks after he had reported to Bravo Company, Sixth Battalion, Twenty-Second Marine Division, as a platoon officer, Gunnery Sergeant Zitzwitz had taken him aside after the morning run. "Lieutenant," he said, "I think you've got the raw material to lead Marines. If you listen to me, run this platoon through me, say only what's necessary, and keep your shoes shined, I will make you the best damn platoon officer in this division." The green first lieutenant had known enough to recognize good fortune and offered his hand and his loyalty to his gunny. The gunny had kept his promise, and that first assignment was the beginning of a stellar career. Morales had good instincts, toughness, and tactical skills that earned the loyalty of his Marines, plus smarts, thoroughness, and political savvy that marked him for staff assignments deemed critical to the Corps. That, plus luck, had taken him to four stars and the highest military post in America: chairman of the Joint Chiefs of Staff.

Most of that career wouldn't make for exciting reading. Oh, he would give his views on leadership, loyalty up and down, the characteristics of a good staff officer. Maybe a few vignettes of well-known figures he had served for and for in the Pentagon and on the National Security Council. But he would focus on his one combat tour, battalion command during Desert Storm, draw out the lessons, strains, rewards, and emotions of leading Marines in war. And there was the night he had made the acquaintance, at knife point, of Naved Singh, regimental sergeant major in the Pakistani Army. That had been the improbable beginning of a relationship of mutual respect that had been critical, years later, to identifying North Korea as the source of a nuke in the hands of Fahim al-Wasari. That and the stoic heroism of his Marines, who had scrapped house-to-house in one of the towns where Saddam's army stood and fought.

And there was one other moment that Morales, despite his self-effacing instincts, acknowledged had been high drama: his resignation as chairman of the Joint Chiefs of Staff. He had acted as a matter of conscience when, despite his factual warnings and strenuous objections, President Glenna Rogers had ordered a rapid withdrawal of the majority of troops from Iraq. He believed that not only the timing but the procedures for this would lead to unnecessary casualties and loss of much that had been gained with the blood of men and women like those he had led there during the First Gulf

War. When he did not prevail in his petition, he resigned, not in anger but because he could not support that decision.

His secure cell phone chirped with a call identified as "White House." Coming out of his reverie, he answered, part of his mind chiding himself for *still* having written nothing.

"Morales."

"Ray, this is Bart. I'm calling with an urgent request from the president. The NSC has just concluded a full assessment of the situation in the Middle East, including of course Ghorbani's view of it and our own intel. The community now believes there's a substantial possibility that Israel is indeed preparing a deep strike on Iran. The president is prepared to act to prevent that, but he needs harder evidence of Israel's intentions. So far, Ghorbani has offered none. He needs you to go back to Ghorbani and press him for his evidence. Ideally, the president needs physical or documentary evidence. Can you do that?"

Morales's demeanor changed instantly from this injection of excitement, recognition, and power. He belonged again. His drifting was over. He had a mission. And one more thing.

I'm going to get my shot at evening the score with Ghorbani!

Chapter 54

TEHRAN, ISLAMIC REPUBLIC OF IRAN

WHY DO PEOPLE BETRAY THEIR countries, their homelands, their comrades? The question was merely an excursion, a distraction from a profound, looming decision, but Adel Ghorbani welcomed it.

Face it, Adel, you're not ready to make the real decision yet.

So he let his mind wander. Some spy because they believe in the cause they are serving by spying. Some because they hate the country or organization or person they're spying on. Some are being blackmailed; that was an especially rich vein to mine: shame, danger to loved ones, fear for their own lives. Some spy for money. Some are driven by an ego so huge that they do it to demonstrate their superiority.

Fifteen years ago, Ghorbani had been a spymaster. He had encountered nearly every motivation. He preferred spies motivated by money, which was usually the most reliable incentive. A straightforward transaction. Not without its risks, however. You hoped your spies had the self-discipline not to flash wealth, but sometimes they didn't. And an agent motivated solely by money (and of course survival) was one of the easiest to turn. Outbid the current employer, and you have a double agent. Still, money was the best.

Although those days were behind him, he had inquired about Iran's agent inside the Israeli air force munitions organization. She spied for money. That was a plus. And she thought she was spying for her birth country, America; all face-to-face meetings had been during her visits to her parents. She'd been working for Iran—and maybe for others—for seven years. Her product had been high quality. Sometimes her information had been incorrect but never in a way that suggested she was a double. But she might be. You could never rule that out. And she might be wrong. But she had provided photographs of engineering drawings she said were of Israel's MOAB. She had also photographed the weapons themselves. All of that could be faked, of course.

So Ghorbani was back where he'd been many times in his years of serving Iran: back to relying on his gut. And his gut said this was true.

Today his housekeeper, Caspara, had the day off. She had cooked his dinner the evening before and left it for him to reheat. Ghorbani rose and crossed his small, well-appointed apartment, needing some distracting physical action to free his subconscious mind to examine and reexamine the decision he would not yet admit he had made. He focused his conscious mind on the simple motions of dinner preparation, moving from refrigerator to microwave to dish. He put his meal on a tray and took the tray to the living room, where he settled on a couch...

Again he weighed what he knew and what he believed that meant. The Israeli Air Force's C-130 cargo planes were practicing a maneuver more like dropping a huge bomb than delivering cargo. A reliable agent reported that Israel was secretly manufacturing very heavy deep penetration bombs, which only the C-130s could lift. Other agents had seen early-model F-15s with new conformal fuel tanks that doubled their range. Some C-130s were being converted to refuel F-15s and F-16s. El Al had pulled its new long-range Boeing 737s from regular service, supposedly to reconfigure their cabins. But by withdrawing all of them at once, they had maximized disruption to their commercial flight schedules. What would be so important that they would do that? Maybe using them as airborne refuelers? And just yesterday Lajani had reported that the Jews were relocating their Patriot anti-missile batteries from sites chosen to defend cities against attacks from Gaza to positions that appeared chosen to defend cities against missiles coming from Iran. Israelis whose neighborhoods were being hit from Gaza would be very angry. Why create that political problem?

Ghorbani sighed, chewed, thought, and returned his dishes to the small kitchen. This set of occurrences could be a coincidence. But what were the odds of that? And if *not* coincidence, what could they mean except that

Israel is preparing for a large air strike deep into Iran and girding for Iran's response? *Nothing! There's nothing else they can mean.*

And if that happened? The Supreme Leader would order him to retaliate with the three nuclear bombs his engineers had assembled, as yet untested but from a proven Chinese design. And Israel would respond twofold, or more. It would be the end of both countries.

If I tell the Supreme Leader, he will order me to strike Israel first, and the death spiral will begin.

Ghorbani was certain the only way to prevent this was to stop the Israeli attack. And only one person could stop Askenazi: the American president. But how to convince him to act?

Through Morales.

But Iranian intelligence at VAJA was alert now, and contacting Morales could mark Ghorbani as a traitor. He must assume from his surprise warning in the park that VAJA was now scanning specifically for his number and Morales's number. The regime had learned from the Green Movement in 2009 that cell phones were critical to organizing protest demonstrations. Since then, cell service had become tightly monitored, with help from the Chinese, the world's best at it.

It wasn't possible to walk into a store in Iran and purchase a cell phone. Phones and SIM cards were available only through a government agency that was the sole provider of cell service throughout the country. Records were kept; it was nearly impossible to make an anonymous cell call in Iran. Of course, Quds had access to sterile phones and SIM cards for its clandestine operations, but these, too, were on record with the bureaucracy as issued to Quds. The obvious solution of using burners to remain in anonymous contact with Morales was not available to Ghorbani.

He considered risking a call from a phone registered to Quds but not to him. Still, the risk would be great. Any cell phone would give VAJA his location relative to the nearest cell tower. If they decided to investigate the call, for any reason, he'd have only minutes—or less—before VAJA troops would be on him. And even if he avoided that, VAJA, a rival of Quds in Iran's security structure, would make a stink about phones issued to Quds being used by a traitor.

Too risky. I've got to find another way to reach Morales!

* * *

ARLINGTON, VIRGINIA

When Ray entered their apartment, Julie saw, as she always did, that he was wrestling with a problem in their lives. It was something about the set of his shoulders and the veiled look in his eyes. She knew he would be groping for the right moment to broach the subject, and he knew she anticipated something, so unspoken tension accompanied their dinner.

The time came after dinner as they cleared the table. "Julie, I've had a call from Bart. The president, and the country, are in a tough spot right now. Ghorbani raised the alarm about a preemptive Israeli attack on Iran's missile and nuclear programs. But since then, he's gone silent. If Ghorbani's claim is true, the president *must* intervene with Askenazi to head off the attack. Because if the attack comes, Iran—according to Ghorbani—will use weapons of mass destruction to retaliate. That response would cause the Israelis to pull their nuclear trigger. It would be mutually assured destruction."

Julie put down their plates and stood stiffly. This moment, she thought, is like when the dentist says, "This may hurt a bit." She said, "And this means *what* for you, Ray? For us?" Her right hand began twisting and worrying the wedding band on her left.

Ray moved to her and said, "The president needs me to reestablish contact with Ghorbani and get proof of his claim right away. I can't do that with a phone call. I've got to meet him."

"A phone call was enough before; why not again?"

"I don't have the means to call him. No secure number. We're pretty sure that he broke off the conversations because he was coming under suspicion. He would have trashed the phone he used to call me long ago." Ray shrugged.

"So meet him someplace safe," said Julie, scowling.

"If he's under suspicion, he would be closely watched during any travel outside Iran."

Wide-eyed, Julie said, "So, you're telling me you're going to go to him? *In Iran?* Ray, that's *nuts*! You're a well-known, sixty-six-year-old public figure. You don't look Persian and can't speak a word of the language. You'd be spotted and arrested the minute you got off the plane. How can you even *consider* that?"

His big hands beseeching reason, he said, "That's not how this would work, Julie."

She stalked to the kitchen window and gazed out, arms crossed, back straight, breathing deeply. "Work? There's no way it would work!"

Ray's voice rose. "Yes, Julie, it *can* work. Just hear me out, please!"

Slowly she turned but didn't meet his eyes.

"Here's how this would work. I allow myself to be captured in the Strait of Hormuz, like those US sailors who got lost there about seven, eight years ago. That area is the responsibility of the Revolutionary Guard. They'll take me to their base in Bandar Abbas. Ghorbani will be informed immediately. I'm betting he needs this meeting as much as we do. He will come at once, supposedly to interrogate me. Under those circumstances we get to meet without causing suspicion of him. He'll provide his evidence, and a SPECOPS team will bring me back with it."

"Ray, that's a setup where everything depends on Ghorbani, a man you don't know and don't trust. How can you put yourself in that position?"

Ray rubbed the back of his neck. "Because there's no other way."

"Why *you*? This is a job for a trained operative."

Ray shook his head. "Ghorbani won't come for anyone else."

She looked straight at him for the first time and said, quietly, "And if Rick Martin doesn't have the evidence he needs to handle Askenazi, there will be nuclear war in the Middle East."

"Yes."

Julie looked away, then met his gaze and said, "Ray, this is the last time! I didn't marry Ray Morales the young Marine deploying to dangerous places all over the world. I *wouldn't* have married that Ray Morales. I don't see how military wives *stand* that strain. I married the Ray Morales whose days in the field were behind him. Then came Idaho and now *this*!

"Ray, no more. After this, I'm *done*. Promise me you'll never again put yourself at risk like this!

Ray started to speak, then stopped. He squared his shoulders. "I promise."

Chapter 55

THE PERSIAN GULF

SEATED IN HIS CHAIR, *AGERHOLM*'s captain adjusted the focus of his binoculars, bringing the deck of the minesweeper *Sentry* into clearer view. He saw a coverall-clad figure, wearing a blue hardhat, clip a hoisting cable onto the remote operating vehicle resting in a cradle, then signal for it to be lifted. It was swung over the side and into the green, greasy-looking waters of the Strait of Hormuz and released to hunt mines. Readjusting his binoculars, Captain Greenhouse swung them to his left, where he saw through the pilothouse windows the grayish smudge of Larak Island with its Iranian garrison and missile launchers.

Greenhouse put the heavy 8×50 binoculars on his lap. *Agerholm*, *Sentry*, and a Chinese destroyer and minesweeper to seaward of Larak Island were clearing mines from international waters. They were chips in a poker game, out on the table to be scooped up by the winner of this hand. The little flotilla had been at it for a week, and the White House's bet that the Iranians wouldn't interfere hadn't been called. They had made considerable progress in clearing a mine-free path.

Picking up the binoculars again, Greenhouse focused on a hulking shape hull-down at the horizon: the battleship *Iowa*. Her huge guns and Harpoon missiles, plus the aircraft from *Stennis* orbiting ceaselessly nearby, would be unleashed if the mine clearance operation were attacked. That was encouraging, but he had no doubt that his ship would be heavily damaged if the Revolutionary Guard on Larak Island launched a swarm of missiles.

The intercom to the right of the captain's chair crackled, then spoke:

"Captain, TAO. Marathon reports a pair of Iranian F-14s airborne from Chabahar and heading our way. They're now about sixty miles northeast of us, in Iranian airspace."

Marathon was an air force E-3B airborne warning and control aircraft, usually referred to as AWACS. It was engaged in surveillance, identification, and the tracking of everything that flew within two hundred miles of its position in international airspace above the Persian Gulf.

Greenhouse felt a tightening in his stomach.

* * *

USS JOHN C. STENNIS, INDIAN OCEAN

Lieutenant Kaycee "Pecos" Jenkins was bored even though she was sitting in the cockpit of her F/A 18E Super Hornet strike fighter on seven minute alert. The boredom had set in an hour or so ago in the Ready Room of her squadron, VFA 124, while she was beating Lieutenant (Junior Grade) Jim "Steamboat" Gandy at Ace Combat 7. Steamboat was good at the video game but in flight, although he was fleet qualified in the Super Hornet, or "Rhino" as pilots called it, he had a lot to learn. Real aerial combat was a combination of procedure, improvisation, and stamina. It required a surgeon's knowledge and precision plus a gunfighter's instincts and quickness, even as the pilot's body and mind strained to function despite powerful G forces while flying a fighter to the limits of its performance. Gandy was a nugget, an inexperienced pilot on his first deployment and today he was her wingman. Right now he was sitting in the cockpit of another strike fighter on the catapult next to Jenkins.

They had assumed the alert seven duty about twenty minutes ago. Reaching her aircraft, and settling into the familiar pocket of the cockpit, Jenkins had run through prestart checks. Not only was that standard operating procedure; she was a big believer in preparation. She'd been raised on a ranch in Pecos County, Texas, first sat in a saddle around age three, and had been the West Texas Junior Barrel Racing Champion two years running. After that came a couple of years in the lower divisions of pro rodeo. You couldn't ride a quarter horse at full tilt, careening around barrels where a mistake could cripple or kill you, unless you were prepared.

You had to know yourself and your horse and exactly what you were capable of on that particular day.

"Launch the Alert Seven fighters," bellowed the flight ops announcing system, those words triggering a practiced rush of men and women on the flight deck to get the two F/A 18 Super Hornets airborne within seven minutes. The bright colors of the shirts they wore identified their various roles in the drama of launching and landing jets aboard *Stennis*.

At that announcement, Jenkins removed her right glove, spit a wad of gum into her hand, and stuck it on the right side rail of the cockpit. It was one of her preflight rituals, like putting the picture of her husband and daughters in a certain spot on her desk before heading for the Ready Room. Each time, she marveled that she had survived the risk-taking and full-throttle living of her rodeo years. Hornet pilots thought they were tough, and they were, but they had nothing on barrel-racers or bull-riders.

At a signal from the yellow-shirted taxi director, she tapped the throttles of her F/A 18E, squeezed the nose wheel steering button on the control stick, and maneuvered the twin-tailed jet into position on the inboard angle catapult of the USS John C. Stennis, now steady on aircraft launch course at twenty-five knots. One more signal from the yellow-shirted figure ahead and left of her aircraft, and she nudged the throttles slightly, while riding her brakes, just enough to bump the nose wheel into the catapult shuttle. A green-shirted figure completed the aircraft's attachment to the catapult, then signaled to Jenkins to ease off on her brakes.

Behind her aircraft—radio call sign Slingshot 301—jet blast deflectors rose from the flight deck to protect the busy area from the hellish blast about to issue from the aircraft's twin engines. Beneath the aircraft, a red-shirted ordnance man and a brown-shirted plane handler darted purposefully about, then scrambled clear, each signaling completion to a figure in a black-and-white checkered shirt on the flight deck to Jenkins's left. The catapult officer, or "shooter," wearing a yellow shirt, otherworldly in helmet and goggles amid a cloud of steam from the catapult track, made a vigorous circular motion with his right arm.

Jenkins advanced the twin throttles to full power, her eyes scanning the cockpit display screens. With a flick of her wrist she cycled the control stick, confirming that rudder, ailerons, and stabilators were functioning. Once the catapult began its rush toward the bow, any issue with flight controls or engines would probably kill her. Satisfied, she pushed the throttles past the detent and into afterburner, snapped a salute to the catapult officer, grabbed the "towel rack" grip that kept right hand clear of the stick, locked her left elbow to ensure she didn't accidently pull the throttles back when the G force hit her, and pushed her head back hard against the high-backed ejection seat.

From this moment until a few seconds after launch, Jenkins's life would be entirely in the hands of others: those who maintained and operated the catapult, the shooter who would make a last check and give the signal to fire, the green-jerseyed figure far to her left who would actually fire the catapult, the computer programmers who had written the code that would control Slingshot 301's autopilot until several seconds after the plane had been flung off the carrier's bow. She hated this time when she had no control.

Seeing her salute, the catapult officer, who had dipped one knee to the deck and was pointing upward with an outstretched arm, slashed it down to touch the flight deck, then raised it to point toward the bow. The catapult yanked Slingshot 301 forward, accelerating to 165 knots in three hundred feet. Jenkins, punched into her seat by five Gs, allowed the Super Hornet's computer to fly the aircraft for the first few seconds. Then, relaxing her left arm to a gentle touch on the throttles and grasping the stick with her right hand, Jenkins took flight control from 301's computer and put her aircraft into a climbing left turn as her wingman, Gandy, launched in Slingshot 317.

"Departure, Slingshot three oh one, airborne."

"Three oh one, take heading one two five and angels six point five. Switch to Strike Control on button eight."

"Departure, Slingshot three one seven, airborne."

"Three one seven, take heading one two five and join three zero one at angels six point five. Switch to Strike Control on button eight"

When Gandy had guided his aircraft into position, Jenkins said, "Strike Control, Slingshot three oh one, flight of two checking in, request vector to station."

"Three zero one, radar contact, take heading three one five, angels fifteen point five. Switch to Marathon control on button thirteen."

"Roger, switching."

"Marathon, Slingshot three oh one, flight of two Rhinos for your control, over."

"Roger, three oh one, radar contact, say your state and weapons."

"Three oh one, in the green, state eleven point five, on board Maverick and Rockeye, plus Fox two, Fox three, and twenty mike-mike."

"Three oh one, hot vector two eight five. Switch to Checkmate control on button ten as BARCAP. Be advised: Iranian F-14s orbiting about twenty miles inland from Bandar Abbas."

"Wilco, switching."

Feeling a jolt of adrenaline, Jenkins nudged her throttles to intermediate power, accelerating to five hundred knots. A glance to her left showed Gandy on her wing.

Damn! This is going to get interesting.

* * *

USS Agerholm's air intercept controller ordered the Hornets to position themselves in a barrier patrol between *Agerholm* and the Iranian F-14 fighters.

"Checkmate, this is Slingshot three oh one, flight of two Rhinos, on station, request vectors to the Iranian fighters."

"Hold your horses, three oh one. Weapons tight. Those guys are in Iranian airspace. Stand by and maintain BARCAP."

"Three oh one, wilco," replied Kaycee Jenkins, disappointment in her voice.

Jenkins squirmed in her ejection seat, hoping to relieve the numbness in her butt from over an hour in the cockpit. Slight relief obtained, she focused on the left panel of her cockpit display screens, her fingers flitting among the vertical rows of buttons on either side known to the pilots as "chicklets." Soon she had a tactical display of the entire eastern region of the Persian Gulf, data-linked from Marathon. The Iranian fighters were about forty miles away, putting Jenkins and her wingman within range of their missiles. She knew the F-14 Tomcat, which had been purchased from the United States before she was born, was obsolete but still dangerous in this situation. It was armed with active radar-guided missiles, perhaps old Phoenixes but more likely modern Chinese PL-12s. Those missiles could eat up forty miles in thirty to forty seconds.

This could really be the OK Corral. ROE don't let me shoot unless they shoot first. Quickly, she glanced at the screen where warning of an inbound missile would appear, feeling a familiar combination of eagerness and fear, as though she were waiting for the starter to launch her into another barrel-racing course.

Switching briefly to a private frequency known as Squadron Common, Jenkins said, "Steamboat. Here's how this goes. We're going to set up a weave so that one of us always has the angle to lock 'em up. If they lock us up with fire control radar, we lock them up. If they shoot, we evade, and then we go get 'em. Also, even if only one of them shoots, we take 'em both out. Got that?"

"Wilco, Pecos."

Feeling prepared, Jenkins turned her aircraft to the right, being careful to keep the Iranians within the detection arc of the radar in her aircraft's nose.

The attack happened so quickly that Jenkins had no time to think. She reacted as she had been trained. The stabbing missile warning symbol and the warbling in her earphones meant death was coming for her at over three thousand miles per hour. Jenkins wrenched her Hornet into a hard break turn to the left and throttled back, forcing the missile to deal with a different target aspect, reduced closure rate, and change of bearing. Breaking to its right, the missile streaked in pursuit but was now required to travel farther to kill its target. Simultaneously Jenkins's left thumb triggered the chaff button repeatedly, ejecting bundles of thin aluminum strips, creating false returns for the missile's radar that might lure it away from her aircraft.

They did not. The missile warning system continued to flash red and warble, and she fought the panic of being pursued by a remorseless, inhuman killer. With a flick of her right wrist she rolled inverted, then pulled the stick back, sending her aircraft plunging toward the Persian Gulf. That forced the missile's active radar seeker to look down, where its tracking ability was reduced.

"Marathon, Slingshot three oh one. The Iranian launched a missile at me!"

Now in a vertical dive, Jenkins shoved the throttles into afterburner, feeling the jolt of ignition. Within seconds she was at six hundred fifty miles per hour, headed straight down, nothing but the waters of the Gulf visible ahead. Reversing her aircraft's turn, she fought the crush of seven and a half Gs and felt her cheeks peel back. She swung toward a course at right angles to the missile's present path and began a delicate dance with her flight controls, juggling speed, turn rate, and angle of dive to control G force so that she didn't black out or tear the aircraft apart. The G-suit squeezed her hips, abdomen, and thighs; her ribs ached with the effort of breathing. Pursuing tenaciously, the missile was forced to change course repeatedly to maintain a lead angle, and with every turn it gobbled fuel and lost speed. Physics and aerodynamics were on Jenkins's side because the lower the two raced, the better the aircraft's performance was relative to the missile's. The pursuer was tiring, while the pursued grew stronger. At ten thousand feet Jenkins began pulling out of the dive and, by six thousand feet, was level over the gulf at nearly seven hundred miles per hour and pulling away from the missile, now out of fuel and chasing her on lift and momentum alone. Sweat-soaked and hyper-alert, she could see it dead astern of her Hornet, falling back, and felt sweet triumph. She next felt killing rage.

"Steamboat. You good?"

"Pecos, I'm on your four o'clock at ten miles and closing."

"All right. Let's get those bastards!"

"Checkmate, Slingshot three oh one. Picture?"

"Slingshot three oh one, Checkmate. Hostiles zero three five for twenty, angels twenty-three. Weapons free."

Fingers flying over the buttons on the stick and throttle, Jenkins set up for a missile shot at the closest F-14 Tomcat. When the head-up display showed the Iranian in the missile target basket, she twitched a finger and saw a flash to her right as an AIM-120 missile motor ignited. The sleek shape streaked ahead, leaving a faint smoke trail. It pitched up sharply, climbing into the blue sky and disappearing.

"Fox three," she radioed, and seconds later heard Steamboat announce his own shot.

Now at twenty-five thousand feet, engines and afterburners hurling them ahead with forty-four thousand pounds of thrust, Pecos and Steamboat charged toward the Tomcats at Mach one point two, one hundred twenty percent of the speed of sound. A flash told them one of their missiles had hit. But there was no second flash. Jenkins bared her teeth beneath her oxygen mask and strained for visual contact on the second Tomcat. Sweat stung her eyes, and she blinked to clear them. Suddenly, she saw the Tomcat!

"This is Slingshot three oh one. Splash one Tomcat; tally the second."

"Roger three oh one. Be advised you are approaching Iranian airspace. Do not enter Iranian airspace. I say again: do not enter Iranian airspace."

"Bullshit, Checkmate! That sumbitch shot at us. I'm authorized under hot pursuit rules."

"Three oh one, you are not authorized to pursue into Iranian airspace. Turn starboard, now! Take heading one two six for home plate."

Jenkins ignored that order to break off. She had the remaining Tomcat in sight. It was in a tight left turn, seeking to deny her the up-the-tailpipe shot she wanted, but the Hornet easily turned with the Tomcat, and Jenkins kept it in her cone of attack. The Sidewinder's heat seeker growled happily in her earphones as she twitched her index finger. The little missile flashed across the short distance and buried itself in the F-14's left tailpipe, which erupted. The Tomcat staggered, then dipped its left wing and lost altitude rapidly. When the aircraft had dropped several thousand feet, Jenkins saw the pilot and radar intercept operator eject and become tiny specks descending beneath white canopies.

"Splash the second Tomcat," crowed Jenkins.

Squadron Common came alive: "Pecos this is Boots. You will RTB immediately and report to me."

"Aye, aye, skipper," responded Jenkins to her squadron commander, still filled with the fierce joy of turning the tables on someone who had tried to kill her. Seventy minutes and an aerial refueling later, after catching the three wire and jolting to a stop on the flight deck of USS Stennis, she was only slightly less elated. She pulled the throttles back to idle, raised the Hornet's tailhook, and taxied to her parking spot. After shutdown and a brief word with her plane captain, she strode confidently, with a hint of swagger, to her meeting with Boots.

Chapter 56

TEL AVIV, ISRAEL

YA'EL BARAK FEARED FOR HIS nation's survival. Every Israeli always felt some concern for the survival of the country, but this was more. Far, far more. Over an early breakfast this morning, General Dan Rivkin had given him news that Barak feared was one of the last nails needed to close Israel's coffin. And this was not an abstract fear. Barak knew his wife and three kids and his parents and his wife's widower father would die after Operation Persepolis, as surely as the sun would rise the next day. Oh, and he would die, too. But that would be a mercy after the annihilation of his family and his country.

The news? That Jordan and Saudi Arabia had agreed to allow Israeli warplanes to traverse their airspace en route to and from Iran. He had met Rivkin over a breakfast of poached eggs and Israeli salad. They were not close; even in so small a nation as Israel, their paths had not crossed often as each rose to great responsibilities, Rivkin's defined by law and regulation, his own by seventeen years' loyal and brilliant service to Joshua Askenazi.

"Ya'el, the Saudis, and Jordanians have agreed. They'll ignore our strike aircraft and tankers on the day of Persepolis."

"Do you trust them to do that?"

"Yes, because it's in their interest that Persepolis succeeds."

"*Will* it succeed?"

"I believe so. It will at least delay the deployment of their nuclear missile force. It might stop it. Do you know about our Tunis strike back in eighty-five?"

"Yes, of course. You flew that mission, didn't you?"

Rivkin smiled. "Yes. Operation Wooden Leg. And that strike, like Persepolis, was thought to be beyond Israel's ability. Just too far away and too likely to generate worldwide condemnation. Arafat thought he and his lieutenants had safe haven in Tunis while their PLO thugs ran wild.

"By bad luck, only luck, we didn't kill him. But we flattened his headquarters building, killed several of his top henchmen, and sent a message: No one and no place is beyond our reach when Israel's survival is threatened. Under those conditions, no risk is too great for us to take. And you know what? Arafat behaved for quite a while after that."

"Yes, but Persepolis is a strike at well-defended targets in a nation of eighty million people, with military forces much larger than ours. Iran's people are willing to support long, bloody warfare when attacked. We saw that in the eight years of war after Iraq invaded Iran in the eighties. And unless Persepolis destroys any nukes they already have as well as their capacity to make more, they could respond by destroying cities, if not our nation itself."

"Barak, you could be right. But, number one: What are the consequences of allowing Iran to deploy a nuclear missile force? Because that's what Iran will do unless we stop it. And where does that leave us? How are we better off allowing that?

"Number two: We have enough nuclear weapons ourselves, now, and several ways to use them against Iran or any other enemy. We have aircraft, sub-launched missiles, and land-based missiles. It would be impossible for Iran to prevent at least some of those weapons from detonating over Tehran, Qom, and elsewhere. Khamenei knows this well. He will not risk it by using a lone nuke or two that might escape Persepolis.

"Bottom line: Operation Persepolis sends the message that Israel will *never* allow Iran to possess nuclear weapons. Best case, Persepolis destroys any nukes Iran now has and the means to make others. Iran retaliates in some manner but gives up its attempts to become a nuclear power. It will still be a very dangerous enemy, but it will not possess the means to carry out its threat to destroy Israel. Worst case, Iran manages to shield some nukes from destruction and resolves to continue to develop that force, but its deployment is set back for years. Iran of course retaliates, as in the best case, but does not dare do it with nukes. In the worst case, we might have to do another Persepolis, but we have prevented Iran from becoming a nuclear power in the next year—or less."

"Dan, there are lot of assumptions in Persepolis. If those assumptions are wrong, our two nations will destroy each other. Surely you realize that!"

"Of course I do, Ya'el. But the risks of accepting a nuclear-armed Iran outweigh the risks of Persepolis."

The two stared at each other across their breakfasts gone cold.

"So you're going to do this, Dan?"

Rivkin snorted. "If the PM gives the order, of course I am! I have a duty to obey the PM's orders. *And* I believe this is our best course of action. I will carry out Persepolis to the best of my ability. And Israel will be better off because of it!"

Was this how it felt living in the Warsaw ghetto in 1942? thought Barak. Was it as clear then as now that Jews were on a conveyor belt to oblivion? Only now their own leaders would be responsible.

* * *

Barak entered his boss's private office during a break in the PM's schedule, about eleven fifteen. Joshua Askenazi looked up expectantly.

"Well, what of it?"

"They have agreed."

Askenazi smiled and got a faraway look. Then he was fully present again. "It is ready." His strong baritone voice dropped to a whisper that Barak barely heard but recognized as a passage from the Nevi'im: "No one shall be able to resist you as long as you live. As I was with Moses, so I will be with you; I will not fail you or forsake you. Be strong and resolute, for you shall apportion to this people the land that I swore to their fathers to assign to them."

Barak felt as if someone had stepped on his grave.

* * *

NEAR THE STRAIT OF HORMUZ

Ray Morales sat on the uncomfortably hot plastic seat of a small navy patrol boat as it motored northeast through low, undulating waves near the Strait of Hormuz. He felt the warm breeze and smelled the odor of crude oil, patches of which he saw bobbing here and there. The sun had heated the boat's hull until it was too hot to touch as they set course for Iran, on a path south and east of the minefield. At least he hoped it was clear of the minefield, the true extent of which only the IRGC knew.

He was now committed to a plan of action many thought was crazy. But Ghorbani would only speak to him, and what he was doing was the only way they could meet without compromising Ghorbani.

I may be the biggest fool in creation. The trackers in my boot and in my belt buckle let our guys see where they take me, but if this is a trap, they will only help them find my body.

"Here they come, sir," said the SEAL chief petty officer at the controls of the boat, pointing to the white rooster tail of a boat near the horizon to starboard.

"Do it, Larry," the chief said to another SEAL, who busied himself at the engine, removing the fuel pump and replacing it with a defective unit.

"About time for us to go over the side," said the chief. "We'll put a pinger on their hull, and there's another team waiting near Bandar's entrance to follow from there. If this thing goes south right here, bang the hull twice, and we'll pop up and lend you a hand."

"Got it, Chief. Thanks for the company." Morales heard the engine sputter and die as the SEALS flipped over the side and disappeared. A small submersible, called an SDV, would return them to shore. As the Iranian boat bore down on him, he recalled his confident assertion to the incredulous special ops planners that Ghorbani would quickly learn of his capture and come to him. There was a team standing by to extract him once Ghorbani had freed him and provided proof of the allegedly impending Israeli attack. But that would be of no avail unless Ghorbani took control of the situation before Morales was dragged off for display in Tehran.

* * *

Al Udeid Air Base, Qatar

"Looks like the party's beginning," said the major monitoring the video feed of an MQM-9 Reaper drone. He pointed to the monitor in the Ops Center.

"About time," said a compact man next to him. "Those guys don't run very good surveillance."

"This is a crazy scheme, if you ask me," said the major. "But, of course, nobody asked me."

"I've seen crazier," said the other man, who was a SEAL lieutenant. "But never with a guy like Morales hanging out there. If something goes wrong on the water, we can probably get him out. But once he's in Bandar Abbas ... after that, all we can do is keep eyes on the pickup site and wait for him to get there."

"What if he doesn't get there?"

"Way above my pay grade, boss."

* * *

NEAR THE STRAIT OF HORMUZ

The Iranian patrol boat, around twice the size of Morales's craft, slowed about a hundred yards away, then moved toward him at idle speed. Morales saw a heavy machine gun on the foredeck, a crewman keeping it trained on him. He heard a shout, and then the machine gun fired a long burst over his head. When the Iranians had closed the distance by half, they began a slow circle around Morales's boat. They were suspicious, wondering if this boat with its unknown occupant was the bait in a trap.

Morales raised his hands above his head and shouted, "My engine has quit. I can't start it."

The patrol boat pulled alongside, several of its crew pointing weapons at Morales. He heard a burst of a language that he didn't understand, but the speaker's gesture was plain. Morales raised his hands again.

Adopting a relieved expression, Morales said, "I've been drifting for hours. I don't know what's wrong with it."

The Iranians said nothing, but two clambered down into the boat, their pistols pointed at him. One holstered his weapon and handcuffed Morales with zip ties pulled painfully tight. Both Iranians then manhandled him aboard their patrol craft, where he noticed the Iranian flag flying from a stubby staff above the helm position. One of the Iranians spoke again, and Morales was hustled below, accompanied by his two guards. The boat's engines roared, and the boat leapt ahead, the motion throwing him to the steel deck, where, unable to break his fall, he split his lip. His captors laughed as he struggled to right himself without use of his hands.

Chapter 57

BANDAR ABBAS, ISLAMIC REPUBLIC OF IRAN

THE ROOM WAS ALL HARD surfaces and sharp angles, as if designed to reinforce its purpose. The walls had once been white but were now grayish and splotched with patches of mildew and blood. The concrete floor beneath Ray Morales's bare feet was stained, scuffed, and cracked; an unforgiving sight to the many prisoners who had gazed at it to escape the scouring eyes of their interrogators. This room was humid with pain and fear and stank of sweat and tobacco smoke.

Morales, dirty, bloody, and dozing fitfully in a chair with his hands and feet manacled, was awakened by a commanding voice in the corridor and then the scrape of the door. With quick, angry strides Adel Ghorbani, clad in his greenish uniform of a Revolutionary Guards general, moved to him and delivered a backhanded slap that echoed off the concrete. Morales's head rocked to his right, and his eyes narrowed. Another welt appeared on his left cheek.

"So, your boat broke down?" shouted Ghorbani in Farsi. "You think we are stupid enough to believe that story?"

He grabbed Morales's grimy, blood-spattered tee t-shirt and yanked the man toward him. Thrusting his face down to nearly touch Morales's, he whispered, "I'm going to get you out of here. I have a message you must carry to your president."

Morales spat in his face.

With the quickness of a striking snake, Ghorbani's fist crashed into

Morales's nose. Blood dribbled from the American's nostrils, making its way through the stubble on his upper lip to drip onto his lap.

"You fool!" roared Ghorbani, resuming his native tongue. "I know all about your plan to infiltrate and kill our nuclear scientists! And now I'm going to parade you through the streets of Tehran after Friday prayers, in chains."

Swinging both hands, Ghorbani delivered an ear-ringing clap to Morales's temples and leaned close again.

"This message is worth both of our lives—understand?"

"Yes," mumbled Morales, through swollen lips.

Again in Farsi, Ghorbani roared "I'm going to make you crawl, American!"

After delivering another slap, Ghorbani turned, strode to the heavy steel door, and pounded on it. It flew open, and he exploded through it, shouting in Farsi.

Morales let his head sag, his gaze on the floor and his blood-spotted camo trousers. He was careful not to show that a huge surge of adrenaline and relief was having its effect.

Ten minutes later Ghorbani returned, accompanied by a pair of his Quds Force commandos and a frightened prison guard. The guard hustled to Morales and released him, the manacles clanking as they fell to the concrete floor.

At Ghorbani's command his men grabbed Morales by each arm and rushed him out the door and down a hall lined with cells, each marked by a door with a peephole. The smell of blood, urine, and despair was in the air. Soon, Morales was seated in the front passenger seat of Ghorbani's Chinese-made Tiguan SUV, and three Quds commandos were aboard another.

Ghorbani was silent until he had maneuvered the SUV out of the narrow, twisting streets of Bandar Abbas and into the countryside. Abruptly, he swerved to the roadside, parked, and turned to Morales. The sudden silence emphasized the change of mood.

"We meet again, General Morales," he said in a conversational tone. "I thought we might, someday. I had to hit you back there—I'm sure you understand."

"I knew it wasn't going to be a picnic, General," said Morales, with an energy that belied his beleaguered appearance. "I'm here because President

Martin sent me to convey his message to you for the Supreme Leader: if Iran attacks Israel with nuclear weapons, not only will the response be Israeli nukes, but we will also encourage and assist the Saudis to take control of what's left of Iran after that attack. And, should Iran use nuclear weapons against American forces, the president will respond in kind, as he did against North Korea."

Ghorbani's eyes flashed anger and he made a dismissive gesture. "You Americans are foolish to make common cause with the Saudis! As Sunnis are inevitably marginalized by Iran and our Shia brothers, they will grow ever more desperate and soon cause the very war you want to prevent."

He looked away, then back at Morales, and said evenly. "We are not fools. We have no reason to use a nuclear weapon against American forces— unless you give us one by attacking us."

"But," he continued, "that's not for today. Today, I have this message for President Martin: the nuclear missile warheads that will destroy Jewish cities are ready. Yes, we have never tested them. But others have. They will work, and you know it. The Israeli attack is now only days away. I have seen the intelligence, and I believe it. Tell your president we will use our missiles before they can be destroyed.

"If he wants to save the people in those cities and many thousand other lives," continued Ghorbani, "Martin must prevent the Israeli attack. And the information I have for you should be decisive when he tells that fool, Askenazi."

"I will deliver that message, General. But tell me, why are you so sure Israel will attack? President Martin will demand evidence before he approaches Askenazi, *if* he decides to do that."

"The evidence is here." Ghorbani pulled an envelope from the space between the front seats and gave it to Morales.

Ghorbani said, "So you've accomplished the first part of your mission. Now you must return. How can I help you?"

"Give me a pen and paper," said Morales. He wrote a set of GPS coordinates and handed the paper to Ghorbani. "Just get me there and leave."

"I will do that, and my men will ensure that no one interferes."

Ghorbani keyed the coordinates into his GPS, then said, "Ah ... the Gabrik Rural District, between Bandar Abbas and Chabahar. Not many people—good choice. I'll have you there in about six hours." He started the SUV, made a U-turn, and headed for a road junction they had passed earlier. The SUV with Ghorbani's men followed. Morales opened the envelope and scanned its contents. Then he fell asleep.

* * *

CREECH AIR FORCE BASE, NEVADA

"I have eyes on two vehicles approaching the pickup point." The air force captain who said those words was seated in a dimly lighted room of the base. His windowless environment was maintained at the chilly temperature and low humidity relished by the thousands of semiconductor chips that enabled the officer to observe and act in the Persian Gulf. It was lit mostly by the glow of video monitors and the flight instruments of the MQM-9 drone he was piloting in a lazy, looping figure eight just outside Iranian airspace. Not far away a pair of F-35 pilots orbited, scanning their radarscopes and the cloudless sky, hoping that one of Iran's fighters would go for the drone.

"Roger that," replied a major in the disciplined hubbub of the Tactical Operations Center. He glanced at a compact man in desert camo, John Deere green baseball cap pulled low over his eyes, dozing in a plastic chair against the cream-colored wall. He decided not to wake him yet.

* * *

GABRIK RURAL DISTRICT, IRAN

As the SUV approached the grid coordinates, swaying and bumping over rough ground, Ghorbani eyed Morales and said, "I think it took a brave man to come here as you did. There was no certainty your capture would turn out as it has. And last year you showed courage"—Ghorbani smiled slightly—"and perhaps foolishness, in going after Fahim personally.

"You were prepared to die bravely, fighting unarmed against Fahim's knife. I've fought and killed many men. Some of them just gave up; I could see it in their eyes. But others ... you are one of the others."

Morales looked at Ghorbani with hooded eyes, suspicion warring with curiosity, then said, "Sometimes there's no choice. You know that, I'm sure.

"But why did *you* risk coming to America? Why were you after Fahim, too? Surely the Supreme Leader wasn't unhappy that he was terrorizing the Great Satan."

"Just as you said. Sometimes you have no choice. Think, General. You now know what Fahim planned with the tanker and the nuclear power plant so near the LNG terminal. After Nine-Eleven, America invaded the two countries it held responsible and hung the leaders of one of them. After Fahim destroyed Las Vegas, you destroyed a North Korean city with nuclear missiles. What country would you have invaded or bombed if Fahim's plan had worked, and that nuclear reactor had contaminated the Chesapeake Bay and much of Maryland, maybe even Washington? We believed you would have struck Iran. To protect Iran, Fahim *had* to be stopped. And since you Americans were failing at that, my men and I had to do it."

Morales looked angry, then puzzled. "But Fahim had no connection to Iran. He was a Sunni. He was a Brit with Palestinian roots who radicalized and fought with Zarqawi in Iraq. What made you think we would blame Iran?"

"When the truth is inconvenient, politicians will invent another one. Iraq had no connection to Nine-Eleven. The Saudis did. Yet your president chose to invade Iraq and take no action against the Saudis."

Morales looked skeptical. "I know President Martin. He wouldn't have repeated Bush's mistake."

Ghorbani shrugged. "So you believe. And you might be right. But we could not take that chance."

Morales nodded. "OK, I see that.

"But," he continued, "what happened on the Chesapeake Bay that day?" It *was* your guys who stopped Fahim's men from blowing up the tanker as it docked at Calvert Cliffs, wasn't it?"

Ghorbani smiled. "Yes. We had a team at Crisfield monitoring LNG tankers in the bay, which was easy to do because they were required by your navigation rules to broadcast their movements."

Morales scowled. "Was it your team that murdered the Coast Guard security boat crew?"

Ghorbani's expression hardened. "I don't know because no one in that team returned from their mission. But I don't think so. They would have had no reason to do that as long as the tanker was safe. Fahim's men would have had to deal with that security patrol in order to seize the tanker. The mission of my men was the same as the Coast Guard's: to protect the tanker. And they did. You should be grateful, not accusing them of murder!"

Ghorbani looked at his GPS display. "We have arrived." He braked the SUV.

"At our first meeting I saved your life. Now you are saving mine— by saving the lives of the Persian people and the existence of our Islamic Republic itself. We are even now, General. I wish you well."

Not quite even, thought Morales, but he said, "You're going to have a lot of explaining to do after it becomes known that you took me out of that prison but didn't deliver me to Tehran. We can pull you and your men out now; there's a backup aircraft that can be here in thirty minutes."

"No, General Morales. My men and I can take care of that. Iran is surrounded by enemies, and I am needed here. Like you, I long ago accepted that serving my country might cost my life. And besides, I am more powerful than you know. I have the loyalty of Quds, the most powerful fighting force Iran possesses. The Supreme Leader needs me, and he knows it.

"Once again we part company, General Morales. You *must* convince your president to stop Askenazi and his Operation Persepolis!"

"We may need to talk again before this is over," said Morales. Ghorbani frowned, but Morales said, "I have a safe way to do that. Give me something to write with."

Ghorbani produced a notebook from his pocket and handed it to Morales. Morales wrote as he spoke: "At this location in Qeytariyeh Park next Thursday you will find three untraceable phones. The one with the lowest SIM serial number is for the rest of this month. The second lowest is for next month, and the third for the following month. No call longer than five minutes."

After returning the notebook to his pocket, Ghorbani stepped back and offered a salute. Morales returned it.

A few moments later, he stood with three Quds soldiers, waiting for extraction. He watched Ghorbani's SUV head toward Bandar Abbas; Morales knew it was being tracked by an armed American drone. And he also knew Ghorbani would assume that because it's what he would have done in Morales's position. Once aboard the pickup aircraft soon to arrive, Morales could give the order, and Ghorbani's SUV would be transformed into burning wreckage. Quds would become leaderless again and less dangerous, for a while, as a result. But the United States would lose its only direct contact within Iran's senior leadership, someone who, at least in these circumstances, wanted to prevent war. So Morales would not give that order. The decision pleased him. He would spare Ghorbani's life for the same reason Ghorbani had spared his. Knowing Ghorbani knew that let Morales feel whole again.

* * *

Al Udeid Air Base, Qatar

The major in the Ops Center of Al Udeid Air Base was on the radio with the drone pilot at Creech Air Force Base. The pilot had zoomed in the drone's video camera on one of four men standing next to an SUV in a treeless, sandy area. He wanted the major to confirm his identification.

The major picked up a photograph of Ray Morales, compared it to the screen, and said, "I make him as General Morales." The major then turned to the SEAL dozing in a chair near him and said, "Saddle up. Your passenger is waiting."

Chapter 58

THE SITUATION ROOM

"SIR, THE ISRAELI GOVERNMENT HAS what it believes is convincing evidence that Iran has assembled three nuclear bombs and is preparing to mate them with Shahab-3 missiles."

"How can the Israelis know?" replied the president to Aaron Hendrix, director of national intelligence.

"Communication intercepts. They claim to have overheard a conversation between one of the Chinese missile engineers in Iran and a warhead engineer in China where they discussed a problem with accommodating the warhead on the missile."

"Do we have anything of our own to corroborate that intercept?"

"No, sir. Israel monitors Iranian communications more closely than we do, ordinarily. Since receiving this information, we've committed additional assets."

"Do you believe it, Aaron?"

"We've had our folks go over the recording of that intercept. NSA ran the voiceprints through its files, and the voices do match those of two Chinese engineers known to be involved in Iran's ICBM program. So, yes, I believe the conversation took place.

"But," he continued, "the question is, what does it *mean*? To Mossad it means Israel is in imminent danger of nuclear attack. But I come back to the fact that Iran has never tested a nuke. And why would they risk certain Israeli nuclear retaliation by preempting with only three weapons?"

"We can't dismiss his threat out of hand," said the president, Ghorbani's words to Morales very much on his mind.

"But sir, that intercepted conversation told us there's a problem mating the warheads to the missiles," said Easterly.

"Aaron, when did that conversation take place?" said Martin.

The DNI tapped on his keyboard, looked intently at his computer, and said "six days ago, sir."

"So we can't rule out that since then some engineer has solved the problem. Or that one might solve it tomorrow. I'm not going to ignore this."

There was no rejoinder.

Breaking the silence, the president said, "But as Aaron said a minute ago, the issue right now is, What does that intercepted phone call mean to Askenazi?" continued Martin.

"Apparently he's taking it seriously, Mr. President," said the director of national intelligence. "Israel's Patriot missile defense systems are being relocated to provide maximum protection against Iranian missiles. The Israelis keep one sub with nuclear cruise missiles always at sea. The next sub in rotation has been put on deployment alert. And their third missile sub, which is undergoing routine repairs and updating, is now being rushed to completion twenty-four seven. Plus, the other unusual activities we spoke of earlier continue, for instance the C-130s performing what may be a bombing maneuver. And of course, the Israeli memos, blueprints, and photographs of a possible MOAB that Ray brought back from his meeting with Ghorbani. However, the manufacture of MOABs by Israel could be either the *result* of increased activity in the Iranian nuclear missile program or the *cause* of increased activity in the Iranian nuclear missile program."

"Lord," said the president. "We're one mistake away from a nuclear war between Israel and Iran, a war that will kill millions, destroy at least two countries, and shut down the flow of Middle East oil—maybe for years. And it looks like Askenazi is about to make that mistake!"

Martin's eyes swept the group in the Situation Room: John Dorn, Anne Battista, Eric Easterly, Mac MacAdoo, Aaron Hendrix, and Bart Guarini. Vice President Griffith, testing the political waters in the state of *Iowa*, loomed from one of the video screens. Knowing that soul-wrenching decisions lay ahead of him, Martin wondered why Griffith, or anyone, would want to be president. He was tempted to put Griffith on the spot by asking for his recommendation, but prudence stopped him.

"Ideas?" said Martin.

"Well, sir, most of Israel's aircraft are American-made," said MacAdoo. "Our planners know their capabilities and limitations well—except for what the Israelis themselves have added. We train with the IAF in Exercise Red Flag. So we might be able to get inside their heads about how this strike they seem to be planning will go down. In fact, we've reviewed the matter several times over the years when this issue came up as tensions rose."

MacAdoo paused, deliberately giving his boss a chance to jump in. The secretary of defense was prickly about the close working relationship between the president and the general.

"That's right," said Easterly. There are two big problems facing the Israelis: They have to know where the Iranian nukes are stored, and they have to fly a long way with a heavy bomb load to reach all of the likely places. Refueling is crucial, and that's why we've never sold them our KC-135 tankers."

Martin looked impatient. "Yeah, I've been briefed on all that. They must have solved those problems, or think they have, or they wouldn't be about to attack. So how do we get them to call it off? For sure, I will call Askenazi. But what else have we got?

"Perhaps cyber, Mr. President," said John Dorn. "General, with what we know about IAF aircraft, is there some way we can degrade their computers? Is there a back door into the computers aboard the aircraft we sold them?"

Mac looked startled, then thoughtful. "Offhand, I don't know. I'll get our people on that right away. But if we *could* do that, say, mess with their mission planning software, we could create some chaos in the strike; that's for sure." MacAdoo motioned to a staff officer seated behind him, who went to one of the secure phone niches in the room and called the Pentagon.

"It's not enough to create chaos," said Anne Battista. "We need to get them to call it off. An ineffective strike will be just as likely to cause the Iranians to retaliate and leave them more to do it with."

"You're right, Anne," said the president. "But so far, it's all we've got, so let's work on that angle. Maybe something will come up. But what else could cyber do—Aaron?"

"Mr. President, my people are working with CYBERCOM on that, but the answer will probably be 'not much.' Except in fortuitous circumstances, cyber isn't a quick-reaction tool. It takes months or more to prepare a cyber-attack that will do more good than harm. But we do have some capabilities on the shelf called 'zero-day vulnerabilities.' That's the term for a flaw that we have discovered, or have bought from the person or entity that found it, which we can use to hack into or bring down a network. CYBERCOM and the intelligence community are reviewing zero-day vulnerabilities now."

"What about GPS?" said the vice president. "Doesn't most of the world use our GPS satellites? If the IAF had no GPS information, wouldn't that disrupt their plan?"

All eyes turned to General MacAdoo. "Yes, it would disrupt the operation. But I expect that the Israelis practice, just as we do, operating without GPS. Even so, that would degrade the coordination of a big long-distance air strike. And it would mean their GPS-guided bombs wouldn't find targets."

"You know, I just take GPS for granted. Who runs the system, anyway?" said the president.

"I do, sir," said Easterly. "But I'll have to admit that I've also taken it for granted. I'm sure we could shut it off completely, but as for other options, I'll have to get someone to brief us." His military assistant hustled over to a phone niche.

"Well, I don't think we'd want to shut it off completely," said Guarini. "Just consider the potential downsides: airliners getting lost and running out of fuel over the ocean, the disruption to world commerce, millions of American voters losing a service they find very convenient—and all with no notice."

Optimistic expressions faded around the room.

"But could we just mess up the Israelis' use of GPS?" said Vice President Griffith.

"Probably not," said Hendrix. "Unless we have a zero-day vulnerability that applies to the Israelis alone, I don't see how we could be selective in denying GPS."

The room was silent. Then Martin said quietly, "I'm going to Israel. I can stop this, or at least try to. We can't just watch it happen!"

Looking around the room, Martin saw surprise, alarm, disapproval. Everyone except Bart Guarini was stunned by his decision. Guarini said,

"You figure that if you can get Askenazi to stand down, the Iranians won't use those missiles."

Martin nodded. "Yep."

Anne Battista was the first to react aloud: "Mr. President, that's a bold and courageous step to take. It may well work. But consider the risk and the downside. You are assuming that the Supreme Leader has tight control over the nuclear missiles. But he might not. Some lower-level fanatic might launch them, even with you there—maybe even *because* you're there. She raised her arms, palms up, and looked at the others for support. Easterly and MacAdoo nodded.

Martin held up a hand, then said, "The missiles, if they are actually operational, are almost certainly under Ghorbani's control. Based on Ray Morales's conversation with him, I believe Ghorbani accepts that it would be suicidal for Iran to attack Israel before it has a second-strike nuclear capability as strong as Israel's. He's dedicated his life to the Islamic Republic. He'll wait to fight Israel another day, a day when Iran can win."

Martin paused and then spoke more slowly, weighing his argument as he made it: "Yes, it *is* risky. But so many signs point to an imminent Israeli strike on Iran, a strike based partly on fear that otherwise Iran will strike Israel first."

Martin paused, then, in a tone that signaled decision, said, "I think stopping this thing is too heavy a lift for anyone but the president of the United States, in person, sharing the risk with Askenazi and the people of Israel if negotiation fails."

Martin looked at MacAdoo and Easterly, seated side by side to his left. "This is one of those 'all in' moments. Wouldn't you agree?"

MacAdoo replied immediately: "Yes, sir."

Easterly paused, then said, "Yes, it is. But this isn't sending in a SEAL team or some other expendable group. You are the president. If you're killed, we have no choice but war."

"You're damn right!" said Griffith.

Easterly glared at the vice president and continued, "In that case we would be even worse off than if you had tried and failed from here to prevent the Israelis and Iranians from going at it."

Martin blinked. He hadn't expected caution from Easterly, but that wasn't going to stop him.

"Objections noted. You're all welcome to put them in writing for the record. But I think the risk is acceptable because of what's at stake. A nuclear war in the Middle East would kill millions and destroy most of the infrastructure for exporting oil from sixty percent of the world's known oil reserves.

"Bart, start setting up a trip to Tel Aviv; I want to leave immediately."

He paused, solemnly eyeing the vice president and the others. "I'm going to travel light because, if those bombs go off, I want Bruce to have you with him as he does what he has to do. Mac, I want you with me. It's possible that military-to-military will be the way we shut this attack down. Also Ray Morales. His personal knowledge of Ghorbani will be important. And no public announcement until I've called Askenazi. Thank you all for your counsel."

Martin rose and left the room.

Chapter 59

JERUSALEM, ISRAEL

Joshua Askenazi's tendency toward insomnia had increased. There was no denying it. Now he hardly ever had a full night's sleep. He felt Shara's absence—and sometimes her tenuous presence—the most at night. Having given up on sleep, he sat in his study.

Askenazi was frozen. He could not move on. Every possession of Shara's remained where she had placed it: clothing, toiletries, books, and knick-knacks. Every morning he arose at his usual five a.m., drank coffee, and read the Torah for an hour in his study. At six a.m. he padded into the kitchen, prepared English tea in Shara's cup, and took it into their bedroom. He set it on the table beside her side of their bed, breathed deeply of the aroma, and stared into the darkened room, willing himself to pretend she was there, asleep until the aroma awakened her as usual. For the first week he had required that the housekeeper prepare Shara's breakfast tray, exactly as she had specified, with a fresh rose and a copy of the *Jerusalem Post*, folded just as she liked it. He had rescinded this order after he noticed the housekeeper looking at him with fear as well as pity.

Occasionally, he could complete this morning ritual without tears, but usually it ended in wracking sobs. After minutes of hopeless agony, the sobs became rage at her killers, a rage that possessed him as had nothing else in his life, even his ambition to become prime minister. It was a rage that he caressed, that gave him strength and direction and, in a way, pleasure.

Since he couldn't sleep, he was working his way through documents that Barak had assured him he could sign without study. Still, he would at least skim them.

Askenazi heard a sharp sound upstairs in the residence. It was a sound he knew: the toilet seat being dropped down. Shara did that on mornings when he had left it up, an unspoken scolding for his carelessness.

He listened intently but heard nothing else. After arguing with himself—he knew that he was alone in the house except for security officers on the ground floor and patrolling the small garden—he climbed the stairs. The toilet seat was indeed down. Had he left it up? Or unconsciously put it down out of long habit? Askenazi's skin prickled. He looked around, feeling sheepish but certain he had heard the sound. He stood still, looking and listening, hyper-alert. Nothing out of the ordinary. Except the toilet seat. Still …

Feeling foolish but strangely comforted, Askenazi returned to his study.

He turned his attention to the next document, titled "Memorandum for the Prime Minister from the Minister of Infrastructure, Energy, and Water." *Avraham* again, he thought. The man actually thinks he should be prime minister. That he *could* be prime minister. Askenazi's grimace said what he thought about that. This job is so much beyond both his intellect and his balls that he has no idea! Pushing back slightly from his desk, he looked at a row of framed photos on the wall to his right. *There* with Ming Liu, he thought. *There* with Rick Martin. *There* with Viktor Volkov, president of Russia.

How could pygmies like Avraham find support for their ludicrous ambitions? The press. Newspaper editors and television producers continually fabricated news. They constantly created accusations of corruption. Yes, he and Shara had rich and powerful supporters. Yes, these supporters often provided upgraded tickets and hotels when he and Shara traveled abroad because the Knesset failed to appropriate funds adequate to provide for the travel of a head of state. Yes, some gave cases of champagne and jewelry for Shara and Cuba's finest cigars for him. These were just gifts from friends, really just trifles from men whose skill and determination had earned them so much. He was sure they had never affected his decisions and never would! Journalists, pursuing their own objectives, not the interests of Israel, constantly defamed him.

Then the telephone—the secure telephone—rang.

"Sir, President Martin is calling."

Startled, Askenazi replied, "Put him through."

"Joshua, I apologize for the hour, but we need to talk right now. I've just received an intelligence report that Israel is preparing to attack Iran. All the signs are there: your subs rushing to sea, relocation of Patriot batteries, and reconfiguration of aircraft as tankers. You must not do this, Joshua! It will start a fight to the death between Israel and Iran, and Israel cannot win that fight."

Askenazi's heart raced. If he knows, do the Iranians know? "Mr. President, I have given no such order. You are mistaking a readiness drill for an attack. And it is the Supreme Leader you should be calling. Iran is constantly threatening to destroy us. The Iranians' bomb program has continued in secret. They have lied to you, Mr. President. They have at least three nuclear warheads and, even as we speak, are working on the engineering details of mating them to Shahab missiles. You know that. So don't accuse *me* of threatening a war!"

"Prime Minister, I agree that Iran has warheads. There may well be more than three. And that is why you must not attack. Israel's chances of destroying all of Iran's nuclear weapons in a single air strike, one carried out at extreme range for your aircraft, are zero. Zero!

"I know that Israel has its own deep-penetrating bombs. But you don't know where to use them. You cannot possibly know the location of every underground facility that might contain one of those weapons. And after you have failed to destroy all of them, your cities will begin disappearing beneath mushroom clouds. Consider, *please*, Mr. Prime Minister, that neither you nor I know exactly how many nuclear weapons Iran has. If you launch this doomed attack, you will find out how many by counting the Israeli cities destroyed.

"And there's another risk to Israel's survival. General Ghorbani has, at great personal risk, told us the Iranian government has seen clear signs that Israel is on the verge of attacking and is prepared to preempt; to use its nuclear missiles against you before you can destroy them. Israel and Iran are about to destroy each other,"

"You once told me," continued Martin, "that since I had no skin in the game, I couldn't understand what you face. You were wrong about that. And to show you that America has skin in this game, I'm coming to Tel

281

Aviv. I will come and sit with you in Tel Aviv, risking whatever you risk from Iran, and we will work this out, provide for the safety of Israel without war, a war that would become nuclear. And then I will go to Iran. As much as the Iranians may hate Israel, they know you have a nuclear second-strike capability that would mean the utter destruction of their nation if a nuclear war occurs. The Supreme Leader is not a stateless jihadi. He is not seeking martyrdom. We don't know it, but he may well have authorized Ghorbani to reach out to us. You and the Supreme Leader both have everything to lose in a nuclear exchange, everything you have worked for in your lives. We can prevent that. Together, the three of us will find a solution."

Askenazi felt frustration surge like a river overflowing its banks. His mind raced. Having America's president, who did not understand Israel's situation, in Tel Aviv yammering at him about finding common ground would be a distraction—or worse because, to protect its president, America would put Israel and Iran under close surveillance. That could tip his hand. But to refuse Martin would likely raise American alarm to a higher level, and that, too, would bring surveillance meant to find out what he was hiding.

But the highly publicized presence of a presidential peace mission would lull the Iranians; after all, Israel was less likely to attack Iran with America's president sitting in Tel Aviv. As for Ghorbani's claim, it was a bluff the naive Americans had believed. And even if, against all odds, Ghorbani were telling the truth, the Iranian government would not dare launch a nuclear attack while Martin was in Israel. A rare smile lightened a face habitually sad since Shara's death. With a little luck, Martin's visit could be the ultimate deception of Iran.

Askenazi made his decision.

"Mr. President, I regret to say that much of what you have said is wrong. For the past few moments I have been refuting you in my mind, point by point. But I would never reject an opportunity to improve Israel's security through negotiation. So come ahead. I welcome you."

After the conversation ended, Joshua Askenazi knew the hand of God had just moved the chess pieces. He was keeping His promises to Moses and Joshua, as Shara had been so sure He would.

* * *

JOINT BASE ANDREWS, MARYLAND

"Another grave crisis in a presidency marked by crises," said the reporter doing a stand-up with Air Force One looming behind him. "We all recall that, during his first term, President Martin had to deal with nuclear terrorism enabled by North Korea, and after diplomacy failed, he became the first president since World War Two to order a nuclear strike, one that spelled the end of the Kim family dynasty. And then, as he was running for reelection, the terrorist mastermind Fahim al-Wasari brought jihad to America, and that was followed by *another* crisis with North Korea involving Kim's successor."

"Yes, Jim," said the anchor, "and that's not even to mention the mystery surrounding the defeat of Fahim's attempt to blow up an LNG tanker. There's a lot more to that than we've been told."

"Well, Carleton, you've put your finger on one of the hallmarks of this administration," replied the reporter. "It's addicted to secrecy. Now this trip to Israel, and perhaps Iran, revealed to us only hours ago in a brief White House statement. Clearly something has happened, something we have not been told, which requires this sudden trip. All we know is that, quoting the statement, 'events in the Middle East have reached a very dangerous and volatile point, and the president is going to the region to meet with all parties in order to build momentum for a peaceful settlement of the strait closure.'"

The anchor teed up another line of conflict; after all, it was conflict and fear that drove ratings: "And no one is more critical of President Martin than the man who lost to him a year and a half ago, Governor Walter Rutherford."

"That's right, Carleton. The governor's reaction, expressed only hours ago in an exclusive interview with our Lindsey Padua, is critical to say the least."

"Let's take a look at that," said the anchor.

Rutherford appeared on video: "As I've said many times, our current president is way too fond of diplomacy. He would rather negotiate than use American power. And not only that, but by scuttling away from the joint American-Chinese ultimatum to Iran, he has cast doubt on America's resolve."

"Some would say he is playing the best cards he has left after China insisted upon giving diplomacy more time." said Padua.

"Well, that illustrates another flaw in his worldview. President Martin is way too fond of collaborating with China's president, Ming Liu. The Chinese can't be trusted. Their plan is to weaken America and become the dominant world power. Martin walked right into another situation where the United States—the greatest power since Rome—gets snookered. The next president is going to have a mess to clean up."

"And might that be you, Governor?"

"I think the American people will see more clearly three years from now than they did a year ago."

"What do you make of that, Jim?" said the anchor.

"Clearly the governor intends to use the next two years to actively build the case for a Rutherford presidency. And that spells big trouble for Vice President Bruce Griffith. He must support Martin's policies and actions, even though, as sources tell us, he doesn't fully agree with them. And his almost certain opponent, Governor Walter Rutherford, clearly intends to lay what he will call 'the failures of the Martin administration' right at Griffith's door."

Chapter 60

TEL AVIV, ISRAEL

YA'EL BARAK HAD BEEN HAVING the dream for several days and thought about it as he dressed. He was once again serving in the army, in parachute training. Shuffling behind the soldier ahead of him, he moved to the door of the C-130. The light above the door winked green, and the jumpmaster slapped the shoulder of the soldier in front of Barak, who stepped into space and was yanked from view by the slipstream. Barak glanced to his left, toward the jumpmaster standing beside the door. It was Joshua Askenazi, who motioned impatiently for him to move to the door. Obediently, Barak complied as he had been taught. There was a pause, then the jumpmaster's slap on his shoulder, signaling him to jump. He did so, and as he fell away, he saw that Askenazi had unhooked his static line, the line that would jerk taut and trigger his parachute. Down, down, down he fell, fingers digging frantically in the mass of equipment strapped to his chest for the D-ring that would release his reserve chute. But he couldn't find it. He *knew* it was there, but he couldn't grasp it. He tumbled as he fell, seeing sky, then onrushing ground, then sky, then ground, ever closer. He woke up just before striking the ground.

Important though he was, Barak had no security detail waiting to whisk him to the prime minister's office, where he occupied a small room adjoining Askenazi's. He smoked, worried, and cursed the traffic as he made his way through the usual chaotic morning rush in his five-year-old white Hyundai. After close examination of his car, he was waved into the heavily guarded parking garage.

As usual, he was in ahead of the prime minister. Today, of course, was all about the arrival of the president of the United States. The prime minister had been vague about the reasons for the visit, which Barak knew from experience meant his boss was up to something. In Barak's overnight message queue was Askenazi's revised schedule for the visit, with a striking change: Air Force One was to land at Tel Aviv's Ben Gurion International at eleven a.m., but nothing of the visit was on Askenazi's schedule until two p.m. The prime minister's time until then was scheduled as "Luncheon and Briefing—General Rivkin." Impatiently, he called Protocol and learned that the change had been ordered by the prime minister himself, last night. Furious that Protocol hadn't notified him immediately, he chewed out the unfortunate staffer who had answered his call, then hung up.

Jabbing speed dial, Barak called Rivkin's personal number. After ten rings had gone unanswered, he hung up. His next call was to Rivkin's office number. The secretary to the chief of defense staff, who, Barak was sure, had been there since before he was born, politely but firmly refused his request to speak with her boss. The general was doing the final review of military security measures for the presidential visit and could not be disturbed.

After returning the phone to its cradle with more force than necessary, Barak hunched his shoulders, gnawed on a fingernail already damaged by years of such mistreatment and scribbled on a sheet of yellow legal paper. He was in this posture when Joshua Askenazi swept by, his energy palpable, and entered his office. As he passed Barak, he said, as he had a hundred times before, "Ya'el, you shouldn't do that. It's bad for your manicure." Barak looked up, saw Askenazi settle behind his desk, then rise and close his door.

* * *

Askenazi removed a red file from his safe, then returned to his desk. He felt confident about the day ahead. He glanced at his wristwatch. In an hour, President Martin would be part of Operation Persepolis, perhaps the most crucial part. The Americans—that such power should be combined with such naiveté! He patted the folder.

He had lain awake grieving Shara last night, as he always did without a sleeping pill. He had heard again the snap in her voice when she said,

"Remember, Joshua, just as no one could stand against Moses or Joshua of old, no one can stand against you. You will be bold and resolute, for God is with us." He rose and began to pace.

* * *

Within the unsuspecting man's body, under the unceasing pressure of blood returning to his heart, the blood clot began to sway, tugging at its fibrin threads and eventually snapping them, a few at a time. With each broken thread, the movement of the clot increased, until it snapped the last of its moorings and joined the blood flow. Oblong in shape, rusty-red in color, it trailed a few fibrin threads in its wake. Rotating slowly about its long axis as it rose within his deep femoral vein, the clot headed for a rendezvous that was now inevitable.

* * *

A knock immediately followed by the opening door broke the prime minister's concentration, and he looked toward the sound with irritation. It was Ya'el.

"Prime Minister," said Barak in the tone Askenazi knew he reserved for the most serious matters, "I don't see how this schedule revision can work. You've left President Martin waiting three hours for his first meeting with you."

"Yes, I have, my friend. But *I* haven't kept him waiting; Persepolis is responsible for that."

Barak lurched as if he had been punched in the stomach. His face flushed, and his eyes flashed. "Persepolis? You are launching Persepolis while President Martin is in Tel Aviv to prevent war?"

"But he cannot prevent war. Relying on allies is a failed strategy for Israel. The Iranians are determined to destroy us. We must remove that threat. And I am the one anointed to do that. Shara told me, but I didn't believe her until they killed her. On that day I understood and accepted my destiny."

Barak saw Askenazi's eyes cut to Shara's portrait, and a corner of his mind noted that it was as though Askenazi was looking for her approval.

"*Anointed?*" blurted Barak, "*You* may be anointed, but our pilots are not! They will *not* be able to destroy all of Iran's nuclear bombs. And *that* will be the end of Israel. You must not do this!"

The prime minister's neck flushed, and the red spread to his face. His eyes hardened. But his voice was soft as he quoted from the Nevi'im: "But only be brave and resolute. None can stand against you because I am with you and will never forsake you."

* * *

A few minutes after attaining its freedom, the clot entered his larger femoral vein, glancing off one wall as it did, then moving steadily upward again. Soon it entered the external iliac vein, then the inferior vena cava. It was then the equivalent of an uprooted tree in a surging river just upstream from a spinning mill wheel. Arriving at the midline of its unknowing host's chest, the clot was carried in a sweeping one-hundred-eighty-degree turn as the lower vena cava delivered its contents to the right ventricle of his beating heart. The clot paused briefly in the right ventricle and, with the next contraction, exited via the pulmonary valve and plunged into the pulmonary trunk. By pure chance, the clot was swept next into the right pulmonary artery. There it began a dive into his right lung, as deadly as that of a ballistic missile. Soon it smashed into a smaller artery and lodged there, severely reducing blood flow to the right lung and creating back pressure in the pulmonary artery. The effect on his exquisitely balanced cardiopulmonary system was like that of an eighteen-wheeler driven into a china shop.

* * *

The prime minister picked up his phone. Barak reached out and wrenched it from his grasp. Then he grunted, made a gurgling sound, and dropped the handset, which struck the desk with a crash and hung over the edge by its cord.

Barak's pulmonary artery, its passage for the blood surging in with every heartbeat greatly reduced by the clot, experienced back pressure. This pressure was quickly manifested in the pulmonary trunk. It overcame the pulmonary valve, and his right ventricle swelled rapidly with blood. Soon it impinged on the left ventricle, further reducing arterial blood flow. Barak's brain, receiving signals that blood pressure was dropping, ordered his heart to speed up. But now the heart itself was not receiving enough oxygenated blood. The heart stopped, and its tissues began to die. Ya'el Barak's life ebbed, then ended.

"Ya'el, Ya'el," Askenazi said softly, sorrow modulating his normally robust tone. "God smites those who do not trust that He keeps his word, those who do not obey."

Swiftly, the prime minister moved to the door and locked it. Returning to his desk, he picked up the handset and pressed speed dial for General Rivkin. Glancing around as he waited for Rivkin to pick up, he imagined Shara, leaning against the door, smiling.

Chapter 61

USS JOHN C. STENNIS, PERSIAN GULF

K AYCEE JENKINS WAS PISSED OFF and gloomy as she hung around VFA-124's Ready Room aboard *Stennis*. She was the squadron duty officer, SDO, which meant lots of administrative work and no flying. This was especially galling today, when a max-effort flight schedule had been laid on to cover the sudden visit of the president of the United States to Israel. In fact, she was the SDO every day because she had been grounded for disobeying the order to break off her attack on the Iranian F-14. A Field Naval Aviator Evaluation Board, universally referred to by a mashup of its initials as "Feenab," would decide whether or not she would ever fly a Hornet again.

Immediately after she had landed aboard *Stennis*, having just become the only squadron junior officer with kills in aerial combat, she and her squadron skipper, Commander "Boots" Bossert, had presented themselves to his boss, the air wing commander and officer in charge of the eight squadrons assigned to *Stennis*. Known by the traditional title "CAG," Captain Stevenson was a veteran pilot with twenty-five years of flying and more than a thousand carrier landings. His consistent success at both leadership and airmanship had put him on the path to admiral.

As Jenkins stood at attention, CAG examined her with flinty eyes, as if he were looking at a weed just before yanking it out of his garden.

"Jenkins," the CAG said, drawing out the *S* like the hiss of a blade descending to decapitate the pilot before him, "how long have you been in the fleet?"

"I'm on my third cruise, sir."

"Your third cruise. Have you learned nothing? Do you not understand the Rules of Engagement?"

Jenkins met his gaze, sweat popping on her forehead. "Sir, I do. I know what I did was wrong. But at the time—"

"At the time?" The CAG's face was beet-red. "Listen, Jenkins; there is no 'at the time' in naval aviation. There is only one time—*all* the time. We don't have one standard for when you feel happy and one when you're scared and another when you're pissed off. There is *one* expectation: that you do the job, *all the time, every time.* So don't even begin to give me and your skipper that 'sorry, lost my head' bullshit!

"When you or I or your skipper launches, none of us can have a bad day. Pilots who have bad days get people killed. The wrong people. I won't have pilots like that in my air wing.

"You're not the Lone Ranger riding in on a white horse to clean up the town. You're an instrument, an instrument of the United States government. The government didn't give you that white horse—that sixty-million-dollar fighter—to right wrongs. Sometimes you get to do that, and it feels damn good. Other times you have to watch while the bad guys run wild. That sucks. And," his voice got softer, "sometimes you have to do something you believe is wrong. That *really* sucks."

His voice hardened. "But it's what we do. And if you can't or won't do it, you don't belong in a navy cockpit. Am I clear?"

"Yes, sir."

"Commander Bossert," CAG continued, "you will convene a Feenab to determine whether or not"—he spat the words—"Lieutenant Jenkins keeps her wings."

"Aye, aye, sir."

"Jenkins, you're dismissed. "

She saluted and fled, pale-faced, head spinning.

Take my wings. Oh, God, no, not my wings.

After Jenkins had left, CAG Stevenson said, "Grab a chair, Boots, and tell me about her."

Stevenson dropped into his desk chair and put his feet up, gazing expectantly at Bossert, who sat across the desk from him.

"She's one of my top lieutenants. Excellent landing grades, tough dogfighter, pretty damn good at bombing. She's a leader, respected by her fellow officers; she never does stupid stuff on the beach. Married, two kids, no family issues. I'm really surprised that she pulled such a dumb-assed stunt out there. Although, as we both know, when somebody shoots at you, it sends you to another place for a while. I think it was a combination of first time in a real dogfight and the aggressive temper that makes her a good fighter pilot."

He paused, then said, "I think she could have my job someday, maybe yours."

"So you want to save her wings, Boots? OK, I'll give you that. But she gets the Feenab—you figure how to handle it. Just know that if she screws up again, she's not going to be the only one who gets busted.

"It took about fifteen minutes for her ROE violation to make it all the way to Washington. I was getting my ass chewed by the strike group commander, but he had to break off to get *his* ass chewed by Admiral Watson, who probably got a blast from CENTCOM, who … You get my point, I'm sure."

* * *

And receiving her reprimand, Jenkins had nothing to do but wait for time to be found in the busy flight schedule to convene a board of senior naval aviators. She suspected, rightly, that the delay was part of her punishment. She could only hope—no, *pray*—that the board wouldn't pull her wings, disqualifying her from navy flying.

The phone at the SDO desk rasped, and Jenkins answered. In seconds her expression went from boredom to worry.

"Yes, sir. I'm on my way."

She hurried to Commander Bossert's office, skillfully taking the steel "knee-knockers" of ship's framing that crossed the 03-level passageway every few yards in stride like hurdles in a track race. When she arrived, she found the skipper and the executive officer, both in flight gear. They stared at her as if she were something distasteful left behind by a dog.

"Jenkins," said the skipper, pointing his index finger at her like a dagger, "I'm gonna take a huge chance on you. Screw this up, and you'll be admin officer for a patrol squadron permanently deployed to Iceland. You know about the presidential support mission, out of the blue. We need everybody up there, so I'm temporarily returning you to flight status. You're flying the next cycle, but when this op is done, you're grounded again until your Feenab."

Jenkins barely stifled a war whoop.

"The XO here is going to be on your Feenab. He might, just might, be able to save your wings. But not a chance if you pull another cowboy stunt. Now get moving!"

Kaycee Jenkins, a fighter pilot again, saluted and hustled for her flight gear.

* * *

ABOVE THE PERSIAN GULF

US Air Force Captain Brad Thompson was excited. He'd been deployed to Al Udeid for two boring months as mission controller for the odd-looking aircraft known as Marathon. In flight, his job was to supervise thirteen airmen engaged in identifying, tracking, and reporting everything that flew over the Persian Gulf and much of the Middle East. But today wasn't boring. There had been a different atmosphere in the morning mission brief because today the president of the United States, traveling to Israel aboard Air Force One to defuse a crisis, would be under his team's protection. Well, under their supervision; the protection would be provided by fighters from *Stennis* and, if needed, by two squadrons of F-15 Eagles, four of which were on strip alert at Al Udeid. If necessary, he would take control of them as they roared off the airstrip in afterburner to investigate a suspicious or threatening aircraft.

Feeling a little embarrassed about his excitement and hiding it carefully, Thompson gazed at the master ops console. Airspace over the Middle East was busy, as always, with airliners and the military aircraft of six nations moving to and fro, their symbols cluttering the video screen and clustering around major airports. Rolling the cursor to the symbol identified as Air Force One, Thompson noted that it was ninety-seven miles from its destination, Ben Gurion International Airport.

"Control, Commo. I'm getting an unusual amount of chatter on Israeli Air Force frequencies. The Yellow Bird and Desert Giant squadrons, mostly."

"Roger, Commo."

Thompson remembered that those squadrons were the IAF's transport and refueling aircraft based in the Negev desert. The Birds flew the twin-engine C-130 Hercules, and the Giants were aging Boeing 707s converted to aerial refueling. Some of the Hercs were also refuelers, he knew. Glancing at his ops display, Thompson observed clusters of video around the base as aircraft climbed skyward. Typically, these aircraft headed north toward the Mediterranean, above which they would ply their trade pumping fuel into thirsty IAF fighters.

Today, however, their video symbols moved east, toward Saudi Arabia. Thompson paid a bit more attention. Was he going to witness a border violation? The symbols representing the Israeli aircraft continued to march eastward.

"Control, Commo. Now we're getting something weird. The Birds and Giants are checking in with the Saudi ADIZ."

"What are they saying?"

"They seem to be filing to prearranged positions, like 'Anchor three' and 'Anchor six.'"

The lead Israeli aircraft crossed into Saudi airspace. No new video appeared. The Saudis weren't launching interceptors. Thompson almost forgot Air Force One.

* * *

Al Udeid Air Base, QATAR

Brigadier General Seth Wilcox, commanding the 324th Expeditionary Air Wing at Al Udeid, was composing an email to his wife when his phone bleeped. After a brief conversation, he saved the file, grabbed his hat, and headed out into the heat for the short walk to the Ops Center. Entering, he was met by the major in charge of the ops team on duty.

"What's up?"

"Sir, Marathon is reporting unusual Israeli air activity, apparently in cooperation with the Saudis." The general's eyebrows shot up.

"What activity? What sort of cooperation?"

"Almost all of their tankers are now in Saudi airspace, some orbiting, and some still tracking southeast. And there are a lot of launches under way at the IAF's fighter bases.

"So the IAF is mounting a max-effort strike?"

The lieutenant colonel who was operations officer of the wing appeared at the general's side with a clipboard. "That's what it looks like, sir. Here's a draft message to alert CENTCOM, JCS, and NSC." The general read it, added several lines, and returned it to his ops officer. "Add Chairman JCS, SECDEF, and SECSTATE," he said. "Get it out flash precedence." Then he walked over and climbed into the pedestal-mounted commander's chair, his eyes scouring the air situation depicted in symbols and letters on the large plasma screen mounted on the wall before him. Picking up the handset nested in the console to his right, General Wilcox said, "NMCC watch commander, flash red rocket. "

In less than thirty seconds Wilcox heard, "This is Rear Admiral Klebert, NMCC watch commander."

"This is Brigadier General Wilcox, commander of the 344th Expeditionary Air Wing at Al Udeid. Hard copy follows with details. It looks to me like the IAF is mounting a maximum-effort strike on Iran. IAF aircraft are now in Saudi airspace and in comms with the Saudis, who are not opposing the incursion."

"Hold for the Situation Room, General."

Chapter 62

AIR FORCE ONE

MAC MACADOO WAS IN THE senior staff cabin talking baseball with Ray Morales as Air Force One crossed the Mediterranean coastline enroute to Tel Aviv. Mac was a Phillies fan, and they were debating the wisdom, or lack thereof, of Washington letting slugger Bryce Harper go to the Phillies several years ago. The intercom spoke: "General MacAdoo, there's an urgent sivitz for the president from the Sit Room that we are linking up now. The president asks that you and General Morales join him."

The two exchanged curious looks and made their way forward to the president's in-flight office, bracing slightly as Air Force One banked gently in its final approach to Ben Gurion International. On their way to his cabin, they were intercepted by a first sergeant from the comm center who handed General Wilcox's flash precedence message to each. As they entered, the president waved them to seats. The president observed the documents they carried and motioned to Mac for his. Morales then pushed his own toward MacAdoo, and the three read General Wilcox's initial report simultaneously.

"Mr. President," came a voice from the ceiling speaker. "This is your sivitz on the evolving military situation in the Middle East. The NMCC and CENTCOM headquarters are in the net. Mr. Dorn is on his way to the Sit Room."

"Well, Mac," said the president, "you're the only fighter pilot in the room. What do you think?"

"Sir, if the Saudis remain passive, as they apparently are, that means this is no navigational screw-up or some IAF squadron going rogue. It means this is a pre-agreed operation, and the only reason I can think of for that is the Israelis are going after the Iranian nuke program."

"With the president of the United States in Tel Aviv?" blurted Battista over the sivitz link. "That's crazy!"

"Maybe crazy like a fox," said Easterly over his link. "If anything could encourage the Iranians to back down a little, it would be just that."

President Martin and his companions felt and heard Air Force One land.

After General "Rifle" Remington, the CENTCOM commander, summed up the situation, there was a moment of silence as everyone tried to absorb the picture he had painted. Then Martin spoke: "I'm going to call Askenazi. Each of you reach out to your counterparts. One message—call those planes back."

Ten minutes later they reconvened. "Askenazi wouldn't take my call!" said Martin, anger and shock on his face. "I got the defense minister, but he claims to know nothing about it!" said Easterly. "Same for the foreign minister," added Battista. "And General Rivkin wouldn't take my call, either," said MacAdoo.

"General Remington," said the president. "What are my military options for stopping this attack? Do I even have any?"

The CENTCOM commander stared grimly from the video screen. "Because of the buildup to force open the strait, and your own trip, we have the *Stennis* air wing and two wings of air force fighters in the area. We could order them to prevent the Israelis from refueling. That would certainly disrupt their attack plan; might even kill it."

"Prevent the Israelis from refueling," repeated the president. "How exactly would you do that, General?"

"General Krongaard?" said Remington.

A thin-faced man with short, red hair appeared on the video. "Sir, we could start by having our fighters take up positions directly behind the tankers, as if they were going to refuel. That would block the Israeli fighters from plugging in. But it would make those aircraft of ours sitting ducks if the IAF decides to attack them."

"So what are the odds the IAF would do that, would open fire on our aircraft?"

Krongaard replied, "Sir, from my perspective that's unknowable. The Israeli airmen are tough bastards. They wouldn't hesitate if ordered to shoot. But I don't think the commander in the air would make that decision on his own authority. It's really a political judgment."

"You said we could start with blocking," said the president. "Is there any other option, General Krongaard?"

"Yes, sir. We could order our fighters to shoot down the Israeli tankers."

"Kill them in cold blood, you mean," said the president.

"Yes, sir. That's what it would amount to. The tankers are big, slow, unarmed, and full of fuel."

"Mr. President." Colonel Roberts's familiar voice issued from a speaker. "Ben Gurion ground control has informed me that there is a security alert, and we must remain aboard until it's taken care of. I'm to taxi to an area protected by the army and await further instructions."

"This stinks, Mr. President!" said Bart Guarini, who had joined the group in the Sit Room. "You're being confined until their attack is past the point of no return."

Eyes flashing, Rick Martin grabbed his telephone handset. "Colonel, tell the Israelis that the president of the United States demands to speak with Prime Minister Askenazi at once. *At once.*"

Eyes sweeping the cabin and the video screens, Martin said, "Ideas, anyone?"

"Mr. President," said Anne Battista, leaning forward as if she could stare directly into Martin's eyes. "If this strike hits Iran, the chain of retaliation will destroy two countries and cut off the flow of oil through Hormuz for who knows how long. And that's only what we know for sure. There'll be devastating second-order effects we haven't thought of. We've got to do whatever we can—whatever it takes—to prevent that strike!"

The president let the silence reign as he continued to look at each of his advisors.

"OK, I'll keep trying to reach Askenazi. But that may be too late. So, Eric and Mac, what's the best military option?"

The secretary of defense rubbed a hand across his face, then folded both hands on the Sit Room table. "Put our fighters on the tankers. If the IAF opens fire, we take the tankers out. The strike aircraft have no chance without the tankers, so they won't go. They'll have to turn back."

"Mac, anything to add? Do you agree?" said Martin.

"I agree; we sit on the tankers and hope we don't have to shoot," said the Joint Chiefs chairman. "I don't know their chief of staff, General Rivkin. By reputation he's analytical and pragmatic, so I'd be very surprised if he's in favor of the deep strike. And since their ministers of defense and foreign affairs apparently didn't know about this, it looks like the prime minister's personal decision, on his own authority. It just may be that we can get Rivkin to stand this down when he sees his refueling plan stymied."

"Ray, do you know Rivkin?" said the president, causing MacAdoo and Easterly to bristle.

"We were in the same class at National War College and had beers a few times after playing softball; I doubt that would mean much now."

"Okay," said Martin. "Then these are my orders, General Remington. Block the refueling, without firing if at all possible, but if attacked, respond and prevent the refueling by force.

"And Mac—keep trying to reach Rivkin."

Chapter 63

BEN GURION INTERNATIONAL AIRPORT, ISRAEL

"ENERAL RIVKIN'S OFFICE."

MacAdoo wished once again that he had made a greater effort to get to know Israel's top military officer. Their relationship was correct but not cordial. And because his staff hadn't given Rivkin the number for Mac's direct line, Mac didn't have Rivkin's now when minutes, even seconds, mattered.

"This is General MacAdoo. I need to speak to General Rivkin *immediately*."

"One moment, please."

MacAdoo gripped the radiotelephone with a suddenly sweaty hand. Realizing he needed to make notes, he stretched for a legal pad across the table and pulled a ballpoint from his shirt pocket. After about twenty seconds, he heard a series of electronic switching tones and then a wary voice in heavily accented English: "This is General Rivkin."

"General, you and I are not close. I regret that, because we're going to have to trust each other with the future relations between our two countries and the lives of millions of human beings. The United States is fully aware that Israel is in the process of launching a deep strike against Iran, with the cooperation of the Saudis. And you are attempting to use the arrival of the president of the United States to mask your attack."

MacAdoo continued, struggling to keep his tone even. "General, you must stand down. Give President Martin the opportunity to speak with Prime Minister Askenazi. The result of this attack will be the nuclear destruction of both Israel and Iran. I'm sure you know that. Give the order to stand down, now, I implore you!"

"I have my orders from the prime minister, General. I'm sure you understand that I must obey them."

MacAdoo wanted to shout his response but didn't: "Do you realize, General Rivkin, that you are giving the same rationale for killing millions of Jews tomorrow—when Iranian retaliation hits—as the commandant of Dachau gave in 1946 on trial for his butchery? *I have my orders?* This attack will result in the destruction of Israel. I know you must have argued against it. Stand down the deep strike and save Israel, General. We have solid intelligence that Iran already has nuclear weapons deployed in Israel and they will be detonated in reprisal. Then your submarines will fire their nuclear missiles at Iran in retaliation for *that*, and two nations will become radioactive ruins.

"*And* the attack will not succeed. As you undoubtedly know by now, American fighters are sitting right behind your tankers as they orbit over Saudi. These are their orders: if your tankers attempt to refuel your outbound strike package, our fighters are to shoot them down."

Sweat rings marked the armpits of MacAdoo's light blue shirt. "Please, General—do what your mind and your heart are telling you is the best for Israel. Carry out your Masada oath by saving Israel, not by beginning its inevitable destruction!"

Silence.

MacAdoo realized with rage and sorrow that Rivkin had hung up.

Chapter 64

SAUDI ARABIA AND ISRAEL

"A MERICAN FIGHTER ASTERN OF THIS aircraft, move away. You are interfering with our operation." The voice over Guard, the universal military air frequency, was imperious and heavily accented.

Kaycee Jenkins grinned beneath her oxygen mask. Switching her transmitter to Guard, she replied, "I know that, Desert Giant. That's why I'm back here. And I'll stay until you head for home."

Five miles astern of her, Jim Gandy flew cover, maneuvering in a zig-zag that allowed the fighter's radar to search behind them as well as ahead.

"Bogey, bogey inbound, nine o'clock!" called Gandy. Jenkins jerked her head left, saw nothing at first, then a speck that grew rapidly as it lanced toward the port side of her aircraft. Going with her intuition, she held position behind the Boeing 707 tanker. An Israeli F-16 roared close overhead, crossing left to right. The American fighter was jolted by the F-16's turbulence. Grimly, Jenkins nudged her Hornet back into its blocking position.

"Slingshot three oh one, this is Marathon. Was that as close as it looked from here?"

"It was, Marathon. Close enough to mess up my 'do," responded Jenkins.

* * *

The listeners aboard Air Force One, isolated at Ben Gurion International far from the terminal and surrounded by Israeli troops and army vehicles, exchanged startled looks.

"So, Mac, what's going on?" said the president.

"Sounds to me like the Israelis are pushing back, sir. I think one of them just made a pass very close to one of our fighters."

"So now we find out just how far the Israelis are willing to go," said Easterly.

* * *

Aboard Marathon, mission commander Brad Thompson saw video materializing near several Saudi air bases. Many Saudi aircraft were taking off. He keyed his mike. "Ninety-nine, the Saudis are launching."

For Slingshot 301, the Saudis were a problem for later. "Pecos, we've got another bogey inbound, closing from astern," said Gandy. "I'm going for a visual." He pulled back the stick, and as the Hornet's nose passed the vertical, he rolled one hundred eighty degrees while climbing three thousand feet and leveled on the opposite course. Soon he passed above an Israeli F-16. He pulled the Hornet's nose up, flipped the jet to the right, then upside down in a barrel roll swooping in behind the Israeli, who continued to close in on Jenkins and the tanker.

"Whaddya think, Steamboat? I'm not seeing any lock-on—are you?" said Jenkins.

"Nope, he's Israeli, and he's slowing—plus, I'm on his six."

"OK, I'm staying put," said Jenkins.

Time passed slowly. Then Gandy: "Five miles out, overtaking slowly. I think he's making an approach to tank."

"American aircraft astern of our tanker, move away. You are interfering with my refueling."

Jenkins ignored the demand while watching the Israeli's video creep closer on her display. Eventually, through her rearview mirrors, she saw that the aircraft was an F-16 laden with bombs, missiles, and drop tanks of fuel. She keyed her mike on the mission primary frequency. "Marathon, Slingshot three oh one. I have an Israeli F-16 on my six at about two hundred yards and closing. I intend to hold my position."

"Roger, Slingshot three oh one. We copy all. Continue to hold position."

"Three oh one, wilco, out."

Gandy's voice came sharply over the radio. "Pecos, he's pulling out to starboard, looks like he's going to overtake." Jenkins, concentrating on flying formation with the big Boeing, shot a glance to her right, seeing an F-16 with the blue and white insignia of Israel. It pulled even with the American aircraft, and she noticed five small flags, each representing a kill, painted below the cockpit. She saw its pilot gesturing that she should move left. Jenkins raised the middle finger of a hand to him and continued to hold position.

The Israeli fighter began to edge closer to the American. "Marathon, Slingshot three oh one. This guy has pulled alongside and is closing the standoff distance. Looks like he's going to try to push me out to port."

As the Israeli fighter moved steadily closer, it climbed slightly, allowing the wings of the two aircraft to overlap without touching. Her gaze cycling between the tanker ahead and the fighter to her right, Jenkins could see that if the Israeli kept sliding closer, his port wing was going to contact her canopy. She prepared mentally for the aftermath if it punched through.

Jenkins heard the warble of her radar warning unit, announcing an active homing missile inbound. "Breaking left!" she barked to Gandy while punching the chaff button. She shoved the stick forward and left, wrenching Slingshot 301 into a diving turn to port. She felt a jolt as her Hornet's right stabilator clipped the left wingtip of the Israeli fighter.

As she maneuvered to evade the missile, which had been fired from ahead of the three aircraft, Jenkins struggled with the effects created by the torn and missing metal of the stabilator. A ball of red-orange fire flashed above and behind her as the Boeing tanker exploded. The missile had found its target and the blast wave shook Slingshot 301 so hard that Jenkins's helmet struck the canopy.

At his console aboard Marathon, Brad Thompson saw the video for one of the Israeli tankers disappear. Seconds later he heard Jenkins: "Marathon, three oh one, the tanker's gone. Big fuel explosion. I doubt anybody got out. Who fired?

"Unknown at this time, three oh one."

Jenkins considered telling Marathon he was supposed to know that shit but instead said to her wingman, "Steamboat, look me over for damage. I'm showing a hydraulic caution, my right stabilator is X'd out, and I'm having a tough time keeping the plane level."

After maneuvering carefully around Slingshot 301, Gandy said, "You lost about ten percent of your starboard stabilator ... and it may not be done yet. There's metal working in your slipstream."

"Marathon, this is Slingshot three oh one. I have damage to my starboard stabilator, and flight controls are a little erratic. The aircraft is flyable, but I need to bingo for Al Udeid."

"Roger three oh one, your course zero eight five. Be advised the Saudis are up, intentions unknown," replied Thompson.

* * *

His face pale, General Dan Rivkin dialed Askenazi's direct line. He was furious at the Americans, whose naiveté and arrogance had created this mess, and shaken because Operation Persepolis hung in the balance. It was essential that the strike aircraft refuel over Saudi Arabia on the way to and from their targets. If this American blocking tactic was allowed to succeed, many of his strike aircraft would not be able to reach their targets in Iran and return. There would be no point to going on as planned. He was confident that if he gave the order to use force to clear the Americans out of the way, his pilots would prevail. But that was a decision for the prime minister. He had to reach him immediately. The phone Rivkin held continued to ring.

Turning to his aide, Rivkin said, "Get Barak for me!"

The general and his aide held their phones and listened to ring tones as the seconds passed. Stabbing his finger at an air force major nearby, Rivkin said in a strangled voice, "Get Shofer for me," referring to Brigadier Mordechai Shofer, the prime minister's military aide.

A minute later General Rivkin pressed the major's phone to his ear.

"Shofer."

"Mordechai, what the hell is going on there? I need to speak to the PM immediately, but neither he nor Barak answer."

"I don't know. His door is locked, and he's not answering us either."

Rivkin heard the sound of splintering wood.

"The security detail is breaking in now."

"Well, I need to speak to him immediately. *Immediately, do you understand?*"

"One moment, sir."

Rivkin wanted to smash the phone, to kick over the chair he had just vacated, to shout his frustration and rage.

After a long silence that actually lasted only about a minute, Rivkin heard General Shofer's voice. Shofer was a paratrooper and former Sayeret Matkal, but there was fear in his tone: "The PM is sitting at his desk, looking at Shara's picture and reading aloud the Book of Joshua. Barak is unconscious, maybe dead. No sign of a struggle."

Rivkin slammed down the phone and growled to the colonel at his side: "Call it off. Bring them home."

* * *

Thompson stared at his operations display, trying to make sense of the swarm of new video indicating Saudi fighters. Intercom broke into Thompson's speculations: "Control, EW. We're picking up many new fire control radars in acquisition mode." These guys are on the hunt, thought Thompson. But who are they hunting? The video of an Israeli aircraft disappeared, and then a Saudi winked out.

A moment later his question was answered by Saudi air defense control: "Marathon, this is Falcon Control; you will direct all your aircraft to leave our airspace at once!"

That Saudi demand completed the picture for Thompson: the Saudis were going after the intruding Israelis. Moments later, he heard General Wilcox: "Marathon, clear all US aircraft from Saudi airspace immediately!"

* * *

"Did you see that, Ari?" said the pilot of the Israeli F-16 lately alongside Jenkins. "The American shot him down. She just murdered a dozen of our guys. She doesn't get away with that!" He wracked his fighter into a diving turn toward Jenkins and Gandy. He turned too sharply, and his first burst of twenty-millimeter cannon flashed between the two Americans, the red streaks of tracer rounds an unmistakable announcement that they were being attacked.

306

Knowing Jenkins's aircraft was limited, Gandy yanked the stick back and shoved his throttles into afterburner, going after the F-16 to protect his wingman. The Hornet climbed vertically, and he searched for their attacker. G force mashed him; with great difficulty he turned his head left and right, scanning for their ambusher. There! The F-16 was above and to his right in a diving turn that would put him behind Gandy, who forced his Hornet into a tighter turn intended to let him rake the Israeli fighter as the latter crossed ahead. In the few seconds that Gandy's head-up display showed his attacker was vulnerable, Gandy fired, feeling his aircraft shudder and hearing the Vulcan cannon's six barrels belch. His bullets missed.

To avoid overstressing the damaged stabilator, Jenkins had eased her aircraft into a climb but was soon below and behind Gandy and the Israeli. Inching her throttles forward and slowly feeding in back stick, Jenkins increased her rate of climb, trying to find a way to get into the fight. The other two became no more than specks against the blue sky, but Jenkins's data link system kept her apprised of Gandy's range, bearing, and altitude.

Above and to the east of Jenkins, Gandy and the IAF pilot wove back and forth in a scissors pattern, each trying to get in killing position. For half a minute this dance continued, each pilot putting all his concentration and experience into gaining deadly advantage but not succeeding. Then the veteran Israeli pilot yanked the nose of his aircraft upward. That maneuver slowed him rapidly, and Gandy sped past, putting him in the Israeli's gunsight. The Israeli got off a long burst, and the port engine of Gandy's Hornet began to trail fire.

In the shuddering cockpit of his wounded Hornet, fire warning shrieking, Gandy verified fire suppression systems were operating and put the burning aircraft into a dive. With only one engine, that was the best move he could make to escape his pursuer. Intent on finishing him, the Israeli followed. Seeing this, Gandy yanked the handle of his ejection seat and was flung from his aircraft. Satisfied, the Israeli pulled out of his dive as the Hornet plunged for the desert below, trailing fire and smoke.

Jenkins had lost sight of her wingman in the distance but was maneuvering to close the range to him, guided by the data link. Now the link showed Gandy's Hornet descending rapidly, and that was quickly followed by the sound of an emergency beacon on Guard, the military air distress frequency. Jenkins felt a chill run down her spine as she realized that Gandy had ejected from his disabled fighter.

Jenkins's alarm for her wingman was replaced by utter concentration as her fingers flowed over the weapon system controls on the throttle and stick. She designated the radar contact close to Gandy's aircraft as hostile and set up to engage it with one of her AIM-120 radar homing missiles. The Hornet's targeting radar locked on to the Israeli fighter just designated hostile and passed its range, bearing, altitude, and speed to the sleek missile riding a pylon beneath the Hornet's right wing. The head-up display centered atop the cockpit dashboard showed all firing parameters met, and Jenkins pushed the weapons release button, much harder than necessary.

Descending under his parachute canopy, Gandy saw the Israeli aircraft disappearing to his right. A few seconds more, and he saw the shrinking dot that was his assailant became a fireball. As Gandy continued down, he saw a massive fighter battle around him as the Saudis and the Israelis had a reckoning many years in the making. One of the many silvery dots in view began to grow, and Gandy feared it was an Israeli come to finish him. But then it banked and began to circle him as he descended.

It was Slingshot 301, and the plane remained nearby until he hit the desert, with more force than he expected. His right ankle twisted beneath him as he toppled. A gusty wind yanked his chute, threatening to drag him until he unclipped it. As Gandy dug out his survival radio and switched it on, he watched the chute balloon and then blow away, its long white shroud lines writhing as if alive.

Suddenly feeling the pain and weakness in his right ankle, Gandy assessed his situation. He felt like his body had been a punching bag for the heavyweight champion of the world. He wouldn't be able to run or even walk far on that ankle. And he was in the middle of the desert.

Hearing the growl of engines, Gandy twisted his torso around just as Slingshot 301 approached. It thundered overhead, its stabilator damage visible and wings wagging.

He raised the radio to his ear and immediately heard "... boat this is Pecos, Pecos, over."

With a grin, Gandy transmitted, "Pecos, this is Steamboat. I've got a bum ankle, but otherwise I'm fine."

"Roger, Steamboat. I gotta go, but help is on the way. See you back on the boat."

* * *

Aboard Air Force One, the president and his advisors, hearing Marathon and Falcon Control, sat motionless, frozen as they processed the Saudi action. The president looked at MacAdoo, who muttered, "Son-of-a-bitch!" then said, "The Royal Saudi Air Force is going after the IAF."

"What does that mean for us?" said President Martin.

"Tactically, sir, it means the IAF attack is off. Sending our fighters to block the refueling worked. But it goes way beyond that. If the Saudis and the Israelis chew each other up today, Iran will be a big winner."

"Do you think that will happen?" asked the president.

"Sir, ordinarily the Saudi Air Force would be no match for the IAF. But right now, most of the Israeli planes are loaded for bombing and suppression of Iranian air defenses, not dogfighting.

"So the Saudis switched sides—why?" said Martin.

"Well, a couple of possibilities come to mind, Mr. President," said Secretary of State Battista. "There may have been a palace coup. The Saudi royal family is very large and full of rivalries. It may be that cooperating with the Israelis, even to weaken Iran, was too much for some cabal of princes to accept.

"Or switching sides may have been a calculation by the current regime to *avoid* a power grab by royal rivals. Maybe they figured they could take the heat for cooperating with Israel if—*if*—the strike destroyed Iran's nuclear program. But they couldn't survive the anger if they were seen to have cooperated in a failed effort, an effort that many would say was foolish. When they observed us interfering with the refueling, they knew that doomed the IAF strike plan, so they switched sides. They probably figure on claiming self-defense against an Israeli attack."

"So now Israel and Saudi Arabia are duking it out while the president of the United States is in Israel! Talk about guilt by association! How's that going to play?" worried Martin aloud.

"Not well in some quarters, Mr. President," said Battista.

"What do you think, Ray? Did Ghorbani set us up?" said the president.

"I'll bet he'll be pleased with this outcome, but I don't see how he could have predicted the Saudis would change sides. With your permission, sir, I'll call him now. We've done our part of the deal. Now it's for him to take their missiles off hair trigger."

"Do it. I'd like to speak to him."

Ten minutes later the technicians of the White House Communications Agency had Ghorbani.

"Yes?"

"General, it's me. On the line with me is my commander-in-chief. We've prevented the Israeli attack. Now it's time for you to do your part. Stand down your missile launch crews."

"I will keep my word, General. You will understand, of course, that I will wait for independent confirmation, but as soon as I have it, I will do as you ask."

Martin spoke: "General Ghorbani, this is President Martin. You also said that Iran would enter negotiations with Israel to limit nuclear weapons. We expect that, as well."

"Unlike the missiles, that is not under my direct control. But I will make the recommendation. And now, we must end this call."

Ghorbani was gone. Martin looked at Morales, eyebrows questioning.

"Yes, he will stand down the missiles, but as for further negotiations, we'll just have to see," said Morales.

The president and his advisors sat silently for a moment, thousands of miles apart but united in their surprise at what they had just witnessed. Then Easterly said, "So why don't you just leave, Mr. President?" Your bird should have enough fuel for the hop to Italy or Spain, so why sit there like a prisoner? I can have a fighter escort with you by the time you're over the Med."

The president called the flight deck.

Chapter 65

QOM, ISLAMIC REPUBLIC OF IRAN

ADEL GHORBANI'S FACE WAS IMPASSIVE, concealing the triumph he felt as he entered the Supreme Leader's office. They were so close now, so close to becoming the dominant power in the Middle East without firing a shot. But the Supreme Leader's red face and fiery eyes showed this conversation wasn't going to be easy.

"I should have had you brought here under arrest!" said the Leader, shaking his fist and glowering beneath his black turban. "I know you helped that infidel pig Morales to escape. Why? I demand to know why!"

Rage nearly took possession of Ghorbani, but he held it in check. Standing confidently before the Leader's desk in his general's uniform, he said, "Leader, your bold stroke with China would have been undermined if I had not. I did not let him go; I *sent* him with a demand for his president, a demand that forced the Great Satan to capitulate to your will. Your clever agreement with Ming Liu left the Americans powerless to attack us. You saw how they backed down from their foolish ultimatum. *You* did that, Leader! Morales was merely our unwitting tool, sent back to America with a story to confuse and hoodwink President Martin."

"And now we will destroy Israel before they can attack us," said the Leader eagerly. "Your missiles are ready as I ordered—correct?"

"We have no need to do that, Leader. The Saudis tore the heart out of the Israeli strike force. They no longer have aircraft capable of reaching and destroying our nuclear sites. And the Israelis, in return, gravely damaged the Saudis' air force. You are now the most powerful leader in the Middle East. And you did it by stealth and guile."

The Supreme Leader's color had returned to its normal pasty white, but his lips twisted in a pout: "All the more reason to destroy the cursed Israelis, now, when no one can challenge us."

"I think not, Leader. The Israelis are useful to us in their weakened state. They will no longer be aggressive toward Hamas or Hezbollah. With Israel weak, we can increase our influence in Syria even more and create a corridor to the Mediterranean."

"Pah!" We could attack Israel and still take the corridor."

"We could, indeed, Leader, but that would force the Americans to defend Israel. And the Americans don't want that. They want a weakened Israel so dependent on them that it can be forced into giving what the Americans call 'justice' to the Palestinians. Recall, Leader, that Askenazi made Martin a tool of his plan to attack us. He used the distraction of Martin's arrival in Tel Aviv to launch the attack. Even though Askenazi's duplicity brought him disgrace and Israel a new government, Martin will never forgive what happened. So long as we don't force his hand by attacking Israel, Martin will leave Israel weakened by refusing to provide it further funding or to sell it military equipment. This is yet another way your genius has guided our Islamic Republic to dominance."

As he watched the Leader's body language, Adel Ghorbani's pulse began to drop to normal. The man who ruled Iran absolutely was smiling and leaning back in his chair.

"You are a thorn in my side, Adel Ghorbani," said the Leader, "but you have exceptional merit, so I tolerate you. But do not try to push me too far!"

"I would never do that, Leader," said Ghorbani, concealing the power he felt.

Chapter 66

THE WHITE HOUSE

R AY MORALES PULLED THE CAR into West Executive Drive and stopped at the gesture of the black-and-white uniformed federal policeman. Lowering his window, he handed his military ID card and Julie's driving license to the man, who smiled and then, unexpectedly, saluted. "Semper Fi, sir. Staff Sergeant Owens, Bravo Company, Three-Two." Morales grinned and returned the salute. "Semper Fi, Marine." He pulled into visitors parking and handed over his keys.

As they walked to the South Entrance, Julie said, "How are you feeling about this, Ray? I mean, the four of us together?"

"I'm a little nervous. And I've never been big on bury-the-hatchet dinners. But they invited us, we've got a long history, all of it good until recently; why have our parting be angry?"

"Our parting?"

"Yeah, that's how I see this. We're done with government service; they have just two years to finish all they came to this town to do."

"But how about you, Julie? How do you feel about this?"

"Well, I'm in a different position. Like Rick, I'm the spouse done wrong. I still get my hackles up around Ella. Maybe *she* can just forget what happened, but I can't. But I grant what you just said, and the circumstances, either for you two or the country, will never occur again. So, on balance, I'm OK with this."

She smiled. "As long as you don't gobble your food."

"I'll be as couth as a Marine can be," he said, taking her hand.

When the elevator doors opened, the president and the First Lady greeted them in the light and cheerful anteroom leading to the family quarters. Ella and Julie faced each other for an awkward moment, then hugged stiffly. Ray shook hands with the president and saw Julie stiffen as he kissed Ella's offered cheek.

After they were seated on the Truman Balcony with drinks, Rick said, "I think we all feel awkward. I certainly do, and I hope we can begin by clearing the air. We've all had to reexamine ourselves and the state of our marriages. We may never be able to put Camp David behind us, but I hope we will, and this evening will be the beginning."

That sounded rehearsed to Ray, but he acknowledged that he would have done the same in the president's place. He replied into an awkward silence: "I—we—hope so, too, Mr. President."

"Yes," said Julie, looking at Ella, "as long as we all remember the potential, we should forget that night—as best we can."

Rick Martin smiled—uncomfortably, Ray noticed—and said, "Yes. And please, Julie and Ray, in here it's Rick."

"There's something else," said Julie. "Arlene Gustafson. *We* can agree to put this behind us. But what about her? As long as she has that picture and her misplaced hatred ..."

"We don't need to worry about her," said the president. "Bruce has something on her so big that he can control her. And he will, because he wants to run on the record of a scandal-free administration."

"So that's how he got me off the hook with her committee." said Ray, looking at the president quizzically. "What's he got?"

"I don't know," said Rick. "He didn't tell me, said 'you don't want to know,' and insisted I must have deniability. Bart agreed, so I didn't push it."

Dinner arrived, and they settled around the table. It was set family-style, with a salad bowl, a large covered dish of lasagna, a basket of fresh-baked crusty bread, and bottles of Chianti. Candles glowed softly as daylight faded. From her chair Julie saw the spire of the Washington monument, its top aglow in the last sunlight. After the Chianti had been passed, the president lifted his glass, his gaze resting on each of the diners in turn.

"To friendship and healing," he said. They touched glasses and then sat quietly, each in their own way drawing a curtain across the lapse that had nearly destroyed two marriages and a deep friendship. It was only a short stillness, but it was enough. The elephant was no longer in the room.

While they ate, they spoke comfortably about their shared past. Of fifteen years ago when Ray and Julie were newly married, General Ray Morales was a rising star in the Marine Corps, and first-term Senator Rick Martin and Ella were learning the ways of Washington. They laughed until tears came as Rick recounted his naive and disastrous first encounter with Arlene Gustafson. Ray regaled them with tales of the scrapes that some of the young Marines in his company had gotten into and the ingenious and sometimes hilarious methods by which his gunnery sergeant sorted things out.

As Rick went to the sideboard to fetch another bottle of Chianti, Ray caught Julie's eye, slowed his chewing to a crawl, and winked.

The four also spoke of crucible events that had bonded them. Fahim's destruction of Las Vegas nearly six years ago, using a nuclear bomb purchased from North Korea. Of Ray's persuasion of newly elected President Rick Martin to accept a duty that demanded, against Rick's every previous belief, ordering the nuclear destruction of a North Korean city. Of Ray's tenure at the Department of Homeland Security, of the long and frustrating hunt for Fahim even as he directed a terror campaign across America from his lair in Idaho. Of the raid on Fahim's base that Ray led and of the intervention of Adel Ghorbani and Quds Force.

The meal passed in companionable conversation, leavened by delicious food and more Chianti.

Over after-dinner drinks in the living room, the president said, "Ray, what about Ghorbani? What's your opinion of him now? Is he someone we can work with going forward?"

"He's definitely an advocate of using Iran's power. And he's no friend of America. That said, he's one of the few Iranian leaders who seems to look at international relations through the same lens we use."

"That could be useful," said the president, "because power has just shifted so rapidly after Israel burned its bridges with me and the Israelis and the Saudis beat up each other's air forces. And now that we've cleared the Strait of Hormuz, China is buying all the oil Iran can produce."

"Ray," the president's tone shifted, "John Dorn has an opportunity to take over at The Brookings Institution. He really wants to do it, so I agreed.

There's no one I'd trust as much or work with as well as you. I need you to become my national security advisor."

Ray's eyes widened, and his lips set in a straight line. Did he want a job that was twenty-four seven at this stage in his life? Did he want to be in the West Wing, at the president's beck and call and only a small organization to call his own? And how would this sit with Julie? He looked at her, and she was smiling.

"You want me after Ali Hadrab? We don't see eye to eye on that, sir. And I may not be confirmable."

"Ray, let me worry about confirmation. I want you *because of* Ali Hadrab. You arranged that knowing you could be prosecuted because of it, knowing it could ruin your reputation, knowing it would take a chunk out of your soul. You did it out of duty to this nation. I sometimes need reminding about duty. You're the voice I want in my ear when I have to make the hard calls."

"Mr. Pres—Rick, I'm flattered, but I need some time for Julie and me to talk."

Julie said, "Ray, you know you're happiest when you're busy and in the loop. And I'll be traveling a lot for Booz Allen. If you want to do this, do it!"

"What about that, Rick?" said Ray. "Back when I became JCS chairman, Julie gave up her career to support me and to avoid any appearance of a conflict of interest. I won't ask her to do that again."

"I've already run that by the White House counsel. Provided Julie recuses herself from national security engagements, no problem."

The president offered his hand. "Will you come aboard, Ray?

With a grin as big as the guilt and self-doubt he had finally sloughed off, Ray accepted the president's hand and the duty that came with it.

AFTERWORD AND
ACKNOWLEDGEMENTS

T HE PLOT FOR *CODE WORD: Persepolis* formed in my mind as I was sitting in an airliner flying cross-country. Next to me was my wife, Janie, who at once became the first person to encourage the book and is the first I want to thank for helping birth it. The plot took its initial written form in notes I jotted on the back of a Southwest Airlines napkin. I still have that napkin and the book is pretty much what I sketched out then.

That flight was three years ago and the journey from napkin notes to completed manuscript was more difficult than I expected it would be. Working with familiar characters has a downside I had not realized: when characters are established in readers' minds, an author has less freedom to maneuver during subsequent adventures. And when one plots, as I like to, in close alignment with the real world, one can get stymied by what happens in that real world. Since American foreign policy changed a lot during the period of my writing, this book strays farther from current reality than do the first two. But there is fun in that, too. For example, it left me feeling free to envision the recommissioning of the battleship USS Iowa. That would be virtually impossible—but it felt great to put old guys like me and my shipmates back in the fray and let IOWA'S 16-inchers roar again!

Many people enabled my journey to publication. More than a dozen helped by reading drafts, sharing their comments and suggestions and encouraging me to keep at it: Betty and Mark Adler, Bob Bishop, Rick

Catterton, Bud Cole, John Dill, Linda and Phil Ferrara, Forrest Horton, Joe Kirby, Nino Martini, Janie Norton, Ranger Norton, Greg Nosal, and Andy Updegrove. Thank you all! Without your direct and substantial help there would be no book.

Several people shared their specialized expertise: Air intercept controller, Master Chief Petty Officer Ernesto "Cabby" Caballero, USN Retired; Dr. Larry Cavaiola, Ph.D.; Lieutenant Colonel Denny Clements, USAF Retired, F-4 Phantom fighter pilot; Rear Admiral Greg Nosal, USN Retired, F/A-18 strike fighter pilot, air wing commander, and carrier strike group commander. Captain Don Norton, USN Retired, my brother, who is a docent aboard The Battleship USS Iowa Museum. ICU Nurse Margaret Kirby Mead, my granddaughter, who described for me the physiology of the pulmonary embolism that killed Ya'el Barak. Many thanks to you all! If I screwed something up, it's on me.

Once again I was happy to place the result of my blood, sweat, and tears in the hands of Editor Robert Brown and of the book design team at Streetlight Graphics. It's a real comfort to work with such seasoned pros!

If this is the first of the *Code Word* series that you have read, I hope you'll pick up the preceding books, *Code Word: Paternity* and *Code Word: Pandora*. To sample them, read on.

CODE WORD: PATERNITY

THE PRESIDENT OF THE UNITED States was sitting in a puddle. The south-east wind gusted and President Rick Martin happily steered up into the puff, his tiny sailboat heeling and accelerating immediately as the wind hit its green-striped sail. He straightened his legs, hooked his feet under the leeward gunwale, and hung his dripping butt over the side, counterbalancing the sail's pull so the boat wouldn't capsize. Rick shifted the tiller extension and the sheet into his left hand and reached out his right, fingers trailing in the bay.

He lost himself in the rippling sound and the slick, smooth sensations of the warm water streaming past the small Sunfish he was sailing at the mouth of the Gunpowder River where it meets the Chesapeake Bay. The sky was an inverted blue bowl, just darker than robin's egg at its zenith and milky around its rim. To the west a fringe of low white clouds curled around the horizon like the remains of a balding man's hair.

A bit over six feet tall and wiry—the build of a swimmer or runner—Rick Martin looked streamlined. His salt-and-pepper hair was graying at the temples, but his face was quite unlined, except when he smiled. After six months in office Rick still projected the optimism, lively intelligence, and likeability that had fueled his rise from Maryland congressman to president. He appreciated Camp David but favored another retreat from the pressures of office: the Chesapeake Bay. The VIP guest house at the military's Aberdeen Proving Ground made a perfect base for the sailing he loved.

He guided the boat, reflecting that sailing was one of the few things in his life that had purity and integrity. It's not that I expect politics to have either one, he thought. I take the hidden agendas and exaggerations and outright lies as they come and, let's be honest, do my share. But it's such a pleasure to enter a world, even a very limited world, where things are as they seem. The wind blows from where it blows—no man can control it or influence it. This little boat gives immediate and honest feedback.

Honesty ... I should be grateful to Glenna Rogers. Had I beaten her back then for the Democratic nomination, I probably would've made the same mistakes she did as president. Those mistakes left her vulnerable as few first-term presidents have been, as Jimmy Carter was, and for the same reason: Most Americans don't like feeling that the country has been humiliated, and when that happens they hold the president responsible.

* * *

As Las Vegas receded at a mile a minute, Fahim fretted, the I-15 ahead of his car as crisp and stark as fresh black paint on the yellowish, desolate soil. There was nothing he could do now, so he should put it out of his mind. But he could no more ignore it than his tongue could ignore a bit of food between his teeth. He knew he was taking a chance, but he had backup. The young man driving the truck would get his wish for martyrdom in any case, although he didn't know about the timer or the bomb's secret. Fahim, who didn't want to be a martyr, had directed the man who did to press his button at 10:35 a.m.

Interrupting his drive to California at 10:25, Fahim pulled to the shoulder and sat in the air conditioner's blast, sweating anyway. The sweat overflowed the barriers of his eyebrows and stung his eyes, which matched the black color of his hair. He compared his worries to the opening night jitters of an actor playing the West End the first time. Thinking of London theater brought to mind his father, a university professor of history who disapproved of his violent embrace of the cause but was nonetheless willing to admit he was cultured—for an engineer. He smiled at the memory of their fond arguments, his wiry body relaxing slightly.

Waiting for the event that would henceforth define him, he muted his humanity, burying it beneath hatred. He remembered the tens of thousands of Muslims America had killed. He remembered the suffering of his own Palestinian brothers at the hands of the Israelis, who owed their existence to Americans. He remembered the humiliation of Muslims at Abu Ghraib prison. He remembered Guantánamo.

Suppose he failed? Some stupid oversight? The Sheikh's memory would be mocked instead of glorified. Heart pounding, he gripped the wheel as if crushing it would ensure success.

At 10:30 a flash brighter than Fahim had imagined stabbed his rear-view mirror, which he had set for night to protect his eyes. He cried out, mouth a rictus that was part astonishment, part orgasm, then slumped in release as triumph embraced him. I have just struck the mightiest blow ever against America!

And I am going to do it again.

* * *

The harsh sounds of jet skis and helicopter rotors were startling. Rick looked around and saw his secret service detail closing fast from their escort positions fifty yards away, followed by a small Coast Guard patrol boat. A familiar Marine helicopter was landing at the shoreline.

Agents surrounded his little sailboat. All but the one who spoke looked away, scanning for danger, hands on the waterproof bags he knew held weapons.

"Mr. President, there's a national security emergency and we need to get you to the helo! Get aboard behind me, please."

Feeling a stab in his stomach, but also a thrill, Martin clambered aboard, mind racing. Another Russian incursion into the Ukraine? Something involving Israel? Maybe Korea? Whatever it was, it might be his first crisis and he was secretly eager to tackle it, more than ready to be tested.

The crew chief jumped out of the helo—its rotors continuing to turn— trotted in a crouch to the president, and led him toward it. As if by magic the head of Martin's secret service detail, Wilson, appeared with a submachine gun and trailed him, followed by an officer carrying a briefcase. Rick moved to his familiar place, saw National Security Advisor John Dorn belted in nearby. The moment the president's soaking shorts squelched into his seat, the helo leaped skyward.

Martin, buckling his lap belt, looked at Dorn, saw his pale face, and said, "What!" in a sharp, flat voice that made it not a question, but a command.

"Sir, a nuclear bomb has exploded in Nevada, in or near Las Vegas! Because we haven't detected any missiles or unidentified military aircraft, we think it was a terrorist act. We have no communications—"

Dorn's lips kept forming words, but Martin's mind had stopped, like a sprinting soldier halted in mid-stride by a bullet. He sat back in his seat, folded his arms across his chest, and stared at the forward bulkhead. His gaze rested on the Great Seal of the President of the United States.

That's me.

He recalled, in a flash, his thoughts from many years past, thoughts that came immediately after he had once tumbled into a ravine, breaking an ankle while winter hiking alone in the wilderness during college: *Later this is really going to hurt, but right now you've got to put that away and figure out how to stay alive.*

Holding a satcom handset tightly to his ear against the chopper's noise, Martin asked General "Mac" MacAdoo, chairman of the JCS, "Do you have any doubt this was nuclear?"

MacAdoo responded from the Pentagon, "No sir! Two DSP satellites picked up a flash with the unique characteristics of a nuclear explosion. Besides, we have satellite imaging showing such destruction that it had to be a nuke, plus what they saw from Creech Air Force Base, about thirty-five miles away."

"Okay, Mac, but what's the chance that this was a ballistic missile attack and NORAD just missed it, somehow didn't detect a lone missile coming from an unexpected direction?"

"No chance, Mr. President. The old BMEWS radars might have missed one, the way you said, but now we have interlocking, multi-sensor coverage from six satellites. It's possible the warhead was put into Vegas using a short range missile, or an artillery tube, but if so the firing point had to be within the U.S., probably within the state. It's also possible it was aboard a commercial aircraft."

"I understand ... thanks."

Martin hung up and looked numbly out the window.

Well, now it begins. Nuclear terrorism was a nightmare and now it's real and mine to deal with. How vulnerable is my administration: did we fail to connect the dots?

How do you deal with tens of thousands of bodies on a radioactive rubble pile?

Who did it?

Why Las Vegas?

What's next?

CODE WORD: PANDORA

WITH THE TV RUNNING IN the background, Secretary of Homeland Security Ray Morales read the second draft of the speech he was to give to the Western States Association of Police Chiefs and sighed. Although he relished every opportunity to speak to street cops, border patrol officers, and first responders, he hated talking to senior groups of local law officials. Each had a wish list, little of which they actually needed, in comparison to their need for patrol officers. But the gadgets were paid for by federal dollars while beat cops' salaries and benefits came with local price tags. He was expected to hand out some grant money at each of these gatherings and did, but he regretted it.

Ray sensed the changed tone of the network anchor's voice before he registered the content of his words. His TV monitor displayed a mob spilling from a New York subway exit, their panic blurred but visible through the smoke overtaking them from below.

The anchor said, "Twitter is reporting an explosion in a New York City subway. This is the feed from a traffic cam, and we are seeing the East Forty-second Street exit from the Seventh Avenue line."

As Morales watched, a firefighter appeared and began shouldering through the throng, looking like an astronaut in the Scott Air-Pak face mask.

His secure smart phone bleated.

"Morales."

"Watch officer, sir. At this point that traffic cam is the best eyes we've got, but FBI's on the way. So is the NYPD bomb squad. I'll—"

After interrupting himself in order to listen to someone, the watch officer blurted, "Sir, we just got a report of active shooters in a school in Denver!"

Morales returned his attention to CNN, saw the crawl scrolling " ... shooter. Police are on the scene" below a slightly agitated anchor man, who was handing off to a helo-borne reporter above the school.

"Sir!" said the watch officer. "A bomb, maybe a pretty large one, has detonated at O'Hare terminal three."

The ten-foot display screen behind the anchor now showed three active incidents. The anchor had one hand to his earpiece and his expression said, "Slow down—this is too much, too fast." Gamely, the anchor picked up his pace, but his words became gabble. A fourth incident scene popped up on the screen behind him, displaying masked gunmen stalking shoppers in a mall. He stopped midsentence, his eyes vacant as he tried to absorb several voices in his earpiece, each pouring out information about a different incident.

Morales heard the double bleep of call waiting and saw "White House." He mashed the button, putting the watch officer on hold, and heard, "Hold for the president, sir." Ray knew Rick and Ella Martin were on a campaign swing, California today, he thought.

"Ray, what's going on?"

"Right now CNN knows as much as I do. That'll change soon, but at the moment I'm monitoring the situation and waiting for word from response teams. FEMA is on the move, and I'm sure FBI is rolling. I haven't heard from Justice, but I'm betting the Hostage Rescue Team is moving out for the mall incident. But for a while, sir, it's the first responders' ball game."

"Well, I can't tell the press that!"

Morales waited, frustrated that Martin seemed to believe the campaign rhetoric that a president was all-seeing, all-powerful, and could fix anything from potholes to the Arab-Israeli conflict. His own experience was that, in battle, you had to let the commander on the ground carry out his mission.

Besides, it rankled him that the lead agency for response to terrorism, the FBI, wasn't under his control. When Martin had asked him to leave Congress and take the job, Ray had argued for shifting the FBI from Justice to DHS but lost as Martin bought the civil libertarians' argument. Now he felt like saying, "Tell the press this is just the occasional price we pay for honoring our founders' insistence on keeping federal power diluted so our democracy will not be endangered."

Instead he said, "I'm sure Sam and Bart have something for you, sir. And you might remind the press that the effectiveness of those first responders they're watching has been greatly enhanced by training and funds from the federal government."

"This could hardly have come at a worse time! It could knock me down in the polls!"

Morales stifled his irritation at the president's political nature. He reminded himself that Martin had made an incredibly tough decision after Six-thirteen, one he feared would cost his soul. The president made it out of duty and contrary to the beliefs of a lifetime, taking on the label of murderer in some parts of the world and also in, so Ray thought, his own conscience. Of course the president's reaction was political! This could become the day that made Rick Martin a one-term president.

Ray heard voices in the background and was pretty sure one of them was Martin's campaign manager, Winston Hernandez.

"Win and Sam are here to work the statement. Keep me informed!"

The line dead, Morales picked up the holding line, wondering if the watch officer was still on. He wasn't, which pleased Ray. His watch officer in the National Counterterrorism Center had better things to do right now than sit on hold.

Glancing to the TV again, he saw a fourth incident on the screen behind the anchor: EMS and police were surrounding a figure sprawled on a bloody sidewalk. The crawler announced a man had been shot on the street in Coronado, California.

The anchor had wisely ceased attempts to comment on each incident, letting the news crawlers tell the tale while he framed the shocking events.

"We've had five apparent terror attacks, in widely separated locations across America: a New York City subway, a Denver school, Chicago-O'Hare—the nation's busiest airport, a Baltimore shopping mall, and the shooting and beheading of a Navy SEAL on the streets of a California city near the base where SEALs train."

The anchor pressed his left hand to his earpiece, then said, "Shit!"

The anchor grimaced at his breach of professional decorum before saying, "Another attack, this one an apparent truck or car bomb outside Washington DC's Union Station."

The screen behind him had morphed into a two-by-three grid, where the latest addition, in the lower right, showed the façade of Union Station blasted to rubble and people staggering or running from the scene as first responders moved in.

Morales's smart phone bleeped again.

"Ray, this is the vice president. Based on the authorities granted to me after Six-thirteen, I'm taking charge of the national response to these attacks until the president can return to Washington. I'm convening a meeting of the Homeland Security Council immediately."

For a moment Ray Morales was speechless at the effrontery of Vice President Bruce Griffith. The president—aboard Air Force One—was unharmed, informed, and able to direct the full resources of the government.

"Mr. Vice President, you are way out of your lane! The president is fully capable of performing his duties. Have you spoken with him about this matter?"

"I don't need to speak to him to know that someone needs to take charge at the seat of government, and because of my role after Six-thirteen, I'm the one best prepared to do that."

Warily, for Bruce Griffith was clever and ruthless and on a recorded line, Morales said, "With all due respect, Mr. Vice President, you should stand down. As you know, this administration has procedures in place to deal with this situation, procedures that supersede the temporary authorities the president gave you and later withdrew. I sympathize with your passion to protect Americans, but unless we all hear otherwise from the president, we need to follow those procedures."

"Ray, I'm surprised you don't see that the president needs to have a single point of contact in Washington now. He can't be calling every cabinet official who has a piece of this and telling them what to do!"

He does, and it's me, thought Morales.

But now was no time to have that fight—even though he would win it—so he said, "If the president wants *a cabinet officer* in overall charge, he'll say so. If you're so sure your plan is right, call him. I have to take a report from the Counterterrorism Center now. Goodbye, Mr. Vice President."

Shattered.

That was how Ray imagined the schoolchildren's parents and grandparents felt. He and Julie had married in their forties; he had no children but saw the faces of his nephew's kids, seven and nine. He imagined their bodies riddled with automatic weapons fire. He knew very well what an AK-47 did to human flesh. A long time ago in years, but not in emotions, he had seen and smelled it, had left his footprints in the gore of it. He had held the dying as they bled out, unable to save them because high-velocity bullets had shredded their bodies.

And today, the bodies belonged to kids. He imagined the pain rippling out through their families as the news traveled. *If that happened to Maria or Carl* … He looked at their picture on his desk. So eager, so confident, so trusting that the world was good. That people were good.

Without warning, his shoulders shook and his breath came in gasps, a tsunami of unexpected personal grief. Tears streaked his cheeks. Snuffling, Ray wiped a big hand across them, then fumbled in a desk drawer, found a tissue, and blew his nose twice.

It's him again. It's that same monster who got away after doing Las Vegas—I can feel it. This time we've got to get him. As head of Homeland Security, that's on me. I'm going to find that sorry bastard; I'm going to find him and make him pay. And I don't care what it costs me. Whatever it takes.

Doug Norton

Doug Norton draws on both experience and research to pen the Code Word Series. As a warship captain during the cold war Doug held launch codes for nuclear weapons and was prepared to use them, but he also participated in high-stakes international negotiations to reduce their numbers and the chance of nuclear war. In Geneva, Brussels, London, and Washington he experienced diplomacy and politics in tense meetings, glittering receptions, and deadline-driven all-nighters.

A graduate of the Naval Academy and of the University of Washington, Doug was a Council on Foreign Relations International Affairs Fellow and Director of International Studies at the Naval Academy. After serving more than twenty-five years, Captain Norton retired from the navy and was an executive recruiter for fifteen years. Doug and his wife live in Annapolis, where he volunteered with the Coast Guard Auxiliary in search and rescue and Anne Arundel Medical Center in the emergency department. He loves to meet readers and has signed books in bars, hospitals, and hotels as well as book stores, libraries, and book clubs.

CPSIA information can be obtained
at www.ICGtesting.com
Printed in the USA
LVHW020936290721
693966LV00003B/288